Marriage Training

GOLDEN ANGEL

CLEiS
PRESS

Published in the United States by Cleis Press, an imprint of Start Midnight, LLC, 101 Hudson Street, Thirty-Seventh Floor, Suite 3705, Jersey City, NJ 07302.

Printed in the United States.
Cover design: Allyson Fields
Cover photograph: iStock
Text design: Frank Wiedemann
First Edition.
10 9 8 7 6 5 4 3 2 1

Trade paper ISBN: 978-1-62778-294-4
E-book ISBN: 978-1-62778-507-5

Library of Congress Cataloging-in-Publication Data is available on file.

PROLOGUE

IN THE LATE HOURS OF THE EVENING, THE glittering facade of London's finest gave way to a decadent, erotic underbelly of depraved lust, if one knew where to look for it. Lord Gabriel Cecil, Earl of Cranborne and son of the Marquess of Salisbury, never had to look very far—it was always around him. Known as the Dark Angel to the *ton* for his darkly handsome good looks, piercing, green-flecked grey eyes, rakish pursuits, and sinful reputation, he knew they didn't have the slightest inkling how far his passions took him. There were others within the *ton* with the same . . . interests. It was at those private gatherings, those intimate parlors, where he would meet with his friends—many of whom were the sons and daughters of his father's friends.

Tonight's private party was in celebration of George Howard's wedding on the morrow to his fiancée, Mary Dermont. The women draped about the room in various states of undress were not whores, but ladies and expensive mistresses with particular tastes. Some of them had their husbands or protectors with them, some of them did not, but they were all there for the same thing.

Already the gathering had begun to devolve into licentiousness. An earl was braced over the back of a sofa as his mistress whipped him with a crop while he begged for more. In the far corner, the Duke of Marbury was engaged in a passionate kiss with his lover, a young man by the name of Vincent Pennybrooke, while his mistress had both of their cocks in hand and was taking each of them into her mouth in turns. Somehow, the erotic antics around the room weren't quite as titillating or as appealing as they had been in the past. There was something lacking in the interactions; rather than enjoying them, Gabriel felt more and more disconnected from the actions and the pleasure.

"Gabriel, you made it!" George Howard's voice boomed out behind him, just before a hand came down on his shoulder.

Turning, Gabriel couldn't help but grin at his friend. Lord Winchester—George—was the opposite of Gabriel in looks, with his straw-blond hair and blue eyes, and his opposite in temperament as well, except at parties such as these. Where Gabriel tended towards solitude and impatience, George was tolerant and a bon vivant; where Gabriel was cutting and disdainful, George was witty and cheerful. Only in the confines of these parties, or the bedroom, did George's more authoritative, stern side come out.

"George, Mary," Gabriel said, giving a short bow to the petite young woman tucked into George's arm. With her pale hair and grey eyes, Mary Dermont looked quite delicate, but Gabriel knew she wasn't—otherwise, George would never be marrying her. Those pale eyes took in the debauchery around the room without flinching. In fact, when her eyes landed upon the duke's erotic trio, they positively lit up.

"Oh my," she murmured, leaning into her husband-to-be even closer. George and Gabriel both turned to see where she was looking, and George chuckled. The duke and Pennybrooke had ended their own kiss and now held the duke's mistress between them. Her dress, flimsy though it was, was bunched around her midsection, baring her breasts for her benefactor to play with while Pennybrooke was on his knees before her, holding up her skirt and eagerly lapping at the juncture of her thighs. "How . . . intriguing. I never knew . . ."

Mary's interest piqued Gabriel's, as if he could see the tableau through her eyes and appreciate it because she did. The tawdriness slid away, and he could see what might interest her about the duchess's pleasure in her two men.

"Is that what you'd like tonight, my dear?" George asked, nuzzling his lips against her hair. "Two lovers paying attention to you?" Catching Gabriel's eye, he smiled. "I've promised her whatever she likes tonight, as a wedding present."

Giving a delicate little shiver of arousal, Mary smiled up at her soon-to-be husband before looking back at the amorous trio. "Mrs. Cunningham's school never talked about anything like *that* . . . but no, thank you, darling. It is quite delightful to watch, though, isn't it?"

Her voice wobbled slightly, her attention turning back to her betrothed, as if seeking his approval for her interest in the scene. The inherent submissiveness in her need for his permission struck a chord with Gabriel, giving way to a moment of envy. While he might play with the women at these gatherings, and they would submit for the time, none of them looked to him for approval the way Mary was currently looking at George. Even with a mistress, there hadn't been that kind of connection between him and another woman, not the way he could see it between George and Mary. Perhaps that was the difference; there would always be an end to a mistress's attentions, but a man could keep his wife forever.

Out of the corner of his eye, he saw George lean down and whisper in Mary's ear. The two of them were already lost in their own little world, totally involved in each other. The other exchanges were so much less intimate— people brought together by common needs and desires rather than tangible emotion, like that between George and his fiancée.

The next morning, Gabriel found himself more envious of George than ever. His own night had been rather unsatisfying. Just another mutual evening of using each other's bodies to find what they wanted . . . nothing like the connection he'd seen between Mary and George. Mary was passionate, eager, entirely submissive, and completely connected to her fiancé.

A virginal harlot.

The idea piqued his interest in a way nothing else had for quite some time.

Mary's very newness, her innocent passion, was something to be envied, but it was the way they looked at each other that Gabriel had found himself wanting the most. In some ways it reminded him of his father and stepmother, whose loving relationship he had always thought to emulate once he married. Of course, he'd always thought of marriage as being a very distant thing, for some time in the future . . .

Now, he felt a strange stirring as he contemplated George's forthcoming nuptials. So far, though, he hadn't met any woman with whom he'd want to enter that state.

Not that he'd truly been looking. His interactions with women had been confined to the wild parties he attended or the occasional events he was required to attend with his family. None of the debutantes he'd encountered during the latter had incited the slightest hint of lust in him, but perhaps he'd been unfair in his observations. After all, they were all virgins and not looking to provoke desire; they were looking for marriage. Perhaps if he took a closer look at some young, unmarried ladies, he could find a hidden gem like Mary.

The wedding was a stunning affair, packed with members of society. As the blushing bride was kissed by her husband, murmurs of approval for the union were heard all around. Everyone remarked on how sweet Mary was. A few gentlemen made some ribald jokes about how that sweetness wouldn't last after tonight. She was so pure and fresh-looking, as if even the knowledge of sexual relations had never touched her. Little did they all know.

Gabriel's own unrest had continued today, as he'd looked through the throngs of well-wishers at the wedding breakfast, wondering if he'd ever find a woman to whom he could commit himself. The idea of the usual, bloodless, *ton* marriage had even less appeal to him now that he saw George's happiness. He craved it for himself.

The marquess, his father, had been wildly in love with Gabriel's mother until she passed, and he was now just as in love with and satisfied by Audrey, Gabriel's step-mother. Certain inclinations, especially in the bedroom, had been passed down from father to son, and Gabriel didn't see why, if his father could find such satisfaction twice, he shouldn't be able to find it for himself at least once.

Doing his best to avoid the giggling debutantes, he made his way through the crowd towards his own circle. Many of the young ladies at the breakfast were just out of the schoolroom and eager to catch a husband, and weddings always made them and their mamas more aggressive.

On his way to the safety of his circle of friends, he stopped to congratulate George. His friend looked at him with just a bit of concern in his eyes. "Sorry about last night, old chap. We looked up and realized you were gone. I hope you didn't feel too left out."

"No, just envious," Gabriel said, teasingly, but also truthfully. "Mary is absolutely delightful. Best keep an eye on her so I don't steal her away."

George chuckled. "Doubtful. My Mary loves me too much, and I her."

"She's quite the treasure." The envy in his voice was palpable, however hard he tried to hide it.

"It's the school," George said, grinning widely. "Best investment I ever made, that finishing school. Gave me the perfect bride, and unlike most gents, I'm actually going to thoroughly enjoy my wedding night. And all the nights thereafter."

Unfortunately, they weren't able to talk any further as George was pulled away by another well-wisher. Gabriel let him go, knowing his friend would be trapped doing the social rounds for the rest of the breakfast, until he was able to escape with Mary.

Sighing internally, Gabriel dodged several frothy skirts of respectable young misses and managed to reach the safe haven of his friends. Flirting with a rake was a dangerous pastime for debutantes, but there were always a few fascinated by men of his reputation. He had no interest in them, although he was starting to wonder if perhaps he'd written debutantes off too quickly. In the past, he'd always thought when he married, it would be to an adventurous young widow, or perhaps a young woman with an already ruined reputation. However, if he could secure a marriage with a debutante like Mary . . . well, that would be an entirely different matter altogether.

The idea appealed to him, especially after last night. Gabriel wanted a passionate wife who looked at him with the same focused tenderness that Mary had for George, the same adoration and love. He also wanted one who was well-matched to his particular proclivities.

As he pondered the conundrum, his attention barely on the conversation between his friends about the latest horse race, a bright flash of red caught his eye. Not crimson like a rose, but the fiery orange-red of a sunrise. Quite beautiful and eye-catching, although red hair was supposedly unlucky. The sunrise-red stood out like a beacon through the more subdued shades and the boring pastel dresses of the other debutantes.

Intrigued, Gabriel shifted his position so that he had a better view of the owner of the sunrise hair.

She was young, too young to have her hair up, which meant that she wasn't out of the schoolroom quite yet, but old enough that she would be very soon. Definitely she was of the age when the young misses started planning their debuts and tactics for husband-hunting. The glorious bounty of locks was pulled back from her face, showing off her quiet beauty. She was wearing a pale green dress, which covered her trim little figure completely, but hinted at the woman she would become. Her pale, youthful face was pretty, almost like a doll's, with brilliant green eyes, a straight nose, and a rosebud mouth. Quite striking, all put together, but her looks weren't what held his attention.

It was the way she was sitting. Her eyes were downcast, properly, as a young lady's should be, but unlike most young ladies, she wasn't peeking through her eyelashes at the people around her. Instead, she seemed content to sit at her mother's side, only speaking when directly addressed, a small smile on her face. At one point, particularly raucous laughter nearby drew her attention to a group of young rowdies, and she looked up, but when her mother reached out and put her hand on her daughter's arm, the young woman returned to her previous pose. More importantly, she did so without the slightest hint of resentment at the direction; in fact, she gave every evidence of relief at her mother's guidance.

Submissive? Or just well-behaved?

Certainly, she was different from the other young ladies, who simpered at their mothers' commands but were otherwise resentful of their elders' attempts to rein in their behavior. Her composure was intriguing, as were the sweet smiles she directed to the company around her. Despite several attempts by the nearby rowdies to get her attention—and Gabriel was sure it was her attention they were after—she didn't glance at them again. Many young ladies would be flattered by such antics and would try to escape their mothers' attention; he'd seen it time and time again. Women who were drawn to the excitement of rakes either ended up ruined or married to respectable men only to bear them an heir or two and then spend the rest of their lives enjoying rakes in their beds.

Definitely not the kind of marriage Gabriel wanted. As an accomplished seducer himself, he didn't in general relish the idea of a woman who was constantly after the attentions of men. Seeing the young redhead actually following her mother's direction and ignoring the young men was a novelty.

Gabriel moved closer, stealthily, still watching her every move. He knew part of his interest was because of Mary's example, as he normally would have no interest in a young innocent who hadn't even officially come out to society yet, but it didn't stymie him now. Despite the young woman's youth, she was old enough to attend the wedding, which meant she would probably be making her come-out next season. Besides, he truly doubted his sudden fascination would last past a few minutes of close observation.

As he watched, the young woman waited patiently to catch her mother's eye, and then leaned in to murmur something. Her mother nodded and the young woman stood gracefully. Perhaps she wasn't different from other young ladies at all; she was going to escape her mother now.

Instead of the expected walk that would take her by the laughing young men, she turned in the direction of the ladies' retiring room. There were no sly glances to any of the men, no invitation in her eyes. Was she truly everything she seemed?

Completely losing interest in the conversation going on

around him, Gabriel slid away from his friends, stalking after the young redhead like a hunter through a forest.

She was headed straight to the retiring room, and he was within a few feet of her when she tripped over something on the floor and stumbled against George's back as he and Mary moved away from a conversation with one of the guests. George and Mary turned around, catching her from falling over completely, and Mary smiled delightedly at the young woman. Fortunately, Gabriel was close enough to listen in to the conversation. He prudently shifted his stance so he could still study the young woman without appearing to actually be looking at her.

"Vivian! Are you all right, dear?"

"Yes, Mary," she said, blushing deeply. The pretty pink on her cheeks clashed adorably with her fiery hair, Gabriel thought. *Quite enchanting.* Vivian, as he surmised that was her name, looked up at George. "I'm so sorry, Lord Winchester, please excuse my clumsiness."

George smiled genially down at her. "No need to apologize, it's a complete crush in here."

Reassured by his demeanor, Vivian's lovely green eyes lowered again. Gabriel was charmed as the red in her cheeks actually deepened at George's reassurance. She was relieved. Pleased. Trusting.

Gorgeously, naturally submissive. Sweetly innocent. He felt the urge to move even closer to her. There was something indefinably seductive about her, and not just in an erotic sense. Something about her called to him, intriguing him, even though he'd only just seen her. Gabriel had always scoffed at the notion of love at first sight. However, attraction or interest at first sight he couldn't deny, because he was currently experiencing it.

That she wasn't presented was a small dilemma, as he couldn't even ask for a formal introduction yet, much less court her.

But she could be worth waiting for.

The thought whispered across his mind.

When she excused herself from them, gesturing towards the hall, he continued to follow her, feeling very much like he was on a hunt.

Blushing, mortified by her clumsiness at her first official adult outing, Vivian Stafford scurried to the retiring room. As her parents were not particularly influential, nor wealthy, they were not often invited to events of this magnitude, and Vivian had been both thrilled and anxious when her mother had stated her intention to bring Vivian. After all, Vivian would be making her debut next year.

She was wearing a new dress for the occasion and new slippers. Well, the dress was new for her. It was actually one of her mother's old silks, but it had been cut down to fit her and redone in the latest style so that it looked brand-new. The pale green complemented her perfectly— even if her coloring wasn't fashionable—and Vivian was in love with it. It was the nicest dress she'd ever worn, even if it wasn't *new*-new.

Vivian didn't begrudge her parents the reuse of her mother's old dress. After all, they were pinching pennies to give her any kind of debut, and she knew they were both anxious over the prospect. She was feeling rather anxious over it herself. Even an event like this, where no one was paying much attention to her, felt overwhelming. She couldn't imagine months of parties and balls, with men looking over her to see if she'd make a suitable bride.

Looking in the mirror in the retiring room, she patted the unfashionable locks of her hair, which were pulled back from her face and hung down her back. She made a face at herself, wishing her hair wasn't so blazingly bright. If she'd been old enough to have her hair up, perhaps the overly bright color wouldn't have been as noticeable.

Patting her hair again, although it did nothing to change its hue or length, Vivian pasted a demure smile on her face and forced herself back out of the room to return to the party. She'd barely stepped out of the door before coming to an abrupt halt as an incredibly handsome man practically melted out of the shadows across the hall, his dark eyes fixed on her.

Everything about him was dark, from his black hair, to his eyes, to the nearly unrelieved black suit he was wearing. It was far too formal for a breakfast, and yet it suited him. The stark white of his collar and the charcoal grey of his cravat were the only variations of color in his attire. He was intimidatingly attractive, with broad, muscular shoulders and a strong jawline, and wreathed in an aura of confidence. Everything about him screamed *danger* to a young, unwed innocent like Vivian. A voice in her head called for her to run, but she stood there, as if her slippers had nailed themselves to the floor.

"Hello there," he said, his voice deep and almost hypnotic.

Vivian looked back and forth down the hall, unsure of how to respond. They hadn't been properly introduced, after all, and she was sure this was exactly the kind of man her mother had warned her not to be caught alone with. Young ladies' reputations were so easily ruined—

just talking to him alone could be the end of her before she'd even debuted. Her heart pounded so hard it felt like the organ might burst from her chest, and yet it wasn't just from fear. She also felt excited.

She focused on him again, folding her hands in front of her and twisting her fingers together nervously.

"Good morning," she said softly, trying to keep her trembling in check. She glanced up and down the hallway. "If you're waiting for someone, the retiring room is empty."

"I think I might have been waiting for you," he said, his voice sounding almost contemplative. Vivian's breath caught in her throat as he stepped forward. She trembled, she quivered, but she didn't run. He approached her slowly, studying her, and she stared back at him, completely entranced. When he reached out towards her face, she froze. Two fingers pressed against the bottom of her chin, tipping her face up.

He was so close she could see his eyes weren't actually black; they were grey with hints of green flecks in them. He stared at her so intensely, she felt as if he could see into her very soul. She wondered if she'd fainted and this was some kind of dream she'd somehow stepped into.

"Are you a good girl, my dear?"

Vivian flicked out her tongue, licking her dry lips, her heart stuttering when his gaze dropped to observe the small movement. There was something in his eyes. "I try to be, my lord."

She didn't know why she tacked on the "my lord." It was pure assumption, but it fit.

A small smile of acknowledgement made his lips curve, somehow making him even more breathtakingly handsome, which she hadn't realized was possible. He moved closer, and Vivian's chest constricted. She imagined she could actually feel the heat of his body through their clothing. She'd never stood so close to a man who wasn't a family member. And she'd never stood next to a man like *this*.

"How old are you?" he asked, his thumb tracing over her lower lip.

"Seventeen, my lord," she said, her voice barely more than a whisper. It was all she could manage when she could hardly breathe. "I come out next year."

"Would you like for me to look for you then?"

"Yes." The word was out before she could think; a breathy, honest answer to his unexpected question. Heat filled her cheeks as she realized how brazen she sounded, but he looked pleased.

Stepping back, he took her hand, bowing over her glove and then kissing the back of her hand. "Till we meet again, my dear."

And then he turned and walked away, leaving Vivian feeling strangely drained, as if all her energy had flowed out of her like a river. Her legs were trembling so badly it felt like it would take hours before she was able to move again, but when she returned to the breakfast, no one had noticed her absence. Everything was as it had been. When she looked around, she didn't see the handsome stranger anywhere; it was as though he'd melted away into the shadows of the hall from whence he'd come.

A week later, at home and in her familiar surroundings, she wasn't entirely sure she hadn't imagined the entire episode.

MARRIAGE TRAINING

When George returned from his honeymoon with his new bride, there was a note waiting for him on his salver.

Tell me everything about the finishing school Mary went to.

~Gabriel

CHAPTER ONE

MRS. CUNNINGHAM'S FINISHING SCHOOL, the school Mary had attended before her marriage to George, was located two miles outside of London. It resided on three square acres of land and included a pond, a riding course, a large garden and hedge maze, and a hunting lodge. On the rare occasions men stayed over-night at Mrs. Cunningham's Finishing School, they were required to stay in the hunting lodge, so as to ensure the reputation of the school and its pupils.

The majority of the young ladies at Mrs. Cunningham's Finishing School were the daughters, nieces, and grand-daughters of viscounts, barons, and younger, untitled sons of titled nobles. These young women were looking to marry above their current stations and so needed the proper training if they were to marry an earl, a marquess, or as one notable graduate did, a duke. The funds earned by providing the proper training for these young women to enter into advantageous marriages netted a tidy sum of profit; however, not nearly as great a profit as the much smaller minority of sponsored students provided.

Of course, the general public knew nothing about the

special arrangements for sponsored students. There was not even a hint of gossip among the *ton* that the advantageous marriages the occasional sponsored students made were anything but respectable marriages of financially disadvantaged but beautiful and accomplished young women to particularly wealthy noblemen—noblemen who didn't need their nonexistent dowries. Sponsorship was always handled discreetly and was assumed, by society, to be at the behest of a wealthy but distant relative. There were rarely more than one or two sponsored students a year, and sometimes none at all, so they attracted very little attention.

Not a single person ever suspected the funds for the sponsored students came from the pockets of their future husbands, or that a large amount of the profits made from Mrs. Cunningham's Finishing School came from those select students. There were a few who were sponsored by distant family members, but only a very few, and their fees were not so great. Men who were part of the secret accounted for nearly all of the sponsored students, and quite a bit of the school's intake, as they were paying for very specific services.

Miss Vivian Stafford, daughter of the impoverished Baron Charles Stafford, had been completely unaware of the special services the school offered when she began attending the school on a sponsorship several months following the wedding of George and Mary Howard, and currently remained so. Although that was all about to change.

Possessed of an innate sense of grace, Vivian was considered a model student. She fairly floated whether she was walking or dancing, she could hold a steady curtsy for hours, her skill at pouring a cup of tea was the envy of all the other students, and she was a rather dashing rider on a horse. She excelled at the pianoforte, archery, pall mall, and water colors, and was the most sought-after partner for any game of charades.

Two days before her eighteenth birthday, Miss Stafford attended a tea party. The formal tea was one of the events Mrs. Cunningham provided for her older students who had been at the school for at least a year, allowing them to make their first appearance before the matrons of society. In that setting, they were able to practice their polite conversation and attempt to make a good impression on those women of the *ton* who could—and would— make or break their futures. Although her flaming red hair and green eyes were not at all fashionable, Vivian Stafford was wonderfully charming, impressively elegant, and modestly demure, emerging from the pack of students as the veritable queen of future daughters-in-law. The matrons were charmed and immediately applied to Mrs. Cunningham to discover when she would be making her debut, already plotting to push their sons into making her acquaintance.

With a small smile, Mrs. Cunningham managed to neatly sidestep their questions, as Miss Vivian Stafford was already spoken for, although the young lady did not know it yet. As far as Miss Stafford knew, a distant relation was paying for her to receive some extra schooling before her debut, which had been pushed back to allow for extra training.

So Vivian had returned to the school, flush with triumph and dreaming of the dashing young men who would, hopefully, be one day falling all over themselves to court her. If she were lucky, one of them would not only love her, but be willing to assist her family financially. All six of the young ladies who had attended the tea were aflutter with excitement over their eventual debuts, but Vivian was the only one whose family desperately needed her to marry well.

Occasionally she would dream of her future husband, who would save her family from their financial straits. Often, in her imagination, he looked like the stranger who had approached her at cousin Mary's wedding. Sometimes she wondered if she had imagined him as well.

On the day of her eighteenth birthday, Vivian was called to Mrs. Cunningham's office. She was, as always, accompanied by her companion for the meeting. Mrs. Banks was a rather attractive young widow in her mid-thirties; she attended Vivian at all times in order to provide advice and correction as needed, although Vivian only occasionally required the former and rarely the latter. Mrs. Cunningham would not allow any young woman under her care to have even the slightest hint of impropriety attached to her, so each student always had a companion at her side.

In Vivian's case, it was especially necessary, as her companion was about to become her most trusted confidant as well as her tutor.

Vivian sat down gracefully in the chair in front of Mrs. Cunningham's desk, aware of Mrs. Banks's presence, but not looking at all flustered. However, behind her demure social mask her insides fluttered wildly. She'd been a fairly new seventeen when she was delivered to Mrs. Cunningham's school, and Vivian was well-aware of the difference it had made in her life already. Her father had kissed her forehead and told her to be a model student and to make him proud, which she'd endeavored to do.

She had no idea the plans that she'd laid out for her life were somewhat different from those others had laid out for her.

"Vivian, dear," said Mrs. Cunningham with a maternal smile that looked odd on her stony face. The years had not been kind to Mrs. Cunningham, and it was reflected in the harsh lines of her face and body, despite her fashionable dress. "I wanted to personally wish you happy on your birthday."

"Thank you, Mrs. Cunningham, how thoughtful of you," Vivian replied with one of her brightest smiles. As Mrs. Cunningham was the power in the school, Vivian always made it a point to stay on her good side. Vivian had always been easily led by the authority figures in her life; she was happiest when she knew what was expected of her and was able to meet those expectations.

"I also wanted to have a little talk with you. Now that you're eighteen, we're going to be moving you into a new area of study here at the school we call marriage training."

Vivian blinked, surprised out of her usual social mask. "Marriage training? But I've never heard of it. I thought I would be debuting with the other girls."

"Most girls do follow that program," said Mrs. Cunningham smoothly. "But you are one of our special students. When your father brought you to us he did not have the funds to pay for your schooling; your schooling, since you arrived, has been sponsored by a benefactor."

"Oh," said Vivian as her world realigned itself slightly. She'd known she was a scholarship student, but she hadn't realized that would mean following a different school program.

Mrs. Cunningham continued, not giving Vivian the chance to ask any questions. "As a sponsored student, your marriage has already been arranged, in this case to your sponsor, the Earl of Cranborne. He agreed to pay for your schooling, and the marriage settlement agreed upon with your father is very generous. As long as you become his wife, there is no need for you to ever concern yourself over your family's circumstances, as he will settle all their debts. To that end, you will be trained to be exactly the kind of wife the earl requires."

There was a long pause as Mrs. Cunningham gave Vivian a moment to assimilate this information. She obviously needed it; her heart-shaped face had paled to a chalky white as Mrs. Cunningham had explained. Vivian hadn't realized the arrangements for her marriage had already been made without her knowledge. Nor that she owed the past year of her life, not to mention the well-being of her family, to her future husband. It was rather frightening, even though she knew that, especially among the upper echelons of society, arranged marriages were the usual way of doing things.

On the one hand, her marriage was going to be quite a coup—the daughter of a country baron to what must be an exceedingly wealthy earl. She wasn't just moving up socially, she was making a leap in title and fortune. There had always been the chance that she might have to step *down* in terms of social status in order to bring money into the family. Although she'd raised her hopes that being a premier graduate of the finishing school might allow her to marry within the *ton*, she hadn't expected to reach as high as an earl. Gratitude over her family's new situation, combined with relief that she would not need to brave the marriage mart, swamped her. She need not attract a wealthy husband; she already had one.

However, on the other hand, not knowing who he was or what he might expect from her caused her quite a bit of anxiety.

Mrs. Cunningham continued, her next words both stirring and disturbing.

"This additional training will prepare you for the private duties of a wife, in which the earl has very particular tastes. As such, this training is of a rather intimate and physical nature, and you will be allowed to glimpse the secrets of the bedroom—knowledge no other well-bred young lady in this school can lay claim to. It is likely you will occasionally find yourself uncomfortable, frightened, and even pained by the methods we utilize, but all of your training will be conducted with the utmost care and the eventual goal of making you as comfortable and happy with your marriage as the earl will be."

Vivian's brow was beginning to wrinkle in confusion again, but Mrs. Cunningham pressed onward with her speech.

"Because of your family's financial straits, the earl understands you might feel beholden to complete your training, even if you find it not to your liking. That is not the earl's wish. He requires a wife who is as enthusiastic about the private side of marriage as he is himself. Therefore, you are to be assured that you may dissolve the marriage contract at any time, with no ill feeling, no need to pay him back for your schooling, and no fear of retribution on his part. All you will have to say is 'I want to call off my marriage to Lord Cranborne' to myself or to Mrs. Banks."

"And . . . then I would not have to marry him?"

"Exactly," Mrs. Cunningham said. "Of course, that will also be the end of your time at this school, but you have enough of the traditional training we provide to make an exemplary wife."

If Vivian could catch a husband, as poor as her family was. But if she completed this new training, then she wouldn't need to. She would have a husband, one whom she'd been specifically trained to accommodate in the private sphere. Training that was certainly highly unusual but not a deterrent in and of itself.

Still, she couldn't help but worry over Mrs. Cunningham's description of the training as uncomfortable, frightening, and painful. Her mind was awash with confusion and new pressures. All this time, she thought she had been diligently applying herself in order to please her parents and to make a good marriage. Instead, it turned out that she had been doing so to please a husband that she had never met or even seen. Now she would be embarking on a new course of study, one which had been specifically requested by her new husband—again, sight unseen.

"Once you near the end of your training, the banns will be read, and then you will be wed upon completion of your training." Mrs. Cunningham smiled, trying to look sympathetic, seeing that Vivian felt quite overwhelmed by all the information she'd just heard. "I suggest you do not mention your new course of training to the other girls. None of them are sponsored students and they might not understand."

By which she meant Vivian would not want to mention

her family's financial situation to the other girls. Vivian's presence at the expensive school masked that, but if she let it be known how her schooling was paid for, it would reflect negatively on both her and her family, which was why she'd been very quiet about it from the beginning. It could harm her sisters, certainly, as they would be making their come-outs in a few years and would need the family's reputation intact.

"May I ask a question?"

"Of course, dear," said Mrs. Cunningham. About half of the young ladies wanted to ask a question at this point; some were too flummoxed by their situation to gather their wits together. It didn't surprise her that Vivian belonged to the former group.

"The earl, what's he like?" That was the question foremost in Vivian's mind. It was easy for her to accept her family's future and fortunes rested upon her shoulders—she'd known that from the start. Less easy to swallow was the embarrassing fact that her schooling had been arranged by her future husband. That, combined with her anxiousness over being betrothed to a man she'd never even heard of, much less met—one who had mysterious and "particular" tastes—made her stomach slightly queasy. Other than her family, she'd had very little interaction with gentlemen, and even less since her arrival at the school.

"He'll make you a good husband," said Mrs. Cunningham, being as comforting as she could, considering she truly didn't have a maternal bone in her body. "His father is the Marquess of Salisbury. He's twenty-eight years old, wealthy—obviously—and ready to settle down with a wife."

"What does he look like? Is he kind?" Vivian didn't quite know what to think, hearing how young he was. She would have made the best of a marriage to an older gentleman. In fact, she'd initially assumed a man who had picked her out for a bride would be an older gentleman in need of an heir. But that a young man should want a bride like her . . . Was there something physically wrong with him, which made him unattractive on the marriage mart? Or was he possessed of a mean temperament, which made him unable to find a bride by the more conventional process of courting her?

"Pish, what kinds of questions are those?" asked Mrs. Cunningham with a disapproving frown that made Vivian wilt a bit. "The important thing to know is that he's taken care of both you and your family. Be grateful for what he's given you." The sudden shift into scolding had Vivian quite off balance, as it was meant to.

Mrs. Cunningham had every intention of making it quite clear how much Vivian owed the earl, therefore instilling in her the motivation to please him. Not that she would need much motivation, as Miss Stafford was already one of the most naturally submissive and eager-to-please young misses the school had ever had. Deciding it was time to end the interview, Mrs. Cunningham picked up an envelope on her desk with Vivian's name on it. "This is a letter from your father, to be given to you today. You have the rest of the day free to do what you please in celebration of your birthday. Mrs. Banks will accompany you if you wish to walk around the grounds. Enjoy your afternoon, Miss Stafford."

Biting back any further inquiries, Vivian took the envelope with her father's letter and made a small curtsy before leaving the room, moving as though she was in a daze. The door to the headmistress's office closed with a decisive thud. A light touch on Vivian's arm called her attention to her companion.

"Are you all right, dear?" asked Mrs. Banks, her gentle blue eyes looking rather concerned. Although she was much younger than Mrs. Cunningham, Mrs. Banks had a comforting air about her, like an older sister who was vastly more experienced and knowledgeable than the young ladies she was paired with. She was the kind of woman a young lady felt she could depend on and confide her secrets to, which was why she was always the companion to the sponsored students. It was often quite easy for her to establish a rapport with her students; by the time they commenced their special training, they trusted her instinctively, which was necessary since she would be their primary instructor in their new skills.

"Yes, I'm just . . . I'm a trifle overwhelmed," said Vivian. With a bit of effort, she managed to summon a weak smile as they moved through the halls of the school, which was really more of a large manor house. Quite without realizing it, Vivian headed for the front door and the grounds. She needed to go outside and walk for a bit, read her father's letter, and take the opportunity to think.

"Vivian!"

She turned, recognizing the sound of her friend Emily's voice. With a rush of relief, Vivian turned to face her.

"Don't tell her too much," Mrs. Banks murmured behind her, but there was no threat in her voice, it was a true and compassionate warning from one woman to another. While Emily Warpoole, daughter of the Marquess of Deane, was probably the best friend Vivian had at the

27

school, she would have no understanding of the kind of circumstances Vivian found herself in.

"Happy birthday," said Emily as she drew closer, thrusting a small package at Vivian. They were opposites in many ways, and not just because of their differences in social station or finances. Emily was a hoyden who struggled with having a ladylike demeanor. Most of the other young ladies would have never dared call out another's name as loudly as Emily had, or rush to meet the other, but Emily's social status, as well as her natural charm and energy, allowed her to get away with what others could not.

She was a pert young lady, with more curves than was fashionable, freckles across her slightly upturned nose, and just the slightest tint of sun to her skin, as she spent most of her time outdoors either on a horse or doing some other activity about the grounds. Keeping Emily indoors was a chore that her companion, Miss Norton, despaired of. Emily was energetic, and it was that energy that gave her almost plain features the vitality needed to render her attractive. Ordinary brown eyes sparkled, cheeks flushed with good health, and a kind of vibrancy to her every movement made Emily quite the original. With her social standing, dowry, and natural friendly charm, there was no doubt she would take London by storm when she debuted.

"Emily, you didn't have to get me anything," Vivian said as she took the small package and undid the ribbon. Emily practically bounced with exuberance as Vivian opened the box. "Oh, it's beautiful!"

"Isn't it lovely? I thought you could use it on one of your debut gowns."

Emily clapped her hands together excitedly as Vivian

picked up the lace, doing her best to keep the smile on her face at her friend's inadvertent barb. There would be no debut gowns for Vivian, but the lace was still beautiful. Perhaps she could use it on her wedding dress. Her stomach churned nervously at the thought, as she still was not quite accustomed to the idea of being married so quickly.

"Thank you so much," she said, but her voice wavered a little and Emily's bouncing stilled as she peered into Vivian's face.

"Are you all right?"

Realizing she wouldn't be able to hide everything from her friend, and that some events would come to light soon enough, Vivian thought quickly about what she could and could not tell Emily. "I would love to wear the lace for my debut, but I'm not going to have one," she said, trying to sound more enthusiastic than she felt. Emily's eyes grew round with shock, but before she could say anything, Vivian continued, not wanting her friend to ask too many questions. "Mrs. Cunningham just told me—I'm betrothed. Once I leave the school we'll be wed immediately, so there's no need for a social debut. But I would be happy to wear the lace on my wedding dress."

"Oh yes! How wonderful! Let me be the first to wish you happy—if I am indeed the first." But Emily's face remained somewhat concerned, even as she smiled encouragingly. "Is this . . . Are you sure?"

"I'm just a bit surprised," Vivian said smoothly, feeling Mrs. Banks radiating approval behind her. "I wasn't expecting it you see. I hadn't realized—"

"No one told you?" Her friend sounded a bit outraged on her behalf, and Vivian realized she was going to have to do better to soothe her friend's ruffled feathers.

"Mrs. Cunningham just did," she said with a light laugh, pretending an indifference that she didn't feel. She was a bit put out that no one had told her either. It was like being the only one who didn't know a secret, one that affected her entire life. "She gave me a letter from my father, which I'm sure will explain things in more detail." Vivian held up the envelope and Emily made a little "oh" noise, her indignation on Vivian's behalf quickly subsiding. "I'm just disappointed over the loss of my debut, of course." She said the words almost teasingly.

"Oh, but the whole point of a debut and the balls is to find a husband," said Emily reassuringly. She smiled in delight at Vivian, immediately finding the best possible way of viewing the news. "You'll be entering society without any of the pressure the rest of us will! I can't tell you how relieved I would be if my parents were to tell me I had a match and the whole thing was over and done with." The most wonderful part about Emily's reassurances was her obvious sincerity. "Well, as long as the man wasn't unbearable. Who is your husband?"

"A . . . an earl," said Vivian. "I'm sure I'll know more once I get a chance to read my father's letter." At least she hoped so. The name "Cranborne" didn't mean anything to her. Emily would surely know something, but Vivian wanted to read her letter before she requested Emily's opinion.

"Ah, well then, I will leave you so that you may read your letter," Emily said with a laugh, her infectiously high spirits rising again. She and Vivian clasped hands and touched each other's cheeks, mimicking the gesture of affection they'd seen their mothers use with their closest friends. Vivian thanked her again for the lace and then Miss Norton dragged Emily off to practice her embroidery while Vivian and Mrs. Banks headed outside.

Ensconced beneath a tree, with Mrs. Banks fanning herself on a bench a few yards away, Vivian read through her father's letter. It contained a birthday greeting, words of obvious joy at hearing of her excellence in her studies, and an apology for not telling her sooner about her betrothal to Lord Cranborne.

Lord Cranborne had apparently seen her at a wedding breakfast and been instantly smitten. The only wedding Vivian had attended in her entire life was that of a distant relation, a cousin several times removed named Mary. That had been only a few months before her father had brought her to Mrs. Cunningham's school, but she felt quite sure she hadn't actually met any earls there. *Unless* . . . But she was so sure *he'd* been a figment of her imagination.

Sudden uncertainty and even a bit of hope welled up in her. Except the dark-haired man had said he would look for her when she debuted. So even if she hadn't imagined him, he probably wasn't the earl of Cranborne. But why would a man who'd never spoken to her be willing to assist her family so greatly with their finances?

She should feel grateful, but instead she felt more anxious than ever. She had been a little frightened of her debut and the pressure to marry well, so she should have been relieved that those burdens had been taken from her. But now she felt anxious about what her husband-to-be would expect of her and whether or not she could please him.

Of course, it seemed that Mrs. Cunningham thought

she could mold Vivian into exactly the kind of wife that would please Lord Cranborne best. Vivian had excelled at her studies ever since arriving to the school. Now, she vowed she would continue to do so with this new course of study.

Lord Gabriel Cecil, the Earl of Cranborne and son of the Marquess of Salisbury, came to Mrs. Cunningham's Finishing School early in the morning the day after Vivian's birthday. His dark, wavy hair, just a bit longer than the fashion, fluttered gently in the breeze as he rode up on his horse, Lucifer. It had amused him to name his horse after the devil, and it was an apt name, considering Lucifer's temper. Only an experienced and skilled rider would be able to handle Lucifer; he was Gabriel's favorite mount.

Gabriel had waited impatiently for this day, for the beginning of his future wife's training. Ever since seeing her at Mary and George's wedding, he'd practically become a monk. He'd never replaced his mistress, and he'd found that even the temptations of private parties had begun to wane. In fact, it had been nearly a year since he'd indulged in the pleasure of a woman. He didn't plan to share his wife with any other man, and it seemed hypocritical of him to spread his favors with other women just for appearance's sake.

He hadn't been able to get Vivian out of his mind. The way her green eyes had filled with cloudy desire when he'd touched her. The innocence in her every move. The inherent submissiveness he saw when she'd stayed in place under his touch, rather than running, the way she'd undoubtedly been told to do. The obvious attraction between them had drowned out his passion for any other woman.

Discovering Vivian's family's financial situation had made everything even easier. Both George and Mary had raved about the school's curriculum, and Mary herself said it was the best way she could have imagined to be introduced to the pleasures of the marriage bed and George's particular preferences. As much as Gabriel would have liked to train Vivian himself, he ultimately decided it would be best to have her fully trained by professionals with experience, so as to ease her into it.

The time since George and Mary's wedding had crawled by as Gabriel had looked forward more and more to Miss Stafford's birthday and the commencement of her new training. Brokering the negotiations with the baron had been the easy part. Waiting had been much more difficult.

Today, he would talk to Mrs. Cunningham more specifically about the training he wished his future wife to receive and he would finally be able to see Vivian for the first time since that fateful day at the wedding.

He handed Lucifer over to one of the grooms, who looked askance at the feisty horse, and was then escorted up to the school and to Mrs. Cunningham's office by one of the footmen. The severe woman was already seated behind her desk, and she immediately popped up and curtsied as he entered the room.

"Mrs. Cunningham," Gabriel said, taking her hand and bowing over it elegantly.

"My lord," she said, the almost simpering expression on her hard face looking quite at odds with her usual demeanor. Gabriel had that kind of effect on women, and Mrs. Cunningham was not immune. "Thank you so much for coming this morning."

"Of course," Gabriel said, smiling. "I wouldn't have missed this for the world."

He was finally going to see his bride-to-be again.

CHAPTER TWO

THE DAY AFTER HER BIRTHDAY STARTED out like any other day. Vivian woke, dressed, arranged her hair in a simple but elegant chignon, and broke her fast in the dining room with Emily and their friends Charity and Lily. They chatted and Vivian told them the little she knew about her intended husband, which they were much more interested in than anything else. Especially once they found out who it was. Lily recognized the name immediately.

"They call him the Dark Angel," she practically whispered, glancing around to make sure none of the companions were too close. Sometimes the older women took a dim view of gossip, though Vivian considered it more informative than anything. "They say he's devilishly handsome."

"That's what my mother said," Emily said, jumping into the conversation, although her whisper wasn't nearly as low as Lily's. "I've heard he has no need of padding for his shoulders or thighs."

"Emily!" Although she knew she shouldn't encourage her friend's scandalous observations, Vivian couldn't help but laugh. Lily and Charity were giggling just as hard at Emily's scandalous description.

"He's said to be a bit of a rake, runs with a wild crowd," said Emily. "Mama won't allow Sarah to go near him or his friends." Sarah was Emily's older sister—already into her second season, she would know everyone who was respectable. Of course, from the expression on Emily's face, the danger of a wild, forbidden man was thrilling. But then again, Emily wasn't the one marrying him.

"I'm sure that if he wants to be married, that means he'll be settling down," Charity said sympathetically, her hazel eyes warm as she looked at Vivian.

"Or maybe he'll just keep to his wild ways on the side," Lily said, in a voice so low they could barely hear her. "My mama says that it's a relief if the men take their wildness to their mistresses."

"My husband won't have a mistress," Emily said fiercely, glaring at Lily. "Your mother shouldn't let your father get away with it, either. If my father did something like that, he'd be booted out of the house."

"I think my mama really does prefer it," Lily said, a bit defensively, although she looked glum. "I didn't say I wanted it . . . unless I don't like my husband. Then it'd probably be a relief."

Ignoring the conversation going on between Emily and Lily, Charity turned her attention back to Vivian. "If you don't remember meeting him, how does he know who you are?"

"Apparently, he saw me at a wedding, but I'm not sure I remember him." She sighed, trying not to show her disquiet over Emily and Lily's words. As far as she knew, her own father had never kept a mistress. But she had to wonder, would she know? She didn't think she liked the idea of being married to a man who would have other women in his life. The man she'd met at Mary's wedding popped back into her head. Would a man like that be content with her for a bride? Still, she wasn't convinced it was him, so she hadn't mentioned him to Emily or any of the other girls.

"But he remembered you!" gushed Emily, clasping her hands in front of her in excitement. "How romantic!"

Looking at it in one way, Vivian realized it was rather romantic. She had to wonder why the earl had chosen her, a poor girl of much lower social standing, after only meeting her once. If he had met her at all. Objectively she knew she was considered beautiful, even if her red hair wasn't fashionable, but was that all a man wanted?

Well, of course not, she told herself sardonically. If that was all a man wanted, then there would have been no reason for the future training Mrs. Cunningham had told her about. The other girls gushed about the romance of having a man fall in love at first sight, but Vivian still wasn't sure if that was it. Knowing he was handsome and desirable was making her have more dire thoughts.

What if he just wanted a bought bride, one who wouldn't protest? He could do whatever he wanted with his life and wildness and other women, while having his heirs with a respectable woman. What other reason could a man of his social standing, age, and attractiveness want with someone like her?

Obviously, she could not disclose her family's financial circumstances to any of her friends, not even Emily. Even if Emily were to keep it a secret, Vivian couldn't bear the shame of her friend knowing that the earl was paying for

her schooling and for her family's upkeep in return for . . .
well, whatever she would be learning during her training.

After breakfast, she retreated to the music room to
vent some of her feelings on the pianoforte. Today she was
rather manic with it, pounding her way through Chopin's
Nocturnes in a manner that was not at all ladylike. Mrs.
Banks said nothing, just sat in a nearby chair, reading
the book she always kept in her skirt pocket, apparently
understanding that Vivian was discomposed.

Far too soon, however, Mrs. Banks looked at the clock
on the mantle and closed her book. "Come dear, we need
to dress you for luncheon."

Vivian's fingers faltered over the keys. "Dress me?"
she asked. The sudden silence made her voice seem louder
than usual.

"Yes, you'll be having lunch with your fiancé today,"
Mrs. Banks said calmly, as if her announcement was
completely commonplace. Vivian's fingers came down on
the piano with a crash of sound as she clutched at the
instrument. Her head was suddenly whirling.

"Why didn't anyone say anything?" she cried out.
Panic, dismay, anxiety—her chaotic emotions were too
turbulent to pin down any single one. The slight peace
she'd managed to achieve during her playing had been
wrecked.

Mrs. Banks gave her a quelling look, though her blue
eyes were as kind as they always were. "Would you have
been able to relax at all this morning, dear, if you'd known
that you were to have luncheon with him? I didn't want
you to work yourself into a panic, and I decided the less
time you had to do so, the better."

Put that way, it made sense. Part of Vivian still wished

she'd known beforehand to give her more time to mentally prepare herself, but the other part of her was glad she'd had an anxiety-free morning. Who knew what emotional state she'd be in if she'd spent the morning fretting about the upcoming lunch.

Half an hour later, Mrs. Banks and the maid had Vivian dressed in lavender muslin with green trimming, her coppery hair piled in a loose coiffure. She did her best to hide her trembling as Mrs. Banks led her to the front parlor. The door was closed, and the closer Vivian stepped to it, the larger and more intimidating it seemed to appear. She stopped several feet back, grabbing onto Mrs. Banks's sleeve and looking up at her imploringly.

"What do I say?" she whispered, anxiety making her feel almost faint. It felt like she could barely drag enough air into her lungs to live, much less speak. "What do I say to him?"

Seeing the panic in Vivian's eyes, Mrs. Banks drew the younger woman into her arms, hugging her comfortingly. "Speak to him as you did to the matrons at the tea a few days ago. He's not going to expect anything from you but conversation. Ask him about himself, if you'd like."

"Can you stay with me?" Vivian asked, clinging just a bit. After the success of her tea with society's matrons, she'd been feeling quite mature. Now, she felt like a little girl again, uncertain and terrified that she might misstep.

"Of course, I'll be with you," Mrs. Banks said with a little laugh. "Even if he is your future husband, you won't be allowed to socialize unchaperoned with him on school grounds." The companion didn't mention that training was not considered socializing; it wasn't something Vivian needed to know just yet.

Taking as deep a breath as she could, Vivian straightened up, pushing down her panic. She trusted Mrs. Banks; the companion had never steered her wrong before.

The other woman opened the door.

Entering the room, which Vivian was already familiar with, her eyes went immediately to the small table set up near the window, where a man stood up to greet her. Her eyes widened in surprise. It was *him*. The man from Mary's wedding. *Not* a figment of her imagination.

Young. Tall. More than attractive, he was darkly handsome with piercing eyes. He looked like the hero of one of the gothic romances by Mrs. Radcliffe she and Emily loved to read. Mrs. Cunningham frowned upon those books and didn't keep them in the library, but Emily's mother kept her well-stocked, sending her a new one almost every month. Emily always let Vivian read the newest one when she was done with it, and they giggled and whispered over their favorite passages.

It was all too easy for Vivian to imagine swooning into Lord Cranborne's arms, only to be carried away to some dark, distant castle where he'd keep her captive until she agreed to marry him. Except that he didn't need to do that, did he? The marriage was already assured.

But the fantasy brought color to her cheeks and sent a shiver down her spine. Even after the shiver went through her, her body felt as though it was still trembling; tingling almost, in her lower belly.

"Lord Cranborne," Mrs. Banks said with a curtsy. Scrambling for her wits, Vivian immediately followed suit, lowering her eyes. The dark, piercing gaze of the earl as he approached made her feel incredibly uneasy— at least, that was the only explanation she had for the sudden butterflies in her stomach. "May I present my charge, Miss Vivian Stafford."

"Miss Stafford," he murmured in a deep voice she felt all the way down to her bones. Vivian nearly gasped as he reached out to take her hand, feeling his touch like a lightning bolt even through her glove. "A pleasure."

"You're too kind, my lord," she said automatically. Her legs were unaccountably weak as he kept his hold on her fingers. It was all she could do not to fall to her knees in front of him. There was something incredibly dominating about his presence, overpowering even, like he sucked all the air from the room just by standing in it. He acted as though they were just meeting for the first time, and she didn't know what to do.

Of course, technically, this would be the first time they were being properly *introduced*.

"Look at me, Sunrise," he said in a soft voice. The fingers of his free hand came up and pressed against her chin, making her gasp at the presumption of his touch. It was Mary and George's wedding breakfast all over again, except this time she was even more aware of him because he wasn't just a stranger. He was the man who was going to be her husband. Mrs. Banks said nothing, so Vivian could only conclude that it didn't break the bounds of propriety for him to be so free with his fiancée. Her eyes met his grey gaze, the dark silver orbs flecked with green, framed by thick lashes.

His thumb caressed her cheek, making her swallow nervously. Her mouth was suddenly dry. A swipe of her tongue across her lower lip had his eyes lowering, something sparking in them that made her feel quite breathless in response, though she didn't know why.

"Sunrise?" she asked, her voice coming out in a whisper. More color flooded her cheeks. The second sentence out of her mouth and she couldn't even speak correctly!

A small smile tilted his lips, crinkling the corners of his eyes and making him look slightly less intimidating. "Your hair. It's the color of a sunrise."

Vivian blinked at him, too astounded to censor herself. "I think that's the nicest thing anyone's ever said about it."

His smile widened, relieving her. Normally she didn't speak quite so directly, and she really had wanted to make a good impression on him. But he didn't seem to mind. "Not everyone is a slave to fashion, Miss Stafford. There are those of us who adhere to our own preferences." He held out his arm, offering it to her. "Come, I'd like to sit and talk with you."

"Thank you," she said, a bit in a daze. Whatever hazy expectations she'd held in the back of her mind, this domineering, highly desirable man with his surprising compliments was not it. While no one had ever said anything outwardly cruel about her hair color, she was constantly receiving suggestions on how to make it more fashionable, less garish and less bright.

But he liked it. He called her "Sunrise."

A happy little hope rose in her heart as he led her to her seat.

"How would you like your tea?" she asked, picking up the pot, taking some comfort in the expected rituals. She really had no idea how to start a conversation with him. With another lady, it would be easy. What did one say to a man who was soon to be her husband?

"Just a bit of cream," he said, watching her pour. He made her nervous, but she managed not to spill any, even if she trembled a bit. Adding cream to his and cream and sugar to hers, she breathed a sigh of relief when she passed him his cup. At least she could successfully serve tea. Thankfully, he ignored her trembling hands.

Looking at him, her face solemn, she lowered her voice. She had to ask, but if she were wrong somehow, she didn't want Mrs. Banks to overhear. "Have . . . We have met before, yes?"

"Not formally, no," he said, a slight twinkle in his eye that made him much less intimidating. "But yes, at my friend George's wedding. I believe you're a cousin of his wife, Mary."

"Yes . . ." Vivian's voice trailed off. She couldn't believe he was real. That moment had been real. Like before, everything felt too surreal to be possible.

"I'm told Mrs. Cunningham informed you that you are my betrothed?"

The shiver that went through her nearly caused Vivian to upset her own cup of tea as she lifted it. She hadn't expected him to be quite so forward, although perhaps she should have. As he clearly didn't follow the fashions, he didn't seem to adhere to the expected social niceties either.

"Yes, my lord," Vivian said quietly. "Yesterday."

"Your birthday," Lord Cranborne said, holding his saucer in one hand. Avoiding his eyes, Vivian nodded. She found herself horribly intimidated by him. She didn't know what he wanted, and yet she was supposed to please him.

More than that, now that she'd met him, she desperately *wanted* to please him. There was something about his commanding demeanor that garnered instant respect, and he'd been so complimentary about her hair, and he made her feel so warm and tingly inside . . . and she had no idea what to do.

"Yes," she said, wishing she could think of something better to say.

Lord Cranborne reached into his jacket and pulled out a small package wrapped in white tissue paper, placing it on the table between them. "Happy birthday, Sunrise."

With trembling hands, Vivian put down her saucer and teacup and picked up the package. She glanced up at the earl through her eyelashes. The expression on his face was one of anticipation, but he wasn't looking at the box. He was looking at her bosom. Heat flickered through her, and she immediately dropped her eyes. Beneath his gaze, her nipples puckered and tightened, and she felt a strange throbbing between her thighs that made her press her legs together.

Doing her utmost to ignore the strange reaction her body was having to him, Vivian unwrapped the package. A book fell into her hands and she gasped with pleasure, meeting his eyes completely on her own for the first time.

"Thank you! How did you know?" She cradled the precious book, Mrs. Radcliffe's latest gothic romance, so new that even Emily hadn't received it from her mother yet.

A small smile played on his lips at her pleasure, which only made her feel guilty. After all, she owed him. Shouldn't she be the one finding ways to please him? "Mrs. Banks wrote to me of your reading preferences. I'm glad you like it."

"I love it," she said, wrapping her fingers around it as if she was afraid it might disappear if she didn't hold it tightly enough. "My parents can't . . . I mean, I often borrow the books from my friend Emily, but I usually have to wait until she's done with them. Which is only fair, as they're hers, but it's lovely to have the latest novel as my own."

"So you enjoy reading Mrs. Radcliffe's works. What else do you like to do, Sunrise?" The way he asked the question made it seem as if he were implying something, but Vivian was unsure of what.

"I like to paint watercolors—no, I truly do," she said, catching the slight change in his expression. "I know all the young ladies here are taught to say they do, but most of them really don't. I love painting and seeing a picture slowly being created out of a blank canvas, every brush stroke bringing it one small step closer to being a complete image."

The look the earl gave her now was filled with a bit more respect. He leaned forward. "May I tell you a secret?" he asked, his low voice inviting her to lean forward as well. Feeling helpless to the spell he seemed to be weaving around her, Vivian leaned in, expecting at any moment that Mrs. Banks would say something about their proximity to each other. "I sketch . . . and I feel the same way."

Vivian blinked and then smiled at him, feeling a touch of kinship. It wasn't that unusual for a nobleman such as himself to have a hobby like sketching, but it wasn't exactly common, either. Then again, he'd already professed himself to not care about what was fashionable. She suspected he'd wanted her to lean in to be close to him, not because he actually cared whether or not anyone knew that he sketched.

"What do you like to draw?" she asked.

"Whatever I find beautiful," he said smoothly. The

look he gave her warmed her from the inside out, while at the same time making her shiver. "In fact, I think you might be my next subject, sweetheart."

The warmth inside of her blossomed at the second compliment. He must truly think she was beautiful. There was no reason to charm her or court her. After all, they were already betrothed and she and her family owed him a great deal. Although Vivian wasn't used to thinking of herself as particularly beautiful, there could be no doubt of the earl's truthfulness.

"What else do you like to do?"

"I like to play the pianoforte," she said shyly. "I was playing this morning, before this. I also like to walk out on the grounds in the gardens. While there's always something to do in the school, whenever there's sunshine, I try to go outside, even if it's only for a few minutes."

Remembering she was supposed to ask questions as well, she did her best to turn the tables on him. They both talked about their families, and she learned his mother had died of an illness when he was younger, after his second sister was born. A few years ago, his father had remarried—to his daughters' governess, no less. It appeared the earl's disdain for convention and the opinions of others was a family trait. Marrying a governess wasn't a complete scandal, but it was certainly something that would cause quite a bit of talk. Most of it unkind.

In return, Vivian told him a little about her younger sisters, Persephone and Rose, and her little brother, Alistair. She was in the middle of a story about Rose's determination to study the same subjects as Alistair, when Mrs. Banks cleared her throat and stood.

"I'm sorry to interrupt, but Miss Stafford needs to

return to her usual schedule for the afternoon," Mrs. Banks said.

The sharp pang of disappointment that Vivian felt was reflected on her face for just a moment before she covered it with the usual social mask. She'd managed to relax and had been enjoying talking to the earl, forgetting, for a bit, to be nervous.

"Of course," the earl said, exchanging a look with Mrs. Banks as he stood. He held out his hand to help Vivian up, and, to her shock, pulled her close to him as he did so.

They were standing so close that if she breathed too deeply, her chest would brush against his. For the second time that day, her breasts were tingly and sensitive, and she felt completely breathless. Which was probably good, considering that a deep breath would put their bodies in contact, and then she might just faint.

Bringing her hand up, the earl looked into her eyes as he kissed her palm through her glove. There was something achingly intimate about the gesture, and it certainly crossed the bounds of propriety. But Mrs. Banks didn't protest and Vivian felt too dizzy to consider saying anything.

"I expect to hear you've been applying yourself to your studies," he said in a low voice. His eyes bore into hers. It was like being caught in a predator's gaze, as if he was one of those exotic snakes brought back from India. Heat surged inside her. She was acutely aware of her hand in his and his other hand on her waist. "Be a good girl for me, Sunrise."

"Yes, my lord," she whispered. For just a moment, his eyes lowered to her lips and she wondered if he would kiss her. Mrs. Banks cleared her throat, and instead he stepped back. Vivian almost regretted the need for a chaperone, but she knew that she also would have never become comfortable in the room with the earl if Mrs. Banks hadn't been there from the beginning.

"Come along, Miss Stafford," Mrs. Banks said.

As she exited the room, Vivian glanced over her shoulder to see the earl watching her go, a contemplative expression on his face.

Once Mrs. Banks and Vivian were gone, Gabriel sat down and waited for Mrs. Cunningham to come fetch him.

He thought the first meeting with Vivian had gone very well. In the time since he'd last seen her, she'd matured into an attractive young woman, more than ready to be married. Ready to be initiated into the rather decadent and debauched world he inhabited.

When Mary had found out Gabriel's plan, she'd endorsed it quite enthusiastically, saying she'd found great comfort in learning so much before she and George were expected to be intimate together. Apparently the "talk" she'd had with her mother the night before her wedding had left a great deal to be desired. She thought the school's methods were much more informative, and less frightening for a young woman about to embark on marriage.

Mary's mother had told her to lie back and let her husband do as he wished and hope he didn't desire to do it very often. She'd assured her daughter that it would probably be over with quite quickly and that after the first time it wasn't as painful, although it could be tedious if it took too long. Therefore, it was best to just be as still as possible and let him get on with it. Mary had done a spot-on imitation of her mother's condescending tones, interspersed with wild giggles. Both George and Gabriel had been appalled. It made him wonder what his step-mother had said to his sisters, because he couldn't imagine Audrey saying anything like that.

If that was the kind of advice mothers gave their daughters . . . well, Gabriel was glad he'd heard about the school from George and Mary. Otherwise, his needs and desires might have frightened the hell out of Vivian, even though he would have tempered them for her at first.

Considering Mary's recommendation, and knowing that his own desires when it came to the marriage bed were broader than that of most men, he knew having the school prepare Vivian was the right thing to do.

CHAPTER THREE

"WHAT DID YOU THINK OF MISS STAFFORD, my lord?" asked Mrs. Cunningham once Gabriel had settled himself in one of the comfortable chairs in her office. She had three seats arranged in a circle to facilitate the necessary conversations that took place there. Mrs. Banks would soon be joining them.

"She's just as delightful as I remembered, perhaps more so," he said, smiling fondly. Sweet, gentle, submissive, and every inch the perfect young debutante.

"Miss Stafford is quite lovely, and, if I may say so, is a well-chosen subject for the training we provide," Mrs. Cunningham said, smiling. "Ever since she arrived at the school she's been cooperative, very eager to please, and inherently submissive. I think she will be quite easy to train and will be one of the school's most accomplished students."

The description aligned very closely with the impressions Gabriel had received, both when he'd first met Vivian and as he'd spoken with her today.

"I think we must discuss exactly what you would like the training to achieve, once Mrs. Banks arrives. We would like to match her to your desires as precisely as we are able to."

"How so?" asked Gabriel, curious.

"Well, for instance, some men prefer their brides come to them obedient but partially untrained so that they might finish the training themselves. Some prefer that their brides become accustomed to being constantly penetrated. Others want a bride who will obey any command instantly, some want their brides to associate certain punishments with pleasure, or being bound with pleasure. It all depends on the particular gentleman. And, if he so wishes, the desires of his particular bride."

"Will I be able to participate in any of the training?"

Mrs. Cunningham hesitated. "It is not unheard of, although I do not recommend it for at least the beginning of training. You will, of course, have regular meetings with Miss Stafford, but at the outset it is likely she will be overwhelmed with her new studies and adjusting to new revelations about what a marriage entails. During that time, she will cling to her companion for explanations and reassurance; once she begins to accept the new aspects of her life, it will be easier to transfer her obedience from Mrs. Banks to you. It's possible she might go through a period of resentment, especially if she earns any punishments, and it will be best if she has time to accept her new situation before you become a part of that aspect of her training."

Disappointed, but realizing that Mrs. Cunningham made a very good point, Gabriel nodded and sank back into his chair to think. Seeing that he was focused inward, Mrs. Cunningham did not press him. Instead, she waited with her ear cocked towards the door, listening for Mrs. Banks.

A few minutes later there was a cursory knock at the door before it opened and Mrs. Banks walked in. Both Mrs. Cunningham and Gabriel stood; after all, he could not remain seated while there were ladies standing, his higher rank notwithstanding.

"Mrs. Banks, please join us," said Mrs. Cunningham with a sweeping gesture at the awaiting chair.

The companion murmured a greeting to Lord Cranborne as she took her place. Gabriel's keen gaze swept over the woman who spent so much time with his future wife and who would be responsible for guiding Vivian through the beginning of her intimate education. Mrs. Banks was younger than he'd expected, perhaps only a few years older than himself, with honey blonde hair, bright blue eyes, and an attractive oval face. The blue and cream dress she was wearing set off her good looks and displayed her curves to perfection without being immodest.

Gabriel was immediately struck by what an attractive pair she would make with Miss Stafford. Older, yes, but there were many gentlemen among the *ton* who would pursue Mrs. Banks in her own right. He had not thought about what his reaction to watching his future wife with her companion would be, but he now realized it would be quite a bit more enjoyable than he anticipated.

Mrs. Cunningham turned to give Lord Cranborne an ingratiating look. "So, my lord, what would you like Miss Stafford's training to achieve?"

Shifting in his seat to a more comfortable position, and pushing away the erotic images now titillating his imagination, Gabriel took a moment to consider his words. "I'd like her to keep as much of her innocence as possible," he said, deciding to be bluntly graphic. "I shall enjoy her blushes and attempts to preserve her modesty, and I don't want her to lose that before we marry. I don't mind if she protests, as long as she is obedient when she is given an order."

"That is quite easily done," said Mrs. Banks, nodding. Her soft smile brightened her countenance even further. "We shall allow her to indulge in her natural reactions without punishment. If she is given that small amount of latitude, while being trained into obedience, she will cling to those reactions for as long as possible."

"Wonderful," said Gabriel, a slow, pleased smile spreading across his handsome face. "I would like her to become accustomed to being in restraints as well as holding herself in position without the restraints."

"Of course," said Mrs. Cunningham. "Our training also usually includes accustoming the young women to the combination of pleasure and pain, unless you would like to keep them separate. It depends on what you'd like her punishments to be."

"She'll be spanked on a regular basis, for both pleasure and minor infractions," said Gabriel, leaning back into his chair with an anticipatory gleam in his dark eyes. "Larger infractions will be punished with a strap or a cane. I plan to use her bottom as well, for both punishment and pleasure. I want her to become accepting of it as a punishment, but not accustomed to it. I would also like her to be trained to please me orally, but I'd prefer she actually practice on me."

"I can start her out sooner than that, if you'd like, without involving another man," Mrs. Banks said smoothly, obviously understanding that Gabriel was reluctant to share the favors of his bride-to-be. Indeed, she looked as though she were anticipating the lessons just as much as Gabriel was. "If she is introduced to the techniques beforehand she will progress much faster and be less resistant when confronted with doing such a thing on a man. I can use my fingers to simulate the act and therefore I will also be able to guide her more definitively."

"That's acceptable," he said, giving the widow a roguish grin.

The group discussed further methods of Vivian's training for the next quarter of an hour, before Gabriel had to be on his way. However, by the time he left the school he felt fully confident leaving the instruction of his bride in the capable hands of Mrs. Cunningham and Mrs. Banks. Although, of course, he was also understandably frustrated at the long wait he had ahead of him before he would be able to participate in Vivian's training.

CHAPTER FOUR

A KNOCK ON THE DOOR HAD VIVIAN SITTING up abruptly. She'd just been about to drift off to sleep, despite all the thoughts whirling around her head, and the unexpected knocking sent anxiety shooting through her. The nervousness quickly turned to relief as the door opened and Emily stuck her head in.

"How are you?" she asked, quickly sliding in and kicking the door shut behind her. They weren't supposed to be in each other's rooms at night, although Emily and Vivian did it often enough. Of course, Emily came to Vivian's room much more often than the other way around, always being the more daring of the two. "Mrs. Banks said you weren't feeling well."

With a lacy robe covering her dressing gown, Emily scampered across the room and sat down on Vivian's bed, not at all deterred by Vivian's supposed illness. The little slippers she was wearing were embroidered quite prettily. It occurred to Vivian that many of her own things, ever since she'd arrived at the school, were nearly as good in quality as Emily's. For the first time, she realized that it must be because of Lord Cranborne.

"Oh, ah, I'm feeling much better," Vivian stammered, realizing that Mrs. Banks must have fibbed for her after Vivian had requested some time alone. The day's events had thoroughly disoriented Vivian in a way that she'd never experienced before. She was enamored of her husband-to-be already, and yet she couldn't shake Mrs. Cunningham's warnings about her new training from her mind. She'd just wanted to be alone with her thoughts for a bit.

"You look a little flushed," Emily observed, looking her over carefully. "But not feverish."

"It's been a rather interesting day," Vivian said. "I had lunch with my betrothed today. The Earl of Cranborne."

Emily squealed loudly, bouncing on the bed, before clapping her hand over her mouth. Her brown eyes sparkled above her fingers as she hunched, both of them automatically waiting, expecting one of their companions to open the door and catch them in a misdeed. When the door didn't open, both let out the breaths they'd been holding and smiled at each other.

"What was he like?" Emily asked, whispering the question so loudly that she might as well have spoken in her normal tones. "Was he as handsome as I remembered?"

Opening and closing her mouth, Vivian realized she didn't have the words to adequately describe him. "Very handsome. Powerful. He looks like one of Mrs. Radcliffe's heroes." She flushed with pleasure. "He brought me one of her books for my birthday."

Vivian picked it up from the little nightstand next to her bed, where she'd set it for reading. She couldn't wait to get started on it, but tonight she'd been too unfocused to even make the attempt.

This time Emily's squeal was much quieter. "Oh, how thoughtful! This time I might actually have to borrow a book from you if my mother doesn't send me a copy quickly enough." Her eyes sparkled with happiness for Vivian. That was one of the most wonderful things about Emily: despite her high social position, she was an incredibly generous and sweet person, with not the slightest hint of artifice about her. "Did you like him? Did he say why he chose you?"

Vivian hesitated for just a moment. "He said . . . He said he saw me and he felt a connection," she said. Which, he'd implied, in a manner of speaking. Of course, she couldn't tell Emily too much about it, without treading on dangerous ground. As to Emily's other question . . . Vivian's lips tilted up in a helpless smile. "I do think I like him, yes. He's frightfully intimidating at first glance, but we had luncheon together and he was very polite and easy to talk to after a while." In truth, she had been drawn to him, the same way the heroines in Mrs. Radcliffe's books often were.

Emily clapped her hands in delight. "I'm so happy for you, Vivian. Out of all the girls in this school, you deserve it."

Somehow, the way Emily said it made Vivian feel uncomfortable; she could almost swear she saw hidden knowledge in Emily's eyes of the Staffords's financial situation. But, if she was aware, of course she would never say it outright. Still, Vivian felt it best to change the topic.

"Thank you," she said, smiling at her friend to cover her own unease that perhaps her family's problems weren't as well-hidden as they'd thought. "What did you do with your day?"

Not at all perturbed by the change in topic, Emily chattered about the lesson she and several of the other young women Vivian usually studied with had in a new embroidery knot that afternoon, which Vivian had missed due to her luncheon. Since Vivian recognized the knot as one her mother had already taught her, she knew she would have no work to make up for. Emily, on the other hand, always had trouble with anything that involved sitting still for long periods of time and had no patience for embroidery.

"Miss Norton said that I'm hopeless with a needle, but I can't imagine a man actually choosing to wed me for my embroidery skills," said Emily laughing. The gossip had restored Vivian's equilibrium and she laughed along with her friend.

"And riding a horse will make you more appealing?" Vivian teased back.

"As long as he enjoys riding, it will," said Emily staunchly, although her eyes were twinkling merrily. She glanced at the clock and sighed. "I must be getting back to my room, in case Miss Norton decides to check on me."

"Thank you for coming to see me, I'm glad we had a chance to talk," Vivian said, as Emily leaned over to give her an affectionate kiss on the cheek.

"Of course. I'll see you in classes tomorrow." Catching the look on Vivian's face, Emily frowned. "Won't I?"

"Um." Vivian faltered. "I might be having some special classes from now on. I don't know what time they're to be held, though. Mrs. Banks says that there will be specific things I need to know as Lord Cranborne's wife." Things she didn't dare mention even obliquely to Emily, both because of her scholarship status, and because Emily would be full of questions that Vivian couldn't answer yet—and wouldn't even once she could.

Obviously, her worry communicated itself to her friend, because Emily smiled reassuringly at her. "You're going to be an amazing wife, Vivian. Whatever special classes you need, I'm sure you'll be brilliant at them."

With that Emily gave her a quick hug before sneaking back out the door and down the hall to her own room.

The next morning, instead of going to the usual dining room, Vivian was taken to Mrs. Cunningham's private rooms to break her fast. When Mrs. Banks had come to fetch her and told her where she would be having her meal, she'd been quite shocked. She'd never heard of another young lady having a meal with Mrs. Cunningham.

The beautiful vivid blue gown she wore gave her some measure of confidence, yet she felt as though both Mrs. Cunningham and Mrs. Banks were studying her every movement much more closely than ever before. It was an unnerving sensation, but she did her best to smile and engage in the light social repartee as they had taught her. They discussed the weather and the newest fashions, and complimented each other's dresses. It was all what Vivian was used to, but suddenly it felt like a charade.

Having met the earl yesterday, she could only assume Mrs. Cunningham wished to speak with her about her upcoming training. Engaging in meaningless social chatter was becoming almost tiresome, making her more and more anxious to discuss what they were really there for.

As the meal ended, Vivian felt her emotions winding up tighter and tighter as if she were being stretched and pulled like wool around a spindle. So far, nothing out of the ordinary had happened, and yet that did not comfort her. Why would Mrs. Cunningham invite her for a private meal only to discuss fashion? There must be some purpose behind her presence here, especially after the events of yesterday, and she was becoming quite desperate to know what.

Finally, she couldn't take it anymore.

Putting on her social smile the way a warrior might don his armor, Vivian raised her emerald eyes to meet the hard agates of Mrs. Cunningham's. "Thank you so much for the invitation to break my fast with you, Mrs. Cunningham," she said. "It was quite an unexpected honor."

Mrs. Banks and Mrs. Cunningham exchanged pleased smiles. Not only had Vivian lasted much longer than most of the young woman in inquiring about her presence, but she had done so subtly and politely. Some young women became quite aggressive at this point, and others never got up the gumption to say anything at all.

From her reading of Lord Cranborne, Mrs. Cunningham was becoming more and more assured that Miss Stafford was exactly the right kind of young woman for his lordship. Submissive but spirited and with a well of inner strength that would make her final submission to him all the more glorious.

"But one well deserved," she replied to Vivian. "After all, you have proven yourself to be one of the most exemplary students at this school. Now that you've been informed of your upcoming training and had the chance to think things over, as well as meet the earl, I wanted to speak with you again."

"Thank you," she said carefully, trying to decide how to word her myriad of questions. "I do appreciate it."

But before she could ask anything, Mrs. Banks reached across the table to rest her hand on Vivian's.

"Tomorrow your training will begin in earnest," said Mrs. Banks. "During the day, you will join the other young women in a practicum we have created to give you all experience in the actual running of a household. In the evening, you will forgo the usual activities to begin your marriage training."

"Not all of it will be pleasant," said Mrs. Cunningham, her voice cutting through Mrs. Banks's softer tones. "But some girls have found a good deal of pleasure in their training. You will be punished when necessary, and rewarded as deserved."

"I'm sure you'll do wonderfully," Mrs. Banks said, giving Vivian's hand a squeeze. Vivian's heart jumped and she bit down on her lower lip, made nervous by Mrs. Cunningham's words even as Mrs. Banks had sought to reassure her.

"She'd better," Mrs. Cunningham said acerbically. "We have a reputation to uphold."

"Of course she will, she'll be a credit to us all."

It didn't occur to Vivian that the scene being played out before her was well rehearsed, designed to both set her off balance and realign her emotions positively towards Mrs. Banks. The handsome widow's support bolstered her spirits in the face of Mrs. Cunningham's doubtful tone and foreboding expression.

"I will certainly do my best," said Vivian truthfully, not wanting to let down Mrs. Banks's confidence in her. Mrs. Cunningham nodded her head as if to say she knew that Vivian would try her best, but that didn't entirely convince her that she would do *well*. Mrs. Banks gave Vivian's hand another squeeze.

"Wonderful, my dear," Mrs. Banks said, giving both her and Mrs. Cunningham a brilliant smile. "Now, come along. Your new lessons don't begin until the morrow, but there are still things to do today."

Gabriel swirled his scotch around the bottom of his glass, listening to the musical clinking of ice against crystal as he stared out into the night. After his meeting at the school, he'd come to his father's house in London to have a visit with the family. They were, of course, all eager to hear about the woman that he'd finally chosen as his bride.

Both of his younger sisters had married before him, both to men who were also part of the wilder set. In fact, Jonathan, his youngest sister's husband, had been one of his good friends since they were at Oxford together. They'd both spent time at the private parties that catered to the clandestine activities their group enjoyed.

Taking a sip of the scotch, his eyes fell to the pad of paper in front of him. A sketch of Vivian, as he'd seen her at luncheon yesterday. Softly feminine, with a sparkle in her eye, her lips slightly parted as if about to ask a question. He'd been sitting here for an hour and he'd already drawn three sketches of her, the itch in his fingers impossible to ignore.

One of the sketches was of her nude, but obviously it was not drawn from memory, as he hadn't yet had the opportunity to see her languishing in front of him, eyes sleepy with feminine pleasure. The Vivian that he'd drawn in his sketch was the one he would eventually have, with her lush curves, inviting smile, and submissive eyes.

"Gabriel! Why are you hiding away in here when you're supposed to be visiting us?" Henrietta, his youngest sister, impish and impulsive as always, grinned at him as she burst into the room, practically skipping across it to reach him.

"Hello, poppet," he said, grinning at her as she bent down to kiss his cheek before plopping down in the chair across from him. "I see that a few months of marriage to Jonathan has done nothing to curb your unladylike behavior."

Calling Henrietta a hoyden was a vast understatement. Being married to Jonathan had barely slowed her down. Their father had had the same trouble disciplining her; it never kept Henrietta subdued for long. She had a penchant for trouble, especially if it involved eavesdropping or spying, the little sneak.

Henrietta snorted. The soft copper of her dress set off her brown hair and hazel eyes quite prettily, and Gabriel could only marvel that she was now a married young woman. Although she was the same age as Vivian, he still had trouble seeing Henrietta as anything other than a rosy-cheeked little nuisance in pigtails.

"Who is this?" she asked, leaning forward with interest as she looked at the sketchpad he'd been using. "Is that Miss Stafford? She's beautiful!"

"She is, isn't she?" Gabriel asked, putting his fingers atop the page so that Henrietta didn't get any ideas about seeing what else he'd been sketching. The nude of Vivian definitely needed to be hidden from her. He looked down at the picture, smiling at the visage that he'd created.

There was such a softness, a sweetness to Vivian. He hadn't quite managed to capture it in the drawing, but he could still see it in his mind's eye.

"Oh, that's lovely."

Jerked out of his thoughts, Gabriel glanced at his sister and raised his eyebrow when he realized that she was looking at him and not the picture. "What is?"

"You. When you were talking about the marriage at dinner, you made it sound like a business arrangement, but you care for her." Henrietta's laughter chimed and she shook her head at him. "I can see it in your face." She stood and held out her hand to him. "I'm glad, brother. You deserve happiness. Now come and talk with everyone— you've spent far too much time in here mooning over your fiancée as it is. Pining away won't make her finish her schooling any faster."

"Imp," Gabriel said, standing up with a sigh and offering her his arm, which she took. The grin on her face didn't fade at all, despite his scowl at her. Mooning, indeed. He wasn't mooning. Or pining.

He was just feeling a bit impatient.

"Good morning!"

The overly bright, cheery voice of a maid roused Vivian from a most unexpected dream. The earl had been holding her, whispering sweet words of love in her ear, when suddenly he'd whispered that she had been a very bad girl and he was going to punish her. Vivian didn't know what that meant, but her entire body had tightened in an odd sort of exquisite anticipation.

"Time to wake up, miss," the maid said, pulling the blue damask curtains apart. Brilliant sunshine filled the room and Vivian groaned, throwing an arm over her eyes to protect them from the sudden light.

"Is it earlier than usual?" she asked, blinking her emerald eyes in sleepy confusion.

"Oh, yes, miss, a full hour earlier. Please, miss, you'll be late if we don't get started."

"I don't understand," Vivian said as she dragged herself from the warmth of the bed, shivering slightly from the morning chill when she was wearing nothing but a thin night rail. The gossamer fabric did very little to warm her, and her nipples stuck out in pink little points, rubbing against the silky inside of the garment.

"You're starting the practicum today, right, miss?" the maid asked as she steered Vivian towards the stool in front of her vanity.

"Yes, I believe so." Vivian's thoughts were a bit hazy, but she did remember that she was starting a new course of study today.

"Well, that starts a full hour earlier than the normal run of lessons, as you have to travel to the house," the maid chattered. Vivian stifled a groan as the maid began to unpin and re-curl her hair. Why hadn't Mrs. Banks or Mrs. Cunningham mentioned the earlier time? What house was the maid talking about?

Blearily she stared into the mirror as the maid did her best to give some life to her hair. Scrubbing the sleep from her eyes, Vivian allowed the maid to help her dress. The difference of one hour's worth of sleep was more than she could have ever realized; her body had become acclimated to the normal schedule of the school, and this one unexpected change was brutal. She felt almost as though she were sleepwalking.

"There you are, miss, you'd best hurry, you're already two minutes late," the maid said, practically bustling Vivian out the door. She'd been dressed in a smart morning gown of blue muslin.

Vivian gave herself a little shake and walked towards the front of the house. She didn't pick up her steps until she was at the top of the staircase and saw two other young women waiting in the foyer with their companions, one pair being Emily and Miss Norton, as well as Mrs. Cunningham and Mrs. Banks. Another older woman, Vivian assumed she was a companion, was waiting there too, and she felt a surge of relief that she wasn't the last to arrive. Sweeping down the stairs, she joined the group at the bottom.

"Good morning!" said Emily as Vivian reached the bottom of the stairs. She was looking almost annoyingly chipper, dressed in a sunny yellow morning gown, and far too bright-eyed. "Isn't this exciting?"

"Is it?" asked Vivian, slightly confused. She still wasn't entirely sure what was going on.

"You missed the explanation because you were late," Emily said, grinning. Mrs. Cunningham must have explained what the practicum was. Vivian winced.

"Yes, Lady Emily, she did." Mrs. Banks cut into their conversation dryly. "If you'll excuse us, I'd like to speak with Vivian."

Emily shot Vivian a sympathetic look as Mrs. Banks drew her off to the side.

"Miss Stafford, you're five minutes late," Mrs. Banks said in a stern voice. Vivian shifted uncomfortably under the widow's hard gaze.

"I'm sorry, Mrs. Banks. I didn't realize that I needed to

be awake so early." Although she was apologizing, there was a hint of reproach in her voice.

"That's part of the practicum," said Mrs. Banks, raising her eyebrow at Vivian. "Your studies are moving on from the theoretical to the practical, and you will actually be taking turns with the other young ladies in running a small household. One of the first things you will need to learn is to be flexible and to be able to adjust to any change in your routine. Who knows what emergency might crop up in the early hours of the morning? You must be prepared to deal with it. It would behoove you to remember that." The look she gave Vivian clearly showed she had not missed the implication of blame Vivian had placed on her. Vivian wilted a bit, knowing Mrs. Banks was right and that she'd already disappointed her companion in this new course of training. "We will discuss your punishment for being late when we return to the school this evening."

Punishment? Vivian almost felt faint. Yes, Mrs. Cunningham had said something about punishments, but Vivian hadn't properly heeded the warning. Had her dream been somehow prophetic? Not once, in all her time at the school, had she ever earned a punishment. Certainly not for something as trifling as being a few minutes late.

The shock must have shown on her face because Mrs. Banks's expression became slightly more sympathetic. "You are no longer a child, Vivian. You are a young woman and you are going to be married soon. Being late is no longer acceptable; it is a measure of disrespect towards the people you are meeting. What is acceptable for a child is no longer acceptable for you."

Never had Vivian been so thoroughly chastised, and

she blushed bright red, feeling quite miserable. Since coming to the school she'd always been a model student, indeed she'd strived to be so. Perhaps she had become complacent.

Footsteps came rushing down the stairs and Vivian turned her head to see the last young woman joining them, looking flushed and contrite. Her immediate apology to the group was in sharp contrast to Vivian's unconcern. Mrs. Banks gave Vivian a significant look and then they were sweeping out the door to the awaiting carriages.

The return home that evening saw all four young women completely exhausted. Even Emily had lost the habitual sparkle in her eyes and was leaning her head heavily against the side of the carriage she was sharing with Vivian, Miss Norton, and Mrs. Banks. If it weren't for the jerks and bumps along the road, Vivian was quite sure she would have fallen asleep right where she sat.

Which would surely have made for another reprimand from Mrs. Banks.

It had been a day full of reprimands. For all the young women. They were sharply chided, their mistakes loudly pointed out every time they made one. The classes had taught them how an effective household was supposed to run, but the practicum was already showing them they could not rely on theories. Mrs. Cunningham had explained, before leaving them at the practice house, that all the scenarios they would face during the practicum were taken from actual events in other households.

The experience had been eye opening. The day had been sectioned off by hours, with each young lady assigned a section during which time she was in charge.

Each day they would rotate sections so that each was able to practice running the household during the morning, luncheon, afternoon tea, and dinner. Today, Vivian had been given the morning section, which had started out smoothly enough but had quickly gone haywire when a maid burst in on the group as they were being given a tour of the house, shrieking that there were rats in the kitchen.

Vivian had had no idea what to do.

The other young ladies were allowed to give suggestions, but two of them had become so hysterical at the idea of rats that they had been utterly useless. Eventually Vivian called for several footmen to go on a rat hunt, but the fracas had ended up delaying lunch. Which, she'd been able to tell from the look on Mrs. Banks's face, had been unacceptable.

Each of the companions had a pad of paper on which they took notes about their students, and Mrs. Banks had had an ominous expression as she'd scribbled down several things on hers. All of the companions pointed out the myriad of mistakes each of the girls was making, flustering them further.

All in all, it was not a pleasant day. Hers wasn't over yet. She hadn't forgotten that her marriage training was to begin this evening. Nibbling on her soft lower lip, she glanced over at Mrs. Banks, who was staring out the window of the carriage. Somehow, she didn't think her companion would be willing to postpone the first lesson for a later date. After all, once she was married and the lady of a household, her duties would be round the clock.

Once the carriage arrived at the school and the young ladies stepped out, Mrs. Banks pulled Vivian over to the side, speaking in a low voice. "I will join you in your room in an hour. You have until then to do as you please."

"Thank you, Mrs. Banks," said Vivian, feeling quite relieved. She wanted to do nothing more than go upstairs to her room and lie down.

"That was awful." Emily joined Vivian as she headed up the stairs, both of them dragging their feet. "I feel like I've been trampled."

Vivian thought Emily had done much better with her portion of the day than any of the other young ladies. The kitchen was still in an uproar when it was time for tea, but Emily had distracted her guests by performing on the pianoforte until the tea was ready. Then, rather than enjoying the tea, they'd all had to follow Emily to the kitchen, where she'd managed to restore order, something neither Vivian nor Rose (whose section of the day included luncheon) had accomplished. The key, as far as Vivian could tell, was sheer bravado. Although Emily had confided to Vivian that she'd had no idea what she was doing, to the others she'd appeared completely confident, and the staff had taken heart from that confidence and the firm hand Emily had wielded.

"You did very well," said Vivian enviously. "I felt like a complete wreck."

"Well, of course!" Emily rolled her eyes. "Who knew they'd give us something so awful on our first day? Before we'd even finished touring the house!"

Vivian sighed. "I suppose that was the point, to teach us we can never expect when such an emergency might occur."

"Kind of like throwing a child in the pond and seeing if she swims?"

"Very like," Vivian said, a little smile curving her face for the first time in hours. Thank goodness for Emily.

"I can't wait to fall into bed. Surely tomorrow won't be as frenzied," said Emily as they reached her room. "Have a good night!"

Vivian continued down the hall, wishing she was like the other students. Trepidation filled her as she wondered what kind of first lesson tonight would bring, and what her punishment would entail.

CHAPTER FIVE

HAVING LEARNED HER LESSON FROM THAT morning, Vivian made sure she was ready early for Mrs. Banks and her training. She'd had the maid help her change into a fresh gown, and had used a wet cloth to wash her face, neck, and arms. Feeling much revived, she sat by the fire to read the book Lord Cranborne had given her while she awaited Mrs. Banks. The story pulled her in immediately; she found herself comparing the dark and brooding hero to the Earl of Cranborne. Picturing a real man made the book much more exciting, especially because she couldn't help but imagine herself in place of the heroine.

As soon as the door opened, she reluctantly set the book down and stood to greet her companion, giving her a small curtsy. It was hard to leave the dramatic happenings of the book, as the hero and the heroine had just met for the first time, the hero leaving the heroine breathless just as the earl did to Vivian. But any other response would be rude.

"Good evening, Mrs. Banks."

"Good evening, Miss Stafford." The older woman

swept into the room, the same notepad in her hand that she'd been carrying during the practicum that morning, probably filled with every critique she'd made about Vivian. Vivian's stomach twisted as she looked at it; there was nothing she disliked more than feeling as though she had disappointed someone's expectations.

Stepping to the side, Mrs. Banks gestured to a footman behind her who was carrying a high-backed chair. It was a sturdy piece of furniture, simply carved from oak, the seat comfortably padded with a dark brown cushion, and it had no arm rests. The footman settled it in the middle of the room as Vivian stared, before giving both ladies a small bow and exiting.

"This is your punishment chair," said Mrs. Banks, gesturing at the chair as she tapped her thumb against the pad of paper in her hand. Her voice was firm but gentle, with a matter-of-fact tone.

"My . . . my punishment chair?" Vivian stared aghast at the thing, completely flabbergasted. Mrs. Banks thought it rather a pity the earl wasn't able to see Vivian's reaction to the piece of furniture he'd provided; with her wide green eyes and open pink lips she made quite a fetching picture.

"Yes. At the end of each day you will present your-self to atone for whatever transgressions you may have committed during the day."

Staring at the chair, Vivian tried to imagine what kind of punishment could include such a chair.

"Is this . . . is this punishment part of my marriage training?" she asked, her mind scrambling to make sense of this turn of events. She had no idea what Mrs. Banks was expecting of her right now and the lack of guidance made her feel both confused and anxious.

Pleased with her pupil's perception and reaction, Mrs. Banks moved closer to curve a supportive arm around Vivian's shaking shoulders. There was a fine line to be walked, of both disciplinarian and comforter; Miss Stafford must learn that the person who doled out her punishment was the same person who would give her pleasure, the same person who would guide her and soothe her when it was needed. The earl intended to be all of those things to his wife, and so Mrs. Banks must prepare Vivian for that eventuality.

"It is," Mrs. Banks said, in serious but encouraging tones as she stroked the soft skin of Vivian's upper arm. "It will not be so bad, as long as you are a good girl and cooperate. Go ahead and sit down, dear."

Relieved to have received a direct order, but still wondering how a chair could be a punishment, Vivian turned and lowered herself into the chair. It was a fairly comfortable chair, although the seat was a bit high, but Vivian couldn't understand why such a thing might be considered a punishment. She looked up at Mrs. Banks, who was standing directly in front of her, consulting her notepad.

"This morning you were five minutes late, so I will give you one spanking for each minute. When we reached the house, the housekeeper had to prompt you to ask for a tour of the premises even though I told you beforehand that you should familiarize yourself with it immediately, so that's another," Mrs. Banks continued, listing each infraction she'd noted on her paper and the amount of spankings it incurred.

Vivian's jaw dropped. She hadn't been spanked since she was . . . She couldn't remember the last time. She must have been quite young. Realizing Mrs. Banks was still listing Vivian's mistakes from the day, she tried to focus on what Mrs. Banks was saying, rather than the revelation of her punishment. There would be time enough to think about that later, but if she didn't want to repeat any of her missteps today, then she needed to pay attention. While she would have listened just as fervently in her own determination to be the perfect wife for the earl, the threat of spankings certainly gave her motivations an edge.

"So that's a total of twenty. Now let me help you out of your dress."

The words punctured the bubble of Vivian's purposefulness and she blinked rapidly, her eyes looking twice their normal size as she clutched at the neckline of her gown. Her heart was starting to beat rapidly, her mind still reeling from the idea of being spanked as a punishment. "My dress?"

"Yes," Mrs. Banks said as she helped Vivian up and turned her around, nimbly beginning to undo the buttons. Moving like a puppet at the end of Mrs. Banks's strings, Vivian's movements were jerky as the shoulders and then waist of her dress gaped and the fabric slithered to the floor. "At the end of each day, I will come here, just like tonight, and you will sit in your punishment chair while we go over why you are being punished. Then you will stand and disrobe, as punishments are most effective when delivered to a bare bottom. Once you're married, Lord Cranborne will be in charge of your correction. This is part of the special training he requires of his wife." The last sentence was said with particular emphasis, reminding Vivian that she could change her mind about fulfilling that role, and almost challenging her to speak up and say that she had. For some reason, that only made Vivian more determined to stay silent.

Blushing, trembling, Vivian stood still as Mrs. Banks began to unlace her corset. She didn't understand what removing her corset had to do with being spanked on her bare bottom, but she didn't protest either. With her stays gone, it was the work of a moment for Mrs. Banks to draw Vivian's chemise over her head. Vivian found herself blushing as she was bared. She closed her eyes as Mrs. Banks drew down her drawers, leaving her standing in nothing but her stockings, exposing the bright tint of the hair obscuring her womanhood. Although she didn't protest, she was certainly beginning to understand what Mrs. Cunningham had meant by telling her that she'd be uncomfortable.

Vivian's mind raced, as she tried to gather the remnants of her sensibility. She realized her days would be spent as an elegant young lady and her evenings . . . Her evenings would be spent entirely in dishabille while she was being *spanked,* of all things. By her husband. Eventually, anyway.

Were the other young women in the class being spanked for their mistakes? She supposed she could ask Emily. But what if the answer was no? What if this was one of those things she wasn't supposed to speak of to the other ladies? What would Emily think of her then? No, she couldn't ask anyone else, not even her best friend. How humiliating for anyone to know she was being spanked like a child if they were not sharing the same punishment. Even if they were, Vivian wasn't sure she would be able to bring herself to ask the question. Emily was the brash, outspoken one, not her.

With one hand wrapped around her breasts, making the mounds of flesh bulge temptingly, and the other covering the shock of red hair at the apex of her thighs, Vivian made a delightful picture in nothing but her stockings with blue ribbon garters. Looking over her charge, who was obviously lost in her own thoughts, Mrs. Banks pursed her lips and decided to keep Vivian in her stockings. It was a look many men enjoyed, after all. Tomorrow she'd strip her down completely.

Settling herself on the chair, Mrs. Banks gave Vivian a reassuring smile. "Come across my lap now, Vivian. Legs on one side, hands on the other, with your bottom in the air."

A little whimper escaped Vivian's lips as she stepped forward automatically at Mrs. Banks's direction, but she couldn't bring herself to lay across the other woman's lap. A spanking? And she would be expected to do this for Lord Cranborne eventually?

"I'm not sure—"

"Don't dawdle, young lady, or we'll add another five spankings to your count for the evening." Mrs. Banks's expression became sterner, almost as severe as Mrs. Cunningham's.

"Oh, please," Vivian begged, face flaming red at the indignity of it all. "Can't I do something else? Lines or—"

"Tonight, and tonight only, I am affording you some leniency," said Mrs. Banks sharply. "You are going to be punished, and you can either lay yourself across my lap or I can call for some assistance if you require."

Hot shame coursed through Vivian at the idea of anyone else seeing her in such circumstances, stripped to the skin and about to be spanked. Shame, and something else. Something that had been tickling at her senses ever since Mrs. Banks had ordered her to disrobe. Something that had been making her feel quite warm inside, especially when she thought about the earl in Mrs. Banks's place. His lap was quite a bit broader than Mrs. Banks's, and she could easily picture his dark gaze in her mind, compelling her to submit. Heat washed through her at the image.

"Cum now, Vivian." Mrs. Banks's voice became more intimate, coaxing. Her stern blue gaze softened as Vivian hesitated, becoming more seductive. "The sooner we begin, the sooner it will be over and you can put your night rail on and go to sleep. I know you must be tired."

"I...I..." She wanted to run, but Mrs. Banks reached out and took Vivian's hand, tugging her forward and over her lap. Vivian's body went stiff, and she almost pushed away, but then Mrs. Banks began stroking her lower back and bottom, soothing her and amplifying her tension at the same time.

Although Vivian didn't know it, Mrs. Banks had spread her legs to approximate the size of a man's lap and to support a good portion of Vivian's body. The strokes of Mrs. Banks's fingers felt good, and Vivian's muscles relaxed, the warmth between her legs growing as Mrs. Banks's fingers moved across her bare skin. Vivian bit her lower lip, closing her eyes and trying not to think about the tingling inside of her that had been growing ever since Mrs. Banks had told her to undress. Why was she having the same feelings she'd had when the earl had touched her, when he'd kissed her palm and held her hand? Why did Mrs. Banks's soft touch stir such strange feelings inside of her? She didn't want to be spanked ... did she?

A rippling shiver went up her spine as Mrs. Banks rubbed the palm of her hand over one of Vivian's creamy cheeks, almost as if preparing the unblemished expanse of skin for the smack that was coming. Although Vivian couldn't see her expression, the companion was smiling in anticipation of the coming punishment. There was always something special about delivering a young woman's first spanking; it created an intimacy between the two participants like nothing else Mrs. Banks had ever experienced.

When Mrs. Banks's hand lifted, Vivian automatically tensed.

"No, dear, you need to relax," Mrs. Banks chided, her voice firm but gentle. Although she tried, Vivian's muscles just wouldn't cooperate. She buried her head against Mrs. Banks's skirts as she felt the other woman sigh. "I was going to wait to put you in the proper position at a later date, but I think it will help you now. Spread your legs. More. More." Cool air brushed against the inside of Vivian's most intimate folds, and she shuddered, knowing how exposed she must look. "That's it."

With her thighs spread so far apart it was difficult to clench her bottom muscles, although there was still a great amount of tension all throughout her body. A small cry escaped her when Mrs. Banks's hand fell upon her bottom, even though the actual slap had not been very forceful. It was more surprising than painful.

As it was her first punishment, none of her transgressions had been particularly great, and she had been fairly cooperative, Mrs. Banks was not going to be overly rough with her. If she'd had anything to compare it to, Vivian might have been quite grateful.

Tears filled her eyes as Mrs. Banks's hand came down three more times, so each of her pert bottom cheeks had two spanks apiece. It was more the humiliation of being spanked like a naughty child than actual pain that affected her, although the slaps did sting.

Slap! Slap! Slap! Slap!

"Oh!" Vivian cried out.

Mrs. Banks's hand returned to the same spots on each cheek, leaving two rosy prints in the center of each globe. While this was going to be a light spanking, comparatively, she did want Vivian to be able to feel it for at least a few hours afterwards, and that meant focusing her efforts rather than giving her bottom an all-over warming. Each subsequent slap meant the pink print turned a little darker and Vivian's bottom burned a little hotter.

As Mrs. Banks centered the next four slaps in the exact same manner, Vivian found herself kicking her legs in consternation. The tips of her toes dragged along the carpet as Mrs. Banks swiftly repositioned her so that her head dangled farther forward and she had no purchase from which to resist.

"Stop! Please!" Tears fell onto the floor beneath her, her muscles clenching and bottom throbbing as the spanking continued. Despite Mrs. Banks's slim appearance, Vivian was discovering the woman had an arm like iron as it lay across Vivian's back, holding her firmly in place.

Lord Cranborne had given instruction that he would expect Vivian to maintain her position when being disciplined from behind, but while he had her over his lap he rather enjoyed a more natural reaction. Therefore Mrs. Banks did not chide Vivian or slow the spanking; instead she adjusted herself to allow for Vivian's struggling response and continued to rain down a flurry of hard smacks upon the protesting bottom.

"Oh, please! Please, Mrs. Banks! Not so hard!" Vivian squealed and twisted, knowing her pleas were useless but making them anyway. The two spots on her bottom taking the brunt of the punishment felt as if they were on fire. Her helpless position made her feel even more like a wayward child, but the only way out of this was to call off her wedding to the earl, and Vivian couldn't do that yet. Not on her first night of training. This was humiliating and painful, but not unbearable.

"Nineteen, twenty," Mrs. Banks counted out as the last two blows landed. Vivian quivered on her lap, crying but not sobbing, Mrs. Banks noted approvingly as she brushed a wisp of blonde hair out of her eyes. An honest reaction. She was pleased Vivian was not holding back her emotions, and also that she had not allowed herself to descend into hysterics over what was, in reality, a very light spanking. It was more Vivian's emotions causing her to cry than any physical discomfort at this juncture. Rubbing her hand over Vivian's bottom, she made soothing noises about what a good girl Vivian had been to take her punishment so well, smoothing some of the pain away with her gentle touch.

Although part of Vivian wanted to return to her feet, she continued to lie across Mrs. Banks's lap, taking comfort in the gentle touch of the woman's hand. The irony in accepting comfort from her disciplinarian did not escape Vivian, but she was used to turning to Mrs. Banks for support.

"Very good, Miss Stafford." The clear approval in Mrs. Banks's voice did more to reassure Vivian than anything else had thus far.

When the woman's hand slipped down to the crease between Vivian's legs, she moaned in embarrassment. Mrs. Banks's fingers found the damp evidence of a reaction Vivian would have never expected. The earl's handsome visage and strong hands suddenly flashed through her mind, and she imagined that it was him touching her so boldly, the fantasy heightening her reaction.

The smarting spanks and the helplessness of her position had aroused her, and she had no defense against the spark inside her that the school was skillfully revealing. If she'd had the opportunity for a conventional marriage, it was quite possible she would have been able to lie back and think of England during her husband's infrequent visits to her bed, her passion remaining forever buried. Instead, those hidden passions were being slowly coaxed to the surface at the experienced hand of Mrs. Banks.

A hand whose fingers dipped and swirled, making Vivian gasp and squeeze her thighs together—to no avail. The rude fingers pressed deeper between her pouting pussy lips, her twitching thighs rubbing the sensitive folds against the probing digits, creating such a deliciously pleasurable sensation that Vivian thought she might swoon. She was already feeling lightheaded, from both her position and her exertions as she'd kicked her legs and struggled, and now the growing need between her legs was making her feel even more discombobulated.

"Oh, please . . . Mrs. Banks . . ." Vivian shuddered, unsure if she was asking her companion to cease or continue. Fingers pressed inside her, invading her tight body, as Mrs. Banks's thumb rubbed against the most sensitive spot on the exterior of her body.

"Please what?" Mrs. Banks asked. "Do you want me to stop?"

Vivian's legs kicked again. No, she did not want her to stop. She was no longer struggling, but she could not control her writhing as the burn in her bottom mingled with the heat in her loins and began to swirl and grow. Her hips moved in instinctive rhythm with Mrs. Banks's thrusting fingers, her hard nipples rubbing against the fabric of Mrs. Banks's skirt.

She had been stripped of everything but her footwear, spanked like a child, and now she was working her way up to a glorious climax. Having never experimented with touching herself, she was defenseless against the sensations streaking through her, and she wallowed in them with all the passionate abandon of an innocent.

"Oh . . . *Oh!* Mrs. Banks! *Oh!*" Vivian wailed as her body tightened and exploded, her tunnel spasming around Mrs. Banks's fingers as the first orgasm of her life wracked her young body. Her head tossed, wayward strands of hair shining brightly against her skin, rosy bottom bouncing as she arched her back and writhed in exquisite ecstasy.

The stroking fingers slowed in their rhythm, allowing Vivian a slow descent down from the peak of her pleasure. Vivian moaned, her hips still jerking with the last wringing spasms of her climax, before she hung limply across Mrs. Banks's lap.

Mrs. Banks allowed her a few moments to gather herself before helping the girl up and leading her through her preparations for the evening. The companion caressed Vivian's hot bottom, murmuring accolades.

"You were such a good girl, Vivian, you took your punishment very well. I'm so proud of you."

Vivian blushed as Mrs. Banks helped put her to bed, tucking the covers in. While she thrilled to hear the approval in Mrs. Banks's voice as she praised her, some part of Vivian couldn't help but feel embarrassed at more than just her spanking, but also at her loss of composure. Yet Mrs. Banks was praising her for losing control of her emotions and reactions, despite the fact that the school had trained her never to do so.

"I don't understand," she said, looking up at Mrs. Banks in confusion. Mrs. Banks sat on the bed next to her, very similar to the way Vivian's mother had when she was a young girl. "Which part was my punishment and which part was my marriage training?"

Smiling, Mrs. Banks smoothed back a wayward strand of hair from Vivian's forehead. The young woman was lying on her side, obviously loathe to lay on her back with her bottom cheeks still feeling tender. "It was all part of your marriage training."

"I don't like being spanked," Vivian said, stifling the urge to rub at her sore bottom cheeks while Mrs. Banks was still in the room with her. She wasn't quite telling the truth, but she didn't want to admit that. "Are the other girls being punished?"

Mrs. Banks skewered her with a hard look, and Vivian bit her lip before the other woman's face softened a bit. "You are not like the other girls, Vivian. You are luckier than they are, because you will be prepared for your marriage. Not all husbands may wish to discipline their wives in the same way your future husband does, but it is not at all uncommon either. Those girls will go into their marriages never knowing what male needs or disciplines await them. You will be prepared as best we can to be the best possible wife for Lord Cranborne. You won't let us down, will you?"

The question was gentle but it appealed to Vivian's pride and determination.

"Of course I won't," she said, setting her jaw stubbornly. Mrs. Banks smiled and bid her a good night, skirts swishing gently as she left the room to go write her report on the day's activities. The report would go first to Mrs. Cunningham and then, at the end of the week, each daily report would be bundled and sent to the earl so he would be kept apprised of Miss Stafford's progress.

Alone in her room with her sore bottom, Vivian wondered what her future marriage would be like. She vowed to be the best wife she could, so her husband would have no reason to punish her. Although once the actual spanking was over, she had found it was not an entirely unpleasant activity. What would it have been like to lay across Lord Cranborne's lap and be spanked? Despite the climax that Mrs. Banks had brought her to, the sensitive area between Vivian's legs throbbed.

Shivering, wondering, Vivian snuggled down into her sheets and her exhausted body drifted into sleep.

CHAPTER SIX

"YOU'D BEST GET UP MISS, YOU DON'T WANT to be late again!" The maid shook Vivian's shoulder, and Vivian stifled a whimper as she tried to burrow back under the covers.

Despite her determination not to have a repeat performance of the day before, Vivian found herself struggling even harder to wake up than she had the previous day. The long day at the practicum, the spanking, the subsequent climax, and the earlier hour than she was used to all worked against her. Gathering her willpower, she dragged herself out of the sheets, stumbling through her toilette as the maid fussed over the bags under her eyes and then practically had to force her to eat a light breakfast.

Her muscles ached, although her bottom wasn't nearly as sore as she would have expected after the spanking. She had sneaked a peek in the mirror when the maid was dressing her and seen that her skin looked perfectly clear, without a hint of pink. It almost disturbed her that there were no remaining visible marks from the punishment, disappointing her in a way. Shouldn't there have been some lingering evidence of her ordeal, more than a faint tingle in her bottom when she sat on the hard chair while the maid hurriedly did her hair?

But the only visible evidence in the entire room was the punishment chair, which was still in its place at the center of the room. Vivian's eyes flicked to it and away, her stomach slowly churning with the memory of her chaotic emotions the night before.

Despite the maid's best efforts and Vivian's slowly burgeoning panic once she began to truly awaken, she knew she was on the borderline of being late. Today she was the second student down the stairs, but Mrs. Banks was already shaking her head and making a note on her paper pad. Looking at the clock, Vivian sighed. Two minutes late, but her bottom already tingled in anticipation of being punished later. Emily came rushing down only moments behind her, breathless and looking nearly as exhausted as Vivian felt.

"When I'm mistress of my own household, I will never rise before eleven in the morning, ten at the very earliest, even when we're in the country," Emily muttered under her breath to Vivian. She was dressed in a deep brown cambric morning dress that looked very well on her. Vivian felt almost overdressed in her green and ivory stripes. "I can't remember my mother ever rising this early while we're in town."

"I rather enjoy early mornings on occasion," said Vivian, smoothing her hands over her skirts to straighten them. "But I enjoy them much more when I *choose* to rise early."

Sighing, Emily patted her hair, trying to get the flyaway wisps under control. Either her maid wasn't as skilled as Vivian's or, more likely, Emily hadn't been able to sit still while it was being done. "Are you ready for today?"

"I hope so. I made more mistakes yesterday than I had realized."

"Me too." Emily rolled her eyes and shot a glance at Miss Norton, lowering her voice even further to ensure she would not be overheard. "She read me such a lecture on my multitude of errors last night that I thought it would never end."

Vivian hesitated for just a moment. She wished she could confide in Emily, but she was too afraid her friend wouldn't understand the situation. After all, Vivian barely understood and she was living it. "Mrs. Banks, too. I thought I was better prepared, after watching my mother run our household. She always made it look so easy."

"I suppose that's why they're giving us the practice," Emily said, making a face. "My mother would allow me to run some things in our house, but as soon as a problem arose, she always took over again. She also helped me, rather than sitting in silent judgment. I swear, it was the looks the companions were giving us that made me so flustered."

"My mother did the same," said Vivian, although she was quite sure Emily's household had been much larger than her own. "She never had any crises that I can remember, but I doubt she would have let me flounder on my own if there had been."

Vivian sighed, her nerves rising again. She wondered how large the Earl of Cranborne's household was and felt a shiver go down her spine. Considering he had the funds to send her to the school and no need for his wife to bring a dowry, she had no doubt he must have at least several estates.

The idea of running his household was even more

nerve-wracking now that she'd met him. She didn't want to disappoint him after he'd picked her out and helped her family in their time of need. Wondering when she'd see him again, she was immediately assaulted by her confused feelings over being spanked. After all, she knew it was because of his desire for her to be trained that she had been disciplined last night, and she still didn't know how she felt about the idea of her future husband being the one to spank her.

She turned her face away from Emily so her friend would not see the flush spreading across her cheeks. The spanking had been painful and left her embarrassed, confused, and . . . tingly. The pleasure that had followed had been overwhelming. Would one always follow the other, she wondered? Would the earl's large, masculine hands be more painful—and more pleasurable—than Mrs. Banks's?

Before she could lose herself too much in her ruminations, the last girl was hurrying down the steps, flushed with embarrassment at being late, and the companions were ushering them out the door to the carriages. Unlike yesterday, there was no chattering of excitement or speculation; they had a basic idea of what was in store for them and had realized it was not all going to be easy or fun. However, none of them wanted to complain where the companions could overhear. Besides, they were all exhausted. Vivian almost fell asleep on the carriage ride.

Relieved she no longer had to start off the day, Vivian watched with interest as Charity, who was the lady of the house for the morning, sorted the invitations that had been received in the "mail," explaining her reasoning for how she sorted them. She handled it slightly differently than Vivian had the day before, arranging them first by date and then by importance before cross-checking with the calendar Vivian had started the day before and seeing what events could be scheduled and whether any that Vivian had originally put in the calendar would be superseded by a more important invitation. At every step of the way, she had to explain what she was doing and why, not receiving any corrections or feedback from her companion until she had justified her reasoning. After that came a planning of the day's menu for the various meals, then a quick walk around the house and gardens for both relaxation and to ascertain everything was in order.

Then Vivian took over the reins, handling the luncheon with the other young ladies and their companions as her "guests." Once they were running their own households they would not have guests every day, but Mrs. Cunningham obviously felt it was important to have as much practice with guests as possible, because those were the situations that were most fraught with the possibility of failure. Yesterday everyone had been quite well behaved, but today two of the companions were obviously impersonating harder-to-handle guests. One kept attempting to steer the conversation in the direction of inappropriate topics—gossip about gentlemen's mistresses, references to what happens in the marriage bed. All completely inappropriate for the young misses at the table, yet, despite being a young miss herself, Vivian was responsible for guiding the conversation back to more appropriate avenues.

The other companion became quite acerbic, very much like one of the *ton's* "dragons," the older ladies who ruled the roost and often cared little for the opinions of others. Vivian had met one at her cousin's wedding, and the companion was doing a very credible impersonation from what she remembered; rudely remarking on the dresses the ladies around the table were wearing, interrupting their sentences. She was actually the more challenging because Vivian had to smooth things over for all parties without offending her.

By the time the luncheon was over, Vivian felt quite battered; it had been a strain not to lose her temper for a bit. The "dragon" in particular had seemed almost gleeful about making things difficult for her.

"Well done, Saint George," whispered Emily, referencing the old story of George the dragon-slayer. She squeezed Vivian's hand in support as Vivian metaphorically passed the reins off to her. "I would have ended up 'accidentally' pouring tea on her."

Vivian giggled, feeling slightly more cheerful, although that faded when she saw Mrs. Banks continuing to scribble on her pad of paper. Oh, what had she done now? It was disheartening to see how much Mrs. Banks was writing, although at least Vivian was fairly certain she hadn't repeated any of her mistakes from the day before. Of course, it would have been difficult to make exactly the same errors, as she'd been in charge of an entirely different section of the day for today's practicum.

But she could now relax, somewhat, as her portion of the day was finished. All of the young ladies were on edge, waiting for something dire or exciting to happen. By the end of the day Vivian felt almost disgruntled when there had been no major catastrophes, and strangely weary from the tension of anticipation.

Thinking it over, on the carriage ride back to the school, Vivian concluded that truly dire situations couldn't possibly occur on a daily basis. And one could never anticipate when one would occur. As always, the teachers were a step ahead of her and the other students. The next crises would happen when the students would be caught unawares. Not while they were on the tips of their toes, ready for any unexpected occurrences.

Vivian shared this theory over dinner, as she and the other practicum students naturally gravitated towards sitting with each other. The other young ladies at the school were still involved with classes; they didn't know the trials of actually putting those lessons into practice. It made for a kind of division between the practicum's young ladies and the other students, and all four young ladies found themselves wanting to be able to discuss their days with others who would understand. They agreed with Vivian's theory and were generally supportive of each other, giving suggestions and commiserating over the lectures they were sure to receive later that evening.

It was pleasurable to chat with them, especially as Emily was in the group. The other two girls she hadn't made friends with before: Astoria and Rosalie. The beautiful blonde Astoria, daughter of the Duke of Somerset, had always been rather snobbish, being even higher in rank than Emily, but unlike Emily she enjoyed lording over other girls, and Rosalie was one of her followers. Now, however, the trials and tribulations of the practicum was giving them all some common ground. It didn't keep Astoria from making the occasional comment about her status, as compared to the others, but it was easy enough to ignore. Emily just rolled her eyes at Vivian.

Vivian did feel a small tinge of resentment as she realized none of them were going to receive anything worse than a stern talking-to this evening, yet they were bemoaning the lectures that were to come. But then she also realized none of them were likely to know anything of the hot bliss that had followed her harrowing experience at the hands of Mrs. Banks. Still, just as there was a division between the young ladies involved in the practicum and the ladies in classes, Vivian realized there was a division between her and these ladies with whom she was sharing her days. None of them could understand everything she was going through; the only person she would be able to confide in about such things was her companion.

Which, of course, was exactly how Mrs. Cunningham intended it.

The sharp rap of Mrs. Banks's knuckles preceded her entrance through Vivian's door. Vivian was seated at her window seat, her book in her hands, thoroughly engrossed. She jumped up as Mrs. Banks entered, her fingers clinging to the book. Just reading it made her feel as though she had a connection to Lord Cranborne, and the story itself was sweepingly romantic.

"Good evening, Miss Stafford," said Mrs. Banks coolly as she swept into the room, closing the door with a solid thud behind her. Vivian put down the book, bookmark firmly in place between the pages, and bobbed a small curtsy.

"Good evening, Mrs. Banks."

They both stared at each other for a moment, Vivian's nerves rising. Mrs. Banks raised her eyebrow and shook her head. "I thought you had a better memory than this, Vivian. Where should you seat yourself so we may begin tonight's marriage training lesson?"

Vivian blushed, feeling quite awkward. Hoping to smooth over her hesitation, she quickly walked to the punishment chair and sat down. "I'm sorry, Mrs. Banks, it won't happen again."

"I'm sure it won't," said Mrs. Banks, her soft voice ominous. Vivian told herself she was just imagining things, and that her anxiety was adding more meaning to Mrs. Banks's words than were truly present. The companion ran a critical eye over Vivian's straight-backed posture, skirts fanned out in a flattering manner, and hands demurely folded in her lap. Apparently finding nothing amiss, she consulted the pad of paper in her hand. "So. Tonight's count. Five for the five minutes it took you to discourage Mrs. Marbury from her discussion on men's breeches, two for . . ." It took all of Vivian's willpower not to protest the list of transgressions. Surely it could not be considered her fault if the companions had been too enthusiastic in their disruptive roles. And yet she knew in some small part it was.

Society would judge her skills as a hostess just as sharply, if not more so. Blinking back the protests that threatened as she listened to all the ways in which she'd failed during the day, Vivian reasserted her vow to improve. After all, if today had truly been a luncheon with society matrons and not just the students and companions, she probably would have been on the verge of tears by the end of it.

Mrs. Banks tapped her notes, finishing her count. "That's a total of eighteen with my hand, plus four with the hairbrush for the two minutes you were late this morning and two more with the hairbrush for not immediately sitting in your punishment chair after greeting me."

"But you didn't tell me to! You can't punish me for

that!" The words burst forth from Vivian's lips before she could stop them. Although, once she'd thought about it, she didn't want to stop them. It wasn't fair she would be punished for not doing something that she hadn't been told to do in the first place.

Indeed, Mrs. Banks frowned at her. "That's another two for protesting. Your punishments will never be decided by you, nor will they be excused for anything other than a situation out of your control. You did indeed know what the procedure was to be for this evening, and instead of seating yourself the way you were instructed to last night, you dawdled in an attempt to regain control over your punishment. If you ever have a true excuse you may present it, or you may beg if you are so inclined, but whether or not you will be allowed a reprieve will be up to me, and, eventually, your husband."

Vivian stared down at her hands and didn't say anything further. She felt so conflicted. On one hand she was indignant that Mrs. Banks suggest she beg. On the other hand, she could feel the truth in the other woman's words. The need to reassert some control over the indignity of what was about to happen had been instinctual, but it was still the action she had taken by choice. The desire to please Mrs. Banks, and ultimately Lord Cranborne, was very strong, but part of her also felt like rebelling.

Against that, she couldn't deny her body was already feeling somewhat excited at the knowledge she would be rewarded at the end of her punishment if she was good. Hopefully her outburst would not deny her that sweet finish.

"I'm sorry, Mrs. Banks," she said finally when the silence seemed to drag out. She truly meant it as well.

"Very good, Miss Stafford," said her companion approvingly, and a little flutter of warmth went through Vivian at the praise. The same words Mrs. Banks had said the day before when she'd put her fingers between Vivian's legs with such delightful consequences. "You may now stand so we may undress you."

Mrs. Banks was pleased with the progress Miss Stafford had already made. She'd expected a bit of resistance still, yet Vivian's innate submissiveness and desire to please had dominated her responses, and she was already beginning to fall easily in line with the program laid out for her. The young woman quietly turned so Mrs. Banks could undo the buttons along the back of her dress, revealing the lacy chemise and drawers beneath, covered by a rose-pink corset with ivory laces. Vivian let out a shuddering breath as her corset was loosened and then removed. Looking down, she blushed as she realized her nipples were already hardened into little buds beneath her chemise, poking suggestively at the fabric. Beneath them she could see the coppery glint of the hair over her mound. Now, knowing the importance of that area, she realized how very suggestive her chemise was; something she had never considered before.

She blushed even harder when Mrs. Banks turned her around and looked down at the rosy swells of her nipples, giving an approving nod.

"Do not be embarrassed by such responses," Mrs. Banks said, noticing Vivian's flushed cheeks and lowered gazes. Cupping Vivian's breasts in her hands, Mrs. Banks squeezed them gently and pinched the jutting nipples, making Vivian whimper and tremble as a current of desire ran through her body. Her thighs pressed together as the area between them suddenly felt extremely hot, the pressure increasing both her excitement and her pleasure. "See how hard and pretty your nipples become? Feel how wet you are? Those are all very good reactions. Your responsiveness, your pleasure in this, is part of what the earl will value about you as his wife."

Such a comment only raised more questions in Vivian's head as Mrs. Banks removed her chemise and drawers, this time also removing Vivian's shoes and stockings so she was completely nude. Would the earl touch her breasts and pinch her nipples?

Did she want him to? The wetness gathering between her legs and the heat in her body certainly seemed to indicate such a desire.

Mrs. Banks settled herself into the punishment chair, spreading her thighs to widen her lap. "Across my lap now, Miss Stafford."

Tonight, Vivian draped herself over Mrs. Banks's legs without protest, and the companion smiled.

"Spread your legs further, Miss Stafford," she directed. "And point your toes inwards." Vivian tensed as she did so, awaiting the inevitable addition to her spanking that came with corrections. "I will not add to your punishment this evening, but if you do not spread your legs to my satisfaction tomorrow then you will increase the number of strokes you receive from the hairbrush." She continued to caress Vivian's bottom, fingers delving down very quickly to test the status of the young woman's arousal without giving her any pleasure. Slick, slightly swollen pussy lips split apart by the positioning of her body. Soon her responses would associate all of this, the positioning and the punishments, with pleasure and respond with a sopping wet arousal that would delight the earl and Vivian alike.

Tonight Mrs. Banks decided to cover Vivian's entire bottom, the slaps coming down with slightly more force than the night before now that the young woman had a better idea of what to expect. She worked her way down one cheek and then the other, making Vivian cry out as her tender sit-spots were also spanked. *Why does that spot smart so much more than any other?* Vivian wondered. She had no time to contemplate the question before her left side was receiving its second line of hearty smacks.

When Mrs. Banks's hand came down on her sensitive crease, Vivian broke position and her legs kicked out a little. Mindful of the earl's desire for a natural response, Mrs. Banks did not scold her.

Besides, the young lady would be kicking even more in a moment.

Panting, heated, and wet between her thighs, Vivian spread her legs again, worried that Mrs. Banks would scold her for the little kicks—although she suddenly realized she hadn't been scolded the night before when she'd been much more active. It was only because Mrs. Banks had stopped that Vivian had immediately started worrying she'd done something wrong. That quality was part of what would make Vivian such an excellent submissive wife to Lord Cranborne, Mrs. Banks knew. It was something Gabriel had instinctively responded to and been attracted by when he'd first met her. The desire, the need to please, in every aspect of her life, in order to be happy herself.

"I have a new brush for you, Miss Stafford," Mrs. Banks said, keeping one arm across Vivian's back as she reached into her pocket for the hairbrush she'd brought with her. "I will take your old brush with me tonight, and from now on you will use only this brush to brush your hair, and it will also be used for your punishments. First mistakes will be punished with my hand to your bare bottom, repeated mistakes will be reprimanded with the hairbrush and you will receive double the number you had the first time."

"What if I make a mistake for a third time?" asked Vivian worriedly, turning her head to look up into Mrs. Banks's stern blue eyes. They softened slightly, even though Mrs. Banks frowned at her.

"Let us hope you never need to find out," said the companion, more to bolster Vivian's motivation than anything else. Fear of the unknown was a powerful tool, and besides, she hadn't decided yet. Quite possibly that would be the time to introduce the young woman to the crop, which would have a more lasting sting. It was best not to set up expectations, so the training could remain flexible and the student kept on her toes.

Indeed, Mrs. Banks's ominous words made Vivian shudder, her buttocks automatically clenching as she tried to imagine what awful retributions such a transgression would invoke. But she did not have too much time to think as Mrs. Banks hefted the hairbrush in her hand.

It was a lovely creation, specially designed and crafted for Vivian by Lord Cranborne once the marriage contract had been signed and she'd been enrolled in the school. The bristles were made of stiff boar hairs that would particularly sting if a reddened bottom were smacked with it—much pricklier than Vivian's current horsehair brush. It was also wider and heavier than her current silver-backed brush, and not nearly as pretty, made out of sturdy wood in a squarish shape that would cover a large amount of Vivian's attractive bottom when used in such a manner. The handle was slightly ridged to assist the grip of whoever was holding the brush. About as thick as three of Mrs. Banks's fingers, the bumpy length was also slightly longer than the average hairbrush handle, which would assist with attaining the perfect swing for a proper spanking.

Applying a sturdy grip on the hairbrush, Mrs. Banks brought it down right across the center of Vivian's bottom. The back of the brush was large enough to catch both of her cheeks, and to Vivian it felt like fire was licking across the area from the heavy wood, an entirely different sensation than the less severe smack of Mrs. Banks's hand.

"*Ah!*" cried out Vivian, sudden tears sparking in her eyes, her body lurching forwards. Mrs. Banks paused just long enough to readjust her arm, securely holding Vivian in place, before delivering a second sturdy smack in almost exactly the same location.

"Oh, please!"

"Four more," Mrs. Banks said, raising her arm and bringing the hairbrush down again.

There was now a red-hot rectangle of smarting flesh right in the center of Vivian's bottom, glowing much brighter than the slight rosy pink that colored the rest of those formerly pristine globes. Vivian shrieked, her legs kicking without restriction now, fingers pressed against the floor as a tear fell to the floor in front of her.

"Please, Mrs. Banks," she begged, her voice high-pitched and slightly panicked. "It hurts too much! Please just use your hand!"

"If it's that bad then it should give you proper motivation not to repeat any of your mistakes a second time," said Mrs. Banks calmly, admiring the way Vivian's bottom marked up so nicely. The hairbrush the earl had made for his bride was easy in her hand, and it made a resounding, meaty noise when it impacted flesh. The rosy red color it immediately provoked spoke to its effectiveness, as did Vivian's pleas. And yet, for all her kicking and squirming, the young woman wasn't making a true attempt to dislodge herself from her companion's lap. While Mrs. Banks had to hold her in place somewhat, none of Vivian's movements indicated a concerted effort to end the punishment.

Thwack!

Vivian squealed, trying to bring her hand back to cover her burning bottom, the throbbing heat of that tormented spot greatly increasing her agitation. She was hindered on one side by the chair and Mrs. Banks's body, and as soon as she got her other hand around, Mrs. Banks grabbed it by the wrist and held it to the small of her back.

"That's three more you've earned, Vivian, in addition to the three you already had left," Mrs. Banks said fiercely, upset more because she hadn't been prepared for such a maneuver and had been about to lower the hairbrush again. "You may beg and plead and kick all you want, but you must never try to cover your bottom. What if I had brought the hairbrush down on your wrist? You could have been injured!" That was something she knew the earl would never stand for. He might want his bride accustomed to a certain amount of physical discipline, but he would never countenance true injury.

"No," Vivian moaned, her hand twitching in the

confines of Mrs. Banks's much stronger fingers. "I'm sorry, Mrs. Banks, I didn't mean to!"

Thwack!

"Well, you certainly won't do it again."

Thwack! Thwack! Thwack!

Vivian's tears fell to the floor in front of her, watering it in the same manner as the night before. She was thoroughly sorry for trying to impede her spanking—it would have already been over by now if she had not! She was even sorrier for the disappointment she heard in Mrs. Banks's voice, disappointment in her for not taking her punishment as well as she might have. Would this mean she would be denied the climax her body so craved? The thought made her almost as distraught as the actual punishment.

You could make all of this stop . . .

Vivian remembered that she could end this punishment if she truly wanted to, and she might never have to go through it again—after all, this was just the beginning of a lifetime of such punishments with the earl. All she had to do was tell Mrs. Banks that she didn't want to marry the earl. But then she'd have to leave the school. Her family would have to sponsor her debut. And worst of all, she wouldn't see him again. He would marry someone else. Was it worth it, to save herself this punishment, and lose her chance to discover the pleasures that such a marriage promised? To lose him? Something inside of her screamed *no,* her heart already aching at the imagined loss. Vivian bit back the impulse and hardened her resolve.

Thwack! Thwack!

The last two smacks with the hairbrush landed against each of Vivian's buttocks in turn, catching the area that had already been thoroughly punished in the center of her bottom, as well as fresh canvas to paint red. Now a wide, red stripe crossed her bottom horizontally, much darker in the center and lightening towards the edges.

Vivian choked back her howls, the fingers of one hand clenched around the chair leg while the other was still held in Mrs. Banks's tight grip. The noise slowly softened to whimpers as the immediate sting eased, leaving her bottom feeling hot and tight, an insistent low throbbing throughout the entire area.

The hairbrush was placed on her back, so she could feel the warmth of the wood between her shoulder blades, while Mrs. Banks's hand rubbed over the beaten flesh of her bottom, causing Vivian to hiss between her teeth as the pain flared again. She quivered, spreading her legs further apart, as if in hopes of enticing Mrs. Banks downwards and away from her sore backside.

"Very good," Mrs. Banks said approvingly. "I know you didn't mean to fight me, Vivian."

Tendrils of red hair wafted around Vivian's face as she shook her head, letting out a relieved sigh as Mrs. Banks stroked along the center of her womanhood. The spanking had heated more than her reddened bottom— her folds were sopping wet with her cream and she raised her hips as Mrs. Banks stroked and swirled her fingertips against Vivian's swollen flesh. It was exquisite bliss, easing the sting of the spanking more than anything else had done, as pain and pleasure mingled in the lower half of Vivian's body.

One finger slid easily into Vivian's wet sheath, causing her to moan and her muscles to tighten around the invader. It pumped back and forth, curving and probing, looking for that certain sweet spot inside of her. Mrs. Banks's other hand started rubbing and squeezing at Vivian's chastened bottom cheeks, further mingling the pain and the pleasure at her core. Vivian whimpered in confusion as the sensations melded, making it almost impossible to discern which was which. Neither deterred the growing tension in her loins, nor her desire for it to continue.

Another finger slid inside of her as Vivian began to move her hips in conjunction with the thrust of Mrs. Banks's probing fingers. The companion's thumb reached down to caress the nubby pearl of flesh at the apex of Vivian's pussy lips, which was shyly peeking forth from its hood. The contact sent a spasm of pleasure through Vivian, and her hips began to move at a faster pace, her rump rising to meet the press of Mrs. Banks's hands.

The companion smiled her pleasure at Vivian's heated responses, and the tightness of her virgin sheath, as she watched her fingers delving in and out of it.

"That's it, Vivian, just let go," Mrs. Banks murmured as she roughly rubbed her other hand over the hottest spot in the center of Vivian's reddened ass.

Lightheaded from her position, Vivian's head arched up and back as she tightened around Mrs. Banks's fingers, the hairbrush falling from her shoulders to the floor, her little clit pressed hard by the pad of Mrs. Banks's thumb. She gasped and trembled as her climax washed over her, and her bottom cheeks clenched and bounced as the convulsions took her. It was a fiery tide of hot-bottomed pleasure, a rapturous release of all the tensions of the day, a wash of pain-tinged bliss as she cried out in ecstasy. The muscles in her arms trembled and collapsed as she rode the wave out, her head hanging above the floor as she went limp over Mrs. Banks's lap.

The heady feeling of satiated exhaustion overtook her, and she groaned a little as Mrs. Banks continued to stroke and soothe her swollen flesh. Mrs. Banks allowed her to lie there like that, her thighs spread and open to receive the soft strokes of her companion's fingers, for several long minutes before she told Vivian to stand. After she helped Vivian dress herself in her night rail for the evening, Mrs. Banks brushed her long red hair with the brush that had just punished her, ignoring the young woman's squirming as she was forced to sit on her sore cheeks throughout the hundred strokes of the brush. At least these strokes were pleasant, even if she was constantly reminded of her punishment throughout them.

When Mrs. Banks left Vivian's room that evening, she took Vivian's old hairbrush with her.

The next few days continued in the same manner, with Vivian's practicum in the morning followed by dinner back at the school, an hour to herself, and then draping herself over Mrs. Banks's lap in the punishment chair for chastisement and pleasure. Her first day after the hairbrush spanking she found her bottom remained quite sore the next morning, her cheeks showing just the faintest hint of pink across the center when she looked in the mirror. She incurred another round with the hairbrush when she attempted to meet Mrs. Banks in a robe rather than fully dressed. The companion scolded her soundly for trying to take control of the punishment again and made her redress before sitting her in the punishment chair for her litany of offenses during the day, and then undressing her again. That one earned her a hefty ten swats with the hairbrush on top of her already sore bottom that evening. The next morning she found herself shifting uncomfortably as she ate her breakfast, although there were no lasting marks.

Each day she made some mistakes, although she was not late again, as her body finally adjusted to the new schedule. It seemed to Vivian that the spankings were becoming harder each evening, and yet her body always had the same response—abject need for the pleasure that followed.

At the end of the week, Vivian returned from the practicum to find an ornate box waiting for her in her room, with mother-of-pearl inlay decorating the top of it. The box itself was a thing of beauty, finer and probably more expensive than any she'd ever owned. Her heart fluttered wildly in her chest as she opened it to find a debutante's posy resting on the velvet lining. It was made up of violets and dark pink roses, trimmed of their thorns, and wrapped with a lacy, navy ribbon.

Fingers trembling, she reached for the folded note that accompanied the posy.

Sunrise,

Although you will not have a come-out as a debutante, I wished to ensure you did not want for the tokens you deserve. Please accept this posy and bring it with you to dine with me at eight this evening in the blue parlor at your school.

Gabriel

Vivian gasped, whirling around to run and ring for the maid. If she was going to be dining with the earl she needed to change immediately. She had to look her best. Any weariness from the day melted away in her anxiety and excitement. For the first time since she'd begun her training, she was going to see the earl!

CHAPTER SEVEN

IMPATIENCE HAD CONSUMED GABRIEL FOR the past few days. Impatience and thoughts of Vivian. He'd already drawn her a hundred times, forgoing his usual social pursuits to sketch her over and over again.

Now that he was finally going to be seeing her again, he couldn't remain still. The blue parlor at Mrs. Cunningham's wasn't a large room, but he prowled restlessly through it like a lion trapped in a cage.

When the door finally opened to admit her and Mrs. Banks, he startled both the ladies with how quickly he whirled around and approached them.

"Good evening, Sunrise," he said, reaching out to take Vivian's hand and bowing down to give it a kiss. Just touching her gave him a sensation of relief, and some of his previous tension drained from his body. She was here and smiling at him, which boded well for their relationship. It was only at that moment he realized he'd been worried he'd misconstrued her character and she'd hate both the lessons and him. The shyly eager smile she gave him, her emerald eyes shining, immediately assuaged those concerns. The grin he gave Mrs. Banks, over Vivian's shoulder, was practically giddy. "Mrs. Banks."

Both ladies murmured their greetings, dipping slightly in curtsies. When Vivian said, "My lord," he clicked his tongue. "Gabriel," he reminded her.

Her cheeks flushed a light pink. "Gabriel."

The way she said his name was still tinged with a touch of awe, and it made him hard as a rock to hear his Christian name pass her lips. The fact that her fingertips were still lightly grasped in his hand didn't help his situation. Just being in her presence had aroused him.

It was immediately obvious to him she had dressed with care for the evening. As he'd paid for her wardrobe, he'd had a hand in picking some of it, and he knew the jade-green silk gown she wore was one of her best. Hugging her body, it was low-cut enough to show a hint of bosom while still being modest enough for a debutante; the color made her ivory skin gleam, brought out the deep green of her eyes, and contrasted wonderfully with her vivid hair.

As he guided Vivian to her seat, Gabriel gave Mrs. Banks a nod, and she left the room. Vivian looked over her shoulder, a bit startled as she realized she was to be left alone with him. Seating himself across from her at the small table, Gabriel enjoyed watching the blush rise in her cheeks. Proper young ladies were never left alone with a man not related to them, as it might ruin their reputation.

However, Vivian had no reputation to ruin, and Gabriel desired to have her to himself. Of course, if she'd been distressed by Mrs. Banks's departure, he would have had the companion return. But while his bride-to-be was nervous, she didn't protest or seem upset.

"You look beautiful this evening," he said, sitting down on his side of the table. His flinty eyes glinted appreciatively as he looked her over, and he ran a hand through his black hair. He'd dressed up for her this evening as well, his coat and waistcoat an austere grey and black that he knew suited him to perfection. They were close enough that he could probably slide his foot over and touch hers, and the thought was tempting, but he wanted to set her at ease first.

"Thank you," she said shyly. For just a moment he wondered if he should call Mrs. Banks back in, as Vivian seemed to have shrunk into herself a little bit. He didn't want her to be uncomfortable. Then she peeked at him through her lashes, the color in her cheeks flaming brighter. "You look very handsome."

"Thank you," he replied with a roguish grin. His Sunrise might have been submissive and, currently, a little unsure of herself, but she had spirit. Pretending to preen, he tugged at his jacket lapels. "I certainly did my best."

Vivian's giggle broke the tension she obviously felt, her eyes lighting up. Normally Gabriel wouldn't poke fun at himself, but right now it was worth it.

"I hope you like the meal this evening," he said as he lifted the covers from their plates. He'd specifically requested no servants attend them tonight, as he wanted to be completely alone with Vivian. Having anyone else in the room might inhibit her, and while he understood she was learning to be a proper lady here at the finishing school, he also wanted her to be able to relax in his presence. That would never happen if she thought she was being watched and judged.

This was time apart from the school, separate—their

own little bubble of the world. That was how he wanted it to be once they were married as well. He'd seen how his father and stepmother behaved in public versus how they behaved when it was just family; and, by chance, when it was just the two of them. Gabriel wanted that same kind of easy intimacy with his bride, and this was the best way to build it.

Vivian smiled in delight as she looked down at her plate of roast duck with plum sauce, Yorkshire pudding, and vegetables in gravy. All of which he knew were foods she particularly enjoyed. "It looks delicious, thank you."

She gave him another little peek from beneath her lashes. She was studying him, perhaps wondering if he'd deliberately had her favorites made.

"Are you enjoying the practicum?" he asked, deliberately phrasing the question so as only to ask about her daytime studies. After all, he wanted her to relax, and he doubted a conversation about the evening activities would assist that goal.

From the way she blushed, he knew she was thinking about it anyway, but she answered calmly enough, despite her pink cheeks.

"For the most part," she said, shaking her head with a little smile. "I do think the companions truly enjoy attempting to fluster us."

"Do they succeed?"

"Often." Vivian laughed and began to tell him about the day's lesson, which included Mrs. Wisp, Charity's companion, pretending to be an aggressively motivated matron, aiming to marry off her son to any of the young ladies present. As Vivian told it, it had been highly entertaining, in some ways, and absolutely horrifying in others;

trying to put Mrs. Wisp off without insulting her or her "son" was a Herculean task. Emily had failed miserably at it, Vivian said, being far too blunt in her responses. Vivian was sure her friend would receive a blistering lecture from Miss Norton this evening. Gabriel chuckled, relieved that his intended was finally beginning to talk to him with more ease.

Vivian was amazed that Gabriel seemed to find Emily's impolite rejoinders just as entertaining as she did. As he chuckled, she abruptly changed subjects, to the "emergency" that had occurred just before tea time, when the kitchen reported the milk had spoiled. Although she knew he was her betrothed, she'd felt a small flash of worry—or was it jealousy?—about his mirth over Emily's antics. He wouldn't change his mind about wanting Vivian, would he? Even if he did, the papers were signed and they would be married, but Vivian didn't want a husband who regretted doing so.

So better to stay off the subject of Emily.

"Have your stepmother or sisters had any similar contretemps?" she asked, turning the subject back around on him. She was desperately curious as to how one of the august ladies in Gabriel's family behaved; after all, she was going to have to live up to their expectations once she and Gabriel were married.

"I've made it a habit never to be around for tea time," Gabriel said, his grey eyes glinting with amusement. "Or when Audrey and my sisters were at home for callers. The few times they caught me and I was obliged to attend, I had to suffer through some very lackluster attempts at poetry by my sisters' suitors, or a bevy of mothers that behaved just like Mrs. Wisp—only towards me about their daughters."

"How ghastly," Vivian said, teasing him. He grinned back at her, pleased she felt comfortable enough to do so.

"Exactly."

Vivian could hardly believe she'd had the cheek to tease the earl in such a manner, but he did seem to be inviting it. She could tell he was doing his best to help her relax, and so she was trying hard to. It did help that he was an excellent conversationalist, truly listening and adding his own comments when she talked, and quite engaging to listen to. Of course, if her mind ever did drift from the conversation, her thoughts would immediately go to the punishment chair in her room and her nighttime lessons.

Having him right there in front of her made her evenings seem even more surreal. The earl was so elegant, even with his slightly mussed black hair. There were tiny flecks of green in his eyes, and his extravagantly long lashes would have made him almost pretty if his square jaw and patrician nose weren't so aggressively masculine. He was every inch the perfect English gentleman, just with an air of danger that came from being a rake. At least, she assumed that was what contributed to the aura around him. It was so hard to imagine he would want her spanked and touched. That he would want to spank and touch her the way Mrs. Banks did.

The idea frightened her, even as it excited her, but she was also finding their conversation was easing some of her anxiety. The earl was not some faceless, terrifying specter of her future. He was handsome, charming, and highly attractive, even if he was also intimidating.

Of course, if he wanted to turn her over his knee right now, she didn't know how she would react. She was grateful he didn't seem so inclined. If anything, he just seemed interested in getting to know her better, which was a relief. Sitting in front of him fully clothed was difficult enough; she thought she would be quite distressed if she'd been expected to bare her bottom for him the way she did for Mrs. Banks.

"You'll enjoy Brentwood Manor," the earl said, as she forced her attention back to the conversation at hand. She smiled at his obvious love for his father's estates, taking another bite of the roast duck as she listened to him expound on the place. "It's the perfect place for painting. There's a large lake with a small copse nearby my grandfather built a folly in, using his travels in Greece for inspiration. It's quite peaceful. I spend a fair amount of time sketching among the columns when I'm there."

"It sounds wonderful," Vivian said, completely sincerely. Her own family's property certainly didn't have anything as nice as a lake or a folly on it. His descriptions made her want to see the estates he was describing, but at the same time she felt a bit anxious.

Why would he want someone like her by his side when his family was obviously so much wealthier and powerful than her own? They were getting to know each other now, but he'd chosen her based on nothing but a sighting at a wedding. It was terrifying to think she might somehow let him down, especially as her family's well-being now rested in his hands. She didn't feel nearly beautiful enough or accomplished enough to be his wife, and yet she was the one he'd chosen.

Emily had said it was romantic, and Vivian supposed it

was in a way, but surely he couldn't already have feelings for her. They barely knew each other. What if he changed his mind? Or never developed feelings for her?

She was sure it would be all too easy to develop feelings for him. She was already more than halfway there, between his solicitous attention, his generosity to her loved ones, and her fantasies.

"Are you all right, Sunrise?"

The endearment made her smile, without having to force it, despite her thoughts. "Yes, I'm sorry, just woolgathering. The duck is delicious, isn't it?"

His eyes narrowed slightly at her as she retreated behind meaningless chatter, but he allowed it. Vivian was relieved; she'd become accustomed to falling back on social niceties when she was unsure of herself. The rest of the meal passed easily, and she relaxed again as he told her some of the gossip from the *ton*. She'd never met most of the people he talked about, but she recognized many of the titles, if not the names. Every tidbit of information was tucked away, because one day she would meet all of them as the earl's countess.

His gossip was very different from what she heard from the other young ladies. They were focused on who was courting, what new fashions were being set, and which titled men were said to be looking for a wife. The earl's anecdotes focused on who had won the latest race, who had bought the finest horses, a fistfight that had broken out after Parliament over the day's debate, and how a pair of mischievous young men had released a flock of chickens onto Rotten Row during the daily promenade. Vivian couldn't help but laugh about that one when he described the looks on the matrons' faces as chickens alighted onto their stately carriages, which were lined up next to each other.

The end of the meal came all too quickly, and her heart fluttered with anxiousness as Mrs. Banks came back into the room. The sight of her companion reminded Vivian of what the evening still had to come—the punishment chair in her room awaited her, at the behest of the man in front of her. Heat flushed her cheeks as Gabriel stood, holding out his hand to help her up.

A large hand. Much larger and stronger than Mrs. Banks's. Vivian could only imagine what it might feel like on her bottom, and her insides did all sorts of flips and turns at the thought. She trembled a bit as she put her fingers in his hand, trying not to think about it because it was all too confusing.

The earl's silvery eyes pulled her gaze to his as he lifted her hand to his lips. He turned her hand, pressing the kiss to her palm. Even through her glove she felt the heat of it, and something inside of her tightened. It was the same sensation she got when Mrs. Banks touched her, after the spanking.

Flustered, Vivian looked at the floor, her face burning so brightly she was sure it was red as a cherry.

"Good evening, Sunrise," Gabriel said, his voice low and intimate. "Tend your lessons well . . . and think of me."

"I will, my—Gabriel."

"My Gabriel," he said, and she could hear the smile in his voice even though she didn't dare peek up at him. "I like that."

Breathless, Vivian practically fled the room when he released her hand. She felt confused, skittish, and elated.

She almost looked forward to the ritual of her spanking before bed. At least she knew what to expect there. It had become routine, safe. Almost comforting.

With tear tracks on her cheeks, Vivian gasped as Mrs. Banks administered the last swat to her burning bottom. Safe? Comforting?

Yes. Strangely, yes. It was.

And between her legs, her womanhood was wet. Slick. Creamier than ever. Because the entire time, she hadn't been able to banish the image of Gabriel from her mind. That magnetic, predatory gaze. His easy, mischievous smile. The way he tried to diminish his confident, domineering aura in order to make her more comfortable. Those strong, broad hands.

She'd almost wanted Mrs. Banks to spank her harder, because she was sure Gabriel would. As Mrs. Banks rubbed her fingers across Vivian's pleasure bud, the earl's image brought the gasping redhead to culmination faster than she'd ever achieved her satisfaction before.

After bringing Vivian to her moaning climax, Mrs. Banks didn't give the young woman the opportunity to lie across her lap as she normally did. Instead, she immediately pushed the lower half of Vivian's body off of her so she was kneeling naked between Mrs. Banks's legs, looking up at her with dazed green eyes, a few tears still clinging to her long lashes.

Taking advantage of the young woman's disorientation, Mrs. Banks put her fingers to Vivian's mouth, the ones coated with the honey from her quim.

"Open up, Miss Stafford."

The command was stated firmly, and Vivian automatically responded with compliance. Mrs. Banks's fingers rubbed along her lower lip and then pushed between Vivian's lips—the musky sweet taste of the juices from her own body exploded along Vivian's tongue. She blinked and jerked back.

"No," snapped Mrs. Banks and she hauled Vivian back up and over her lap, landing four hard slaps to each bare cheek of Vivian's bottom, which were still dark pink from the punishment she'd already received. Shocked by this sudden brutal treatment, her body still tingling from the aftermath of her orgasm and feeling even more sensitive than usual, Vivian shrieked and kicked to no avail. She shuddered as Mrs. Banks's fingers roughly swiped up her slit, and then Vivian was suddenly moved back onto her knees in front of her companion, the dripping fingers with their renewed coating of juices held in front of her lips. "Open up, Miss Stafford."

Her lips trembled as she stared at the fingers. Her tongue rolled around her mouth a little, tasting the strange, musky sweetness, and then she reluctantly parted her lips. Just a tiny bit. Just enough that she had followed the order.

Instead of the reprimand Vivian half expected, Mrs. Banks practically cooed her approval. "Very good, Vivian. Such pretty lips you have, so soft and pink."

Mrs. Banks rubbed her fingers along Vivian's lips, coating them with the orgasmic juices from Vivian's pussy. The musky smell filled her nose and she felt rather light-headed, although she was unsure if it was from the abrupt second spanking over Mrs. Banks's lap or the heady smell of the honey coating her lips.

"It feels nice to have your lips touched, doesn't it? To

taste your cream . . . it's sweet, isn't it?" Mrs. Banks's voice was almost hypnotic, the tips of her fingers pushing just very slightly into Vivian's mouth before pulling back out again and running over her pouty lips, then back in and out and around. Each time she pushed a little deeper, speaking soothingly to Vivian about what a good girl she was, and how nice it felt to have Vivian's lips on her fingers. Eventually she was rewarded when Vivian's tongue flicked against her fingertips.

"That's it, Vivian," cooed Mrs. Banks, leaning forward to establish more intimacy between them. Her blue eyes held Vivian's, almost the way a snake's would, and Vivian found herself unable to look away as she fell under the companion's spell. "Lick my fingers, suck on them . . . Doesn't it feel nice? Don't stop licking while you're sucking. Don't use your teeth except very, very lightly . . . that's it . . ."

She moved her fingers back and forth in Vivian's mouth, mimicking the way the earl would one day use his cock, knowing Vivian had no idea what she was being trained for. The young woman sucked and licked every drop of cream from Mrs. Banks's fingers.

The dream-like haze Vivian was in felt stronger than ever. She didn't know why Mrs. Banks was doing this, or why the earl might desire it be done, yet she did find some pleasure in the act. It wasn't the same kind of pleasure that came from sucking on a lolly, but there was some kind of strange enjoyment in it. Perhaps it was the flush of heat from her bottom that she'd grown so accustomed to, or the satiated glow in her body that always followed her climax, but everything felt good right now. She truly enjoyed having praise heaped upon her by Mrs.

Banks, as well as the stroking of her hair, which always felt good.

Mrs. Banks had Vivian suckle on her fingers for a few more minutes before she helped the young woman to her shaky feet and got her ready for bed, well pleased with the progress her student had made during this first week.

"You will have Saturday to do with as you please," she told Vivian as she helped her into bed. "I would suggest that tomorrow you study with the other girls at some point." Sunday, of course, was spent in church and doing other small, quiet pursuits.

Being the obedient young woman that she was, Vivian did exactly that the next day.

In conclusion, Miss Stafford shows all signs of flourishing under this course of study. She responds to spankings with arousal and pleasure, and it is probable she will respond to other punishments in a similar fashion. As you requested, I have encouraged this response to her spankings by following all of them by bringing her to climax. The most effective way to reprimand her is by expressing disappointment. She strives for praise and is deeply moved by what she sees as a failure to please her superiors. I suspect her inherent responses to her continued training will closely match your expressed desires.

Yours to command,

Mrs. Honoria Banks

Leaning back in his chair, Gabriel re-read the last paragraph Mrs. Banks had penned. Vivian had responded to the training exactly the way he'd thought she would. The school was already bringing out her inner submissiveness and awakening her passions. His cock had been rock hard ever since the night before, when he'd had dinner with Vivian. His glorious Sunrise.

It was a good thing he'd had dinner with her before receiving the report, or he might not have been able to control himself. The meal had been hard enough, thinking about all the things he'd like to do to her, all the things she was learning. But she'd been nervous with him still, too. Certainly it sounded as though she was opening up to Mrs. Banks during their evening lessons, but she was already comfortable with her companion. She wouldn't be so with him. As much as it burned him to wait, he knew Mrs. Cunningham and Mrs. Banks were correct when they said his involvement in those lessons should come later.

Sitting upright, he settled his boots on the floor and began to pen a letter to Mrs. Cunningham, thanking her for the report and asking when he could visit with Vivian again. The more time he spent with her, the better she would come to know him and, hopefully, the sooner she would be ready to have him join her training.

He had just finished writing and sealing the note when his butler knocked on his study door.

"The Earl of Marley is here to see you, my lord."

Ah, his eldest sister's husband. They were going to embark on a business venture together; Alexander was insistent that railroads were the way of the future.

"Thank you, Verner. Take this letter and frank it for

me," he said, holding out the letter he'd just written. "And send Alexander in."

"Very good, my lord."

CHAPTER EIGHT

ON SUNDAY EVENING, MRS. CUNNINGHAM summoned Mrs. Banks to her office. When Mrs. Banks arrived she found the headmistress sitting behind her desk as usual, dressed in a severely cut grey gown that did nothing to flatter her already harsh features.

"I read your report and you've had a wonderfully successful week with Miss Stafford," said Mrs. Cunningham approvingly, flipping through the papers on her desk. "I must congratulate you on a job well done so far."

"Thank you," said Mrs. Banks with a pleased smile. "She's a delight to work with, very responsive and very eager to learn."

Mrs. Cunningham's eyes roved over the last page of her copy of the report Mrs. Banks sent to the earl. "I'd like you to begin on restraints with her this week. I know the earl is eager to join in her training soon and I would like to accommodate him. We must be sure she will not balk. I do not want him to think we have not been thorough in her schooling."

"She has adjusted quickly to everything so far,"

pointed out Mrs. Banks, feeling an almost proprietary need to defend her pupil.

"Yes, but you have been soothing and comforting her the whole way. She cannot be allowed to become accustomed to such comfort every time she's faced with something new. I highly doubt the earl will be willing to do so. If we keep her off balance now then she will become accustomed to having to be adaptable, which will be best for her in the long run, and will also please his lordship."

"Very true," said Mrs. Banks, deferring to Mrs. Cunningham's greater experience in training young women for their future. "She settled into her evening pattern fairly quickly, but it would certainly not do to allow her to become complacent."

Mrs. Cunningham smiled, her entire face softening into a genuine expression of pride and approval. Out of all the companions she'd had help her train young women, Mrs. Banks was certainly the best, and she was more than pleased with the work she did. She glanced down at the note she'd received from the earl.

"Lord Cranborne also wishes to have another dinner with Miss Stafford sometime this week."

"I see no hindrance to that," Mrs. Banks said. "She was quite amenable after her meal with him; I think his visit has given her extra motivation."

"Lovely," said Mrs. Cunningham. "I shall write to the earl this evening. Thank you for coming by, Mrs. Banks."

Thus dismissed, Mrs. Banks stood, dropped a curtsy, and left the room, already planning what changes she would be making to Miss Stafford's evening routine during the upcoming week.

* * *

The practicum on Monday went well enough for Vivian, as she was leading the second portion of the day again. Thankfully, the luncheon had been unhindered by rats or nasty society ladies. Instead, today the problem had been in the morning section, when a shortage of flour was discovered thanks to weevils. Lady Astoria had hastened to send a footman out for more flour, and had quickly and efficiently ordered the kitchen to do everything else they could without it, and so Vivian had only had to stall for half an hour before the luncheon was prepared. She had opted to do so by giving her "guests" a tour of the gardens, where the roses were just beginning to bloom, a solution that had earned her a smile of approval from Mrs. Banks.

Although, of course, that didn't stop the companion from writing a series of notes on her pad of paper as the practicum continued. At least she knew she had done well in one respect, enough so that Mrs. Banks had acknowledged it immediately.

All of the young ladies had done quite a bit better and celebrated it over dinner, talking and laughing and feeling rather proud of themselves.

"The first week was bound to be the worst," said Rosalie cheerfully, brushing a strand of dark hair off the high brow of her forehead, somewhat dramatically. Out of all of the students involved in the practicum, she certainly had one of the best attitudes towards the disasters—once they were over, anyway.

"Miss Norton still took plenty of notes on me," said Emily, making a face. "I shudder to think of the lecture I'll endure this evening."

Vivian and Rosalie murmured sympathetically while Astoria just sniffed. If they hadn't had the common bond of the practicum, Vivian doubted she would have ever spent time with Astoria. The classically beautiful blonde was far too cold, maintaining a cool mask of civility and hardly ever engaging in any of the humor or sympathy the other young women did.

That evening when Mrs. Banks came to her room, Vivian was ready and waiting for her. She moved from the chair by the fire where she'd been reading to the hated punishment chair. After a weekend without a single spanking her bottom was feeling completely back to normal, with not even the slightest twinge of soreness, despite the hardness of the seat. In fact, she felt almost anticipatory, not just for the pleasure she knew would follow, but also the spankings themselves. They hurt, but there was something satisfying about the experience as a whole. Some part of her craved the pain almost as much as the pleasure now, even if she would never admit such a thing aloud.

Mrs. Banks read out the multitude of transgressions she felt Vivian had performed, most of which were minor. Despite her acceptance, and even the hint of eagerness, for her punishment, the young woman was hard pressed to keep from protesting over the amount of spankings she was to receive for seemingly small infractions.

As if she could sense the rebellion in her charge, Mrs. Banks gave Vivian a stern look as she finished up her list. "You seem vexed, Miss Stafford. Do you deny these errors?"

"No, Mrs. Banks," Vivian said. "But they are such small errors in comparison to my offenses before, and yet it seems as though the amount of punishment I am to receive is nearly equal."

"Well, this is the second week of the practicum, Miss Stafford," Mrs. Banks said, affecting surprise at Vivian's attitude. Truthfully she was not at all surprised. Although Vivian was inherently obedient, she also had an innate sense of fairness. "With each week the expectations of your behavior and skill become higher. Were you to make a larger offense, the punishment would be substantially more severe than it would have garnered before. My task is to prepare you successfully for marriage, and you must expect that the more you prove yourself adept, the more shall be required from you."

Vivian frowned but didn't protest, her mind turning over the answer and finding it both logical and frustrating.

As Mrs. Banks helped her to disrobe, Vivian shivered in anticipation and realized she was almost excited to know her punishment had not been lessened. The knowledge was unnerving, but that did nothing to stem her reaction.

Still, when Mrs. Banks sat down on the punishment chair, Vivian found herself balking at the injustice of her reprimands. Her companion frowned at her.

"Come here, Miss Stafford, you know the position."

"I—I would like to discuss this further, please," Vivian said, feeling rather silly, as she was naked and vulnerable and Mrs. Banks was fully clothed, seated, and obviously in full authority. "I don't feel I should be punished so harshly when I've been improving."

"If you hadn't improved, you really would know what a harsh punishment is," Mrs. Banks snapped, standing up.

Vivian took a step back, but then halted, trying to stand her ground. Her chin went up stubbornly. "It's not fair!"

"Perhaps I should have expected this," Mrs. Banks

said with a small shake of her head. "You've been so well-behaved for so long, but I suppose it's only natural you'd feel the need to rebel eventually. If you truly want a harsh punishment, then that is what you'll receive, Miss Stafford."

"No, wait—" Vivian let out a small shriek as Mrs. Banks grabbed hold of her wrist and bodily dragged her over to the chair and across her lap. Mrs. Banks adjusted Vivian slightly on her lap as she retrieved a silk cord from her pocket. Letting out a small, frustrated cry, Vivian kicked her legs, and received a mighty slap from Mrs. Banks's hand onto her buttocks for the effort.

"Miss Stafford, give me your hands."

Sniffling slightly, Vivian looked over her shoulder at a frowning Mrs. Banks. The older woman patted Vivian on the small of her back.

"Put them right here." Her voice was stern, colder than Vivian ever remembered it being.

Awkwardly, Vivian followed Mrs. Banks's instructions, finding it difficult to shift herself so she could put her hands in such a position while she was bent over the other woman's lap. Tension quivered through her as Mrs. Banks quickly grasped her wrists, holding them firmly, and she felt something looping around them.

Immediately, she began to squirm.

"Mrs. Banks, what are you doing?" she asked. Her anxiety spiked again as she felt the knots around her wrists tighten, holding them together at the small of her back.

"Hold still, Vivian! That's five more added to your tally for this evening," Mrs. Banks said fiercely as she renewed her firm grip on the younger woman. "You must learn not to fight every new experience. Do you think his lordship will be pleased with a wife who is constantly questioning him? Don't you already think you've added enough punishment to your evening?"

A small, frightened whimper fell from Vivian's lips. This was not the comforting routine she was used to and the deviation flustered her, along with her anger over the unfairness of it all. Yet now she wished she'd just kept quiet. She'd known, even as she'd provoked Mrs. Banks, that it couldn't lead to anything good.

She felt so dreadfully confused and helpless, even more so than she had before. Why, with her hands tied behind her back Mrs. Banks could literally do anything she pleased and Vivian would have no way to resist.

She had not fully appreciated how much more secure she had felt when her arms had been free. Now that they were bound behind her back, she realized how comforting it had been to have them swinging down before her. There was a terrible finality to having her hands actually restrained.

"Now then," Mrs. Banks said as she felt Vivian tremble but not resist. "Some men enjoy seeing a woman helpless to their eyes, their hands." As if to demonstrate, she began stroking Vivian's back with one hand, the other caressing Vivian's buttocks and thighs. The gentle touch sent a spark of kindling awareness through Vivian's young body, and her thighs automatically parted as if inviting further stroking to her feminine folds. She had already learned the delights that area had to offer, and her body instinctively bared it. "Some women enjoy being so vulnerable, knowing their husband can touch them anywhere he wants, do whatever he wants to her, and she will be helpless to stop him."

Mrs. Banks's words were exciting Vivian in the same way her hands were. In her mind's eye she could see herself bound with her wrists behind her back as a faceless man wreathed in shadows stared at her. Would he touch her like Mrs. Banks was? Explore the expanse of her milky skin with his fingertips? Put her over his lap and delve into her intimate secrets, or even spank her for no other reason than she could not resist him?

Part of her mind was frightened by such an idea, but the rest of her was falling under the almost hypnotic spell Mrs. Banks was forming with her words.

"Such vulnerability requires a great deal of trust. It shows how much a wife trusts her husband to take care of her, to have complete control over her body, her pain, and her pleasure. It can be both frightening and exciting for her, the combination of which can lead to incredible ecstasy."

The companion's carefully modulated tones were seductive, hinting at secret pleasures, planting seeds of dark desires that would take root in Vivian's impression-able mind and grow, carefully nurtured by herself and by Vivian's very nature. Her fingers slid through the coppery curls lining the outer lips of Vivian's sopping wet crevice, and Mrs. Banks was gratified to find her young charge so obviously aroused.

Shocked at her own desire to have Mrs. Banks pleasure her, Vivian let out a small moan.

"Do not forget, Miss Stafford, if you find that this training is no longer of interest to you, all you have to do is say the word and it will end."

With that said, Mrs. Banks grasped the silk cord around Vivian's wrists with one hand, keeping Vivian's hands well above her buttocks to ensure Vivian would not be able to try and block the oncoming spanking.

Smack!

"Oh!" Vivian had expected the slap, of course, but the sound she made was as much a kind of relief as it was in reaction to the sting. In one short week her body had been trained to accept a hearty punishment to her poor bottom, and now it reacted with surging excitement. For her, a spanking heralded pleasure, and the tingling between her legs intensified as Mrs. Banks began to pepper her bottom with hard slaps. It didn't matter that she was bound now—this was what her body was used to. In fact, she was finding it a bit thrilling to try and move her hands and not be able to. The reaction was inexplicable but undeniable.

Not once did Vivian attempt to roll off Mrs. Banks's lap, although her wrists tugged energetically at the silken cord binding them. Not once did she even consider saying the words that would end her punishment. The feelings of helpless vulnerability aroused her intensely, although she didn't understand her response or the physical manifestation of it.

Mrs. Banks spanked Vivian's bottom so hard that the flesh flattened before it jiggled, the young woman's cries becoming quite heated. Tears slid down her cheeks at the biting sting of each swat, but her lower body throbbed with a very different kind of response. Vivian was sure Mrs. Banks was spanking her harder than a week before—a supposition that was quite correct—and yet, despite the pain, it did nothing to assuage the sensual hunger that made her ache in a completely different manner. If anything, it made the need for Mrs. Banks's soothing touch even more acute. As usual, dark spots decorated the wooden floor beneath Vivian's face where her tears had dropped. She wondered if she would ever receive a spanking that didn't reduce her to weeping, even as her intimate areas pulsed with growing need.

Her tears fell freely, her pleas and cries for mercy going unheard. Surely she couldn't take anymore! And yet the spanking continued, unyielding, upon her already roasted bottom. Vivian cried, heartily sorry she had been so contrary to Mrs. Banks. She had no one to blame but herself for her current situation.

Mrs. Banks showed no mercy. She was aware Vivian needed the comfort of knowing her punishments would be delivered exactly as promised. Unresolved punishments would only confuse her further as to what the rules and consequences were.

By the time Mrs. Banks reached thirty-five, Vivian's bottom was glowing a nice hot pink. The young woman wriggled, wrists chafing against the silken cord binding them as she rubbed them back and forth in an instinctive attempt to escape the next portion of her punishment. Ignoring her movements, Mrs. Banks removed the sturdy hairbrush she'd pocketed before helping Vivian disrobe.

The hard, flat back of the wood made such an impression on poor Vivian's roasted bottom that she shrieked the loudest she'd ever done, pushed past the point of caring whether someone might walk by her room and hear her. Not that any unauthorized ears would ever bear witness to her cries, pleas, or sobs. Every companion and servant in the school knew exactly what was happening in her room and would keep any of the other students from ever walking by. Even if they did, there was no guarantee of her voice being heard; the room was specially designed to hold in sound, with a much thicker door and walls than the rest of the building.

"Please, Mrs. Banks! Please, not the brush!"

Vivian's pleas for mercy became much louder as Mrs. Banks blistered her poor bottom with the unforgiving wooden hairbrush. Her tenderized cheeks were pure agony, and she truly began to buck and kick; only Mrs. Banks's firm hold on her body kept her in the companion's lap. Sobbing and squealing, Vivian could barely hear Mrs. Banks's voice counting out the strokes, or even the meaty thud of the brush against her flaming backside.

Now the thought of saying the words that were guaranteed to end this all flitted through her mind . . . but so did Gabriel's face, and she shoved the impulse away. This was painful, but she'd be willing to bear much more to be with him—although she certainly hoped she wouldn't have to.

The last one caught Vivian across both cheeks and she howled, bucking and heaving before falling down limply across Mrs. Banks's lap and sobbing.

The companion made soothing noises as she rubbed her hand over Vivian's glowing bottom, her fingers making her way down to Vivian's wet folds. Vivian squirmed, with both arousal and embarrassment at her reaction to the harsh spanking. Despite the fact that her bottom was flaming hotter than ever, or maybe because of it, her sensitive core was ready to burst almost from the moment Mrs. Banks touched her. The bindings on her wrists added to the hazy eroticism of the moment as slim fingers stroked her up and down, spreading her natural cream down around the sensitive pearl at the apex of her womanhood. Vivian found her bound helplessness even more exciting now that Mrs. Banks was touching her so intimately.

The pain in her bottom mixed with her rising ecstasy, pooling together at her center and swirling into a transcendent mix of molten sensation.

Mrs. Banks began to rub Vivian's clit with slow, circular motions. The young woman across her lap whimpered and moved her hips, thrusting them up and down in response to the direct stimulation. Her buttocks were still glowing, like the most brilliant of sunsets, and Mrs. Banks had the pleasure of watching those sweet little mounds tighten and bounce as Vivian's modesty fell away under the insistent needs of her body. "Your husband is going to be very pleased with how responsive you are. Such a sweet, wet little cunny. He's going to enjoy it very much."

The shadowy fantasy of the earl having Vivian bent over like this, touching her secret parts the way Mrs. Banks was, was enough to send Vivian reeling into her orgasm. She cried out, shuddering and moving her hips quite frantically as Mrs. Banks's fingers rubbed hard and relentlessly over her pearl. The sizzling pleasure had Vivian moaning throatily, her body quivering and panting from the rapture. Mrs. Banks's words of praise as Vivian came apart only reinforced the ideas that had been planted in Vivian's mind the week before, sustaining her impression that this was the correct response to such activities. That she should give over to the loss of control, that her body was Mrs. Banks's to do with as she pleased, that pleasure came from obedience and from giving over her body completely.

"Good girl," Mrs. Banks said as Vivian's cries slowed

and the frantic movements of her body quieted. The beautiful redhead hung down, completely unsupported with her hands tied behind her back. When Mrs. Banks helped Vivian to her knees, the young woman almost swooned as all the blood rushed from her head. She was rather dizzy, but that didn't stop Mrs. Banks from inserting her glistening fingers into Vivian's mouth again. "Remember what we did last week? Clean my fingers, Vivian. Go on, lick them . . . very good . . ."

Dizziness brought on instant obedience. Mrs. Banks's fingers were already moving back and forth in her mouth, coating her tongue with the musky sweetness, and Vivian obediently sucked. Although she didn't realize it, the restraint of her arms behind her back was thrusting her breasts forward enticingly, as if offering them up for Mrs. Banks's perusal. She shifted uncomfortably on her knees, feeling the heat of her bottom against the cool air of the room. She cupped her hands over it and noticed the blazing skin against her palms.

Deciding to press Vivian a little harder, per Mrs. Cunningham's instructions, Mrs. Banks began to fondle Vivian's breast with her free hand. The young woman gasped a little, something like panic flickering in her eyes, but when she looked up into the unyielding blue eyes of Mrs. Banks, she shuddered and submitted to her companion's touch. Her arms twitched in the bindings, as if to come forward and cover herself, but there was nothing to be done as the silken cord held her wrists quite tightly. It seemed as soon as she allowed herself to become accustomed to one thing, Mrs. Banks was introducing something new.

But she could not deny that Mrs. Banks's hand on her

breast, teasing her little pink nipple, felt incredibly pleasurable. The gentle touch stirred something deep in her belly again, but surely she could not need a climax so soon after her most recent one?

Then Mrs. Banks withdrew her fingers from Vivian's pouting mouth and ceased to caress Vivian's breasts, and Vivian was left with those small stirrings unsatisfied. They were not advanced enough for her to be upset, just curious as to the responses of her body under Mrs. Banks's more experienced hands.

"Very good, Miss Stafford," Mrs. Banks said as she helped Vivian rise.

Solicitously she released Vivian's wrists from the bindings of the cord and rubbed the slightly reddened skin with cream. Vivian's chastised bottom received no such treatment. Once she was dressed in her night rail and put to bed, Vivian was unable to fall into a sound sleep the way she normally was.

She tossed and turned, the pain in her bottom seeming to grow as she tried to find the reprieve of slumber. Laying on her back was impossible and even laying on her sides made her feel sore. In addition to the discomfort, she had found the needy ache between her legs had not been entirely satisfied, some remnant lingered, perhaps brought about by Mrs. Banks's gentle fondling as Vivian had sucked her fingers. Tossing back and forth and wondering at the stirrings between her thighs, grimacing at the lingering soreness of her poor bottom, Vivian finally drifted off to sleep much later than usual.

CHAPTER NINE

NIBBLING DISTRACTEDLY AT HIS BREAKFAST, Lord Cranborne frowned at the report his estate manager had given him. Ever since his father had begun to hand over some of the estates to Gabriel to run, giving him experience with the handling of estate matters as well as relieving some of the burden on the marquess, his days had been filled with worries about crop yields, horses, and the tenants. It was a part of the reason he did not have the time to train his future wife in the manner he desired.

But that was why he'd put his trust into Mrs. Cunningham's Finishing School. Just thinking about Vivian and imagining what she must look like as she was put through her training roused his desires. He couldn't wait to actually be a part of her training. Until then, he had to distract himself with other financial and business affairs.

Affairs that needed his attention if he was going to have the estates in order by the time of his wedding. He wanted plenty of time to indulge himself with his new wife, to sate the ardor he'd had from the moment he saw her.

"Good morning, Gabriel," said his stepmother, Audrey, as she drifted into the room. She was quite a beautiful woman, a few years older than him, and very devoted to her family. So far she had not given his father another child, but she seemed satisfied with her stepchildren. Indeed, it had been her devotion to his sisters that had precipitated the events that led to her agreeing to marry his father.

That had been rather a surprise to him. His father had been involved with any number of women over the years, and Gabriel had always assumed he would never remarry. But then Audrey had applied to be governess to Diana and Henrietta; her attractive looks and buxom figure had appealed immensely to his father from the start, and her fiery nature, strong will, and adoration of his daughters had sent his father tumbling head over heels in love. Unable to fathom giving her up when his daughters came of age, the marquess had made her his wife.

Despite the difference in their ages, she and his father were well-matched, and they truly cared for each other. Gabriel didn't see Audrey as a mother figure, of course, they were too close in age for that, but they'd become good friends. He was happy his father had her in his life; she steadied him in many ways, and the marquess had become a much gentler and compassionate person under her influence.

"Good morning, Audrey," he returned, setting down his papers. Normally he conducted his business within his own home, but today he had needed some documents that were only available in his father's study. Since he hadn't seen the marquess yet this morning, he had taken over the room with his work. "How are you today?"

"Quite well," she said, giving him a ravishing smile as she floated around the study, examining the various piles of papers and books scattered about. The burgundy dress she wore set off the red highlights in her chestnut hair and hugged the magnificent bosom for which she was well-known. "Your father and I are discussing taking another trip abroad before your wedding. He said you have already set a date?"

Gabriel had to smile at the cautious curiosity in Audrey's voice. While she had always been confident and strong-willed in dealing with his sisters, she had never quite known how to handle him. Since he hadn't spoken to her at all about his plans to wed—indeed, he hadn't mentioned it to anyone but his father—he could only assume she wasn't sure whether or not she had any right to ask questions about it, but of course that didn't contain her curiosity completely.

"She's at school right now, but we'll be wed on the day she graduates. I look forward to introducing you to her."

Something like alarm flickered in Audrey's hazel eyes. "On the day she graduates? Somehow I didn't imagine you marrying her right out of the schoolroom, Gabriel."

There was more than a hint of reproach in her voice, and he remembered how she'd argued for his sisters to have more time before their own weddings. He wasn't sure if his stepmother would approve of the lessons Vivian was receiving now, in order to prepare her for marriage to him. While he suspected his father's tastes ran similar to his own in the bedroom, that didn't mean the lessons were exactly proper.

"It's a finishing school, she won't be right out of the regular schoolroom. She's eighteen, so she's already older than most of the debs coming out this year. Mrs. Cunningham's school prepares the young women who attend to run a household so they can make advantageous matches."

"And you've already made one with her," Audrey said, crossing to look out of the window as she thought. He could see her nibbling her lower lip. In many ways, Audrey had always been far too astute, picking up on the subtlest clues that someone was hiding something from her. "Have I met her?"

"Doubtful. She was at George and Mary's wedding, which is where I met her, and she's been in school since." Both of his parents were well acquainted with the couple, although they hadn't been able to attend the wedding.

"So you haven't been courting her?" His stepmother turned towards him, eyes flashing dangerously.

Audrey was ever a romantic. He knew very well that she loved his father with all her heart and that she wanted all of her stepchildren to find love. Diana and Henrietta had both managed to, so he supposed he was the last hurdle.

"It's an arranged match, but I can assure you I have strong feelings for her."

Very strong—in fact, he might go so far as to call himself somewhat obsessed with her. He didn't want any other woman, he thought about her constantly, and he desperately desired her to be comfortable with him. Above all else, he wanted to make her happy. Was that love? Perhaps. It was certainly the strongest emotion he'd ever felt towards any woman, and it hadn't lessened at all in the time he'd been waiting for her. If love grew, the way it had for Diana and Alexander, then he would be content. If not, then he would still have passion, desire, and an obedient wife.

"And her?" Audrey persisted. "Does she have feelings for you? Did she have a choice in her bridegroom?"

That had been the sticking point between Audrey and his father when it came to Diana's marriage, her lack of choice. Of course, everything had worked out, as his father liked to point out, but Audrey insisted on maintaining her position that the happy ending had been as much luck as anything else.

"She had a choice," he said a little testily.

Perhaps she hadn't had much of one, considering her family's financial situation, but he certainly wouldn't force a woman into a marriage that she rejected. He knew from Mrs. Banks's report that Vivian was applying herself assiduously to her new training and striving to make herself pleasing to her future husband, and surely she wouldn't do that unless she accepted the marriage, would she? During the time he'd spent with her, she'd certainly seemed accepting of him, although he also knew she might feel compelled to seem that way. But he thought he would know if she wasn't. There was attraction and desire on both sides, whether or not she recognized it for what it was.

"What are you two doing?" His father's booming voice practically echoed through the study. The way he looked over his wife would make a casual observer think they'd only been married a short time. It was a hungry and lustful look. They had the kind of marriage Gabriel wanted. There was affection, passion, and understanding between them that defied the usual restrictions of the *ton*.

"Gabriel and I were just talking," she said, going to greet her husband with a kiss.

Gabriel wondered about the slightly guilty tone in

Audrey's voice and her lack of detail in her response to his father. He grinned wickedly.

"Audrey was quite interested in my future bride," he said casually. *Aha!* A direct hit. Someone wasn't supposed to be bothering him about his personal matters, and now she'd been caught. Audrey glared at him as his father frowned down at her.

"I told you not to bother Gabriel about his wedding."

"I just asked a few questions," Audrey said, almost simpering as she fluttered her eyelashes innocently. Not at all fooled, the marquess choked on a laugh at his wife's antics. He kept a stern face, but even Gabriel could see his father's eyes sparkling in amusement.

Gabriel enjoyed watching Audrey attempt to use her wiles on her husband, who obviously appreciated the attempt even as he ignored it. He wondered if Vivian would ever try something so blatant as a sexual manipulation. Somehow, he didn't think so, and he preferred it that way. While he enjoyed Audrey's company greatly, her temperament was not of the kind he'd like his wife to have.

"What did I tell you was going to happen if you pestered him?" The marquess traced his wife's cheek with a finger. "You already had plenty of say in Henrietta's marriage, let Gabriel's be."

"I just wanted to make sure he's going to treat the poor thing right," Audrey replied, her spine straightening as she abandoned her flirtations and some of the steel the marquess was so fond of returned. Gabriel knew his father liked it when Audrey stood up to him. "Did you know he didn't even court her?"

His father just laughed at the glaring look she gave him.

Although Audrey had settled into her place as marchioness, she had never expected to be so socially prominent, and she still disapproved many of the things the *ton* took for granted—such as arranged marriages.

"I didn't say that exactly," Gabriel countered. "The arrangements have been made and the papers signed, but I've already visited Vivian twice at the school and given her a birthday gift."

Audrey sniffed at him, as if barely mollified by his assertion, but he also saw her lips moving, and he got the impression she was repeating Vivian's name to herself, as if committing it to memory. Internally, he sighed; just what he needed, to give Audrey another daughter to fuss over.

"And now, my dear, we need to discuss your intentional disobedience of my order to leave Gabriel alone," his father said firmly, turning his wife in the doorway to shoo her out. Glancing over his shoulder, he shrugged and smiled at his son. "I should have realized she was up to something when she practically bolted from her dressing room after hearing you were here. I hope she wasn't too distracting."

"Mmm. . . . I'm sure I'll be able to catch up on my neglected work after a few hours," said Gabriel, his face serious.

The door closed behind the couple and he could hear Audrey protesting. Only when the door was firmly shut did he allow himself to grin again. The little game his father and stepmother played was highly amusing to him. Perhaps one day he and Vivian would play similar ones.

For a moment he thought about Vivian, and his groin swelled again. Groaning, he forced his attention back to the papers in front of him.

* * *

That afternoon found Gabriel at his club, having taken refuge from Audrey and his sisters. His snifter of brandy in hand, he let out a long sigh and leaned back in his chair. While Vivian was tucked away at the school she should be safe from his family. He'd really like her to become better acquainted with him through himself and not his family; not to mention, he'd like to establish his authority before his family undermined it.

"Well, hullo, old chap," said a cheery voice. Opening his eyes, Gabriel looked up at George, who was settling down in the chair next to his. "You look a bit worse for the wear."

Gabriel groaned. "Audrey and the girls are hounding me about Vivian."

Chuckling, George signaled to a waiter to bring him his own drink. "You can't blame them for their curiosity. My mother was constantly harping on me about Mary while she was at the school."

"How did you deal with it?"

"The same way you are," George admitted, with a broad gesture at the club. "I got almost daily letters from her, not to mention the occasional visit from one of her friends. Once they met, Mother adored her, so that was well enough."

"I think Audrey and my sisters are more concerned about how I'll suit Vivian than they are about how she'll suit me," Gabriel said, a bit disgruntled. Then again, he supposed he couldn't completely blame them. He did have a bit of a reputation, after all, one which had fallen by the wayside now that he was to be married, not that it stopped women from trying. Another reason he didn't make social appearances anymore—he wasn't just not searching, he was actively avoiding.

"Well, you don't need to worry about how she'll suit you, that's what the school's for," George replied, a note of satisfaction in his voice. The waiter came by with his drink, which he took a sip of before turning his attention back to Gabriel. "I can't imagine having any other wife than my Mary. When I hear some of these other poor blokes talking about their wives, well, it's no wonder they end up seeking companionship elsewhere." He lowered his voice, leaning in conspiratorially. "Westhaven told me he heard his wife mumbling something about place settings while he was trying to do his duty with her. Can you imagine?"

Gabriel cringed. That certainly wasn't the only story he'd heard about the hazards of taking a wife to bed. It was a large part of the reason he wanted Vivian to come to their marriage with her passions awakened and, hope-fully, more comfortable with her body and her desires than the average wife. His own needs were much more complicated than the average gentleman's and would probably traumatize a woman like Lady Westhaven.

The two of them passed an amiable afternoon at the club, eventually joined by Alexander and Jonathan, Gabriel's brothers-in-law. They'd both been pestered by their wives to find out more about Vivian from him, since he'd fled the scene. Doing their duty, they asked, and then dropped the subject as soon as he expressed his unwilling-ness to delve into details about his future bride.

Shifting uncomfortably on the dining room chair, Vivian did her best to attend to her luncheon, despite the ache that lingered in her bottom. Mrs. Banks watched her out of the corner of her eye and she knew she must stop fidgeting so much or it would be listed on the tally of her infractions and her poor backside would pay the price later. Strangely the ache didn't bother her quite so much as it had the day before, despite the fact that it was stronger.

It was almost as if she was learning to embrace the pain rather than fight against it and allow it to distract her.

And it didn't hurt that, for the first time, she hadn't felt rushed in the morning. A small smile played across her lips as she complimented Rosalie, who was playing hostess, on the soup that had been served. Despite the prior evening's harsh punishment, she felt almost blissful. She knew what was expected of her and today she was making her way through each passing hour gracefully.

Her skill on the pianoforte was flawless, one of the companions had complimented her on her elegant script as she'd composed a letter, she'd quickly soothed one of the crying maids who had accidentally spilled a tray during tea—without disrupting the service—and she was always smiling, no matter the provocation. All with a bottom that still stung whenever she sat down. She could practically feel the approval emanating from her companion.

Indeed, Mrs. Banks was more than pleased, and very proud of Vivian. Only once or twice had she caught the slight wince as Vivian sat, proof that the young woman was still feeling the effects of her chastisement, and yet not once had she faltered today.

Looking at Miss Stafford now, in a plum-colored dress that accentuated her narrow waist and a cream and plum hat perched atop her head to keep the sun from her face as they tended to the gardens, one would never know she had been harshly disciplined the evening before. Which was exactly how it should be.

"You seem to be feeling better today," Emily commented over dinner. The other girls were engrossed in discussing the gossip Astoria had received in a letter from her mother, allowing Emily to get in a quick, private aside to Vivian.

"Very much so," said Vivian, smiling. Although she couldn't completely quell her apprehension about her evening punishment, because it always hurt, she couldn't help but feel rather excited, too, beneath the anxiousness. It was as if she no longer had any control over her emotions or her reactions, at least not in the evenings; only today when she presented her cool facade to the other young women in the practicum did she feel in control. It didn't hurt that she knew today's punishment should be less, which meant the pleasure would come faster.

"You weren't at all yourself yesterday."

Vivian smiled ruefully at her friend. She was quite sure Emily suspected there was something Vivian wasn't telling her, and of course she was right, but there wasn't any recourse that Vivian could see. She certainly couldn't tell Emily the truth; what would her friend think? "No, I wasn't feeling very well."

Overhearing Astoria say the Earl of Cranborne's title, Vivian's head snapped to the right, to the other young ladies from their class. Astoria was talking excitedly about how the earl had apparently become betrothed, but no one seemed to know who the lucky young lady was.

"Of course, it might not be true," Astoria said, her avaricious blue eyes hopeful. "After all, my mother said she spoke to Cranborne's eldest sister about it, but she was very mysterious. Wouldn't even tell my mother her name."

Lily opened her mouth, her eyes darting to Vivian and then away. Of course she, Charity, and Emily all knew about Vivian's betrothal, but they hadn't talked about it among themselves since Vivian had shared the news. Lily and Charity didn't know how she felt about it, since Vivian had only shared the earl's visits with Emily. She hadn't meant to keep him a secret exactly, but already being betrothed, rather than readying herself for her debut, was just another thing that made her different from the other students. She hadn't spoken of it to the others since the day after her birthday.

"It's Vivian Stafford," Emily said, inserting herself into the conversation with a sly smile. She didn't like Astoria any better than Vivian did, even though Astoria toadied to her constantly.

"Excuse me?" Astoria said, blinking rapidly, completely taken aback.

"His fiancée's name. It's Vivian Stafford." Emily grinned at Vivian, who smiled back, although her stomach was now churning with anxiety. Rosalie was flat-out staring at her, mouth hanging open in a very unattractive manner. To her left, Astoria glared derisively.

"Very funny, Emily," the blonde said snidely.

"It's true," Charity said, giving Astoria a superior look. "Vivian told us weeks ago." Well, a couple weeks ago, but Vivian didn't begrudge Charity the implication that it had been longer. Although Charity was the niece of a duke, her father didn't have a title and Astoria could be quite condescending to her at times.

"Really?" Astoria drawled the word, eyeing Vivian as if she was some kind of slimy worm that had just crawled out from underneath a rock. "Strange how no one else knows about it, then."

"Are you saying I lied?" Vivian asked, surprised into responding. She usually tried not to engage Astoria at all. Emily couldn't help but bait her, but Vivian usually came out of any verbal sparring feeling at a loss. Astoria had mastered the art of being insulting without actually issuing an insult.

"Of course not," Astoria said airily, although, of course, that was exactly what she meant. "It's just strange, isn't it? You told Charity weeks ago, and yet not one of us heard anything about it from anyone else until now. Very strange."

Which Vivian couldn't take offense to, because it was strange. She would have thought the news of someone as consequential as the Marquess of Salisbury's heir becoming betrothed would have been trumpeted about quite quickly. Unless, of course, he was keeping it quiet for some reason. Was he keeping it quiet for some reason?

She kept her face impassive, not wanting Astoria to see the line of conversation had affected her.

"Perhaps the earl didn't want to subject himself to common gossip," Emily said in a bored tone. "After all, with Vivian here at the school, I'm sure there would be an untoward amount of ill-bred interest in his betrothed. Why, the school would be overrun with gossip-mongers."

Vivian envied Emily's ease of turning the insults back on Astoria without actually coming out and calling Astoria or her mother gossips. It was the kind of thing Vivian didn't know if she'd ever be able to do; she'd been raised with country manners and wasn't used to the sly double-speak the others had grown up with.

Although Astoria's face turned pink with fury at Emily's insinuations, there wasn't anything she could do. Icily offering Vivian her best wishes, the snobbish blonde quickly turned the conversation back to the day's activities. It was one of the few things they could all converse over perfectly amicably.

CHAPTER TEN

THE REST OF THE WEEK PASSED THE WAY the week before had: the practicum during the day, and disciplines for her mistakes at night. Between her earlier hour of rising and the exhausting punishments and pleasures she was receiving in the evening, Vivian slept very soundly every night. To her delight, the earl sent a note on Wednesday, again requesting her company for dinner on Friday. She whispered the news to Emily, who immediately spread it on to Charity and Lily, which meant Rosalie and Astoria knew quickly as well.

The blonde still seemed disbelieving, but she'd been quieter during the week with Vivian. Not as nasty. Whether Astoria believed Vivian was betrothed to the earl or not, Vivian was grateful for the reprieve.

Her evening with the earl was wonderful. He'd brought some of his sketches to show her; ones that he'd done of his family and of Brentwood and the other estates. She'd barely tasted a bite of her meal as she'd exclaimed over his skill and the wonderful sketches. The landscapes were beautiful and the ones of his family made her laugh. He'd drawn his sister Henrietta sitting outside of a door with her ear pressed against a keyhole.

The whole dinner was wonderful.

The dinner was hell.

Although Mrs. Banks had left them alone again, Gabriel was starting to think he would prefer to have the older woman in the room as a buffer. His instincts as a rake made him want to seduce Vivian right there in her chair, to pull the pins from her glorious hair, pull down the front of her dress to reveal her pink nipples, and push up her skirts until he could feast on the cream between her thighs, rather than the cream on the berries they were having for dessert.

With any other woman in his past, he'd seen, desired, and taken. He'd never had to exercise his patience or will-power so greatly, especially when he had all the opportunity in the world to seduce her. There was no one to stop him. No one would blame him. But it would interrupt her training.

More than that, Gabriel was restrained by his concern that it would also distress Vivian. She was naturally modest and a complete innocent, despite her lessons. While he noted the increased pace of her breathing when he touched her, the blush on her cheeks, and the way her nipples puckered beneath her dress, he could also tell she was a bit discomposed by her response to him. Although she didn't shy away from his touch, she always stilled beneath his fingers for a moment, as if gauging whether to stay or flit away.

Young innocents were not what he was used to, but he knew what his honor demanded. Vivian deserved to go to their marriage bed a virgin. Even if it meant his cock ached unrelentingly every moment he was in her presence.

So he tortured himself by pulling his chair next to hers as he showed her his sketches, pointing out little things in each of the scenes for her to focus on. Her delight in them was evident, her smile genuine. He hadn't brought any of his more recent drawings, because they were all of her. As they looked at his work, he fantasized about a day in the future when he'd be able to sketch her while she posed for him. Naked. Bound. Bottom burnished by his hand or a paddle or some other implement. He could think of a thousand different poses off the top of his head he would love to put her in and then draw her.

When they reached the last sketch, Vivian turned her head slightly to look at him, her green eyes shining with happiness. It made him happy as well; he rarely shared his sketches with anyone. It wasn't just the content that was private—gentlemen of his stature were supposed to be more interested in things like horses, hunting, and women. Which he was, but he also liked to sketch.

"Would you like to see my water colors the next time you visit?" she asked shyly. "I mean, if you come again—I certainly don't expect . . ."

"I'd love to, Sunrise," he said sincerely, reaching up to cup her chin in his hand and stop her nervous rambling. She was sweetly adorable and entirely seductive in her innocence, and if he didn't at least take a taste of her tonight . . .

Well, he didn't know what he would do, but it didn't matter because she was in the perfect position to steal a kiss.

Their first kiss.

Gabriel had been with his share of women, but a first kiss had never been so important. Usually a first kiss heralded a sign of success, that the woman would be his to bed, but Vivian was already his. Her body, her passion, her future all belonged to him; there was no need for conquest or seduction. Once they were married he could do what he willed with her.

This was the beginning of something more. The emotion welling in him as her soft lips pressed against his, parting on a gasp and allowing him to slide his tongue into her mouth and taste the sweet berries and cream intermingling with a flavor that was uniquely and definitively her own, wasn't triumph over a conquest. It was deeper. More powerful. Less under his control.

He groaned as her tongue touched his and he deepened the kiss, taking more of her mouth. One hand still holding her head in place, the other reached out to tug her closer to him, so the sides of their bodies were pressed together and his hand caressed her hip. She responded hesitantly but ardently, and her hesitation was the only thing forcing him to hang onto his control.

He pulled away from her before he could follow up on his instincts, but he realized he needed to end the evening immediately. Vivian's eyes were wide, filled with both arousal and fear. While he could seduce her easily, right here and now, they weren't married. She wouldn't sleep in his bed tonight, and they wouldn't be seeing each other again until next week. Too much time for her to question, for her to worry over her ruined state—it didn't matter that they were engaged, it wasn't the same as being married. She would worry and he wouldn't be there to soothe or reassure her.

Which meant they needed to stop now, before he lost control.

"I'll see you next week, Sunrise. I promise."

Seemingly speechless, Vivian nodded as he rose and went to the door, calling Mrs. Banks in and taking his leave of the both of them. Striding out to Lucifer, he knew he wasn't going to go straight home. He needed to go for a long ride, to feel the wind whipping against his face and the freedom that came from moving so swiftly.

Besides, Lucifer could use the exercise.

Sunlight, rather than the maid, woke Vivian. For a moment she felt panicked and sat bolt upright, thinking she was late for the practicum and Mrs. Banks would be using the dreaded hairbrush on her that evening, and then she remembered it was Saturday and she did not need to worry about the practicum. How very strange. Falling back onto her pillow, she let her pounding heart slow as she wondered why the teachers allowed them to have two days off from the practicum. After all, once the students were married and had their own households to run, they would not receive any such break from their duties.

Then again, they would be able to dictate for themselves when they could rest. Even the most social of the *ton* had days when they stayed in and were not "at home" to visitors. That was not an option for the students, of course, as their schedules were dictated by the school and their companions.

Flopping back against her pillows, Vivian shivered a little. Her dreams had been full of the earl and his burning touch, the strong hands that had easily pulled her against him and the kisses that had made her melt. Kisses where he'd put his tongue in her mouth! She'd tried to utilize the lessons Mrs. Banks had been giving her in the evenings, but fingers weren't the same as a tongue, and she'd been so overcome by all the sensations coursing through her that she had barely been able to think.

Being touched by Gabriel was entirely different from Mrs. Banks. Her skin had felt like it was on fire, and pleasure had curled inside of her so quickly, but it was different from the pleasure Mrs. Banks gave her in the evenings. Somehow more encompassing, even though she hadn't climaxed.

If the earl could do that to her with a kiss, what would it be like when he actually did the things Mrs. Banks did to her?

Thinking back about some of the things Mrs. Banks had said about her evening training and how she was lucky, Vivian was beginning to understand what her companion meant. She had known what the strange fluttering and coiling in her stomach had meant when Gabriel kissed her breathless, known that something wonderful could come of it.

Suddenly feeling energized, Vivian decided it would be a waste to spend the day in bed, no matter how delightful the idea seemed. Pushing herself up off the bed, she rang for the maid.

An hour later, her face and neck scrubbed, fiery copper tresses pinned in place, Vivian went to break her fast. As she sat eating her eggs and kippers, Mrs. Banks walked into the room and headed straight for her. Vivian smiled and stood as her companion approached, brushing the wrinkles from her skirt.

No one watching Vivian would ever guess she spent her evenings being spanked for mistakes made during the day, or that she would even enjoy such a thing. Last night had been particularly pleasurable, with her body already humming from the earl's kiss; the spanking had made her kick and cry out as always, but she hadn't cared. It felt like a casting off of her mistakes during the day, a relief from feeling that she'd disappointed Mrs. Banks, and then she was rewarded.

The older woman greeted her, delivering letters from her family before leaving Vivian to enjoy her day off. As soon as the companion turned and walked away, Vivian sat down eagerly; she put the smaller envelope to the side as she ripped open the larger, bulkier one. Several letters tumbled out, all from different members of her family. She reached for the one with the heavier, blockier handwriting first, recognizing it as her father's.

Homesickness welled over Vivian as she read through the letters. To her surprise, she realized Gabriel must be helping her family out financially already, even though they weren't married . . . even knowing she could call a halt to her training at any time and he would never receive his funds back.

While her father and mother were discreet, and didn't come out and say that financially their lives had improved yet again, she could tell anyway from the description of their activities and their talk about preparing her brother Alastair for school at Eton. Alastair's letter and her youngest sister Rose's were the shortest, both talking of the new ponies they'd gotten. Persephone's letter was the most revealing, as she had always been the most outspoken of the baron's daughters and was old enough to realize something had changed. Vivian wondered if her father had read Persephone's letter before sending it—perhaps he should have, because she was quite forthright in describing the various changes around the household.

The ponies are the least of it; it seems as though every week Father is bringing home a new toy for Alastair, and Mother took Rose and me to the seamstress this week and ordered us entirely new wardrobes! After so many years of wearing your cast-offs, I must admit it felt wonderful to be measured for my own dresses and to be able to choose the colors and styles. The library is filled with books again, all the empty shelves replenished, and Mother's wearing her emeralds again. I must admit, I didn't even notice they were gone for so long until she was suddenly wearing them again; her fingers stroke the necklace constantly, as if she's afraid they might disappear as suddenly as they returned.

Father does not say much about where such a windfall comes from, but he has mentioned that your future husband's generosity is partly to thank. I was surprised you have not written me of your betrothal, but I suppose you must be very busy with your studies. I hope perhaps next year I might be able to go to Mrs. Cunningham's, if an earl is the type of husband one can expect at the end of it! When you are able to write you must tell me more about your studies and your future husband.

Love,

Persephone

As she folded up the letter from her sister, Vivian smiled. Obviously her family's financial worries were over and it was all due to the earl. Gratitude welled up inside of her as she silently vowed to do everything she could to learn how to please him.

After all, from what she'd learned in her evening training so far, it would be pleasing to her as well. Even though the spankings hurt, she didn't think she'd want to give them up anymore.

Vivian spent the early afternoon strolling in the gardens. Emily joined her for part of it before heading off to the stables. Her friend could never resist the lure of the horses. For her part, Vivian was content to chat with the other students, trying to distract herself and make the day pass more quickly. Unfortunately, their conversation wasn't enough to hold her attention, and she found herself rudely staring off into space quite frequently. Without classes and the practicum, the hours seemed to drag by. She found her mind wandering constantly back to the night before and her very first kiss.

As much as she wanted to tell someone about it, she also wanted to keep it to herself for a while longer. Almost like a secret. Sharing it with someone else would make it somehow less intimate.

It wasn't until after dinner that she realized she was

feeling almost despondent over the lack of anything interesting happening that evening. Not only would there be no dinner with the earl, there wouldn't even be a disciplinary session. Instead her time just stretched on until she retired, leaving her feeling restless and unsatis- fied. The change in her routine combined with the lack of an orgasm before bedtime meant an uneasy night. She was full of energy she hadn't expended, and her body had become used to achieving a satisfying climax before sleeping.

The sensation was akin to an itch she couldn't scratch. Rubbing her thighs together only provided so much relief to her loins. When she finally fell into an uneasy slumber, her dreams were filled with fleeting erotic images; Gabri- el's lips pressed against hers as his tongue slid into her mouth, his fingers touching her the way Mrs. Banks's did as she bent over his lap, the burning between her legs and on her bottom that a spanking produced. In her dreams the spankings weren't painful at all. All they did was arouse her.

She woke the next morning feeling tired and cranky. When the maid helped her dress it was all Vivian could do to keep from moaning as the silk slid against her breasts and nipples, the little buds turning hard and achy. The whisper of fabric between her legs just made her want to rub her thighs together some more, even though she already knew it was useless. Perhaps it wasn't that she needed the spanking so much as that she needed the release that always followed it, but right now she almost felt as if she would welcome either.

What had happened to her body to make her this way? Had her marital training already changed her so much?

Was this what it meant to be a woman and a wife instead of a miss?

Emily noticed her distraction during the day and prodded her until Vivian explained about dinner with Gabriel and the magical first kiss. Not that she told Emily everything about it, but it was enough that her friend clapped happily and completely understood why Vivian was so unfocused. Of course, it was the truth, but it wasn't the entire truth.

Her body had been stirred by the efforts of Mrs. Banks, and those new desires had been focused by the appearance of Gabriel into her life. Now she was realizing it wasn't just gratitude for what the earl had done for her family driving her, nor some small amount of attraction, nor a sense of responsibility towards her fiancé—it was her own body. Something inside of her had been awakened that she didn't know how to put back to sleep. Even if she could, she didn't want to.

On Monday, Vivian eagerly threw herself back into her studies, looking forward to the evening. Even though she knew punishment would be part of it, her body had already become accustomed to the routine, and she almost craved it along with the pleasure she knew would follow.

The students were all in top form throughout the day, and it was the smoothest day of the practicum to date. By the time they returned back to the school, each young woman seemed to feel supremely confident and satisfied.

The girls enjoyed their dinner immensely, still flush with the glow of victory as they chattered.

"We've all been doing brilliantly," Rosalie said happily, beaming around the table at all of them. "I'd been dreading making my debut before Mama sent me here, but I feel much more confident about my prospects now."

"Mrs. Billings said I'm sure to make a good match of it," Astoria said, pointing her haughty nose in the air, but even she had a smile on her face. While they might not all rub along perfectly personality wise, the practicum had drawn them together as a group; they had to depend upon one another for support. The school had found it was a very useful tool for helping the young ladies make connections they would rely on during their entrance into society.

"Most of the young ladies who come from here do," Emily pointed out, ever practical. She smiled at Vivian. "Some of us already have."

Astoria sniffed as Vivian gave Emily a weak smile. Of all the things she disliked talking about with her fellow students, her mysterious future husband was near the top of the list. Mostly because they had quite a few more questions than Vivian had answers.

That night, Mrs. Banks delivered a spanking as usual, but it wasn't very harsh or long, and she did so with an air of indulgence rather than necessity. It was almost a pleasurable spanking, warming Vivian's cheeks with stinging slaps that did more to arouse than punish. Throughout it all, Vivian imagined what it would be like to experience it with the earl.

On Tuesday a fire erupted in the kitchens right before luncheon, which threw the entire day askew. The startled looks on the companions' faces said this was not a planned emergency, but they required the students handle everything, anyway. By the end of the day all of the participants in the practicum were exhausted from the extra effort that had gone into righting things within the household—everything from reorganizing the luncheon on short notice, to taking an assessment of the damages and arranging for repairs, factoring that into the household expenses, and getting the staff back in working order after all the excitement. Of course, they couldn't keep themselves from whispering back and forth all day about what might have occurred to start the fire.

The companions frowned heavily upon the whispers, as they distracted the students from what they were supposed to be doing, and Vivian knew her bottom would pay for it later, but she and the other girls couldn't help themselves once they'd realized it wasn't a planned emergency. That was much more exciting than the little things the companions would do to throw a wrench into the inner workings of the house.

On the carriage ride back to the school, Vivian noticed some soot that had gotten onto the hem of her lavender skirt and surreptitiously tried to rub it away with her shoe. Fortunately, Mrs. Banks was staring out the window at the time and so didn't notice she'd gotten her dress dirty. Squeezing her thighs together beneath her skirts, Vivian felt a flutter of excitement as she thought about her upcoming evening. Being so excited felt almost a little shameful, like a perverse little secret she didn't want to share with anyone.

Across the carriage from her, Emily sighed and Vivian smiled encouragingly at her. Poor Emily had been the student in charge of the household when the fire had first flared up, she had been the one to throw the household into action to put it out and ensure it didn't spread. Fortunately, she had known what to do, having seen a kitchen fire before, and hadn't let them try to use water—instead they'd smothered the flames with thick cloths.

"I'm not sure I want to run my own household anymore," Emily said rather cheekily, resting her head against the side of the carriage. Her companion rolled her eyes but Mrs. Banks looked disapproving, so Vivian didn't say she agreed with her friend's sentiment.

"It was a rather hard day," she said instead, her voice full of sympathy. "I'm thankful for the practice, otherwise I hate to think what a mull I might make of things."

"Well, it's different for you." Emily laughed and waved her hand, her tired eyes sparkling a little. "You already have a husband and a household ready and waiting once we finish at school. I think I'll wait around a few years after my come-out before I accept one of my suitor's proposals."

"Your father might not allow you to do so," Miss Norton warned, obviously not liking the idea that her charge might be getting ideas the marquess would disapprove of in his daughter.

"I'm sure he'll do whatever he thinks is best for me," Emily said with the air of an indulged daughter who had her father wrapped around her little finger. For herself, Vivian was only a little envious of Emily's better situation. She thought she might have liked to have a say in the man she married, but now she also couldn't imagine wanting to marry anyone but Gabriel, a thought that held her all the way back to the school and to the time for her evening punishment.

Awaiting the arrival of Mrs. Banks to her room,

Vivian shifted back and forth on the comfortable seat of her armchair. The soreness in her bottom was completely gone, but that might not last long. Although she knew she hadn't made very many mistakes today, she knew she had made some. There would be some kind of punishment before the pleasure.

When the door opened to admit Mrs. Banks, Vivian was ready for her. Mrs. Banks smiled at her charge, although her hand hovered over the pocket where she was keeping the small whip she was going to use on Vivian this evening.

As they were more than halfway through Vivian's first month of training, it was time to introduce her to some of the tools of the trade with which she might find herself chastised.

Mrs. Banks pulled her notebook out of her other pocket as Vivian sat down in her punishment chair, looking almost eager for the start of the evening. She glowed as Mrs. Banks praised Vivian for her successes from the day, which Mrs. Banks was not loath to give her; she knew Vivian thrived on such accolades. Tonight, Vivian would need the praise to bolster her, as Mrs. Banks would be moving into the part of the curriculum where Vivian must become accustomed to being punished for no other reason than her disciplinarian's pleasure. It would need to be done carefully, so as not to make her downtrodden or feel as though it was somehow deserved when she'd done nothing wrong.

The list of mistakes was a short one and took very little time before Mrs. Banks announced that Vivian would receive ten spanks and helped the young woman to undress. As was becoming usual, she tied Vivian's wrists behind her back.

Despite the fact that Vivian had done very well during her lessons, and knowing what would happen after this initial spanking, this time Mrs. Banks did not hold back on the strength of her blows to Vivian's upturned bottom.

After last night, Vivian had been expecting a similar, pleasurable spanking. She jerked with each smack of flesh, a small whimper escaping her lips every time, although she did manage to maintain some dignity as she did not kick or sob the way she often had when she was in this position. After all, ten spanks were barely anything at all compared to what she'd received last week! Despite the increase in intensity of the slaps compared to the night before, her body responded with the same excitement.

When Mrs. Banks counted out the last one, Vivian heaved a sigh of relief. The companion's legs shifted beneath her and she heard the slide of fabric, which usually indicated something being removed from Mrs. Banks's pocket.

Mrs. Banks moved Vivian to a standing position and stood up herself. The companion then gave her a surprising order. "Sit down."

Vivian was finding there was nothing she disliked more than a change to her routine. It was disconcerting and frightening. But she didn't protest. Instead she meekly sat down in the punishment chair, hissing as her bottom landed a little harder without her hands to help her do so.

Crossing around behind her, Mrs. Banks used a second length of silk to secure Vivian's bound wrists to the chair back. The position thrust the young woman's breasts forward, rendering it extremely uncomfortable to try and hunch her shoulders. The rosy tips of her nipples pressed out even further, as if offering themselves up.

"Lovely," Mrs. Banks said as she circled around to Vivian's front.

The realization that she was tied to the punishment chair, with her bottom firmly planted on its seat, wound Vivian's anxiety up to almost unparalleled heights. That kind of tremulous agitation was like an aphrodisiac to men of the earl's character; Mrs. Banks recognized its worth.

Mrs. Banks held the small leather whip up in front of her so Vivian could see the delicate creation. It was made of soft leather strands, each about ten inches long, and had been provided by the earl himself. Depending on how it was wielded, the strands could caress or sting. It was not a whip meant for a young woman's buttocks, which could take quite a bit of punishment without any ill effects, but for more delicate areas.

Vivian stared at the whip as if it were a many-headed snake, her mouth going dry as she tried to imagine what was about to happen. "Mrs. Banks?" she asked.

"You will have a total of twenty strokes, I will administer ten on each side," Mrs. Banks said, shifting herself slightly so she was well out of the way of Vivian's feet. While she didn't think the young woman would purposefully kick her, there was no telling how she might react to this change in punishment.

The whip slapped against Vivian's right breast and she drew in a shocked breath; the many strands snapped against tender skin. Most didn't truly hurt except for the strand that landed directly across her nipple, biting into the especially sensitive flesh and causing it to pucker even more.

"One."

Before Vivian had time to do more than gasp with the shock, another stroke landed across her breast. This time no strands hit her nipple, but instead landed on her puffy areola.

"Mrs. Banks, why are you doing this?" Vivian's arched back as she tried to escape this strange new area of pain only made it seem as though she was thrusting her breast out to ask for more.

"Two."

"Why?" the young woman wailed.

"Because sometimes—three—your husband will want to enjoy your pain." Mrs. Banks's voice was low, almost seductive. Vivian shivered as she suddenly pictured a cold, cruel smile on the earl's face, his eyes lighting up as he watched her writhe. "Four—and you must learn to accept whatever is given to you—five—and that you will not have control over your pain or your pleasure."

Vivian tried to listen to the explanation even though it made very little sense to her. She understood the gist, however, which was that sometimes her husband would desire to torment her for no reason at all. That he would find it exciting to have her at his mercy.

Stroke after stroke of the whip snapped against her skin, placing another layer of impact. With each layer the painful sensation grew. Her skin pinkened, becoming more sensitive as the soft strands of the whip bit into it. Every time a strand licked across her poor nipple she cried out. The blows were not nearly as hard as the ones Mrs. Banks applied to her bottom, but they stung and burned in a completely different way.

To add to her distress, the inevitable squirming was inflaming the welts across her buttocks, adding to the sting and making it seem as though the erotic pain was flowing into her from more than one direction.

When Mrs. Banks reached ten she paused for a moment, and Vivian lifted her anxious eyes in hopes of a reprieve. Instead the companion stepped forward, a cool and neutral expression on her face, and pinched Vivian's tender nipple between her fingers.

"Ouch! Mrs. Banks, oh, please!"

Using the tiny nubbin, Mrs. Banks lifted the curve of Vivian's breast. Her tight grip on the bud sent shockwaves of alternating pain and pleasure through Vivian's body, making her gasp and thrust her breasts forward again in hopes of relieving the pressure. She could feel the heavy mound of her breast lifting—for what purpose she couldn't imagine but was about to discover.

Careful to avoid hitting Vivian's thigh, Mrs. Banks flicked her wrist and the strands of the whip snapped upwards against the sensitive underside of her breast. It was the one part of her breast which, until this point, had gone largely unmarked.

"Eight."

With a yelp, Vivian's head fell backwards, her eyes closing as the whip stung her anew. It was only three lashes to the tender underside, her nipple throbbing in the tight confines of Mrs. Banks's fingers, before the companion dropped her breast and allowed it to wobble back into its normal place.

Two tears trickled down Vivian's cheeks, one on each side, and splashed down to her chest, over her breasts. One breast was unmarked, creamy with a pink nipple of pale rose, the other was streaked with lines of pink, and the nipple was darkened and angry-looking. It looked and felt like a ripe cherry about to burst.

"Lovely," Mrs. Banks said, crooning the word. "The

contrast is quite stunning and you're being such a good girl, Vivian. The earl will be so pleased with you."

Vivian moaned, her insides clenching at Mrs. Banks's words.

Then the strands lifted, flew through the air, and snapped against the tender flesh of her previously neglected breast. The new sting and added burden had the tears flowing down Vivian's cheeks to land on her tormented breasts. The dance began all over again, her flesh jiggling, her bottom pressing against the unforgiving seat, her legs kicking as her formerly untouched nipple was lashed and ripened. Throughout, Mrs. Banks voice intoned after each stroke, counting her way to ten.

The pinch and lift of her nipple was almost welcome, a kind of marker for the last stretch of her punishment.

When it was done, Vivian's head hung down, her eyes closed. The twin peaks of her breasts were now matched— the formerly ivory skin turned a darker rose, her nipples cherry red. It was fine work.

A hand landed on Vivian's thigh, softly, gently. Vivian obeyed as a finger tapped on the soft inner skin, and she spread her legs just enough for the hand to slip in, for fingers to search and pleasure her.

The tie that secured her to the chair was undone.

"On your knees, Vivian," Mrs. Banks said gently, helping her down. Standing before her, Mrs. Banks slipped her fingers into Vivian's mouth. They had only the faintest taste of her musky juices on them. Pushing them deep between Vivian's lips, Mrs. Banks teased the back of the young woman's throat. With her face tilted back, cheeks streaked with tears, she looked satisfactorily peni-tent. Beneath that was the erotic sight of her punished breasts, the marked skin and irritated nipples. The position also allowed Mrs. Banks's fingers to delve deeper without the young woman gagging.

After a suitable length of time, Mrs. Banks removed her fingers from Vivian's mouth. Relieved, Vivian ran her tongue around the backs of her teeth. After a while the constant stimulation in her mouth had become rather wearying. It seemed as though Mrs. Banks had Vivian suckling for a little longer every evening.

"Up we go," Mrs. Banks said, leading an almost stumbling Vivian to the bed. "Bend over now, dear."

Vivian moaned as she bent over the bed, partly in fear that her welted bottom was about to receive an unanticipated punishment, and partly because her breasts felt even more sore as they pressed against the covers. The sensitive skin burned anew as her breasts were crushed between her and the bed, her nipples throbbing again as they were pushed into the bed.

"Spread your legs."

The air on the inner lips of Vivian's pussy was cool against the hot, wet skin. Fingers probed Vivian's folds, from both hands, stroking and gliding up and down the slick crevices of her sex, wetting Mrs. Banks's fingers with the sweet cream that Vivian's body had produced in response to her punishment. With two fingers of her left hand liberally coated in honey, Mrs. Banks transferred the attentions of those fingers to the rosette of Vivian's anus. The tight orifice opened as Mrs. Banks pressed forward, causing a different kind of burn between Vivian's flaming cheeks.

Mrs. Banks smiled as she listened to the young woman's small sounds of embarrassed pleasure. The grasping ridged entrance was very tight, but it gave way easily in this position; with her legs spread the way they were, it was very difficult for Vivian to clench her buttocks with any strength. The channel burned inside as Mrs. Banks pressed inwards, her other hand rubbing gently over Vivian's welts and reawakening the sensitive nerves in her skin. The slick press of her fingers invading and retreating felt almost good by comparison, even though the stretch of her rectum stung and tingled.

Moaning, Vivian felt her hips thrust as Mrs. Banks began to play with both her holes, inserting her fingers into them and moving them back and forth in different rhythms. The invasion of her anus tingled as her pussy creamed, her holes tightening down as she began the slow climb to pleasure out of the smoldering embers of her erotic response to punishment.

"Does it hurt, Vivian?"

"A little," she said back, panting as Mrs. Banks twisted her fingers back and forth in circular motions. The sensation was incredibly strange and yet very erotic. The more Mrs. Banks plundered her backside, the wetter Vivian's pussy became. Mrs. Banks pressed her fingers against the little bud of Vivian's clitoris, rubbing it gently.

"How about now?"

Vivian couldn't formulate a response as the manipulation of her clit sent waves of needy pleasure washing through her. Part of her loved the punishment, even as she cried out and begged for it to stop, and the moment any kind of pleasurable sensations began to mix with the pain, it was like a jolt of lightning to her pussy. Immediately her confused senses began to spiral, constricting and releasing. Her inner muscles worked against Mrs. Banks's fingers, tightening down and trying to suck them further inwards.

"Very good, Vivian, squeeze my fingers . . . good. Your husband will like that a lot. Keep squeezing, sweetheart. Doesn't it feel good when you squeeze your muscles?" It did, even though it also increased the sensation of burning friction in her anus as it spasmed.

Despite the strain of having her anus breached, the slick penetration began to feel incredibly good as Mrs. Banks worked her clitoris with increasing speed and intensity. The movements of her body made her sensitive breasts rub against the sheets, and her nipples started to throb for an entirely new reason. It hurt deliciously, her body interpreting it as more pleasure and sending her heart racing faster.

Mrs. Banks thrust two fingers back and forth in each hole, exploring and twisting her digits. Vivian's swollen folds were aching from all the stimulation as pain merged with pleasure. It seemed to happen faster every time now, her body confusing the responses more quickly as it was trained to the erotic torment. The new burn on her breasts, as well as Vivian's emotional reaction, made her need for some kind of release more heightened than ever. She wanted the pleasure, felt she deserved it after the unexpected and undeserved addition to her evening punishment.

With her hands still tied at the small of her back there was nothing Vivian could do but give herself over to the bursts of ecstasy and torment as the erotic pleasure melded with the irritation of her punished parts. Everything burned, everything tightened and tightened and tightened, like a spool of thread that shrank as it wound around.

A press on her insides in a particular spot, and the constricted channel of her asshole tightened even more as Vivian bucked. Her nipples rubbed over the fabric of her sheets and the fire inside her flared as if another stick had just been thrown on it. Her insides burned and tingled until the sensation became too much and the inferno burst outwards, a combustion reaction of beautiful rapture that had her writhing and convulsing in ecstasy.

CHAPTER ELEVEN

WHEN VIVIAN AWOKE, SHE WAS FEELING especially drained after the rigors of her punishment, and the addition of her breasts as part of that punishment. She had become somewhat used to her bottom being sore; the tenderness of her breasts and nipples was an entirely new experience.

"Oh, good, you're awake."

A gentle voice had Vivian turning, and then she squeaked and froze as the sheets passing over her breasts felt uncomfortable and scratchy against her tender skin. Her nipples tingled, but the sensation was not entirely unpleasant.

At the side of the bed, her maid smiled gently at her. "I have your breakfast, miss."

"Thank you," Vivian said, holding her night rail in place against her chest to keep the fabric from moving over her skin.

After the maid had laid out her breakfast, Vivian sat up to eat, moving very carefully. Even the weight of her breasts wobbling slightly felt strange. Would the earl really punish her in such a manner? Would he enjoy doing so?

Giving her an encouraging smile, the maid bustled around the room, laying out everything Vivian needed to ready herself for the day.

Vivian tried to shake off her daydreams of Gabriel as she applied herself to her breakfast. She needed to remain focused, because she had no doubt that Mrs. Banks would punish her assiduously if she made any mistakes today; last night's previous activities notwithstanding.

Reading over the letter Mrs. Banks had sent him that afternoon, Gabriel had mixed feelings. He was pleased to hear of his future wife's progress, and yet frustrated by the current need to stay away. There was a bill in Parliament his father wanted passed and the entire family was focused on garnering support for it. Unfortunately, it meant Gabriel had no time to go to the school and visit.

At night, he dreamed of red hair the color of sunrise, and pale skin that turned pink under his hand. Although rumors of his engagement were making their way round the *ton*, the absence of his fiancée meant more than one marriage-minded mama was still trying to foist her offspring on him. Other ladies, whose interests were decidedly not matrimonial, weren't shy about offering their favors either, but not one of them tempted him.

He wanted only one woman, and the idea of slaking his desires with a poor substitute held no appeal.

Sighing, he put the letter down in the box where he kept all the reports on his future wife, trying to refocus his mind back to what he'd been working on before the letter had been delivered. He would be with Vivian soon enough. Not just the formal visits he'd been making either; soon he'd be a part of her training.

Shifting his breeches to a more comfortable position, Lord Cranborne bent back over the letter he was writing.

Over the next two days, Vivian worked harder than ever. The day after Mrs. Banks had punished her breasts, she'd earned ten spanks to her bottom, which nearly made Vivian sigh with relief at the more usual punishment. Those ten had been peppered and warmed her skin, making her squirm, just not in pain. The back and forth of sensations Mrs. Banks elicited from her was quite confusing and wonderful. Each evening, following her punishment, Mrs. Banks continued to insert her fingers into Vivian's body as she was given her pleasure.

Thursday evening, after her punishment, Mrs. Banks introduced a new device to her training. Vivian had become used to having her bottom fingered; now Mrs. Banks kept the young woman on her lap as she oiled up a rubber contraption. Mrs. Cunningham had found the rubber dilators were just as useful for stretching out a young woman's bottom, replacing the marble and polished wood instruments that had been used in the past.

It came in three different sizes, although the largest was rarely used as they didn't want to stretch out the tight ring of muscle too greatly. Just far enough to accustom the young woman to an intrusion.

The rubber felt strange in Vivian's tight hole. She moaned and clutched at the legs of the chair as Mrs. Banks pushed it back and forth, shoving it deeper with every stroke between her reddened cheeks. Beneath that slim, pumping rod, the lips of her pussy were swollen and wet, becoming even wetter. It tingled and burned as her muscles stretched and pulsed around the invader. She could actually feel the same kind of pleasure building in her pussy, even before Mrs. Banks inserted her fingers into that sopping orifice.

With her bottom filled by the strange dilator and her pussy full of pumping fingers, Vivian had an explosive orgasm over Mrs. Banks's lap before she was put on her knees to clean the companion's fingers. The dilator remained securely lodged between her lower cheeks as she performed this service, a slightly uncomfortable reminder of how little control she had over her own body.

Afterwards, Vivian was laid down on the bed and the dilator was removed before she was tucked in under the sheets. Her bottom felt sore and tingly from being stretched, but it also contributed to the feeling of warm satisfaction between her legs. Sleepily, Vivian smiled at the reward she'd been given.

Saturday had her restless, as usual, especially since she'd had no word from the earl all week. It made her feel pouty, if she were to be honest, but Emily helped to dispel some of her gloom by insisting they go riding together in the afternoon. On Sunday she went to church services with the other students and spent the rest of the day in the school's gardens.

The next week was particularly hard on the young ladies who were part of the practicum as they prepared for their first real social event. The tea they would be holding that Friday afternoon was part of the practicum curriculum, but it was also a chance for some of the respected and powerful ladies of the *ton* to cast their eyes on the latest crop of students before they were introduced to society. Those venerable matrons could hold the key to a young woman's success once she was out, as long as she made a good impression on them. They were to show all the elegance and grace they'd learned at the school, and their companions rode them hard on matters of etiquette, propriety, and demeanor all throughout the week. After all, their performances would reflect upon the school.

None of them were pushed as hard as Vivian, however.

What the young ladies were unaware of was that the ladies who attended the tea would often bring male escorts other than their husbands. Instead, their sons, nephews, grandsons, and various other young male acquaintances would be dragooned into attending with them. For those marital-minded young men, this would be an opportunity to look over the newest crop of young misses.

For those who were less interested in the marriage mart, it was a move made to placate their older female relatives.

Vivian knew from the guest list that Lady Audrey Cecil, the Marquess of Salisbury's wife, and stepmother of the Earl of Cranborne, would be in attendance.

Of course, she wanted to make a good impression on her future parents-in-law, but she felt reasonably comfortable in her manners and social acumen. Facing them would be nerve-wracking, but since she had no idea what they knew of her training, she assumed they would be looking her over to ensure she wouldn't be an embarrassment to their family. She felt fairly confident she could comport herself well enough to reassure them on that part. What agitated her the most was wondering if the earl would also be in attendance.

However, she had plenty of other matters to fill her mind with during the week, between her fantasies of the earl. On Monday evening she was tested again after Mrs.

Banks plied the hairbrush to Vivian's blushing bottom before filling it with the small dilator. Just thinking about the earl being so intimately acquainted with her body had Vivian's climaxes reaching epic heights.

The next day it was even harder to keep up her concentration during the practicum; she found her mental state to be divided between concentrating on the tasks at hand and lost in physical need. She smiled and chatted naturally with the other girls, not one of them guessing her head was filled with thoughts of amorous things she might do with her earl.

That night Mrs. Banks introduced her to the crop. Not because she had been bad; in fact Mrs. Banks reassured her she'd been very good, but in order to introduce her to more of the implements she might be punished with. Rather than being put over Mrs. Banks's lap, Vivian found herself bent over her bed with her body propped up on her elbows so her breasts swayed beneath her. Every jerk in response to the bite of the crop had her nipples brushing against the covers of her bed.

Each mark was harsh, but so small she couldn't decide whether or not she thought the crop was worse than the hairbrush. It was certainly a very different sensation. She sank into the punishment, her pussy clenching every time the crop landed on the rising heat within her bottom. Blows to her sit-spot had her crying out, as the intense sting was particularly painful there.

When Mrs. Banks landed the first strike to Vivian's clit she spasmed, her body bucking hard as the little nub throbbed and swelled. Then the crop landed and stayed, leather rubbing over the swollen, sensitive clit, and Vivian screamed into the mattress as she came hard with a gush of fluid that trickled down her thighs. The climax left her sobbing with ecstasy.

She was almost dazed as Mrs. Banks began to work the middle-sized dilator into her bottom for the first time. The muscles cramped and stretched, so very sensitive in the wake of her climax, as her bottom was pushed open by the bulbous instrument. Vivian moaned and lifted her hips, offering herself up.

"Good girl," Mrs. Banks crooned. "I'm so very pleased with you, Vivian, and the earl will be too."

Fingers pressed against her clit, rubbing knowingly, and Vivian found herself writhing again as pleasure burst through her. This orgasm was gentler and more complete, traveling all the way to the tips of her toes and fingers, as if her entire body was one large sexual organ. Her breath sobbed in and out with the overwhelming pleasure.

Vivian's last hazy thought, as she was tucked into bed, was that she very much enjoyed being a good girl.

CHAPTER TWELVE

TO VIVIAN'S SURPRISE, ON FRIDAY THE MAID came in with a new dress that had been made especially for her. It was a gorgeous creation of mint green and ivory with tiny accents of gold; the exact hues that set off her coloring beautifully and made others murmur that, in the case of Miss Stafford, perhaps red hair wasn't always an affliction. And for those who actually appreciated the unusual coppery red tresses, it raised her to the level of a goddess.

She had no idea Lord Cranborne had commissioned the dress, with the measurements provided by the school, from one of the most well-known and in-demand modistes in London. The soft fabric slithered over her skin, caressing her body, and Vivian shivered with the sensual pleasure of it. The dress was easily the most beautiful thing she'd ever worn. With delicate beading around the neck and bodice, it was cut to accentuate her hourglass figure in an elegant way. There was nothing overtly sexual about the dress, in fact it was quite modest, but it was enticing.

Admiring herself in the mirror, Vivian couldn't help but smile. The dress gave her the extra little boost of confidence she needed, especially since at the tea she was going to be meeting her future parents-in-law. While she had confidence in her manners, she had to admit this was better than she'd hoped to look when meeting them. Not that any of her dresses had been shabby since she'd begun attending Mrs. Cunningham's Finishing School, but none of them compared to this, either.

Finishing off the toast that had been provided for her breakfast, Vivian hurried from her room and to the school's entrance. The other young ladies were gathered there—all of them were early and chattering excitedly. While they were aware that today's tea was a test, they were also in high spirits and feeling fairly confident, which was exactly how their training was supposed to make them feel. They were also all dressed in their finest day dresses, looking splendid as a group. The companions watched with the smug satisfaction of teachers who had every confidence in their students, bolstering the morale of the young ladies even further.

It quickly became apparent that the gentlemen escorting the ladies who had been invited for tea were not their husbands, but their sons. The revelation sent the young misses into even further heights of tension, although they were all too well-schooled to show it. Several of the young men attached themselves quickly to some of the students, while others looked bored as if they desired to be anywhere but where they were, although they were too mannered to say so. Several did a kind of round-robin between the young misses in an effort to speak with each of them. They were spread out on a patio beside the gardens of the house, as the weather was cooperating beautifully, and it gave them a good bit of room to host a section of the party.

All in all, the tea was going well, although Vivian was still on pins and needles waiting for Lady Salisbury to arrive. Would she bring the marquess, her husband, or would she bring her stepson and Vivian's betrothed?

Despite the attentions of several young gentlemen who had arrayed themselves in the group around her settee, Vivian's eyes were constantly flicking to the doorway as her tension ratcheted upwards with every passing moment. Several of the *grande dames* of the *ton* inserted themselves into her group, silencing the young men who waited for the delightful Miss Stafford's attention again. Vivian's demeanor was quite natural and sweet, her manner unaffected, and the *grande dames* found themselves delighted by her, despite the ostentatious color of her hair.

Satisfied, the ladies smiled and uprooted themselves to move on to the next student. As they did so, the men naturally scooted closer to Miss Stafford, each making an effort to be the one to gain her attention now that it was free again—and it was this sight that greeted the Earl of Cranborne when he walked into the room with his step-mother on his arm.

Before he was even announced his eyes had sought out his bride, easily found with her bright hair and the dress he'd commissioned for her. She looked mouthwater-ingly beautiful, vulnerably innocent, and entirely enticing. When he'd commissioned the dress he'd only thought about the effect it would have on him, not on the other swains who would be attending the tea. Their engagement would only make her more interesting to them—when one man was willing to commit himself to a woman, it made the others want to discover why.

Although Gabriel was quite sure none of them would discern his reasons.

Still, he was more than a bit irked to see Viscount Marchland was one of the men seated beside his betrothed. While the others hovering about her were younger and less threatening to a man of Gabriel's stature, the viscount was beginning to garner a reputation as a dishonorable rake. There were unspoken rules among the rakes of Gabriel's set, rules which Marchland and his ilk ignored, often to the detriment of the women they were involved with. Ruining innocents didn't bother Marchland, and there were rumors of worse, yet he was still accepted in polite society because of his father's influence.

He was younger than Gabriel, but that just meant he was closer to Vivian in age. Seeing him seated beside her had Gabriel's chest clenching with the possessive demand to go claim his wife—never mind they hadn't had the ceremony yet.

"Relax, Gabriel," his stepmother murmured, tapping her fan on the arm her hand rested on. Obviously she'd felt the tensing of his muscles. "One would think you're unhappy to be here."

No, he was quite happy to be there, if only to immediately chase off all the young puppies dancing attendance on his bride. Especially Marchland. He didn't see Audrey's lips curve when her words had no effect on her stepson; his entire being was focused on the enchanting young woman in green. Being the romantic that she was, Audrey quite approved of his focus, although hopefully he wouldn't frighten his young bride with his fierce expression.

Vivian was far too anxious to be frightened. When she'd heard the Earl of Cranborne announced, she'd immediately looked to the door and her breath caught when she met his gaze. His dark eyes seemed to burn into her, making her feel naked and vulnerable. Just the sight of him made her bottom—and more intimate areas—tingle. Slightly older than the young men who were gathered around her, he made them look like unfinished clay next to his polished and confident demeanor. Everything about his attire was impeccable, from the unrelieved black of his outer garments to his crisp white shirt and intricately tied cravat.

She was so caught up in his glittering gaze she almost forgot to breathe, although her lungs felt so constricted that air seemed like an unnecessary commodity anyway. Beside her, one of the men was saying something, but she couldn't hear a single word coming from his mouth; all of her attention was on the approaching earl.

She was so distracted by his mere presence, she almost didn't notice the woman on his arm until they were nearly to her area. This was his stepmother? The marchioness was a stunning beauty, looking of an age to the earl rather than old enough to be his mother. She had thick chestnut hair with coppery highlights that glinted in the sunlight, bright hazel eyes, and a classically beautiful face with creamy ivory skin. The beautiful violet dress she wore set off her well-endowed figure wonderfully. Vivian was aware that more than one of the young gentlemen who had been paying court to her were now eyeing the other woman with blatant appreciation.

Seeing the sophisticated and elegant figure the marchioness cut, Vivian was assailed with self-doubt. Could she ever come anywhere close to matching such self-assured beauty?

Vivian managed a beautiful curtsy to the marchioness and the earl, murmuring a polite greeting. When she looked up again, her future husband was looking at her with a hard expression she didn't recognize, whereas her future mother-in-law seemed delighted.

"It's wonderful to finally meet you, Miss Stafford," the marchioness said as she stepped forward and took Vivian's hands in her own. "I'm very much looking forward to welcoming you to the family."

"I'm very honored," Vivian said, feeling as though she might faint. It was all she could think of to say, and she could barely get the words out. The earl was still looking angry, although he'd transferred his gaze to Lord Marchland. At least he wasn't looking at her like that anymore, not that it helped settle her stomach at all. The marchioness smiled warmly at her, which helped to bolster her spirits.

Noticing her stepson's expression, the marchioness sighed. "Gabriel, why don't you take your intended for a walk in the garden?" She smiled at Vivian. "I'll remain here and entertain these young men for you."

"Oh," Vivian floundered, looking towards the wall where she'd last seen Mrs. Banks standing in hope of receiving some guidance. Several of the men had stiffened upon hearing Vivian openly referred to as Cranborne's intended, but Vivian didn't even notice them as she searched for, and failed to find, her companion. The students weren't supposed to leave their designated areas, but how could she deny a marchioness? And Mrs. Banks had certainly been adamant she should always follow the earl's commands.

The man in question stepped forward, proffering his arm, and her decision was made for her. His lips curved into a small smile as her fingers wrapped around his arm.

"Hello, Sunrise."

Hesitation fled as Vivian smiled back up at him, her heart pounding inside of her chest. He covered her hand with his own and pulled her away from the group with one last dark glance at Lord Marchland. When he turned his gaze back to hers, it was distinctly milder, although still intense. The kind of intensity had changed, however. Before he'd looked angry; now the way he looked at her made her feel rather warm inside.

He didn't speak until they were down the steps that led into the gardens. "You look beautiful in that dress."

Coming from a man who looked the way he did, the compliment seemed even greater. Vivian blushed with pleasure, a little tingle going through her belly.

"Thank you, Gabriel."

"Aren't you going to tell me how handsome I look?" he teased, and she relaxed as she smiled shyly back at him.

"Oh, you look very handsome indeed," she said. She felt daring as she teased him back. With Mrs. Banks constantly referencing the earl during their evening activities, she'd almost forgotten the more playful side of his personality. "I would have thought you knew."

"Of course I know," he riposted haughtily, and then ruined the effect by winking at her. "I just had to be sure you knew it, too."

Vivian's laughter filled the air as they moved deeper into the gardens. Although Vivian didn't realize it, Gabriel had been maneuvering them towards the higher plants and bushes since they'd entered them, wanting a few minutes of privacy with his fiancée before he had to return to the party and share her with others. Although he didn't intend to share her very much.

"Your stepmother is beautiful," she murmured, becoming a little more serious. "And very confident."

"She's a marchioness," he replied easily. "The confidence comes with the title. And while she's quite beautiful, I have a certain preference for beauties with hair like the dawn."

Vivian's cheeks colored. She knew she would sound as though she were fishing for compliments, but she couldn't help but ask. "Even though you could have any other woman you want?"

"Perhaps not any woman," he murmured, turning towards her now that they were just out of sight, but still within earshot, of the tea party. "I'd say the princess is a bit above my touch."

"And you're far above mine," she murmured, shrinking in on herself a little, her emerald eyes falling away from his.

Now that was unacceptable. Gabriel slid his hand behind her neck, cupping the back of it and tilting her head back, forcing her to look up at him. Vivian sucked in a breath as their gazes clashed—he'd gone from being almost friendly and teasing back to irritated.

"Sunrise, Vivian, my future wife," he said, and the very sound of her name being uttered in his deep, gravelly voice sent a shudder of pleasure through her. "I did have my choice of any woman I wanted, and I chose you, because you are what I want. And if you run yourself down in my hearing again, I will put you over my knee and spank you immediately."

Now it felt as though her lungs might actually collapse in on themselves. She didn't know it, but her pupils dilated, making her green eyes look almost black. The hand on her chin was firm but gentle. He'd both complimented her and threatened her, and the most astonishing wave of tingling need had gone through her at his words. Suddenly he was indeed the man she fantasized about in the evening, every hint of playfulness gone from his demeanor. The man in front of her was an authoritarian, a tyrant, and she was his kingdom.

Dark eyes bored into hers, demanding a response.

"I'm sorry," she whispered thickly, although at the moment she could barely remember what she was sorry for.

Unconsciously she leaned towards him, an innocent but instinctive appeal for comfort and reassurance; for a kiss. He'd be a fool not to oblige her, and Gabriel prided himself on a distinct lack of foolishness. Gabriel slanted his lips over hers, his free arm wrapping around to cage her body the way his other hand had caged her face.

Warmth bloomed in Vivian's body as his lips pressed down on hers. Her hands came up automatically to press against his chest. The arm wrapped around her body was unyielding, pressing her into him. Everything about him was hard and muscular against her softness, except his lips, which were so wonderfully soft and inviting. There was a hunger and an urgency that made it unlike their previous kisses; she didn't realize it was because they were now completely alone, with no chance of interruption, and with the earl's sexual frustrations of the past weeks riding him hard. The arm around her back tightened, and she gasped. When her lips parted, his tongue thrust into her mouth.

Gabriel groaned and hauled her closer, delving deeper into her sweet mouth and memorizing the taste and feel of her. Vivian's body came to life against the earl's. Her fingers curved inwards around the fabric of his jacket as she shuddered against him, making small, erotic noises in the back of her throat that were muffled against his lips. Tingling awareness filled her, sizzled along her skin, as her breasts grew heavy and full and the area between her legs became swollen and wet. Hunger flared between them. He took possession of her mouth and she let him, feeling as though some need she'd been unaware of during her training was finally being met.

When the kiss slowed, shallowed, and then ended, she whimpered. The earl placed his lips gently, almost reverently, against hers.

Someone, one of the other female students, had a high-pitched laugh that impinged on his senses—the only thing that kept him from pulling Vivian deeper into the garden and exploring her further. Although some liberties would be allowed because of their impending nuptials, such a blatant indiscretion would never be excused. Which meant he had to get himself under control, and exert that control over her. His cock felt like it was fit to burst, but he had no intention of undermining Vivian's sexual education by setting herself up to be humiliated before her peers.

Because it was obvious she was all too willing to follow where he led.

His reaction to her passion had been more intense than he could have anticipated. The fantasies she had fueled in him, for months now, were so close to culmination that it was agony to wait for the actual event. At least he could console himself with the thought that on Monday he would be participating in her training, and he would gain some measure of relief. Not to mention he would finally be able to put his hands all over her in the way he desired.

For the rest of the afternoon, the earl was a perfect gentleman. He danced attendance on Vivian, fetching her a new cup of tea or a new plate of sweets whenever she looked to be in need, charming her with anecdotes about his lands and his family—his sisters sounded delightful—and behaving with such elegant aplomb, she could hardly credit his threat to spank her. His stepmother watched on with amused eyes, her warmth and easy manner helping Vivian relax.

Although she could see the earl obviously enjoyed catering to her needs, he had an innate arrogant confidence, which was well-merited. Any woman below the age of sixty, and possibly some above, would feel at least a faint flutter of the heart when under his gaze.

Everything about the earl's demeanor was possessive; indeed, by the time they had returned from their walk in the garden, Lord Marchland had already quit her area and was sitting with Emily and her entourage. Vivian was rather glad of it, because Gabriel seemed much more relaxed once he saw Lord Marchland had changed his seat. Several of the other young men remained, chatting with both her and the countess (and some of them watching the countess with worshipful, puppy-dog eyes), but none of them seemed to provoke the earl's ire the way Lord Marchland had.

Fortunately, none of the young men seemed to mind receiving little more than an absentminded smile when she forgot herself and dwelled on the kiss rather than on the conversation.

Returning to the school, triumphant and flush with success, the young women had a boisterous and enjoyable dinner together. Vivian managed to have a short, whispered conversation with Emily, sharing the bare-bones of the kiss she and Gabriel had shared in the garden. Afterwards they wanted to spend more time together, but one of the companions informed them that they would be receiving their lectures as usual; plenty of mistakes had still been made that needed to be gone over, even if none of them had been large enough to permanently harm anyone's social standing or reputation. Lady Astoria twitted at Vivian that she would probably be scolded for going off with Lord Cranborne, even if he was her betrothed. Even knowing that Astoria's scathing tone probably had more to do with her jealousy than anything else, Vivian couldn't help but be a bit worried about the possible repercussions if she was right.

Not that she could think of what else she could have done.

Gabriel's carriage ride home was not as comfortable as he might have wished. The afternoon had been akin to torture, to have Vivian so close and yet be unable to even touch her without breaking the bounds of propriety. Their short walk and the clinging kiss had been risky enough. Despite their engagement, blatant misbehavior would still reflect badly upon her and would damage her reputation, which could have consequences for her younger sisters. Such were the vagaries of the *ton*.

Because of that, he was already feeling temperamental, and his emotional state was not assisted by remembering the way Lord Marchland had been sitting so closely to Vivian when he'd first arrived. Originally he hadn't planned to attend the at-homes he'd been informed she and the other students would be going to this upcoming week, but after seeing the men surrounding her, he knew he wouldn't be able to stay away. So more torturous afternoons where he would be able to look but not touch. He hated that he had to wait until Monday evening to truly touch her again, and he would have an even longer wait after that to claim her irrevocably. He wanted peace and quiet to think and to plan and to fantasize about the upcoming week.

Instead he got a chattering stepmother who was practically glowing as she praised his future wife. He was glad Audrey was so excited about her new daughter and that she would be giving his father a favorable report, but he wished she would ride silently and keep her observations to herself. Of course he could always order her to be quiet, and she would, but it would hurt her feelings, and that his father would assuredly not tolerate. So he did his best to nod in appropriate places and keep a tight grip on his temper.

Perhaps it was for the best that Audrey was there to distract him, he thought with resignation. After all, a carriage ride with an unrelenting erection—as would have been the result if he'd been able to think about the upcoming week and Vivian's training—was probably not a comfortable way to travel.

When Mrs. Banks finally arrived in Vivian's room that evening, her neutral expression didn't give away any of her thoughts. Nervously, Vivian stood and went to her punishment chair to hear the list of transgressions. She was almost eager to hear them, on a day that had been a true test of the lessons she'd been learning. She also wanted reassurance that she'd done the correct thing by taking a walk with the earl; part of her wondered if she should confess that wonderful kiss, but she didn't want to. Somehow it seemed like something private, but she didn't want to discover Mrs. Banks already knew about it and that it would be counted among her transgressions.

After all, a kiss was certainly indiscreet behavior, especially given the venue, even if it was with her intended.

But the walk was not included in the list of mistakes Mrs. Banks read off of her notebook. The actual list was quite precise, full of small nuances that were not truly transgressions but were more areas of improvement—such as her obvious focus on Lord Cranborne and her attempts to discover things of a more personal nature when she was directing the conversation among a group. Such was not how a hostess was to engage her guests, and Vivian had known it even as she had done it.

Still, she couldn't regret such behavior, as the earl had seemed pleased by her obvious focus on him, even if the other young men hadn't. And she had found that, almost immediately, she very much wanted to please him. Not just for the sake of her family or the state of her bottom, either.

When Mrs. Banks's recitation came to an end, Vivian perked up a bit in surprise.

"Mrs. Banks?" she asked hesitantly.

The companion raised an eyebrow at her, surprised by Vivian's hesitation. Several weeks into her training,

Vivian had moved seamlessly from recitation to punishment, without interruption. The young woman's usual good behavior meant she must have some reason for delaying her punishment, although if she was doing so for a frivolous reason then Mrs. Banks would just add to it.

"Yes, Miss Stafford?"

Vivian hesitated, not wanting to earn herself extra punishment, but at the same time wanting to ensure she understood why she wasn't being punished for her walk with the earl. "I disobeyed your order to stay in my location during the tea. Am I not to be punished for doing so?"

"Are you looking for extra punishment?" Mrs. Banks inquired, surprised.

"Oh, no." Vivian shook her head. "But I did disobey an order. I just don't understand."

She looked so earnest, so determined to ask even though she didn't want to add to her spanking, that Mrs. Banks couldn't help but smile fondly at her. That was just the kind of reaction Vivian provoked with her sweet submissiveness.

"Any order from your husband will supersede any direction you've received from another party," Mrs. Banks explained. "Including myself. He wanted to stroll with you and therefore took precedence over my injunction that you remain in the location you were assigned. Any time your husband issues you a new order, you will not be punished for disobeying another's."

"Oh."

Mrs. Banks gave Vivian a moment to think that over. She could see the spark and flare of interest in Vivian's green eyes, the slight curve of her lips as she assigned her future husband his place in the hierarchy. Vivian responded automatically to dominance, and to have the earl be the acknowledged top of the heap only made him more attractive to her, although she wasn't consciously aware of it. It was with those thoughts in mind that Vivian disrobed and got into position over Mrs. Banks's lap.

Mrs. Banks used the hairbrush as Vivian cried out, her hands twitching in their bonds, the earl more vivid in her mind than ever. He'd threatened to spank her for running herself down and she'd seen the desire in his dark eyes when he'd said it. The image made her arousal even stronger than usual as Mrs. Banks turned her bottom red.

Every smack made her hotter and hotter, both in pain and pleasure, as she lost herself in the fantasy of the earl, his dark eyes burning into hers, his hands handling her body easily. Her bottom moved up and down, as if to meet the hairbrush as it descended, the front of her womanhood rubbing against Mrs. Banks's thigh, sending trickles of pleasure threading their way through the spanking.

When the brush finally laid its last imprint on Vivian's reddened cheeks, Mrs. Banks tucked it swiftly into her pocket before putting Vivian on her knees to suckle her fingers. Smiling approvingly, the companion watched as the younger woman relaxed, taking comfort from her after-punishment routine. The companion rather thought Vivian would make the transition well on Monday, although she might be taken aback to be presented with the earl's cock rather than his fingers.

Afterwards, Vivian laid out on the bed while Mrs. Banks took some time to fondle the young woman's breasts, sharply pinching the pink, budded nipples until Vivian practically writhed with the need that had grown between her legs. Then fingers slipped down into that slick aperture, rubbing and teasing and probing. One, two, slid inside of her, giving her the delicious sensation of being stretched as other clever fingers plucked at the little pleasure bud that was so swollen and achy.

Vivian climaxed with a scream, her hands fisted in the bed sheets, as she saw the earl's dark eyes in her mind, his hungry look, and imagined the feel of his body pressed against hers.

CHAPTER THIRTEEN

GABRIEL PROWLED AROUND HIS FATHER'S house the entire weekend. He'd gone there rather than staying in his own London home in order to distract himself from the emptiness of his house. Soon he'd be bringing home his bride, but it couldn't be soon enough for him.

Seeing Vivian again, finally being able to touch and talk with her, had only solidified his desire for her. Granted, he'd been close to the point of obsession with her for over a year now, because he'd thought she'd be exactly the type of wife he'd always wanted to have. From the moment he'd met her at the wedding, he'd sensed untapped passion, a keen mind, and the sweet eagerness of a true submissive.

At that moment he'd decided to have her for his wife. It wasn't an uncommon occurrence for men of his stature to decide quickly on the woman they would wed, due to whatever factors they'd decided upon to choose their brides by. Marriages were brokered and bartered within the *ton* on a regular basis, sometimes without the parties having met at all. Gabriel was glad that he'd taken the time to court her through her training, though. Now that he knew her better, he appreciated her passion, her witticisms, her obvious love for her family, her intelligence, and the sweetness that seemed to be built into her very core. Everything about their interactions had demonstrated how well suited they were for each other.

Still, he hadn't expected this overwhelming rush of emotion now that the time was nigh. In some ways he'd wondered if perhaps his anticipation would render the reality anticlimactic; instead, she'd roused a possessive jealousy and tender awe that he'd never experienced before.

Then again, he'd never taken a wife before.

He'd hated every other man who'd received a smile from her lips, a moment of her shining eyes, or a laugh in return for a quip.

While he knew he couldn't sensibly keep her from interacting with other members of society, part of him desperately wanted to. For the first time, he was assailed with his own doubts, especially after seeing Marchland's interest. What if Vivian didn't find him as appealing as he found her? What if her awakened passions included a desire to test the waters with other lovers?

Throughout his entire life, Gabriel had been self-assured and confident in matters of the bedroom. He'd never had a jealous moment in his life or worried his prowess might not be enough to satisfy a woman.

But, he now realized, he'd never really cared if any previous woman he'd been with had ended their association. He would have easily shrugged and moved on. For the woman who was to be his wife, that wasn't an option. Not just because of the difference in their relationship, but because of these strange new emotions that had invaded him.

Insecurity was new to him and he didn't quite know how to deal with it.

He would have to bind her to him in this next week— mind, body, heart, and soul.

The sensation was like a tingling in the back of her neck, one that said she was being watched. Being watched was something she had become accustomed to, because Mrs. Banks was always watching her, but this was different. It was stronger, more disturbing, and impossible to ignore, as if all of her senses were trying to tug her in one direction at once.

Smiling at the matron chattering away in front of her, Vivian tried to shift to the side to see whether or not she was imagining things.

"Lady Cowper," a deep voice purred behind her, and Vivian's neck actually did tingle as all the hairs on it lifted at once. "I see you've met my fiancée."

A warm hand engulfed hers and brought it to his lips for a kiss, dark eyes flitting over her face before turning back to the woman in front of her. Lady Cowper beamed with delighted approval at both of them—to Vivian's relief, not at all put out by her immediate distraction.

"Miss Stafford and I have been getting acquainted," Lady Cowper said, giving Vivian another approving nod. "I must say, Cranborne, you've chosen admirably." She smiled at Vivian and held out her hand, which Vivian immediately took, although it meant relinquishing the earl's. "It was delightful to meet you, Miss Stafford. I hope to see a great deal of you after you finish school." That last comment was accompanied by a look at Lord Cranborne, who let out a resigned sigh and gave a short bow to the lady before she moved away. Vivian couldn't help but smile; obviously her future husband had the usual male impatience with social events.

But then, why had he shown up at this at-home? Since Mrs. Banks had told her she'd see him again, she'd assumed he'd appear at some point during the week, but certainly not first thing at a Monday tea. And he didn't seem entirely pleased at Lady Cowper's implication that she expected to see them at more events following the wedding. Or was it just that he preferred at-homes to other social gatherings?

There was so little she knew about this man she was to marry, she thought as she turned to him, looking up at his face. She didn't know it but her expression was full of curiosity and questions, and she looked to him as if he had the answers. It was exactly the kind of look that called to the deepest, most protective and authoritative parts of him.

"Sunrise," he said, giving her the special smile he seemed to reserve just for her. Vivian blushed as he retook possession of her hand and settled it upon his arm. "Shall we?"

She nodded and they sallied forth together as a couple, mingling with the others and being shadowed by the ever-present Mrs. Banks.

Interacting with other members of the *ton* had already been a stark lesson for Vivian in how the practicum differed from reality, although she was very glad for the lessons, for they gave her a confidence and grace she would not have otherwise had. Being on Lord Cranborne's arm added an entirely new element. He was so very confident, so very masterful, and for the first time, she was attached to power rather than standing back and observing it.

When he spoke, people listened. His opinions mattered. More than that, they influenced others. And he was so very engaging. It was easy to talk with him, both within a group and when he would catch a private moment with her as they walked.

Beautiful women fawned on him, making her feel incredibly insecure, but his stance at her side never wavered. And he took their admiration, their flirtations, as his due, responding with a casual air that nonetheless cut them off at the knees. Men vied for his attention, his approval and advice, and he listened to what they had to say although he wouldn't always appear to be listening very intently.

With Vivian he was much warmer, much more attentive to what she said. It felt, occasionally, as if he were studying her in the way a child might study a butterfly. Under his gaze she felt fascinating, beautiful, and alive. She didn't realize how much she was blooming under his attention, that others could see the way he affected her as well. It caused much consternation among the ladies, who had assumed the rakish earl's marriage would cause no real upset to his usual activities—even if he hadn't had a mistress in quite a while—and among the men who were starting to see Miss Stafford through the earl's eyes.

Or, what they imagined were his eyes. But they only saw her beauty, her poise and grace, her wit and pretty manners. None of them saw deeper, to the abiding need within her that craved approval, the natural submissive passion the school was nurturing and that he would bring into flower.

As much as he appreciated the others' admiration of his future wife, Gabriel also found it harder and harder to rein in his possessive impulses. It wasn't that he truly took the other women's attentions as his due; he didn't notice them because he was too distracted by the woman on his arm. Too wrapped up in ensuring that she didn't lack his attention or admiration, because he knew that lack of affection from their spouses was what caused most of the women among the *ton* to seek out other lovers. Although he would never have a mistress to war with his attention as many of their husbands did, he still wanted to ensure that, in this arena, Vivian's own head wasn't turned by others' attentions.

Not until hers were more firmly fixed upon him.

For Vivian, it was a rather glorious visit, other than when she compared her beauty to the women who were constantly trying to converse with the earl. However, she was somewhat reassured by his obvious preference for her company, although they were not able to speak privately once.

She would have liked to get to know him better, personally, rather than just hearing fascinating tidbits in passing reference. She overheard quite a bit of political discourse, as well as his opinion of the latest play, the finest stables for buying horses from at Tattersall's, and a curricle race he'd driven in a few weeks before. Unfortunately, no one shared details, as it was assumed everyone had already heard the gossip.

So Vivian just smiled and enjoyed hearing about her future husband, fixing in her mind questions for him later when they would have the opportunity to speak privately. Although, if given a choice, she'd prefer to exchange some more kisses before pestering him with questions.

No such private moment occurred that afternoon, but she still thrilled at being seen off to the carriage by him. The other students looked on, envious but excited, as he kissed her hand and helped her into the carriage.

"I look forward to seeing you again," he murmured, so quietly she knew no one had overheard. It was also so quickly she had no opportunity to respond, but he must know she felt the same.

Dark eyes caught hers for a moment, through the window, before the carriage set off. Vivian knew she would dream about those eyes later.

That evening, Vivian was in for the shock of her life when Mrs. Banks entered her room, at the usual time, followed by the earl himself. She'd begun to stand up from the chair she'd been sitting in before the fire, only to find herself swaying as her stomach dropped and her head actually spun. Seeing her unsteadiness, Gabriel practically leaped forward, crossing the room in a few strides, to clasp his hand about her arm and steady her.

With her head tipped back to stare up at him, soft lips slightly parted in surprise, her pale face and huge green eyes made her look almost fragile. There was a hint of pleasure in her expression as well as the shock faded, and anxiety, and a bit of fear too. The combination caused him to harden immediately, something he was growing quite used to when it came to his bride. Fortunately, tonight he would finally be able to soothe some of his wild need.

"I . . . What—what are you doing here?" Vivian's tongue felt thick and awkward in her mouth, stumbling over her words as her mind whirled.

Gabriel smiled, his dark eyes glinting in the firelight.

The contrast of his white cravat and shirt against his black coat and dark good looks was dramatic, making him look like sinful temptation personified.

"This is marriage training, Sunrise," he said, gently but with a thread of satisfaction in his voice. Or was Vivian imagining that second part? "Surely you realized at some point your husband would be a part of it."

No . . . she hadn't. She hadn't thought about it at all, really. Rather naive of her in many ways, but she'd been so focused on her daily activities, working at avoiding too harsh of an evening punishment, that she hadn't seriously thought about what future training might be like. Things had settled into a routine and she'd assumed it would remain so, until after her wedding.

"I . . . I . . ."

"It's all right, sweetheart," he said soothingly, cupping her chin in his hand and running his thumb over her pouting lower lip. Her trembling slowed, touching him with how trusting she was. How much she looked to him for guidance. She required gentle handling when it came to change, just as Mrs. Banks's reports had indicated, but it was well worth it to see her reaction to his soothing. It was a gift, and not one that he took for granted. "I'm mostly just going to be watching, I won't interfere with your normal routine."

Vivian flushed a beet red, her gaze going beseechingly to Mrs. Banks. The older woman just looked at her blandly, making it obvious she wasn't going to intervene, and Vivian remembered what the companion had said about the earl's wishes superseding anyone else's.

"Good girl," the earl murmured as her mouth opened and then closed again, obviously cutting off a protest or a plea. The heat in his voice sent a shiver right through her spine, even as warmth flooded her at the accolade. Somehow it seemed to mean even more coming from him than anyone else.

He stepped back, releasing her arm from his hold, and Vivian felt suddenly bereft, her skin still tingling where he'd touched her.

"Come sit down, Miss Stafford," Mrs. Banks said, interjecting for the first time as she nodded at Vivian's punishment chair. Her voice was gentle but firm, indicating she had some sympathy for Vivian's shock but she expected the young woman to behave herself.

With much more wariness and anxiety than usual, Vivian moved to her chair, feeling as though the air had somehow thickened so she was moving in slow motion. Behind her she sensed the earl moving as well, and when she sat he had moved one of her chairs near the fire closer to the punishment chair, facing it. Heat suffused her entire body and she knotted her fingers tightly in her lap, willing herself not to stand and run.

Of course she'd known that one day her husband would be the one in Mrs. Banks's position—she had even looked forward to it—but even as the weeks passed, "one day" had seemed so far away. She certainly hadn't expected it to come now, tonight.

Feverishly she wondered if he would be the one to spank her, then remembered he said he'd mostly just be watching. She wasn't sure whether she felt relieved or disappointed about that. Although, knowing he would be watching excited her somewhat as well.

"Are you paying attention, Miss Stafford?"

"Yes, ma'am," Vivian said immediately, drawing

herself up in her chair and forcing herself to attend to her companion's lecture. It was not the easiest task, when she could feel the earl's eyes upon her, but she did not want to earn any extra punishment for the evening. Not with her future husband looking on, and especially not if he would be watching the punishment in question.

For Gabriel it was easy to block out Mrs. Banks's voice as he studied Vivian at close range, able to look at her and drink his fill of her features—something he wasn't able to indulge in quite so much during the at-homes. During the day he certainly couldn't allow his gaze to linger on her bosom or the pulsing of her throat or the way her soft lips parted for her tongue to sweep across them. Now he could look at whatever part of her he wanted, so very close and personal.

She was doing her best to behave, to listen to Mrs. Banks's lecture, but his presence made her nervous. Of course, he enjoyed knowing he had that effect on her. That knowing he was nearby made her blush and tremble. It would have been very disappointing to him if Vivian had become completely inured by her training and he didn't have the joy of seeing her questions and hesitations.

When Mrs. Banks finished the lecture and stepped back, waiting for Vivian to stand so she could be stripped, his future wife's big eyes flitted to where he was seated. Although he knew she wouldn't realize it, he was already achingly hard, just from being so close to her and from the anticipation of what was to come. Slowly she stood, trembling, her fingers still twined about each other in front of her, as if she was afraid to break them apart.

"Turn around," Mrs. Banks commanded, realizing Vivian was going to need some help to disrobe tonight.

She had never done so in front of a man—no less the dark, engaging, intimidating man who had paid for her schooling and training, to whom she owed her family's well-being, and who wanted complete dominion over her body. The idea of being completely bare in front of him made Vivian's heart race with a heady mix of fear and excitement.

Somehow, during the daylight hours, it had been all too easy to forget he was responsible for what happened to her in the evening. He was so charming, so considerate . . . and now he was sitting and watching with avid eyes as she was prepared for her nightly punishment.

Vivian avoided his gaze as Mrs. Banks unbuttoned her dress and helped her step out of it. A heated blush filled her cheeks and she felt quite faint as she was stripped down to her undergarments. She'd grown so used to this part of her routine that she hadn't been particularly aware of her nakedness for days, but now she could practically feel her future husband's eyes traveling possessively over her body. It made her nipples harden and press against the soft fabric of her chemise and already wet heat bloomed between her legs.

Just having him sitting there, watching, heightened every pleasurable sensation that went through her, even though she wouldn't look at him.

She hesitated and whimpered a bit when Mrs. Banks tried to put Vivian over her lap for the first time, earning a sharp smack on the back of the thigh from her companion. The positioning would have her bottom and privates pointed straight at the earl, giving him a spectacular view that had not been shared with anyone other than Mrs. Banks. Marriage would allow the earl to view her body from every angle soon enough, but she hadn't been prepared for such a display this evening.

So when she was finally arranged over Mrs. Banks's lap, her hands bound behind her back, with her bottom pointed at the earl, she kept her legs tightly closed as unexpected tears of humiliation sparked in her eyes. It made her feel exposed, even though her pussy got wetter and wetter with each added step of the evening. When she wondered at her body's response, she realized her fantasies were slowly coming to life as if kissed by Pygmalion, and just as unexpectedly as when the Greek sculptor had kissed his statue.

"That will be six extra with the hairbrush for your delays," Mrs. Banks said severely, and Vivian moaned, shuddering. She hadn't wanted to misbehave, but she was just so . . . So . . .

Smack! Smack!

The blows came down hard on Vivian's bottom, one on the center of each cheek, and she jerked, her legs parting automatically. Then she remembered the earl was behind her and quickly snapped them shut again.

Smack! Smack! Smack! Smack!

Although Mrs. Banks was counting out each swat to Vivian's delightfully twitching bottom, neither the young woman nor the earl were paying her any heed. Vivian was too busy concentrating on trying to keep her legs completely shut against the earl's prying eyes, and Gabriel was too busy watching with delight as his future bride's beautiful pink pussy peeked and winked at him. Her flesh jiggled under Mrs. Banks's unforgiving hand, the soft folds of her pussy opening and closing as her legs began to kick.

It was as if the earl's presence in the room had motivated Mrs. Banks to smack Vivian's bottom even harder than usual. The young woman cried out, unable to twist or buck away due to the heavy arm across her back, which kept her held firmly in place. Her bottom was on fire and she no longer cared that the earl was watching. Her legs kicked out with abandon as she wept tears onto the floor. The growing ache inside her could only counteract the painful swats to a certain degree.

Fortunately, she had mostly done well during the at-home, and the spanking didn't go on for very long in comparison to some of the punishments she'd earned in the past. Still, it was no relief to Vivian when it stopped, because she knew what was still to come. There was only a moment when Mrs. Banks shifted beneath her, and then the dreaded hairbrush came down on Vivian's already blushing behind.

Vivian howled as the sturdy wooden implement caught her right beneath the curve of her buttocks, on her sit-spot, which was sensitive even when it hadn't been recently spanked. Gabriel shifted in his seat. Despite her cries and tears, Vivian's pretty pink pussy was becoming wetter and wetter, the glossy slick of her juices already coating the tops of her thighs. He was breathing in time with her, completely caught up in the eroticism of the act, though he ached with envy that she was over Mrs. Banks's lap and not his. Her reactions were completely uninhibited, even by his presence, and the gift of her submission was beautiful to behold. She was everything he'd dreamed she'd be and more, and the need to claim her, heart, body, and soul, was overwhelming.

When the six blows of the hairbrush had finally been

delivered, Vivian lay quiescent across Mrs. Banks's lap, vowing to herself that even if the earl came with the companion to every punishment session from now on, she would not balk at disrobing before him. After all, being naked in front of him hadn't hurt, no matter that he'd seen all of the most private parts of her body. Being spanked with the hairbrush, on the other hand, had hurt quite a bit. As well as being an added humiliation that he'd seen her misbehave and then be soundly punished for it.

It was well she had decided that before Mrs. Banks oiled her fingers and slid one into Vivian's bottom, because the young woman tensed and almost protested again. But the tight, red skin of her cheeks, as well as her thoughts, stopped her before she uttered more than a squeak at having her person invaded before the earl's watching eyes.

Gabriel was in sexual agony, watching how easily Mrs. Banks penetrated Vivian's tight little rosebud. He could tell from the way Vivian's cheeks clenched and then relaxed that she wasn't entirely happy about being so violated, probably because of his presence, since he knew Mrs. Banks had begun performing this service last week, but she didn't try to stop what was happening, either. In fact, after a few moments the bright pink cheeks of her bottom relaxed.

His cock felt like it was going to burst out of his trousers, and he shifted uncomfortably. Mrs. Banks glanced over at him, a knowing look on her face, and nodded. Taking that to mean it was almost time for what he was most looking forward to, Gabriel reached down and released his aching member from the tight confines of fabric. Unlike Vivian, he didn't feel the least bit embarrassed about baring himself in front of the two women; all he felt was relief that his torment of waiting for his future bride would soon be over.

It was all he could do not to run his hand up and down the turgid shaft as he watched Mrs. Banks work a medium-sized dilator into Vivian's little bottom hole. The soft whimpers coming from his bride's mouth only added to his dilemma, but he held himself still, knowing the eventual reward would be worth the wait.

The steady stretch of Vivian's rear entry was both pleasurable and uncomfortable, not in the least because she knew the earl was watching the thick rubber plug as it was worked back and forth in her tight channel. Her muscles strained to accommodate it, as they did every evening Mrs. Banks inserted the thing, until finally they loosened and the most bulbous part of the prod slid into place inside of her. Once it was securely lodged, Mrs. Banks helped her slide to her knees.

But instead of being presented with the companion's fingers, Mrs. Banks stood and gestured for the earl to take his seat.

Seeing her future husband for the first time since she'd begun undressing, Vivian's red-rimmed green eyes grew wide with shock and curiosity. She looked more than fetching as she knelt before the punishment chair. The position made her feel incredibly small as her husband sat before her on the hard chair, the curious, fleshy appendage jutting out of his trousers in front of her face.

It was long and thick, with a rounded head that had a little slit in it where a drop of whitish fluid had gathered; at its base was a trimmed crop of matted dark hair. The color of his flesh there was darker than the rest of him, more reddish looking, and veins ran over its surface.

The rounded, blunt end looked soft and textured. Vivian couldn't take her eyes away from it.

Although she'd known men and women were different, and she'd had some idea of what a man might look like from having seen the animals in the fields, nothing could have prepared her for the reality that was now only inches from her face.

"This is your husband's cock," Mrs. Banks said, stroking Vivian's hair in a soothing manner, as if she expected her young charge to be upset by her first glimpse of a man. Upset wasn't what Vivian was feeling, though; she was more curious than anything else. Curious and aroused, her bottom tightening around the thick rubber as her insides clenched. So close to the earl, she could smell the clean, woodsy scent of his cologne, as well as something muskier, earthier. She wanted to lean into him and breathe in those intriguing scents.

Mrs. Banks pressed on the back of Vivian's head, pushing her closer, and Vivian went willingly. "You are to treat his cock as you have my fingers."

Startled, Vivian looked up, first at Mrs. Banks and then at the earl. The cock was much, much bigger than Mrs. Banks's fingers and Vivian wasn't sure how it was supposed to fit into her mouth. The hungry intensity with which the earl was looking at her quite unnerved her as well.

But the hand on the back of her head was insistent, and Vivian found herself leaning forward. Her mouth pressed against the stiff rod and she was surprised at how hot and hard it felt against her face. Experimentally she flicked out her tongue and licked it.

The earl groaned and rolled his hips, pushing his cock

at her. Vivian was fascinated by the discovery that such a small touch could have such a large effect on him.

"Again," he said, in the deep voice that stirred her insides.

Not at all loathe to continue her experiments, Vivian began to lick up and down the length of his cock the same way she had occasionally done with Mrs. Banks's fingers. While she knew she was expected to put the large appendage inside her mouth, she fervently hoped the earl and her companion would give her some time to work up to it. It was a rather intimidating prospect.

Fortunately, the earl seemed quite pleased by her efforts, watching her with glittering dark eyes as she explored him with her mouth, working her way from the base up to the tip.

Mrs. Banks knelt to the side of and partially behind Vivian. Sliding one hand between the younger woman's legs to seek out the wet folds of her pussy, she reached into the cleft of Vivian's bottom to find the base of the dilator still wedged inside of her. While she would leave Vivian's ultimate pleasure up to the earl, she would tease and build the young woman's climax. It was the best way to ensure Vivian associated this act with pleasure.

As she traced her fingers along the wet folds of Vivian's pussy, Mrs. Banks twirled and pumped the dilator in the younger woman's back door with her other hand. Vivian's eyes glazed over as the sensations washed through her, her hands twitching in their restraints behind her back. Seeing the sensual enjoyment on his future bride's face, Gabriel reached out and slid his hands into her hair, bringing her lips to the tip of his aching cock.

Distracted by the wonderful sensations in her pussy

and the slight discomfort but still enjoyable sensations in her bottom, Vivian automatically opened her mouth to accept the offering before her lips. Her jaw had to open much further to fit his cock into her mouth, but she found something rather satisfying in the act.

Gabriel groaned as his future wife took him deeper, her sultry, wet mouth suckling at his flesh with enthusiasm. He was both envious and aroused at watching Mrs. Banks touch Vivian so intimately, wanting to replace her hands with his own, and yet enjoying the sight all the same.

Soon she would be all his, to touch and caress and pleasure and punish. Already Mrs. Banks was beginning the transfer of dependence from herself to him, manipulating Vivian's body to feel pleasure as she pleasured him, introducing him into their nightly routine. Every night this week they would take her a little further, push her a little harder, until he and Mrs. Banks had switched roles, and she would be the observer and he would be the disciplinarian.

Using the gorgeous, flaming locks of Vivian's hair, Gabriel began to move her head back and forth on the length of his cock. She tried to pull away as he went deeper, almost touching the back of her throat, and he stopped his momentum. While he didn't allow her to pull away, he didn't push her, either, and waited until she had relaxed.

"Breathe through your nose," he instructed her, kneading his fingers into her scalp to help relax her. "Try to swallow me down your throat. You don't have to succeed yet. I just want you to try."

He moved her head again, sliding her mouth until just his head was between her lips, and then forcing her to take him deeper. Mrs. Banks began to pinch at her clit, and Vivian moaned with pleasure around the thick meat in her mouth, automatically relaxing her throat, and to her surprise the head of his cock slipped quite easily into that space. It felt strange and thick, but before she could panic from realizing it cut off her airway, the earl was sliding her off of him again.

And then he pushed her back down, but this time she was prepared. The groans that came from his mouth as her lips slid down almost to the base of his cock made her shudder with pleasure. There was something intensely satisfying about hearing him make such involuntary noises and knowing she was the cause.

The burgeoning pleasure in her own core made her even more eager to suckle on his cock, her tongue and throat working as need built inside of her. It was an almost automatic response, as she had no control over the way Mrs. Banks was touching her, but she had some control over how she sucked on the earl's cock. And the needier she was for climax, the more enthusiastically her mouth worked on his turgid flesh.

Even the stopper in her bottom had begun to feel good as it was pulled and pushed, her insides clenching in delight as every last nerve was pleasurably tantalized. Yet she couldn't quite reach climax, as Mrs. Banks knew the warning signs too well and immediately removed her fingers from Vivian's clitoris and returned to teasing the young woman rather than satisfying her. Feeling almost frantic, Vivian sucked even harder on the earl's cock.

"God!" His head fell back as his hands tightened on her head. "I'm going to cum . . . Swallow it all, sweetheart . . . Oh, bloody hell . . ." His fingers spasmed and then tightened again. If she could have, Vivian would have asked what she was supposed to swallow, but just as she thought of the question, she received her answer.

The rod in her mouth throbbed, expanding and pressing against her tongue, and the underside of it pulsed as spurts of fluid was forced through it and out the tip, straight down into her throat. Salty, bitter sweetness filled her mouth, and she might have spit it out in surprise, but with the earl's tight grip on her head she had no choice but to swallow it down. The hot fluid seemed to burn her throat and stomach, even as her ears were filled with the earl's satisfied groans.

Once the pulsing stopped, the hard flesh in her mouth seemed to soften and shrink a bit, allowing her to get her breath back. The earl's fingers on her head loosened and he rubbed her scalp, making her hum with pleasure again. Her own body was still throbbing with need and she rocked her hips, only to cry out as Mrs. Banks gave her clit one last teasing pinch and withdrew.

"Good girl," the earl said, and a rush of pleasure went through her. She looked up at him, her mouth still wrapped around his shrinking cock, and she didn't know it, but pleading filled her eyes. Fortunately for both of them, her pleasure was already part of the plan, for after that performance he didn't think he could deny her anything. Gently he removed her swollen lips from around his cock, which was still half hard and if she continued sucking on it he knew he'd be back to full mast in a matter of minutes. But now it was time to see to her and her pleasure, to reward her for a job well done. "Come up here, Vivian."

Gently he helped her to her feet and then to straddle his thighs. She blushed as her wet pussy folds were parted by the position, her breasts thrust into his face, but she was too needy to truly care about her modesty. Neither of them noticed as Mrs. Banks quietly slipped out the door. Vivian was too far gone in her erotic need, and Gabriel was enjoying having her soft womanly curves on his lap, her wrists bound behind her and her body completely open to him.

While she knew her position was completely immodest and that she should be embarrassed by the way she was splayed out over his lap, Vivian's pleasure-driven senses didn't care how wanton she appeared. The taste of him was still in her mouth and she couldn't deny that she yearned for his touch on her skin. His hands were larger and rougher than Mrs. Banks's.

"So beautiful," he murmured, cupping her breasts and squeezing them gently.

Vivian closed her eyes. "Thank you," she whispered.

She loved hearing that he thought so. The way he looked at her made her shiver with delight, but she couldn't look at him while she thanked him for such a sentiment. Despite her desperate need, she still had too much ingrained modesty to feel comfortable expressing gratitude over his perusal of her body if she had to look into his eyes while she did so.

The harsh pinch of her nipples had her eyes flying wide open as she let out a shocked cry, her back arching.

"Eyes on me, sweetness," he said sternly, his dark gaze boring into hers. Tears sparked in her emerald depths as she wriggled a bit on his lap. Between his fingers her nipples throbbed, the tight pinch biting into her flesh even as it caused her insides to clench with anticipation.

While she didn't fully understand why a bite of pain

made her pleasure so much more intense, why it aroused her so, there was no denying the reaction. Gabriel amused himself for a moment, tugging and pulling on the rosy tips of her nipples, making her arch forward with little whimpers.

"Please . . . Please . . ."

"Please what, sweetness? Tell me what you need." Gabriel twisted those rosy little buds, watching as Vivian shuddered above him. One day he would be able to spend all afternoon tormenting the tempting swells in front of him, but not tonight. Tonight he wanted to reward her. He knew prolonging the time before her climax would make it that much more intense, especially if her delightful nips had been attended to, but he didn't want to make her wait so long that it became a punishment.

Still, he wanted Vivian to admit what she wanted, needed from him. And if it made her face turn a delightful pink to match the pink of her well-spanked bottom, then all the better.

"I . . . I . . ." Vivian closed her eyes. Her voice lowered to a pleading whisper, horrified he was going to make her speak her desires out loud. "Please, I—I need to . . ." Her voice went even lower, to the barest thread of a whisper. "I need to climax."

Gabriel pinched her nipples tightly again. "Look at me, sweetness." He was met with pleading eyes, and a pink blush that went from her cheeks all the way down to her collarbone. It was quite enchanting. He smiled. "Ask and you shall receive."

Pulling her forward, Gabriel brought her mouth to his, kissing her deeply. To his delight Vivian sank into the kiss eagerly. As she was shorter than him, her position on his lap put their lips on the exact same level, allowing him to easily fondle and kiss her to his heart's delight.

One hand continued to caress and squeeze the soft flesh of her breast while the other went between her legs. He groaned in her mouth as his fingers plunged between her folds, finding her soaking wet with cream. Vivian whimpered against his lips, her body wriggling on top of him, eager and needy. Already his cock was hardening again as he slid one long finger inside her molten heat.

His mouth devoured hers, ravished hers. And his hands . . . *God, his hands*. The sensations he elicited were exquisite. Shattering. Her nipples still thrummed with the sting of his rough treatment, yet she found herself craving it now that he was being more gentle.

The thick finger pushing inside her stretched her muscles deliciously. Her thighs tightened around his as the heel of his hand rocked against her clitoris. Vivian found herself moving atop him, rocking against him as if he were a horse and his hand the saddle. It was better than any of the half-formed fantasies that she'd engineered during her time at the school—more dangerous, more desperate. Indeed, she was absolutely desperate for his touch, his mouth, his approval.

And he did seem to approve.

When his hand left her breast she only had a moment to be disappointed before it had slid down behind her. He gripped one tender buttock, making her yelp against his lips before he pulled her body roughly into his. Fingers worked busily between her thighs as she rubbed herself against him, her sensitive nipples raking across the fabric of his coat, emphasizing his clothed state against her nakedness. It was domination of both physicality and mentality that she didn't consciously realize, but that her body immediately recognized.

Vivian's head fell backwards as he released her mouth. Every inch of her skin was on fire, from the stinging heat of her punished bottom, to the fiery passion between her legs, to the tendrils of flame that licked her senses as Gabriel bent and sucked one of her nipples into his mouth. It was the perfect storm of combined sensations to send her careening over the edge.

She writhed against him, sobbing as the powerful release overtook her body, sending her senses reeling. It was almost too intense to bear, and if she could have begged him to stop, to let her be for a moment, she would have. Instead, all she could do was cry out helplessly as he tugged and twisted on the plug in her bottom, grinded his hand against the wet folds of her cunt, and sucked hard on the proud pink nipple that filled his mouth. Vivian would have fallen from his lap if it hadn't been for his secure hold on her, her passionate writhing making him tighten his grip wherever he held her.

Sobbing, her body bent and arched as wave after wave of passion spent itself. Unlike Mrs. Banks, Gabriel did not stop or slow as she climaxed. If anything his attentions increased, and the peak of her ecstasy broke only to give way to another.

Hot liquid splashed against her stomach as her undulations rubbed her body against Gabriel's cock, and he spent himself for the second time. He would have been embarrassed at his loss of control, but Vivian was too beautiful, too passionate in her responses to him, and he doubted any other man would have fared any better. Seeing her climax for him had been the most gorgeous sight he'd ever beheld, one he knew he would strive for again and again and again. Not that it seemed like it would be difficult.

His efforts exhausted and overwhelmed her. Reluctantly he slowed his movements, allowing for a natural descent down from the heights of ecstasy he'd driven her to. Her cheeks were wet with tears again, her lips swollen, and her face flushed. Both of her nipples stood out proudly on her chest, reddened from his treatment of them.

It burned him that he couldn't take her home with him this very evening.

Still, he got a certain amount of satisfaction out of caring for her. Vivian clung to him sweetly as he untied her wrists and soothed the skin beneath the scarf she'd been bound with, cleaned her belly and thighs of the evidence of their passions, and picked her up to tuck her into bed. Her lashes fluttered sleepily as he drew the covers up around her and he had to fight back the impulse to climb in with her.

If he did he'd never leave.

"Tomorrow," he whispered gently. "I'll see you tomorrow."

A sleepy smile curved Vivian's lips even though her eyes were already closed, and he pressed a soft kiss to them, tasting her for one last time before he forced himself to quit the room.

Mrs. Banks was waiting on the other side of the door for him, forcing him to compose himself and keeping him from returning to the room, as a part of him yearned to do. Straightening herself up as he exited, the companion smiled with encouragement, dispelling any awkwardness in the air.

"I hope you found everything to your satisfaction, my lord."

"Very much so," he said, his mind's eye already going back to the intimacies he'd just exchanged with his future bride and those he was imagining for the future. "Thank you for your assistance."

"It was my pleasure," she said, as she walked with him down the hall. "If you'll accompany me to Mrs. Cunningham's office we can go over the pace of the transition for the rest of the week. Miss Stafford seems to accept your presence eagerly, so I see no reason why we shouldn't hasten to have you completely in charge of her evening punishment by the end of this week."

Well pleased, Gabriel followed without hesitation.

CHAPTER FOURTEEN

VIVIAN WAS A BUNDLE OF JUMBLED NERVES when she heard the Earl of Cranborne being announced at the at-home she was attending the next day. Immediately her face flushed a bright red, as it had been doing at intermittent intervals all day, whenever she thought about the events of the evening prior. Once she'd woken up and the images had come flooding back into her mind, she'd thought she'd die of embarrassment on the spot.

How could she face him again?

He'd touched her so intimately and she'd behaved so wantonly in response. While she'd become rather used to Mrs. Banks seeing her in such vulnerable states, it was completely different when there was a man there. Even if he obviously enjoyed what he'd seen.

Now, as she turned to face her future husband, the man who had seen her completely unclothed and had put his hands and mouth on her body, she wished she could sink into the ground. Could anyone tell? Would anyone look at them and know?

"Good afternoon, Sunrise," he said, stepping in front of her and bringing her hand to his lips. Realizing his broad shoulders blocked the sight of her flaming cheeks from the rest of the gathering, and his words did not indicate any change in his regard of her, Vivian felt her tension unwinding.

"Good afternoon, my lord," she said, falling back on the courtesies of society. Indeed, it seemed the social niceties were designed to help smooth over awkward moments such as this. "Lovely weather today, is it not?"

The earl's dark eyes glinted with approval, and Vivian felt her embarrassment fade even further. "Quite lovely, although I must confess it could be storming outside and I'm not sure I would notice right now."

Vivian's cheeks flushed again, although for a very different reason this time. The compliment thrilled her, as did the obvious appreciation in the earl's eyes. It seemed almost as though they were sharing a private joke, in the midst of all these people, who had no idea what they had done the previous evening. Like a secret between bosom friends, it made her feel closer to him than she'd ever felt before.

She hadn't been sure what to expect from him today, what he might say or do, but it seemed their evening was to remain completely private. Under the eyes of society, their behavior was completely unremarkable, rather enjoyable to watch in fact, as society always tittered over love matches—which the Earl of Cranborne's was now rumored to be, despite the fact the papers had been signed long before his bride had been seen with him in society. The earl's disinterest in the women who were continuing to pursue him, as well as his behavior towards Vivian during the at-homes, was spurring quite a bit of new speculation. Originally the match had seemed completely arranged, considering the age of the bride and the fact that she was still in school and had not yet been presented; no one had expected him to change his patterns of behavior for her. Instead it appeared that his bride had captured his attention and possibly his heart.

Although his stepmother and his younger sisters had informed him of the gossip, it wasn't something Gabriel was particularly interested in. He did not feel that he knew his future bride well enough to say he loved her. When he'd first met her, her submissive nature had called to him and he'd wanted her. The sweetness he'd seen had captured his attention. Knowing he was expected to marry, and so far had not found a woman that he'd be satisfied to have as a wife, he'd made the decision then and there that Vivian would be his.

During her training he'd become obsessed with her sexually—little wonder no other woman snared his attention, although he would not have dishonored Vivian even if one had. That was not his way; he had committed himself and he would stay committed. Having sampled a large banquet of women, he was now quite happy to settle down with the dish that appealed to him the most.

So far Vivian was everything he'd hoped for and more. But did he love her? Gabriel had never been in love before, although he certainly had loved women in general. Vivian was different, though. He felt far more attached to, maybe even obsessed with, her than he ever had been with any other woman. He'd explained it to himself as a response to her position as his future wife, but it felt far more intimate than that. The idea of losing her, of her changing her mind about marrying him, made him feel quite wild. For the first time in his life, he no longer felt as though he had all the power in a relationship with his woman. She submitted to him, but if she wanted to, she could easily bring him to his knees.

Watching her slowly calm under his approval and easy conversation, he was again reminded of what a natural, wonderful fit she was with him. She glowed when she saw him approving of her behavior. The effect he had on her only increased his desire for her; that he could arouse and calm her, that she looked to him for precedent and guidance, and that she trusted him already.

He was so enthralled by just being near her that he didn't notice Lord Marchland's approach until it was too late.

"Miss Stafford," said the handsome rake, bowing over her hand.

Gabriel had to stifle the impulse to snarl and snatch his bride's fingers away from the reprobate. While there were plenty of rakes and willing ladies within the *ton*, there were also rules surrounding the seduction of said ladies. Only the worst of the worst seduced true innocents, which Vivian obviously was. However, wives were fair game. As Gabriel's betrothed, Marchland's advances could follow one of two agendas—either trying to entice Vivian away from Gabriel, or setting the foundation for a seduction after she was married.

Like Gabriel, Marchland had never lowered himself to seducing the innocent young misses that flooded the marriage mart every year, and he seemed in no hurry to settle down, so Gabriel's money was on the latter motivation.

"Lord Marchland," said Vivian, with a little dip of her skirts. "It's a pleasure to see you again."

"Not nearly as pleasurable as it is to see you," returned the smiling rake.

It took all of Gabriel's considerable willpower not to forcibly remove that smarmy grin. Fortunately for everyone involved, Vivian had smoothly recovered her hand and placed it back atop the one already resting on Gabriel's arm. It was almost like she was clinging to him, he thought, with a small spurt of pleasure.

"Marchland," he said sharply, combining his greeting with warning. Beside him, Vivian stirred and peered up at him with those fathomless green eyes.

"Cranborne."

The other man sounded amiable, almost cheerful, as if he knew exactly the effect his presence was having on Gabriel's peace of mind and was amused by it.

"I didn't realize you were acquainted with Lady Hawthorne," Gabriel said, referring to their worthy host.

"My grandmother is a good friend," said Lord March-land with a shrug. "And when the old dragon beckons, a good grandson must do his duty." He smiled at Vivian, as if inviting her to share a private joke, and Gabriel coughed to cover his instinctive snarl.

"That is very good of you, to try and make your grand-mother happy," Vivian said, giving him only the slightest of smiles back.

Although the earl's face gave away nothing, she could feel the tension practically vibrating through him and she knew he didn't like Lord Marchland. It seemed to calm him whenever she would touch him; unfortunately, there was only so much she could do within the bounds of propriety. Perhaps if Mrs. Banks hadn't been hovering on the edge of her awareness she might have been bolder, but she was already clinging to Gabriel's arm in an attempt to help calm him.

She realized with a start that, for the first time, she'd thought of her husband by his first name. And it had felt entirely natural.

The revelation made her smile brilliantly up at him, completely missing the little conversation gambit that Lord Marchland was making. The demonstration of obvious affection for her future husband left him beaming back at her, while Lord Marchland frowned in surprise. Although he'd heard rumors that the match was one of affection, he hadn't truly believed the rumors might have merit until now.

After that, the conversation was quickly over and Gabriel and Vivian were on their way to speak with some of the other guests of the house.

As they walked, Vivian leaned closer to Gabriel.

"Why don't you like Lord Marchland?" she asked. Immediately Gabriel's face darkened and she almost regretted asking the question. Although nothing could take away from his handsome face, he was almost frightening when the storm clouds gathered on his countenance.

"He's a rake, a rogue, and a scoundrel," Gabriel said in a low voice.

A little smile flitted across Vivian's lips, she couldn't help it. "I've heard the same about you, my lord," she teased.

"Ah, but I'm about to be married, so I'm reformed. And my stepmother has informed me that reformed rakes make the best husbands," he teased back, enjoying the way Vivian giggled. She shook her head up at him.

"And I was never in need of reforming, so what does it matter what Lord Marchland does?"

The storm clouds gathered again and Gabriel dragged Vivian into an alcove with only a quick look around to see that no one was watching. Only Mrs. Banks had her eyes on them, and he knew the companion would see to it that they weren't interrupted.

"You will stay away from Marchland, sweet. No," he said, more forcibly as she started to open her mouth to speak. "There are certain men you should stay away from because they would want to persuade you to intimacies. The kind of intimacies only you and I should share." He cupped Vivian's cheek, stroking the soft skin gently with his thumb. "And some of them, if they couldn't persuade you, might resort to force. I will protect you, but you must never be alone with anyone you do not know or that I have told you to stay away from. And you will stay away from Lord Marchland or I will take my belt to your bottom."

Then he kissed her, with all the pent-up possessiveness and aggression he was feeling. He knew he shouldn't, but he trusted in Mrs. Banks to keep them from being seen for at least a few moments and he needed to taste Vivian. To claim her. To imprint himself on her lips.

When he released her again, Vivian's head and emotions were whirling. The idea that other men would want to do those same things she had done with Gabriel last night was surprising. The idea they might try to force her to do so was more than a bit unnerving; having been held in Gabriel's arms and on his lap, she was well aware that she was much softer and weaker than the men around her. But she hadn't imagined any of them would want another man's wife.

The earl's obvious desire for her to share those intimacies with no one but him made her feel quite warm inside, but it had also sparked a new thought.

"My lord," she said, snagging his arm before he could lead her out of the alcove again. "I know what a rake—I mean . . . that you have had intimacies . . . Ah . . ." She blushed a deep red as she tried to get out the words.

Capturing her hand, Gabriel brought it to his lips, thinking of how sweetly adorable she was. "I've had no intimacies with any woman but you for months now, sweet," he said softly in reassurance. "And nor shall I. As you shall cleave to me, so I shall to you."

"Oh." The soft word was almost a sigh, like a heartfelt benediction. "I mean, very well. Good."

Chuckling, Gabriel drew her out of the alcove. More than one person glanced over at the couple, with the blushing young woman. It was obvious from the pristine state of her clothing that her fiancé had taken no liberties, but something must have happened for her to be so brightly flushed.

Vivian was practically floating on air at Gabriel's reassurances. He was such a bundle of contradictions, her future husband. Sometimes dark as a storm cloud, sometimes sweetly tender even as he threatened to take a belt to her bottom, and sometimes so very gentle with her as though she might break, even though he'd ordered the discipline she received nightly.

Just thinking about it made her bottom tingle. She had no desire to discover what his belt would feel like, even though wetness gathered in her nether regions as she imagined being punished by him. Giving him a sidelong glance, she wondered if the feelings she was having now were what created what her mother called "hussies."

She rather felt a bit like a hussy.

* * *

The evening, chatting with the other students, now seemed interminably long. Knowing she was going to see Gabriel made her rather agitated. Instead of trying to remember all her transgressions, she found that her mind was filled with Gabriel and what his hands felt like upon her. Only when she saw Emily looking at her with true concern was she able to focus herself enough to attend to the conversation at hand. It was all too easy to allow her mind to wander back to the night before and her hopes that this evening would be more of the same.

After the evening meal, Vivian went up to her room and rushed to her vanity to ensure she looked her best for when Gabriel arrived. Vivian spent her wait studying her appearance, taming the tiny wisps of hair that had escaped their pins, adjusting her breasts, pacing, and finally settling down in her chair to read. Even so, the minutes seemed to crawl by at a horribly slow pace and she could barely concentrate on the words on the page.

When the door finally opened, she jumped to her feet.

The earl followed Mrs. Banks in, looking as darkly handsome as ever. Even more so than he had during the day, in fact, since he was now dressed for the evening, every line of his fashionable black and white attire in place. With the lack of color in his clothing, the green flecks in his grey eyes stood out even more in stark relief. The smile he gave her warmed her insides and she smiled back, her lips curving even though she knew she was about to be punished.

Unlike the night before, he leaned nonchalantly against her bedpost, just within her line of vision, as Mrs. Banks recited Vivian's transgressions during the day.

Vivian listened as attentively as she could, trying not to be distracted by Gabriel's presence and the way he was watching her.

Tonight she didn't feel nearly as shy about unclothing; it still caused her to flush beautifully, all over her body, but she was excited by it as well.

To her shock, once she was undressed, she turned to see the earl seated on her punishment chair rather than standing against her bed where he had been before. The hungry gleam in his eyes drank in the sight of her naked body and peaked, pink nipples.

"Oh!" she said, shocked, as she took an immediate step back, earning herself a hefty slap on her bottom from Mrs. Banks.

"Stop dithering, girl, and lay yourself across his lap. You know how to."

"B-b-b-but—" Vivian stammered. Part of her wondered why she was so surprised by this turn of events, while the other part of her wailed that she wasn't ready to have Gabriel punishing her yet.

"That's two with the hairbrush for not immediately obeying an order," Mrs. Banks said crossly. "Now place yourself across his lap."

Squeezing her eyes shut for a moment, Vivian tried to gather her courage. Oh, how she wished Mrs. Banks would tie her wrists together and push her across Gabriel's broad thighs! It would be so much easier that way, as well as exciting. Instead, she had to do this herself.

"Four with the hairbrush."

With a short little exclamation, Vivian's eyes popped open and she hurriedly stepped forward, laying herself across the earl's lap, trying not to look at him or think about what she was doing. But it was utterly impossible to pretend he was Mrs. Banks. The thick thighs beneath her were hard like granite, and there was something—his cock, she realized—pressing into the side of her stomach, and she was higher off the ground than she was used to. Her head tipped quite far forward; only her fingers pressed against the floor, and her toes were barely brushing it. Vivian twitched as she felt his strong hands caressing her soft skin, one on her back, the other on the curve of her bottom.

"Very nice, Sunrise," he said approvingly, feeling her tremble beneath his hands. Those little tremors pleased him greatly as he took the time to explore her backside, caressing her satiny skin and gently squeezing her flesh. Soon that sweet, heart-shaped bottom was going to be a bright pink, and he was going to have an up close and personal view this evening. Bringing his hands to rest, one on her back, the other wrapped around her upper thigh, close enough to her weeping pussy to set her heart racing, Gabriel smiled at Mrs. Banks. "You may begin her spanking now, Mrs. Banks."

Vivian didn't know it, but that was a prearranged command, part of the planned transition of authority from Mrs. Banks to her future husband. While she felt relieved that Gabriel wasn't going to be spanking her this evening, and that she would have more time to accustom herself to his presence and his discipline, subconsciously she understood he was now in charge of her punishment and that her companion was acting completely under his authority. Her pussy was wet and ready, and she was especially aware of his hand so close to her cleft.

Being held by him, in this position, was even more

arousing than her fantasies had been; there was no substitute for the warmth and strength of his body, and she'd never fantasized about the way his member would pulse hotly against her, because she hadn't known it existed.

Smack!

She let out a little cry . . . in Mrs. Banks's new position, standing over Vivian's pert bottom, the companion had quite a bit more room to swing, resulting in a much sharper swat to Vivian's creamy cheeks.

While he regretted the necessary position didn't allow him to see her breasts, having her over his lap more than made up for it. He could feel every reaction of her body, smell her arousal, watch as crimson splotches bloomed on her ivory skin. Wetness trickled down to his hand on her thigh and he squeezed it, eliciting a moan from her between swats.

His hand itched. He so badly wanted to be the one spanking her sweet little bottom . . . but Vivian wasn't quite ready for that yet. While he could have forced the issue, he had told Mrs. Banks he wanted his future bride quite comfortable with him before he fully took over her punishments. This afternoon he had enjoyed seeing her discomfiture when she had to face him, but did not want to push her into a rebellion this week. After all, she must learn to trust him, and he would much prefer to reward her consistently with pleasure so that she did so, before any serious punishments became necessary.

Moaning and bucking, Vivian rocked against the earl's lap, the front of her mound rubbing against his thigh. The delicious sensation of pressure against her clitoris was enough to help arouse her as she was spanked, without allowing her to climax. Her legs spread wider as she tried to get more traction against the sensitive nub.

Both Mrs. Banks and Gabriel noticed what she was doing, of course, but Gabriel shook his head when Mrs. Banks looked at him questioningly. He rather enjoyed seeing Vivian torn between the pain and pleasure, questing for an orgasm while she was being punished. From the way she was trying to rub herself against him, he felt quite sure that she wouldn't be able to succeed, but he liked the idea of her working herself into a sensual frenzy in the attempt.

The creamy cheeks of her bottom were now a bright red, mottled with the after effects of Mrs. Banks's sharp swats. The woman had reached the end of the count, which was twenty.

"Very good, sweetness," Gabriel praised Vivian as his hands wandered back to her bottom. She gasped as his palms came into contact with that sensitized flesh, and then cried out in protest as he squeezed the mounds roughly. Ignoring her wordless cries, he continued to knead her swollen cheeks, his cock aching as he did so. "Your gorgeous little bottom is all hot and red, sweetness. It looks absolutely beautiful. I love hearing the way you cry out when you're spanked and watching you squirm under my hands."

Why was hearing him speak with such blunt, crude words so exciting? It shouldn't be, and yet she could feel her empty tunnel clenching as if it wanted to be filled. His rough hands sent sparks of pain to reignite the burn in her cheeks, and all she wanted was for his hand to slide lower and touch her swollen, throbbing core.

Then his hands slid back to their original positions: one on her back, the other on her thigh.

"All right, Mrs. Banks, I believe she's ready for the hairbrush."

Vivian moaned. She would have protested but she already knew it wouldn't do any good. At least Gabriel's warm hands on her felt good, giving her something pleasurable to concentrate on.

Thwack! Thwack!

Two swats of the brush smacked down on the center of each already-reddened buttock, making Vivian jerk and shriek. Gabriel held her firmly in place as twin tears rolled down her cheeks. The hard wood was completely unforgiving and her skin was already sensitized and flaming from the spanking.

Thwack! Thwack!

The last two blows were delivered directly to Vivian's tender sit-spots. She shrieked again and then slumped over the earl's lap, relieved that it was over. Again Gabriel's hands moved to rub over her sore skin and she whimpered, trembling as he squeezed her flesh again. Even as the stinging bite of pain flashed through her, the sensual tension inside her belly coiled and she could feel her arousal rising. The hard length of his cock twitched against her stomach as he abused her poor cheeks.

Gabriel was amazed at how wet and slick Vivian's pretty little pussy was becoming. She was leaking copious amounts of honey, obviously extremely aroused by what he was doing.

"Good girl," he murmured again, leaning down and brushing his lips across each heated mound.

Feeling the scrape of his bristles against the sensitive surface, Vivian felt a bit faint. He had just kissed her bottom! After it had been thoroughly chastised! Why that should make her insides feel so hot and aching she had no idea, but it did. Discipline with the earl was already very different from discipline with just Mrs. Banks; it was more intense, more personal, and even more erotically exciting.

"Mrs. Banks, the oil, please."

A thick, oiled finger pressed against Vivian's anus and she groaned, wanting to hide from the undeniable fact that the earl was now pressing his finger into such a forbidden, dirty place.

"You're so delightfully submissive, aren't you, sweetness?" Gabriel chuckled as he began to work his finger back and forth in Vivian's backside, watching the digit disappearing into the adorable little pink hole between her flaming cheeks. "Being spanked makes you cream yourself, and when I play with your sweet little asshole, you get even hotter, even though you don't want to. You'll squirm and moan, but you don't truly want me to stop. Do you?"

It was frightening how well he seemed to read her, to know the thoughts flying through her mind. His words just made her even more aroused, and her tiny asshole clung to his finger, spasming with the need heating her insides. "No," she whispered.

"When you are my wife, I'll touch every part of your body; spank you, whip you, tie you up and fondle you, just like this, for hours. I'll bury myself inside your mouth, your pussy, and your ass until you're screaming from ecstasy, and then I'll do it all over again." The earl's voice was fierce, his finger pumping faster, ravishing her bottom. His voice was tight with desire and she could feel the strangest sensation growing inside of her, similar to an orgasm but not quite the same—still, close enough to make her wonder, rather wildly, what was happening to her body. Surely his finger frigging her bottom wasn't enough to make her climax?

And yet her lower body was becoming more excited, her inner muscles spasming as he continued to describe debaucheries and punishments in a low, forceful voice. Vivian wasn't even truly listening anymore, her mind was providing the pictures his words created without any active concentration from her.

When he stopped, removing his finger rather abruptly from her bottom and replacing it with an oiled rubber plug, Vivian cried out. She'd been so close to some kind of culmination, only to have it abruptly snatched away.

"Please! Please, please, please," she begged as her bottom spasmed around the plug now filling it. It felt achingly full, but she needed a return of that blissful friction.

Instead, Gabriel turned her on his lap so she fell onto her knees in front of him. "Not yet, Sunrise. First you must show me how sorry you are for your transgressions . . . then we'll see what we can do for you."

Vivian practically fell upon his cock the moment it was released from the confines of his pants. She didn't even notice the way his head fell back as he groaned with pleasure. Normally Gabriel might have liked her to take more time, licking and caressing, but he was too aroused by her obvious desire for him to direct her to temper her eager sucking. Enthusiasm should be encouraged, he thought dimly, weaving his fingers into her hair as she sucked him deep.

Smiling, Mrs. Banks quietly made her way out the

door. The other two occupants of the room didn't even notice her leave, they were so engrossed in each other. For Vivian, it was the beginning of the culmination of her training; not only had she been carefully prepared to please and pleasure the earl, she very much wanted to. Something about him called to hidden desires deep inside of her, the most basic needs of her inner psyche had been unlocked and met when she'd met him. On her knees, with his unfamiliar member sliding between her lips, she felt as though she'd found a missing puzzle piece that fit perfectly into her life.

For Gabriel, Vivian's full submission was the culmination of years of planning. Months of longing and wanting. Weeks of tormenting himself while she was training. He groaned as her innocent mouth moved as skillfully as any woman's, seeking to milk him of his seed. The light in her eyes said she was becoming aware of how she affected him, of the power she had over him, no matter that she had given up her control and her body to him. The dawning revelation was immensely erotic to Gabriel. Seeing her slowly awaken sexually and bloom was the most arousing thing imaginable.

He reached down to caress and squeeze her breasts. Vivian hummed around his cock as he pinched her nipples, creating an intense vibration that traveled all the way along his length and up his spine. For Vivian's part, having him touch her as she performed this lewd act on him only increased her frantic need, and her body undulated as she suckled harder and more fervently. She whined in the back of her throat as the sharp pain of her pinched nipples immediately made pleasure bloom between her legs.

With a loud cry, Gabriel thrust, pulling Vivian's breasts and squeezing them tightly in his strong fingers as he spurted hot liquid down her throat. She swallowed, tasting the same bitter sweetness as she had the night before, and found she was beginning to like it. The look on his face as he relaxed and then caressed her cheek was one of appreciation, warmth, and almost awe.

"Come here, Sunrise. Spread your legs over my lap."

She shivered at the order, lust rippling through her, but she still hesitated for a moment. Only a moment, during which that delightful blush rose high in her cheeks as she realized he was ordering her to display herself, rather than putting her in the position. That she would have to do it herself, which was somehow so much harder than just allowing herself to be positioned.

But the need pulsing inside of her, the wet hunger, was too much for her to be able to resist. Her legs straddled his thighs and her cheeks heated as she tentatively placed her hands on his shoulders, trying to avoid his gaze because their closeness felt almost painfully intimate. His breath was warm on her cheek, and her lashes fluttered as she peeked through them, her breath catching in her throat when he speared her with his intense gaze. She winced as her bottom scraped across the fabric of his pants, reminding her that her cheeks were red and sore. In her excitement she'd almost forgotten. Seeing the wince, Gabriel knew exactly what had caused it, and his cock twitched despite the fact that he'd just climaxed.

Grasping her by her sore bottom, he roughly squeezed her punished cheeks and pulled her forward, eliciting a gasp from her slightly swollen and used lips.

"Does it hurt?" he asked, squeezing and kneading her flesh, making her squirm. The musky, sweet scent of her arousal grew stronger as he played with her.

"Yes," she said, casting her eyes downwards, focusing on his cravat.

Gabriel's grin broadened. "And that just excites you more, doesn't it?"

With an embarrassed little moan, Vivian covered her flaming face with her hands. Immediately Gabriel reached up and grasped her wrists, taking her hands and placing them on his shoulders.

"Don't move them from here, Vivian," he said sternly. The deep, dark voice he used brooked no argument, and it made her body tingle. "Now, answer the question. You feel wetter and hotter inside when you're spanked, don't you? Do you like it when I squeeze your sweet little cheeks?"

She whimpered and then closed her eyes. How could he say such crude things? And why did she love it so much when he did?

"Yes," she whispered, as his questing fingers found the knob of the plug inside her anus. Immediately her cheeks clenched around it and the pleasure shuddered through her.

"There's nothing to be ashamed of, Sunrise," he said. One of his hands slipped between her legs to rub his fingers along her wet folds, igniting the most incredible sensations. He ignored her gasp and the way her back arched, and continued to play and tease, to circle around her swollen clit but never touch it. "I'm happy you like it. I'm going to touch every inch of your body with my hands and my tongue, I'm going to invade you and hurt you and pleasure you and possess you, and I want to know that you'll love every minute of it."

One long finger slid inside her, and Vivian cried out as her body spasmed around the questing digit. His words created a firestorm within her. The images flashing through her head were fuzzy, indistinct, and yet incredibly arousing from the small parts she understood. The finger plunging inside her and the plug in her bottom that he was now twisting gave her some idea of what he might have in mind.

She cried out as the heel of his palm pressed against her clit, and she tightened her fingers on his shoulders. Gabriel applied the pressure and friction she craved as she rode against his hand.

"I'm going to tie you up, and whip you, and take you in every hole until you're utterly and completely mine."

His fingers stroked inside of her, accompanied by a push at the base of the plug in her anus, and every muscle in her body seemed to tighten and then release in a wave of blissful pleasure that had her crying out and clutching his shoulders. Teeth caught at her nipple as she writhed, her splayed legs trying to squeeze together as the relentless rubbing of her clit made her spasm. The little nubbin was almost too sensitive to bear the stimulation, and yet she couldn't even beg him to stop or slow as she sobbed out her ecstasy.

Gabriel watched her fluttering eyelashes, her flushed cheeks, as she came for him. Triumph surged through him, not only at his mastery over her pleasure, but at her obvious arousal at his words. With his finger inside her he'd been able to feel every spasm, every clench, as the impact of his words were taken in.

He rubbed the sensitive folds of her pussy until she slumped on his lap, her fingers no longer digging into his skin through the fabric of his jacket.

"Good girl," he crooned, lifting his honey-coated digits to her mouth.

Testament to her good training, half-dazed as she was, Vivian immediately started licking them clean. Gabriel felt a tingle in his groin, but he forced down his own desires, knowing full well that if he had his way, he would never leave her bedroom. Unfortunately, it was not possible yet.

But soon. Very soon.

CHAPTER FIFTEEN

THE NEXT DAY VIVIAN WAS ON TENTERHOOKS until Gabriel appeared. The young ladies were having their own "at-home" in the practicum house, giving them yet another opportunity to practice being hostesses. This was much more stressful and fraught with opportunities to make a mistake, as they had more responsibility. Their companions had made it clear that more was expected of them now that they'd attended some true at-homes and so should be more knowledgeable.

She still had some trouble understanding how the many faces of her future husband came together to make a whole. There was the confident, attentive gentleman who escorted her about the at-homes and was every inch the *ton*nish earl. In more private surroundings there was the almost playful, teasing man who made her giggle and laugh. On the other side of the equation there was also the stern disciplinarian with the hot, flashing eyes, who oversaw her punishment and enjoyed it. And then there was the gentle, tender man who had cradled and cuddled her last night in her punishment chair after pleasuring her to limpness and had tucked her into bed almost reverently before placing a light kiss on her lips. It didn't seem possible that all those aspects could belong to the same man, and yet they did.

More and more she became obsessed with finding out more about him. While she waited for him to appear at the at-home, she managed to turn her conversation with the visiting ladies to the Earl of Cranborne, so that she might hear some gossip about her betrothed. Some of it made her stomach turn queasily, mostly having to do the women he'd had as mistresses or lovers—not that anyone said anything specific, but the sly hints and vague comments built a picture she couldn't mistake. The rest of it was fascinating. His protectiveness over his sisters, his friendships with their husbands, his championing of his stepmother when she'd first married his father despite her lower status, his reputation as a Corinthian and a rake, and the tales of wild races, hunts, and a few forbidden duels.

When his presence was finally announced it was almost a relief from the deluge of information. Especially as her worries about other women were assuaged, once again, by his demeanor towards her. She believed him when he said there would be no other woman but her now, as he certainly gave her no reason to think otherwise, but she could not help her feelings of jealousy over the women who had been before her. Still, she could tell he felt the same way whenever she was speaking with another man. Gabriel kept her arm pressed to his side every time they were speaking with any other gentleman, whereas he held it much more loosely when they were speaking to a woman.

And all through the afternoon, she found her mind

drifting towards the upcoming evening and her inevitable punishment.

Her punishment was going to be worse than ever, as it turned out. Astoria had spitefully spilled a cup of tea on Vivian's dress, spattering the earl with some of the liquid as well. She was immediately overly apologetic, mostly to Gabriel, and when Vivian returned from patting her dress dry, Astoria was hanging all over him. While Gabriel seemed more amused at the young lady's antics and her obvious eye-fluttering and compliments, something angry and awful had taken hold of Vivian's insides.

Reclaiming Gabriel's arm, Vivian smiled thinly at Astoria's repeated apology.

"I'm so glad to see it didn't ruin your dress," the pretty blonde said with false sincerity. "How fortunate you weren't wearing silk." She brushed her own skirts, flaunting the yellow silk her gown was made out of, as if to emphasize her higher social and financial status over Vivian's. It was not the first time someone had obliquely referred to Vivian's family's status in comparison to the earl's, but it was the first time it got under Vivian's skin.

"I've always considered it a good practice to wear more durable fabrics in the afternoon. After all, it only takes one person lacking grace to ruin a gown."

Immediately Vivian regretted the words. Not because of the look on Astoria's face when she was so blatantly set down—that was delightful—but because the sudden stiffness of the earl's body and the look Mrs. Banks gave her said her bottom would be paying for her rudeness later.

It was so infuriating that an obviously false spill and an oblique insult was acceptable, but because Vivian had been more blatantly insulting in response, she was now the one in trouble. Darkly, she thought there was little chance Astoria's bottom would be paying any kind of price for her maneuver.

Fortunately, Emily, who was the most adroit at social situations, smoothly stepped into the breach with her cheery good nature. "I should say so, I'm sure that's why Mama never allows me silks. I'd ruin them in a heartbeat."

Everyone within earshot chuckled and the tension immediately dissipated, leaving Vivian feeling worse than before. In one sentence, Emily had aligned herself with Vivian and set down Astoria for her comment about the material of Vivian's dress, and at the same time set down Vivian for her comment about Astoria's supposed clumsiness, without being blatant or insulting to either of them. It was the kind of social cue Vivian had absolutely no practice in and obviously needed to learn. Compared to her own response, Emily's had been verbal grace.

Even more so, she could sense the earl's disapproval with her and she felt herself wilting. Immediately she withdrew behind the only social mask she had any practice at; that of the demure, retiring, modest young miss who had very little to say for fear of offending anyone.

Gabriel could sense the difference in her demeanor, but he didn't quite know what to do about it. Vivian had done herself more harm than good with her little comment—not only had she shown that she was not as adept in awkward social situations as she needed to be to successfully navigate the backbiting atmosphere of the *ton*, but she'd also shown a weak spot. He wasn't fooled by Lady Astoria's conventionally pretty exterior; he could tell she was a viper underneath. Women like her would enjoy weak spots like the one Vivian had just displayed.

But he didn't like the way Vivian retreated into herself, either. The sparkle had completely gone out of her green eyes, which looked dulled even as she listened attentively to the story Lord Lilienfield was telling. Her little laugh upon completion of the story was genuine and yet completely lacking the joyous freedom she usually displayed. While he didn't want her to think he approved of her rudeness, which was not only beneath her but also damaging, and he knew she needed to learn a better tactic, he also didn't want her to disappear within herself. Somehow he had to show her some kind of encouragement before she completely closed herself off before his eyes.

As if on cue, the elderly Lord Lilienfield gave her an encouraging smile before his eyes slid to Gabriel. "You're lucky I'm not twenty years younger, Cranborne, or I'd have to steal this gem away from you."

Vivian visibly brightened at the praise.

"You could try," Gabriel said dryly, pulling her closer to him and looping his arm around her back. It was treading the line of propriety to be so openly tactile with her, but as they were at an at-home and the rumors of their lovematch were swirling, not to mention Vivian's small misstep, he knew it would be tolerated. In fact, such a blatant display of affection on his part would be much more interesting to the gossips than any small verbal blunder Vivian had made. "I can guarantee you'd have the fight of your life."

Lord Lilienfield chortled. "Good show, good show. Trust you to recognize when you've got a prize and to hold onto it with both hands."

Still chuckling, the elderly lord ambled away.

"Come on, Sunrise," Gabriel said, loudly enough for everyone to hear the endearment. "Let's get you some refreshments before Lilienfield tries to steal you away from me." His head descended to her ear and he knew everyone would assume he was whispering something scandalous or romantic to her. "I'm going to spank the hell out of you for being rude later, but only because you're better than that. Next time, don't descend to her level."

The encouraging smile he gave her as he lifted his head again and led her to the table of lemonade and small sandwiches helped to raise Vivian's spirits. Her stomach no longer felt as though it had settled in the vicinity of her ankles. While her bottom might pay the price later, she felt better.

"Please, please, please, I'll be good . . ." Vivian let out another shriek of pain as the earl's hand crashed down on her already cherry-colored bottom. More tears joined the twin rivers already flowing down her cheeks and watering the floor beneath her.

The entire nature of her discipline had changed this evening and she wasn't sure how she felt about it. Mrs. Banks's litany of Vivian's mistakes had been quite a list, as well as very specific. And, unfortunately for Vivian, Mrs. Banks was not the one doling out the punishment this evening.

It was the earl who had helped Vivian to disrobe, earning a series of fetching shivers from her. His hands had brushed her skin constantly, and she was sure he was doing it purposefully, as Mrs. Banks's hands never touched her that much. Then she'd been tipped over his lap, just as she had been the previous evening. Again, his hard cock had already been digging into her side, his hands had squeezed and rubbed her bottom to warm the skin.

But then he'd spoken. "So. Twenty-eight swats and then ten with the hairbrush. I expect you to be very sorry by the end of this, Sunrise, and I also expect you to try to improve. I want you to be a good girl for me so we can have enjoyable spankings instead of punishment ones."

Enjoyable spankings? He gave her no time to ponder the idea.

Smack!

Vivian had howled in pain and indignation as the earl's hand came down on her vulnerable backside—harder and stronger than Mrs. Banks had ever managed.

Thwack!

The second swat had taken her breath away; the "warming" he'd done to her bottom had in no way prepared her for the stinging blows now raining down onto her vulnerable backside. His hand was hard, unyielding, and she could feel the flesh of her entire buttocks as well as her thighs jiggling and dancing with every blow. Despite how much harder he spanked than Mrs. Banks, Vivian's body thrilled to be under his control. It was much more arousing, much more intimate, and highly exciting, fulfilling all the fantasies she'd had ever since she'd begun her marriage training.

She didn't understand how she could be so blissfully happy even as she was being punished and her bottom was burning with the stinging pain.

By the fourth swat she was crying, by the seventh her legs had begun to kick, and by the tenth she had started a begging, pleading chant filled with promises. She would be good, she was desperate to prove to him that she could improve. Somehow this was so much more personal than any of the spankings she'd received from Mrs. Banks; and not just because she could feel his arousal pressing into her side as he punished her.

Gabriel could see the high gloss on her pussy lips as her legs kicked out. He loved the way her breath sobbed as she pleaded, the dance of her flesh, the peeks of her swollen lips that he received as she squirmed and thrashed for him. Although he could have easily stopped her kicking, he rather enjoyed seeing his composed and demure Vivian completely lose her control. This was the appropriate setting for it, unlike her sniping insult to Lady Astoria earlier today.

His cock was absolutely rigid, throbbing with desire to plunge into her, as he could see that, despite her protests and begging, she was highly aroused by her punishment.

"Twenty-seven, twenty-eight," he counted out. Vivian slumped over his lap immediately, sobbing now that the spanking was over.

"I'm sorry, I'm sorry . . ."

"Shh." He rubbed his hand over her shoulders gently. "You're forgiven, sweetness. I know you'll try to do better in the future. That's what spankings are for, and once they're over you don't need to worry about being forgiven, because you already have been. You don't need to feel sorry. Only ten more with the brush and then we're completely done."

"No, please," Vivian begged. She couldn't imagine having the hard back of the wooden brush laid over the flaming skin on her bottom. The throbbing heat was already spread out over her entire bottom, her sit-spot, and the tops of her thighs. There couldn't be a single spot devoid of bright color, a single patch of unmarked skin that could take the additional swats.

"Now, Sunrise, you must take your punishment. If I didn't follow through with your promised discipline, then what kind of husband would I be?"

Even as she started crying again, Vivian knew that, deep down, if Gabriel had acquiesced to her plea, some part of her would have been disappointed. Her backside would have rejoiced, even her mind, but another part of her would have seen it as a weakness on his part. And she loved his strength. Instinctively responded to it. Felt relief that he hadn't given in, even if she didn't fully understand her reaction.

She wouldn't even realize until much later that she never once considered saying the words that would end it all.

Thwack!

Gabriel thought he might actually climax from the heavenly feeling of Vivian's body squirming against him as he spanked her. The jiggling red cheeks of her bottom were flattened with every swat of the brush, showing white for a moment after impact before immediately darkening. He fantasized about burying himself in her wet slickness, feeling the press of her hot skin against his belly as he took her.

Thwack!
Thwack!
Thwack!

The meaty thunk of the wooden-backed brush against Vivian's rounded flesh, combined with her cries, pleas, and chanting promises to be good, was the sweetest sound he'd ever heard. Even more so than any of the punishments he'd witnessed, because now she was suffering at his hand, rather than another's. Her bottom was a deep, swollen red by the time he finished.

But the reason he was so inflamed by her punishment was the aftermath, when he dropped the hairbrush to the floor and thrust his hand between her legs. A moment ago they'd been kicking. Now they were draped, slightly apart, with just enough space for him to slide his fingers into the folds of her pussy.

They came away coated in honey, and his cock jerked.

The punishment was effective, as it should be, because Vivian didn't enjoy pain; but she couldn't help her arousal from his dominance over her. And Gabriel was grateful for that, for although he enjoyed spanking a woman, he knew he would not want to punish Vivian nightly—only when she truly deserved it. And, as sweet as she was, he knew she would not deserve it often. He looked forward to when her training was over and they were married and he could give her more sensual spankings they would both enjoy.

But when she needed to be disciplined, as she truly had this evening, he would not hold back. And he was pleased to know her body would still respond.

Pulling her up onto his lap, Gabriel cuddled her for a moment, enjoying her whimpers as she was pressed against his legs. Mrs. Banks gave him a nod before she made her way out of the room. He pulled a handkerchief from his pocket and dried her tears, allowing her to blow her nose, until her crying had stopped. From what he'd seen and heard, he knew his spanking was much harsher—and therefore more effective—than anything Mrs. Banks was able to dole out.

"You did very well, sweetness. I'm proud of you. And you're not going to make the same mistakes twice, are you?"

"No," Vivian said, a little miserably as she clung to him. Part of her wondered how she could want his comfort and the warmth of his arms so much when he was the one who had punished her, but it didn't change the desire. And most of her was too busy enjoying being in his arms to care about the irony. "I won't be rude again."

"Good girl."

The gentle caresses were at complete odds with the roughness of his hands as he'd punished her; they were also stirring the flames that had already ignited when he'd spanked her. Despite the throbbing ache of her bottom, which was much stronger than she was used to, Vivian's core pulsed with need.

Then Gabriel positioned her and let her slide down onto her knees before him, so she could please him rather than quench the hunger growing inside of her. He bent down briefly to brush an approving kiss over Vivian's temple before straightening up to undo the front of his breeches. Vivian's mouth watered as he pulled his cock from his trousers; she leaned forward and pulled him in hungrily between her lips. The meaty taste filled her mouth as she began to move her head up and down, her tongue working busily over the veins and ridges along his length.

Groaning, highly aroused from finally being the one to spank Vivian and feel her flesh quiver under his palm, it didn't take very long before Gabriel was crying out with ecstasy as he pumped thick cream down her throat. She swallowed eagerly. Truthfully, this might be her favorite part of the evenings this week. She loved to see Gabriel's eyes glow almost silver as he watched her, loved to hear his masculine groans, to feel his legs tremble beneath her hands, to feel the rush of power as she attended to his pleasure. Even when her jaw ached, it felt good, and she adored it when he played with her hair while she moved her mouth up and down his rigid length. The warmth in her belly as she swallowed his cum was always accompanied by a feeling of supreme satisfaction.

And the look he gave her afterwards, the almost reverent, tender expression, made her want to do anything to make him look at her like that again.

To her surprise, he didn't pull her back up onto his lap. Instead, he swept her up into his arms and carried her over to the bed. Vivian's heart pounded. Was he going to anticipate their wedding night?

When he sat her down on the bed, he gave her a deep, probing kiss that made her insides tingle, before pulling away.

"Lie down on your back, Sunrise," he ordered. Vivian did so, leaving her legs hanging off the bed in the position he'd left them, parted just enough for him to stand between. She jerked with shock as he knelt down at the edge of the bed, his eyes alight with anticipation, cheeks slightly flushed, and his hair mussed from its usual perfection. "Pull your knees up."

The position left her wide open, and she blushed as she realized he was looking right at her privates. All she could see of him was his head, but he had an extremely intimate view of *all* of her. Immediately her legs started to close again, and she gave a little shriek as he smacked the inside of each thigh.

"Keep your legs open, I like to look at you."

Vivian covered her face with her hands, whimpering a little from the reigniting of pain as he pulled her hips closer to the end of the bed, scraping her sore bottom along the fabric of the coverlet. Hot breath wafted across her swollen flesh and she moaned a little. His face must be so close to her!

"Put your hands down, Vivian," Gabriel said, amused. He wanted to see her expression, to enjoy the dichotomy of her wanton innocence. "I want to see you play with your pretty breasts and pinch your nipples."

Slowly, hesitantly, Vivian's hands drifted down to her breasts, cupping them gently and pinching the little pink nipples between her fingers. But her face remained averted from her body.

"Look at me," Gabriel ordered. His voice had deepened in such a way that it seemed to throb through her, all the way to her core. She couldn't resist that voice, and she found her head snapping into position to stare down at him along the length of her body.

Deliberately keeping his eyes locked onto hers, Gabriel leaned forward and pressed his mouth against her wet flesh.

Vivian shrieked in surprised pleasure, and her hips jerked upwards. His tongue made broad sweeps between her pussy lips, tasting her, learning the shape of her folds. The intensity in his eyes as he watched her writhe for him was akin to the hunger with which he watched her pleasure him with her mouth.

Pain and pleasure mingled as her bottom bounced on the bed. Her insides clenched as Gabriel licked and sucked at her lips. His tongue flicked against her clit and then teasingly moved away again, making her gasp with pleasure. Squeezing her breasts harder, she found herself adding to the heady mix of mingled sensations surging through her body. The sharp bite of pain enhanced her rising ecstasy.

"Oh, please," she gasped as his tongue flicked over the swollen nub of her clit again. "Oh please, oh please, oh please . . ."

When he moved his mouth upwards and sucked her clit between his lips, pulling hard on the sensitive organ, Vivian screamed his name. He slid one finger into her spasming pussy and moved it back and forth, increasing the intensity of her climax as she rode his mouth and finger, her head whipping back and forth in her passion. The storm of sensations roiled through her, enveloping her, until Gabriel's suction gentled and she was able to descend. Her limbs fell limply as she panted for breath.

"Lovely, Sunrise, that's my good girl," Gabriel said again, moving his mouth up her body as he kissed her stomach and breasts, lingering over her nipples. She moaned a little bit; it felt good, but almost too good, as her body still tingled with the aftermath of the intense orgasm. "I'm so very pleased with you, Sunrise."

He desperately wanted to cuddle her again, but he knew if he did so now, in her bed, with her all soft and pleasured the way that she was, that he would divest her of her virginity within the hour. Controlling his hunger for her, he ignored his rising cockstand and tucked her into bed.

"I'll see you tomorrow," he whispered, brushing his lips over hers.

She tasted the musky sweetness of her juices in his kiss, her tongue flicking out along his lower lip as if to catch more of it.

"Yes, Gabriel."

CHAPTER SIXTEEN

VIVIAN WAS BEGINNING TO WONDER HOW often she would find herself in exactly this position, straining to see what her bottom looked like in the mirror.

Sunlight trickled in through her window; she'd awoken before the maid had come. Probably because her body was still thrumming with excitement from the previous night. She'd wanted to see what her bottom looked like when Gabriel had tucked her into bed, but she'd been so exhausted that she'd fallen asleep before he'd even left the room.

Today there was nothing left to see, except a few faintly dark spots on her skin that were sore when she pressed on them; remnants of the hairbrush when wielded by the earl's powerful arm. He spanked so much harder than Mrs. Banks did.

Brushing her fingers over the sensitive skin, which still felt the effects of the spanking even if it didn't show it, Vivian shivered. The earl roused the strangest mix of emotions in her—desire, fear, warmth, want. She craved his attention and approval like no one else's.

And knowing she would be spanked and then forgiven

was a relief. There would be no wondering, with him, whether or not he was angry with her. There would be no emotional turmoil with the earl; he was quite demonstrative in both his pleasure and his displeasure. She would be punished, and then it would be over and they would return to normalcy.

At least she hoped. She was a bit more worried today, as she really had been quite rude to Astoria yesterday. Not that she would apologize, as it had been deserved, but she would not lower herself like that again. Gabriel had been very disappointed in her. She would strive to be more like Emily, more like him.

With a sigh, she turned away from the mirror and let her skirts drop, her neck muscles strained from the way she'd craned her neck. The door to her room opened and Vivian quickly moved away from the mirror, even though she knew the maid would have no idea what she had just been doing. The silk of her night rail brushed against her sensitive bottom as she moved, teasing her senses and causing even more wetness to gather between her legs.

"Good morning, miss," the maid said, her voice more excited than usual. "Look what I have here! Mrs. Banks said you're to wear this today. It was delivered last night."

Curious, Vivian stepped forward and then exclaimed with pleasure at the sight of the green and gold fabric piled in the maid's arms. Reaching out her hand, she flushed with pleasure as she realized the gown was made of silk.

"Yes, no, I don't know, and absolutely not," Gabriel said, rubbing his forehead and wondering why he'd been cursed with not one, but two sisters. They'd been pestering him with questions on the way to the Marquess of Deane's

London house, which was the at-home Vivian and her fellow students would be attending today. Audrey smiled at her stepdaughters, obviously amused by Gabriel's inability to rein in their incessant questions. It was all he could do to keep up with them, considering they'd barely paused to take a breath and allow him to answer anything they asked.

Both of his sisters were thrilled to be on their way to meet his future bride, especially as the rumors had been swirling about his relationship with her. As Gabriel had expected, the gossips had been tittering over his and Vivian's behavior at the gathering the day before, rather than Vivian's and Astoria's quarrel. They were much more interested in the reformation of a rake and his fascination with his future wife than they were in a schoolgirl spat. Of course, the tale of his blatant affections towards Vivian had brought his sisters round this morning, insisting they join him at Deane's.

He wouldn't have agreed except that Audrey was going as well, and he trusted his stepmother to be able to keep Diana and Henrietta more or less in line. Also, he'd spoken with Audrey the night before about Astoria and Vivian, hoping she might be able to take Vivian under her wing the way she had with his sisters. Unlike his sisters, who had been raised within the bosom of the *ton*, Vivian needed guidance when it came to dealing with the poisonous tongues of "polite" society. Audrey was a master at it, considering the number of incensed women and matrons with eligible daughters after his father had married her.

"Gabriel, you aren't paying attention!" Henrietta said petulantly.

"Leave your brother alone," Audrey said. He cast her a grateful look. "You'll meet Miss Stafford shortly and then you can garner your own impressions."

Both of his sisters sighed impatiently, and he couldn't help echoing them. He was more than eager for this entire week to pass quickly. This weekend his bride would graduate from Mrs. Cunningham's Finishing School, on Sunday the banns would be read for the final time, and next Saturday morning they would be married.

Even better, as her parents didn't have a house in London yet, they would be staying with his father and Audrey next week. Although that was no longer his residence, he would be able to move freely throughout it, and as long as he and Vivian were discreet, he didn't see any reason he wouldn't be able to continue to see his bride in private every evening. Keeping himself from anticipating their wedding night would be even harder without the constant chaperonage of Mrs. Banks, but he was willing to pay the price of frustration.

When Gabriel came into the room with two beautiful women on his arms, Vivian felt the most awful churning feeling in her stomach. Even worse than yesterday, when Astoria had been so horrible. At least he hadn't shown any interest in return, then. No other woman had been on his arm at any of these events except herself.

Then his eyes swept round the room, searching her out, and when he found her, his face took on the hungry look he often had when he stared at her, which left her more confused than ever. He said something to the two women and both of them brightened up immediately, looking over in her direction. It wasn't until she glimpsed

the Marchioness of Salisbury behind them that she realized the two beautiful women weren't two of Gabriel's
conquests; they were his family.

She relaxed as they made their way across the room
to her. She was barely able to attend to whatever Lady
Cowper was saying to her—which would probably earn
her extra punishment, but she didn't care. She was too
relieved.

His sisters were both exquisite. The one on his left,
who looked a few years older than the one on his right,
was a ravishing beauty, equal to Astoria. She must have
been considered the Diamond of her year when she came
out. With her mass of dark hair, startling green eyes, and
pale, ivory skin, she was a complete nonpareil. Vivian had
a moment of strong envy. She'd gotten used to her red hair
years ago, but she couldn't help thinking that black hair
and green eyes had a much more pleasing effect than red
hair and green eyes.

The younger sister was a subtler beauty, not as flashy,
with the same black hair as her brother and sister but a
much softer aura. Out of the three of them, her eyes were
the most unremarkable, a soft brown hazel that went well
with her creamy complexion. The effect was just as attractive but not nearly as intimidating as her siblings.

To her delight, Gabriel abandoned his sisters as soon
as he reached her, letting go of their arms so he could
greet Lady Cowper and then stand next to Vivian for
introductions.

The marchioness and Lady Cowper greeted each other
as good friends would and moved away from the group,
towards where some of the other matrons were congre-
gating. Before she went, the marchioness gave Vivian a

supportive smile and nod of acknowledgment, which she returned with a small curtsy.

"Miss Stafford, these are my sisters, Lady Diana Parker, the Countess of Marley, and Lady Henrietta Hervey, the Countess of Jermyn. Diana, Henrietta, this is my soon-to-be bride, Miss Vivian Stafford." He lifted Vivian's hand to his lips, his eyes trained on hers, and she blushed helplessly.

"I'm honored to meet you both," she said, dragging her eyes away from Gabriel's almost playful silver gaze. She could never decide whether he was more attractive when he looked dangerous and brooding or light and playful. Although he didn't let go of her hand, she still managed to bob a respectable curtsy to both of them.

"Oh no, dear, no need to be formal," Diana said warmly, taking charge of both of Vivian's hands, to her brother's obvious disgruntlement. "You must call us Diana and Henrietta and we will call you Vivian. We're delighted to have a new sister." Gently pulling Vivian, she directed her towards the nearest cluster of empty furniture. "Now let us sit and talk. We've been incredibly impatient to get to know you."

"Oh." Vivian sought out Mrs. Banks. "I'm not sure I'm allowed to stay in one place for very long . . ."

"Pish," Diana said, with a dismissive wave of her hand. "The only reason to know the rules is so you know when it's acceptable to break them. Anyone wishing to speak with you will understand why you are not circulating, and they will seek you out."

"Come on, Sunrise," Gabriel said with an exaggerated sigh and a dark look at his sister. "She won't give up, so you might as well give in."

Reassured by Gabriel's attitude—as Mrs. Banks had said, she must follow the earl's orders first and foremost—Vivian smiled and allowed Diana to lead her towards the chairs, with Henrietta bringing up the rear.

The more she chatted with the friendly sisters, the more she relaxed. Several times they were joined by various gentlemen or ladies who were also attending the at-home, and who contributed their own measure of gossip or conversation. As usual there were a few ladies who attempted to flirt with Gabriel, but their efforts seemed halfhearted at best, and they quickly left when they realized his sisters were laughing behind their fans at their efforts, which bolstered Vivian's confidence.

When Astoria came up to sweetly compliment Vivian on her dress, exclaiming over the fine silk, Vivian merely raised her eyebrow and waited for a beat before responding, drawing attention to Astoria's toadying without being blatant about it.

"Thank you," she said. "It's quite the prettiest thing I've ever worn, and I was overwhelmed by the gift." Her eyes drifted over to Gabriel, leaving no doubt as to who had given it to her. As her fiancé, paying for her clothing was pushing the bounds of propriety, and made quite a statement about how he must feel towards her. Astoria's face turned pink as Gabriel covered Vivian's hand with his own and smiled back at her, not at all shy about showing his infatuation with her.

"Very pretty," Astoria murmured again before beating a retreat.

Both Diana and Henrietta nodded approvingly at Vivian. Vivian realized both of them had been ready to come to her defense if needed, and the warm feeling inside of her chest seemed to expand to encompass her entire body.

Being seated next to Vivian, seeing how she'd already begun to learn to deflect the claws of women like Lady Astoria, was an absolute joy for Gabriel. On the other hand, seeing how beautiful she was in the dress he'd sent her, the way her skin and hair contrasted with all that lovely green, the pale curve of her breasts pushed demurely but seductively upwards, was utter torment. Especially as his sisters were obviously amused by every aspect of the situation.

All in all, with him by her side and his sisters easily deflecting any negative attention, Vivian's confidence and beauty had burst forth like a rose in full bloom. She'd been working her way up to it all week, but now it was obvious how comfortable she felt, and that radiated outwards from her. The matrons nodded at both of them, the men looked on enviously, and the women seemed to have finally received the message that Gabriel's rakish days were at an end.

Vivian glowed.

He grinned, shooting a glance at Mrs. Banks. Unless Vivian had done something awful before he'd arrived, he'd decided his future bride was in for a treat, rather than punishment, this evening.

Vivian's eyes widened in surprise that evening when Gabriel came in through her door without Mrs. Banks.

"Good evening, Sunrise," he said.

"Good evening, my lord," Vivian said, twisting her hands about in front of her.

Gabriel shook his head at her as he hung the jacket he was wearing up on the hook by the door. He could tell she was somewhat agitated by the change.

"Gabriel. When we are alone, always call me Gabriel. I will begin taking a hairbrush to your sweet bottom if I need to, in order to help you remember."

Vivian's face flushed and she twisted her hands even more feverishly. "Yes, Gabriel."

She was more than a bit flustered. The chaperonage of Mrs. Banks had always helped to distract from the earl's domineering presence, something Vivian hadn't fully realized until now. Without another party in the room to divide her attention, there was no one to look at but Gabriel, and no one to distract his silvery, hungry gaze from her either.

Seeing the way her breathing had quickened, Gabriel's cock began to harden. He rather liked her both anxious and aroused. The mixture was an erotic appeal to his senses, making him want to pounce.

He unbuttoned his cuffs and rolled his shirt sleeves up to his elbows as he approached her.

"How do you think you did today, sweet?"

"Oh, I . . ." Vivian floundered for words. "Well, I was rather distracted when speaking with Lady Bryant, and asked about her children before I remembered that they've been living with Lord Bryant. I forgot to offer Mr. Smithson some tea before I ordered it. I trod on the hem of Henrietta's dress and gave it a small rip." That had been humiliating, to be so clumsy in front of one of her future sisters, but Henrietta had been incredibly kind about it.

She was sure there were other small mistakes she'd made, but those were the three that came to the top of her head. To her surprise, Gabriel just smiled at her as he finished rolling up his shirt sleeves.

"And with Lady Astoria?"

Vivian tilted up her chin. "I think I handled it well."

"I agree."

"You do?"

The surprise in her voice made him laugh. Vivian had been expecting more punishment, and she realized she had gotten in the habit of only going through her various transgressions. She hadn't thought he might bring up something she had done well.

"I do indeed, Sunrise," he said, putting his fingers under her chin and tipping her head back as if for a kiss. Grey eyes studied her intently, the jade flecks in them seeming brighter than ever. "I was very proud of you."

Pure pleasure shot through her, and her body quivered in response to the tender, intimate tone he used. She felt absolutely buoyant.

"Thank you, Gabriel. I only tried to do what you told me to."

"Ah, but the words were yours alone and you were magnificent. My sisters were perfectly prepared to deal with the little shrew, and then you ended up not needing them at all. It was quite delightful."

The many compliments made her entire body tingle with happiness. Leaning down, Gabriel kissed her very pink, slightly parted lips, the way he had been wanting to all day at the at-home. Vivian leaned into him, her hands delicately placed on his chest, and submissively opened her mouth to receive his tongue. With a low groan, he wrapped his free arm around her waist, pulling her close, while his hand on her chin moved back to cradle her head.

He ravished her mouth with his, indulging in a much more passionate kiss than he'd ever allowed himself before. While he fully intended to be a stern disciplinarian when the occasion called for it, he also wanted to show Vivian more than that side of himself. There was passion in places other than punishment, and the way she kissed him back—enthusiastically if a bit inexpertly, and learning faster with every movement—told him she would be happy to learn this lesson.

With Gabriel's hands caressing her, his fingers cradling the back of her skull as he kissed her deeply, Vivian felt as though she might burn up to a cinder. The kisses she'd received from him before had barely prepared her for this, especially as she knew there was no one to stop him now.

Desire warred with anxiety. Was he going to take her maidenhead now? Before the wedding? And did she want him to?

At the moment, she felt as though she would happily let him do whatever he wanted with her body. Many of the things she had experienced throughout her training had aroused her despite what was happening to her. Now, she was becoming aroused *because* of what was happening to her.

She felt the fabric of her dress slithering down around her and realized he was undressing her, his hands sliding across bare skin and her chemise. This was quite a bit more exciting than when Mrs. Banks undressed her. Throughout, Gabriel continued to kiss her as she clung to him. She only moved enough to help him free her limbs from the garment.

When she was completely unclothed, except for her stockings, Gabriel stepped back and drank in the sight of her naked body with his eyes. The way she flushed at his hungry gaze only made her more enticing. The hard, pebbled nipples stood out from the soft, white mounds of her breasts, begging to be touched.

Controlling himself, Gabriel stepped back and let his hands fall away from her silken skin. He sat himself down in her punishment chair.

"Come here, Sunrise," he said, patting his lap.

Vivian's emerald eyes grew big. "But . . . How many . . ."

"This isn't punishment, sweetness," he said. He held out his hand to encourage her to come forward. Seemingly without realizing it, she reached out to him, her slender fingers pressing against his palm, and he gently drew her to him. Arranging her to his satisfaction over his lap, so that her bottom was high in the air and her upper body far enough forward that she could rest her fingertips on the floor, Gabriel ran his hands over the curve of her buttocks. It always amazed him how much punishment this particular area could take, although tonight he would be spanking Vivian for pleasure's sake. Rubbing his hands over the ample hillocks, Gabriel explained, "Your body already responds to being spanked, to the bite of pain, but tonight you're also going to discover how much you can enjoy the actual spanking. Tonight you're going to love everything that happens to you. You did very well today, Vivian, and you deserve a reward."

Gabriel's deep voice, combined with the little circles he was making on her backside, had become almost hypnotic. Vivian found herself feeling lightheaded and fuzzy. She didn't realize how much her body had relaxed as Gabriel had spoken. She had felt the hot flush of shame when he'd mentioned how her body responded to her punishments, and she truly didn't understand why the pain aroused her so, but she did understand Gabriel enjoyed that about her.

Rubbing his hands over her skin, Gabriel enjoyed the sight of Vivian's sweet bottom and the slightly parted pouch of her pussy as he began to trace small patterns over her soft flesh with his fingers. The gentle touch slowly became firmer, preparing her for what was to come. She moaned as his hands became a little rougher, sending tingles of sensation up her spine and through her core.

When he finally gave her bottom a little swat, she let out a little squeal of surprise. It hadn't hurt. Just a tiny little sting that she barely felt. Then he swatted her again, on her other cheek, and Vivian actually sighed, wriggling on his lap as if to ask for more.

This was so much more pleasant than the punishment spankings she'd received, and she immediately under-stood the difference. His hand was still heavier than Mrs. Banks's, but she was indeed squirming as the little swats stung and then sent flashes of warm arousal through her body. Gabriel smiled as he began to warm her bottom with crisp, firm swats that had very little overall power. He wasn't going to keep any particular count; he was going to spank her until he saw the lust in her eyes, or until his cock couldn't take it anymore. Trapped between her body and his, that aching appendage was already begging for release.

In a little over a week they'd be married, and then he could keep Vivian in his bed for as long as he wanted, satisfying his need for her over and over. Gabriel had thought about taking her to the Continent for a honey-moon, but perhaps they should travel later; after all, if he was going to confine them to one room, then a room in England was just as good as one abroad. He could keep her in bed for a week and not get his fill of her.

Vivian gasped and moaned as the blows rained down harder, stinging just enough to make her squirm, just enough that her pussy creamed and clenched, but not enough that it actually hurt. She realized the slow burn of the way Gabriel had started off more gently and worked his way to harder blows had helped desensitize her skin, the rhythmic spanking contributing to the easiness with which she received it. Gabriel played her body as if it were an instrument, knowing exactly which notes to hit to make her pleasure crescendo.

When he stopped, his hands rested on her bottom, pulling the cheeks apart so he could glimpse the wet folds of her quim.

"You're enjoying this, aren't you, Sunrise?" His voice was filled with lust and supremely male satisfaction.

"Yes, Gabriel." So much so that she was panting. When he ran his finger down the crack between her buttocks, swirling it over the sensitive nerves surrounding her crinkled hole, and then delving down into her pussy, Vivian quivered and whimpered. Her hips lifted in response, seeking more contact from his fingers.

Running his fingers down to the swollen clitoris, Gabriel gave it a slight pinch before moving his hands away. The little pleading whimper that escaped from her throat made his cock throb again.

"On your knees, sweet. I want you to use your mouth on me and then you'll get the rest of your reward."

At this point in her training, Vivian was so used to giving over control of her body that she didn't even question Gabriel's precedence over her. In fact, as she slid to her knees before him, her arousal continued to build, knowing she was going to pleasure him while she ached for her own release. The submissive qualities inherent in her personality reveled in the idea of servicing the dominant man in front of her and then being treated to her own climax.

She opened her mouth eagerly as he freed himself from his trousers. She actually craved the meaty, slightly salty taste of him.

Flicking her tongue over the head of his cock, she enjoyed the way he groaned as she explored the mushroom-shaped tip with her mouth. For once, Gabriel let her have a few minutes to indulge in her curiosity, enjoying the eager way she licked him, before he pushed his fingers into her hair and pulled her mouth down around the length of his shaft. The press of her lips wrapped around him, the suction of her mouth, was heaven.

Having her kneeling, naked, with her bottom delightfully reddened and twitching while she sucked his cock with such innocent abandon was something he wanted to watch one day. He fully intended to set up mirrors all over their bedroom so he could get the full effect of the tableau.

Just the thought sent him over the edge and he gripped Vivian's hair more tightly, holding her down on his cock as he pulsed into her mouth. He could feel the slight movements of her body, of her throat, as she swallowed, drinking him down, and he groaned as he thought of his seed filling her belly. Her tongue and jaw worked, suckling him, until every last drop had been wrung from him.

Opening his eyes again, he loosened his hold on her

hair and stroked the coppery strands tenderly. She looked up at him with those wide, expressive, hopeful eyes.

"You are perfection, Sunrise. My dream come true." He smiled down at her, his voice gentle. "Now up on your feet." Gabriel tucked himself away as he stood, knowing he was probably going to be leaving her room with yet another erection. He truly wasn't going to be satisfied until he'd had her underneath him for at least a full day. "Lie down on your bed, on your back, with your arms above your head."

The slightly wary look she gave him at this new turn of events set his heart pounding. He loved seeing her little hesitations, her uncertainties, and yet knowing she would obey him anyway. That sweet little tongue flashed across her lower lip as she turned away. He enjoyed watching the shift of her rosy buttocks as she walked to the bed and crawled onto it before turning over onto her back.

Following her, he stood by the edge of the bed, enjoying how vulnerable her position made her. And he was about to increase that.

"Put your feet flat on the bed and spread your legs, love."

Vivian's heart surged in her chest. Did he realize what he had just called her? His expression hadn't changed one bit, despite the change in endearment he used for her.

Standing over her, fully clothed while she was completely nude, he looked almost dangerous, with the shadows from the flickering candlelight dancing across his face. Those silvery grey eyes seemed to glow as they traveled up and down her body. Nervous energy shot through her, and she slowly spread her legs and drew them upwards to reveal all of her most intimate areas to his hungry gaze. Fine tremors went through her body; being so brazenly splayed before him had become exhilarating.

Arousal and trepidation were obvious in Vivian's body; her flushed face, her hesitant movements, and the glossy shine of her inner pussy lips. Gabriel licked his own lips, simultaneously hating and savoring the wait between tonight and their wedding night.

"Spread them more."

Her breasts were thrust upwards by the position of her arms, those pert nipples so tightly budded and tempting, and now she was opening her legs even wider to offer another portion of her body to him. Not one inch of her most intimate area was private from him—all her wet, glistening flesh awaited whatever he wanted to do to her.

Gabriel was no longer surprised by the fact that his cock was already hardening, despite having climaxed so recently. That was the effect Vivian had on him, especially when she was naked, splayed, and submissively ready for him.

Crawling onto the bed, he watched her blush deepen as he positioned himself between her feet.

"Good girl."

Vivian bit her lip as Gabriel put his hands on her knees and spread them even wider. It took every bit of her willpower not to reach down and cover herself, but she desperately wanted the reward he'd offered, and she didn't want to risk getting a punishment spanking instead. The spanking he'd given her had heated up her insides along with her bottom; it felt tingly and sensitive against her bed but not at all painful.

He trailed his fingers along her inner thighs, between her knees, and around her wet folds, and she moaned every time he came close to that sensitive area. Teasing her, he never quite touched it, although her hips lifted in silent entreaty.

"Tell me what you want, Sunrise."

Oh, did he have to ask that of her? Her eyes slid away from his as he stared down at her. He looked so dark and commanding, on his knees above her, his shirtsleeves rolled up and the white of his shirt standing out against his darker skin and hair.

When she didn't respond, he reached up and pinched one of her nipples roughly. It stung and throbbed between his fingertips. "Tell me what you want, Vivian."

"That . . . please. On my—on the other one."

Gabriel's lips curved up in a smile as he squeezed and pulled at the nipple currently trapped between his fingers. That hungry look in his eyes had intensified again. "On what, Sunrise?"

She whimpered. "Pinch my other nipple, please," she whispered.

Those blushes were so wonderfully delightful, Gabriel almost wanted to make her repeat the full request, but he recognized that asking at all had been hard for her. So he would reward her.

With both of those little pink beauties trapped by his fingers, he pinched and pulled to his delight, twisting them gently back and forth as Vivian writhed. The feminine musk of her arousal filled the air around them like a heady perfume as her hips lifted, seeking the same kind of stimulation he was providing her breasts with.

Ignoring her writhing, Gabriel cupped both breasts in his hands and squeezed as he lowered his mouth to one of her tormented nipples. Wetting the tip with his tongue, he sucked it into his mouth, enjoying the way she mewled and squirmed beneath his hands.

When he felt her hands on his head, holding him to her breast, he pulled away, *tsk*ing her.

"I told you not to move your hands. Now, you've lost the use of them."

Gabriel pulled a silken length of cord from his pocket and wrapped it around her wrists before securing them to the headboard, leaving her stretched out and completely vulnerable to his hands and mouth.

Relief swept through Vivian that her punishment was so light. She hadn't meant to move her hands, it had just happened when his lips and teeth had started pulling at her sensitive nipple. The sensation had been so wonderfully intense, so incredibly pleasurable and she'd completely forgotten about his orders.

He didn't seem upset as he lowered his mouth to her other nipple, returning his hands to their places on her breasts, squeezing and kneading the soft flesh again. That was when she learned what her punishment truly was.

Vivian writhed, her arms jerking at the cording restraining her, practically mindless with lust. She eventually lost track of how long Gabriel had been at her breasts, alternating his mouth between her nipples, which throbbed as her heart pounded. Her moans and movements were ignored as he indulged himself in teasing her, tormenting her, until she thought she might actually climax from nothing but his hands and mouth on her breasts and nipples.

And every time she begged him, every time she pleaded, he would always ask the same question: "Please what, Sunrise? What do you want me to do?"

Then he'd go back to tormenting her while she tried to overcome her embarrassment at expressing the rising tide of desires overwhelming her. Finally, the need broke through her modesty.

"Please, Gabriel . . . Put your fingers inside me."

He'd started to worry that she'd never ask. Mrs. Banks certainly hadn't had to work this hard to get a plea for pleasure from Vivian, but then again Mrs. Banks was a woman and Vivian's upbringing was the same as her peers—that is, she was well-trained not to speak of anything bodily to a man. Even if that man had her naked, tied up, and at his mercy.

"Yes, love, I will put my fingers inside you."

The way her body rippled as his hand slid down her stomach said she was dying for his touch. He carefully avoided the swollen nub of her clit, smiling as he watched her face and saw the disappointment and the pleading. Dipping his fingers into the font of her dripping juices, he explored those wet folds with long, slow swipes of his fingers. She was so wet that the juices had started to run down the crack of her buttocks.

During her writhing, as he'd teased her mercilessly, her legs had moved quite a bit and so he pushed them fully open again as his forefinger slid down and pressed against her anus.

"Oh!" she gasped, squirming, as if she might be able to get away from his questing digit. "Gabriel, that isn't what I meant!"

"Ah, but you weren't specific, were you, sweet?"

Any response she might have made was lost as he pushed his finger past the clenching barrier of her anus and inside her, incredibly easily thanks to all the lubrication her dripping pussy had provided. Vivian felt the tingling burn of entry, the way his finger rooted back and forth as he explored her tight backdoor, and she closed her eyes against his molten silver gaze. It wasn't that she hated having that area played with—she liked it too much, and she knew it wasn't proper. From the way Gabriel was looking at her, she could tell he knew it wasn't proper either, and the very forbidden nature of the act appealed to him.

Vivian supposed she should have been used to having that particular hole touched and filled by now, but Mrs. Banks had never looked at her with such hungry, devouring eyes when she'd invaded it. With Gabriel it was completely different; he had much more interest than Mrs. Banks ever had.

She moaned as he shifted on the bed. She peeked through her eyelashes. He lowered himself between her legs. The cool air brushed against her wet nipples as they slowly dried, now a dark red from his ardent attentions to the rosy tips.

"You smell so good." His voice drifted up to her ears and Vivian's body clenched. "I think I could just eat you up."

Vivian had never experienced anything like the long, slow, heated swipes of Gabriel's tongue licking along her gaping slit. She shuddered and cried out with pure pleasure as he teased her tender folds.

It was like a banquet of honeyed peaches, spread out for Gabriel's delight. He kept one hand on the inside of Vivian's thigh, ensuring she remained spread and open for him, as he settled himself down to the delights of her body. The tightness of her anus as it convulsed around his finger had his cock throbbing. Gabriel licked and nibbled at the tender lips of her sex, staring up the length of her body and enjoying the way she began to thrash her head back and forth, her breasts jiggling mightily as he worked her towards a quickly impending orgasm.

All the teasing, combined with the sudden storm of sensation on her vulva overwhelmed Vivian. Her breath came in short pants, and then she screamed his name as he sucked her clit into his mouth. The sobbing cries poured down around him as he frigged her tiny asshole hard, his mouth and tongue working to wring every last ounce of pleasure from her quivering flesh.

Unable to stop him, unable to control her own response, Vivian's orgasm raced on out of control, sweeping her up every time she started to fall and setting off another chain reaction of ecstasy. For a moment, everything went dark, and when her eyes opened again she was still in the throes of a physical convulsion that had her crying out Gabriel's name all over again.

One day, he promised himself, after they were married, he would tie her up just like this and wring climax after climax from her gorgeous body until she was begging him to stop.

And that day couldn't come soon enough for him.

CHAPTER SEVENTEEN

FRIDAY WAS THE FINAL DAY OF THE PRACTICUM for the students of Mrs. Cunningham's Finishing School. In the morning they were informed that a celebratory dinner would be held that evening at the house, with their family members in attendance. Vivian's heart leapt—she hadn't seen her family in ages—and then it sank again just as quickly. How would this affect her evening with Gabriel?

At that moment, Gabriel was just as disgruntled as Vivian. He'd just received a note from Mrs. Cunningham informing him Vivian's parents had requested to take their daughter with them after the dinner, rather than waiting for the next day as had initially been planned. Of course he wouldn't deny Vivian time with her parents, nor such a small request on their part, but he'd been looking forward to one last night alone with her.

He felt distinctly thwarted.

At least there was only a little over a week before he and Vivian would be man and wife, and then she would be in his house, in his bed every night. The servants were already setting up the household in anticipation of their new mistress. He'd caught them preparing the adjoining room for her. Deciding that she should have her own space, he'd allowed it, although he'd forbidden them from adding a bed to the room. Propriety be damned, he was perfectly willing to be unfashionable and sleep every night with his wife, and he didn't care who knew it.

Vivian's reunion with her parents was everything she could have hoped for. Unfortunately, her siblings were not attending the dinner; she wouldn't see them until the wedding celebrations the following weekend. But it had been so wonderful to see her parents, to throw herself in their arms. Her mother had wept unashamedly, and even her father had become gruffly teary-eyed.

They'd arrived several hours before the dinner and Vivian had been given permission to take her leave of Mrs. Banks and walk the grounds freely with her parents. It had felt rather odd, like a rite of passage, to have Mrs. Banks see her off with her parents. After tomorrow, Mrs. Banks would no longer be the constant companion of her life.

Conversation flowed easily. Vivian was eager to hear about home and her brother and sisters, and her parents were eager to hear about her schooling. It very quickly became apparent to Vivian that they had no idea her lessons continued on into the evening, which rather relieved her.

As her mother was admiring some of the roses in the garden, her father pulled her slightly aside and just out of earshot.

"Are you happy, sweetheart? The earl has a bit of a . . . a reputation, and I wasn't sure if I was doing the right thing, but we needed . . . We needed . . ." He flushed heavily and Vivian took pity on her poor, dear father.

"I'm very happy," she said, perfectly sincere. "He's very kind to me. And I met his stepmother and his sisters and they've all been perfectly lovely to me as well."

Her father brightened. "Yes, the marchioness is extremely kind and generous. As is the marquess. We're staying with them, you know, until the wedding next week. They've been quite gracious." There was a touch of awe in his voice that such important personages, quite a bit above a mere baron, would be so welcoming to him and his family. Indeed, the baron was still unsure what had prompted the unusual proposal by the earl for Vivian. He'd heard rumors about the man . . . but he could see for himself that his daughter was quite healthy and seemed very happy.

Indeed, she practically glowed in the afternoon light when she spoke of the earl. Even out on their estate, he and his wife had heard the gossip of how the earl had fallen prey to the whims of love. Although he would have used the earl's desire for Vivian for the betterment of their family either way, the baron truly did want the best for his daughter, and was relieved she appeared to be more than content with the situation.

That evening Vivian's two worlds collided, with a surprising amount of harmony, although she couldn't help but blush whenever Gabriel looked at her in her parents' presence. Mostly because whenever she looked at him she was immediately aroused, wondering whether or not he would come to her room that evening. To be in such a state while having a conversation with her family was incredibly uncomfortable.

Afterwards, the ladies retreated to the drawing room while the men stayed in the dining room for their port. It was wonderful to have her mother to herself for a bit. She introduced her friends, and the atmosphere was quite festive. That was when Vivian learned she would be leaving that evening, by special request of her parents. The marquess's London house was close enough for her to return for the graduation ceremony the next day, and her parents desperately wanted as much time with her as possible. The earl and the school had granted the request.

Vivian was conflicted. Of course she wanted time with her family, especially as she would soon be married to Gabriel and would not be returning to her childhood home, but she'd also been looking forward to the earl's nightly visit. Should she feel grateful he'd approved her parents' request, or worried that his interest in her was already waning?

When the gentlemen rejoined them, Vivian knew her doubts were invalid. The way Gabriel looked at her, the hunger in his eyes, proved he definitely still wanted her.

Before the evening came to a close, he drew her aside by one of the windows. They were still within the full view of the room of course, but separate, and as long as they spoke in low voices, no one would be able to hear what was said.

"I'd hoped for another night with you this evening," Gabriel said, his voice low and intimate. She shivered and stepped a little closer to him. Almost too close for propriety really, but she had such an urge to reach out and touch him that she couldn't help it. The green flecks in his eyes flashed brighter.

"I, too," she said softly, tilting her head back to look

up at him directly. "But I'm also glad to spend more time with my family. Thank you for that."

"Oh, Sunrise, you'll be showing your gratitude later, never worry." The wicked, rakish grin he gave her made her knees feel weak. Or maybe that was just the impulse to drop to her knees and do wicked things to him with her mouth. After all, that had become her normal activity for this time in the evening.

"Will you be staying at your parents' house, too?"

"No. But I'll be visiting quite often. And I expect you to be on your best behavior." Gabriel shifted his weight, partially blocking her from the room. His hand came up, cupping her breast. Vivian gasped. Her eyes darted towards the rest of the guests, but she realized Gabriel's broad shoulders effectively hid her from them, and them from her. The way he'd positioned himself also kept any of them from being able to see that he was fondling her so inappropriately.

Of course, anyone could come over at any second and catch them. Her pulse sped even faster.

Gabriel nearly groaned with the unfairness of it all. His bride-to-be was staring up at him with hot, welcoming emerald eyes, not even protesting his manhandling of her. The amount of trust she showed in him was over-whelming. And incredibly arousing.

"I'm going to miss you tonight, sweet. I'll see as much as possible of you over the next week." Finding the tiny, erect bud of her nipple, Gabriel pinched it between his fingers and enjoyed her shocked gasp. He tugged it, and his eyes bored into hers as she bit down on her lip to suppress a moan. "You will be good, or you will pay for it later." With every word, he increased the pressure on her tender bud, pinching it tighter and tighter in erotic warning. "You may touch yourself as much as you want, but you may not climax. I'll know if you do and you will regret it."

Her cheeks paled in response to his words, which obviously both aroused and disturbed her. She sighed as he lessened the pressure on her nipple, simultaneously rolling it between his fingers to change the stimulation. He would bet his title that she was soaking wet right now.

And he would have won that bet, if he'd been able to slip his fingers between her thighs and check. Vivian was achingly aware of how aroused she'd become from his fondling and threat, from the little bit of pain he'd induced in her nipple, and from the remembered pain of her punishments. She had to bite her lip again to keep from whimpering as he released her nipple and shifted away. The little bud ached from the rough handling, and the other pulsed with envy that it remained untouched.

He'd given her permission to touch herself. She wanted to sneak off and pinch her other nipple so the slightly painful ache would at least be the same on both sides.

Instead she followed along, her hand resting delicately on his arm, as they finished out the evening. It thrilled that deep, secret side of her to know Gabriel could touch her so intimately, rouse her so passionately, and none of these people in the room need know. Of course, being returned to her parents' care dampened the thrill a bit, but only a very little bit.

Over the weekend Vivian spent most of her time with her family. The graduation ceremony was short and they didn't stay long at the tea that followed. There were too many things to do. Her mother was thrilled to be able to go about London with her, shopping for the various things they would need for her wedding next Saturday. She was fitted for her engagement ball dress and her wedding dress, which was done in the latest style, gorgeous frothy layers of silver and white, and they shopped for all the items she would need for a trousseau. Lady Audrey, as Vivian called her soon-to-be mother-in-law, accompanied them for some of the trips, adroitly adding her suggestions.

Vivian could tell that both of her parents felt some-what awed and uncomfortable when in the presence of Lady Audrey or the marquess. He had told Vivian to call him by his title, Lord Salisbury, since she couldn't seem to manage his name—the teasing look in his bright green eyes had caught her by surprise. The marquess was much less intimidating and much easier to talk to than his son was; he smiled, teased, and cajoled both Vivian and her parents into a semblance of ease at every meal. Yet she didn't mind that Gabriel was much more serious; it made the times when he was playful or openly affectionate that much more special.

CHAPTER EIGHTEEN

SISTERS WERE THE ROOT OF ALL EVIL IN THE world.

It was Wednesday, the day of his engagement ball, and Gabriel hadn't managed a private moment with his fiancée since his last night with her at the school. All because of his sisters. Apparently bored with their own lives, they'd taken it upon themselves to interfere with his. During the day, Vivian was busy with her mother and Audrey, putting together the necessary preparations for their wedding. In the evenings, Henrietta and Diana came over for dinner every night, attaching themselves to Vivian like limpets.

When he'd suggested they must miss spending time with their husbands, they'd just laughed and retorted they had the rest of their lives to spend with their husbands and they wanted to get to know their new sister. If it hadn't put such a look of pleasure on Vivian's face, he might have asked his father to intervene, but he wasn't going to deny Vivian such a simple joy. It was obviously important to her to have his family's approval, even if he didn't care whether or not they approved. So he gritted his teeth and continued his useless attempts to get her alone enough to steal a kiss. And his sisters continued to thwart him. When he'd obliquely suggested to his father that he spend the night there, his father had just given him an amused look and said to ask Audrey. Gabriel didn't bother.

Tonight, he'd better be able to have a private moment with her, though. Gabriel wanted to feel the silky softness of her skin, smell her sweet scent, and taste her lips, even if it was only for a fleeting moment. While balls often provided plenty of opportunity for clandestine meetings, he knew his father and Audrey would be displeased with him if he stole Vivian away for any real length of time. Much as he might want to.

Standing in front of his valet, he let the man fuss over his cravat. His mind was already churning, wondering where he might be able to sneak Vivian off to where none of his family members would be able to find him, in a house they all knew like the back of their hands.

He was less than pleased when, after he arrived at his parents' house, the first person he ran into was Diana. She smirked at him, ignoring his glare and chattering at him about the decorations. He had to admit, Audrey had outdone herself. The entire main floor of the house was lit with glittering candles; the dining room was elegantly outfitted in deep forest green and ivory, colors that would set off both Gabriel and Vivian's looks despite their very different coloring.

When he finally set eyes on his fiancée, Gabriel's breath caught in his throat. She was riveting, in a gown the color of lilacs, her hair done in an elegant coiffure, exposing that smooth, unadorned throat he wanted to run his lips over. The gown stood out among the forest green of the decor, and heightened the effect of her creamy skin and bright hair.

"Stop looking at her like that, it's not at all civilized," Diana said, nudging her elbow into his side none too gently.

"Like what?"

"Like she's a particularly tasty éclair and you're going to skip all the other courses and get straight to dessert."

"I recall saying much the same to Alexander when he first met you," Gabriel said dryly, and had the pleasure of seeing his sister blush.

"Really?" The delight in her voice was obvious.

"Ah, not so uncivilized now, is it?"

Diana gave him a look and flounced over to Vivian to greet her, forcing Gabriel to follow behind. She hovered while he kissed the back of Vivian's hand, all very correct and boring. There were so many other places on his bride's body he'd like to put his lips.

Unfortunately, he was given no chance. They were seated too far away from each other at dinner, which consisted of a select group of friends and family numbering about fifty. Dinner was superb, but Gabriel couldn't enjoy it because all of his attention was on Vivian as she charmed her dining partners.

The waiting was becoming unbearable.

It wasn't until he and Vivian opened the evening with their first dance, celebrating their upcoming nuptials, that he was able to hold her in his arms and speak semi-privately with his bride. It was the most he'd managed to touch and talk with her in days.

"Are you well, my lord?"

Gabriel's silver eyes glittered, and Vivian almost

wished she'd held her tongue. But she was nervous; he'd looked so dark and brooding every time she'd seen him for the past few days that she was beginning to worry he regretted his decision to wed her.

"I believe I told you what would happen if you called me that when we're in private," Gabriel said, his voice low and disturbing. All of her senses tingled as he held her closer, much too close for propriety even during a dance as scandalous as the waltz. It had become quite a fashionable dance, but Vivian had never danced it quite like this when she'd been practicing with the other young ladies at the school.

"But we're not in private," she protested.

"Closest we've come all week."

He sounded rather disgruntled, and Vivian looked up at him in surprise.

"I thought we weren't supposed to be alone before our wedding . . ." Her voice trickled off as Gabriel growled.

"My sisters are a plague."

But the dance ended before he could fully explain why he took issue with his sisters, and the marquess came up to claim Vivian's hand for the next dance, a quadrille. After him, she danced with her father, then Diana's husband, then Henrietta's, and then the other guests began to fill in the rest of her dance card. She saved the waltzes for Gabriel, but the rest of the slots were quickly filled.

Unaware of the way her beauty had riveted the attention of the men in attendance, Vivian assumed they were being kind to her because it was her engagement ball, or because they were Gabriel's friends. She didn't realize that many of them were curious about the woman who had tamed the Earl of Cranborne—or that they were attracted to her in their own right. Gabriel did, so as he did his turns with Audrey, his sisters, and Vivian's mother, he made sure to stay close to wherever Vivian was dancing.

More than one man received the unspoken message that the earl was quite possessive over his fiancée. Henrietta twitted him about grinding his teeth, although that was in part because when he was dancing with her, Vivian was dancing with Lord Marchland.

And he didn't realize Vivian's attention rarely strayed from him. She was truly enjoying this ball, as she'd never had a come-out or a season. Content with that, she was still thrilled by the attention and the glittering *ton*. She barely noticed when her feet began to hurt or when the ballroom became stifling.

It wasn't until she stumbled while she was dancing a simple country dance with Viscount Rawlings that she realized how out of breath she'd become.

"Careful, Miss Stafford," said the viscount, looking worried as he assisted her over to the sidelines of the dance floor. "Are you all right?"

"Yes, I'm so sorry," she said, fanning her face with her hand. "I don't know what came over me . . . Is this what they call a 'crush'?"

The viscount laughed, his boyishly handsome face coming alight. "It is indeed, in fact I'm quite sure that your engagement ball is going to be proclaimed one of the highlights of the season."

"Oh."

"Are you sure you're all right, Miss Stafford? Perhaps we should step out onto the terrace to get you some air."

"Oh yes, please, that sounds lovely." Vivian felt almost pathetically grateful as Rawlings escorted her from the dance floor and over to the doors leading to the terrace. The gardens of Salisbury House in London were not extensive, although they were quite beautiful, and she knew they were open for the guests to wander if they wished.

On Rawlings's arm, she allowed herself to be led down from the well-lit terrace towards the gardens as they exchanged the polite small talk that was expected. Already Vivian was feeling much revived, as well as more aware of her sore feet.

"I heard you graduated from Mrs. Cunningham's Finishing School," Rawlings said, leading her down one of the garden paths.

"Yes, I was lucky to be able to attend," Vivian said with a smile. The viscount was not the first to obliquely comment on the fact that Gabriel was marrying her basically straight out of the school room.

"It has quite an interesting reputation."

Something in Viscount Rawlings's voice made Vivian feel uneasy, and she found herself shifting away from him. He was a handsome man, but in the moonlight and shadows he looked more threatening than attractive. It suddenly occurred to her that she was, for all intents and purposes, alone with Rawlings even though they were out in the gardens and there were other people milling about the pathways. There was no one on their current pathway.

Gabriel was not going to like this.

"It's a very good school," she said, hoping her voice didn't sound as shaky as she felt. Taking a step back the way they'd come, she looked around, hoping to see someone so she wouldn't be truly alone with a man who wasn't her fiancé. "We should probably go back inside. I'm feeling much better now."

"Not so fast," Rawlings said, grabbing her arm and pulling her into his body. Vivian gasped, her hands on his chest as she tried to push him away. "I want to see what you learned at school. I've heard it's very good at teaching brides to . . . behave." The sneer in his voice made Vivian quiver with fear, but she struggled and opened her mouth to scream, anyway.

"Unhand her. Now."

The dark voice cut through the night, alive and thick with the threat of violence, before Vivian could even utter the tiniest squeak. With another sneer, Rawlings pushed her away so hard, she almost stumbled. Luckily, an arm wrapped around her waist and jerked her back upright.

"You should have done a better job choosing your bride," Rawlings said derisively. "The chit was begging for it. Or maybe you're just not man enough to satisfy her."

"That's not true!" Vivian protested, clinging to Gabriel. He put his hand over her mouth and she turned her face away, burying it in his shoulder as tears welled up in her eyes. What if he didn't believe her?

"Get out. I don't want to see you within ten feet of her, ever again."

Menace seemed to emanate outwards from Gabriel, although the arms circling her were completely gentle. Vivian trembled; she'd never heard anyone sound so cold, so threatening. If he turned that awful voice on her, she didn't know what she would do.

Thankfully Rawlings didn't say anything further in his defense; she heard the click of his shoes on the pathway as he retreated away from them.

Pulling her head away from Gabriel's shoulder, her face

wet with tears, she looked up at him, hoping he would realize she hadn't meant to go against his orders, and she certainly hadn't thrown herself at Rawlings. "What he said wasn't true, Gabriel, I promise. I was just so over-heated in the ballroom and he suggested we go outside and I didn't realize we were alone until . . ."

"I know," Gabriel murmured, holding her securely with one arm while he drew a handkerchief from his pocket to dry her tears. Gently he wiped them from her face. Rage still surged inside of him—*she could have been hurt tonight!*—but he managed to contain it. "I know he lied, sweet. You aren't the type." He could feel her relax in his arms, sighing with happiness as she leaned against him. That trusting sweetness could have been turned against her tonight. The very thought made him want to chase after Rawlings and pound the man into the ground, but Vivian needed him more right now. "Did he hurt you at all?"

"No," she said immediately, to Gabriel's relief, shaking her head. "He frightened me, though."

Gabriel blew out a long sigh of breath, trying to contain his fear and anger. "You should not have left the terrace with him."

"I know, I'm sorry. I tried to turn around once I real-ized we were alone. I'm so sorry, Gabriel."

Those big wet eyes lifted to his again, pleading with him to understand. And he did. But even though she had come down into the gardens with Rawlings out of ignorance, Gabriel was determined that in the future she would think before stepping away from any gathering with a man who wasn't him. Now that he was assured she was unharmed, he would have to deal with her disobedi-ence. Later, he would find a way to deal with Rawlings.

"What did I tell you I was going to do if you went off alone with another man?" Gabriel asked, holding her firmly about the waist with one hand and using his other to tip her chin up to look at him.

The way he was bending down kept his eyes hidden from her in the shadows, making him look like a creature of light and dark, so very attractive and yet frightening. Vivian shivered.

"You said you would belt me," she whispered. Emotions flicked through her, every one of them evident on her face—fear, excitement, wariness. Heat flooded her core at the thought. It had been too many days since she'd been punished or pleasured. She hadn't touched herself after the first night alone, realizing that teasing herself without the hope of climax only made her feel more anxious. And she wasn't going to disobey Gabriel and bring herself to climax.

"And so I shall. When you retire tonight, dismiss your maid and do not get into bed. I will come once she has left your room."

Anxiety threaded with arousal trembled through Vivian as Gabriel lowered his lips to lay a very gentle kiss on her. It was sweet, tender, until her lips parted and he tightened his arms around her, kissing her more desperately. The idea that she had been in danger, at their engagement ball, had adrenaline pumping through him at high speed. But there was naught he could do now; Rawlings would have quit the field already, and he wouldn't punish Vivian until after the ball was over. She should be able to enjoy the rest of the evening, now that Rawlings was gone.

Pulling himself away, he grimaced as his body

protested. But if they didn't return soon then his father and Audrey would be after them, and he doubted Vivian's parents would be very pleased either.

"Come," he said tersely, forcing himself to ignore the way his cock throbbed. Just a mere kiss and he was randy as a callow youth. "We need to return."

Quietly, Vivian put her hand on his arm and allowed him to lead her back to the ball. She couldn't decide whether she wished time would pass slower or faster before the evening ended. The idea of Gabriel belting her, punishing her for the first time outside of the school, was both frightening and exciting.

She clung close to his side for the rest of the evening. The next morning the gossips would be chattering about how very devoted to each other the soon-to-be-wed couple obviously was.

While Vivian waited nervously in her bedroom, Gabriel had a quick word with his father to tell him what he would be doing that evening. His father just gave him a look and told him that he'd better not anticipate their wedding night under his roof. That was an easy promise to make, since it wasn't part of Gabriel's plan anyway; from the beginning he'd wanted to keep Vivian *virgo intacta* until their wedding night. Despite the circumstances under which he'd arranged their marriage and her training, she deserved to come to her wedding night as other young women had.

Of course, that didn't mean he would go without pleasure tonight.

His emotions were running too high to deny himself that. Absolute fury at Rawlings, for trying to accost

Vivian where she should have been safe. If Rawlings knew what was good for him, he would quit London for the rest of the season, because if Gabriel saw him again he was not going to be able to contain his ire.

It grated on him that Vivian had been frightened on his father's property, during her own engagement ball, when she should have been utterly safe. Although he supposed in some ways he should feel grateful; he doubted that after tonight she would make such an innocent mistake again, and it was almost better that she had been lured away tonight when Gabriel's entire attention had been on her for the whole evening. He'd come following almost imme-diately, making his way across the ballroom and into the gardens after them. On another night, in the future, perhaps he wouldn't be quite so obsessed with knowing where Vivian was at all times.

Or perhaps he would be.

But tonight it had served him well. Vague images of what could have happened, had he not followed them, only exacerbated the emotion. Of course, it wasn't Vivi-an's fault that Rawlings and other men of his ilk were such bastards, but he'd be damned if he didn't do every-thing in his power to keep her safe.

When he reached her room, he lay his head against the door frame and took several deep, calming breaths, forcing his tense muscles to relax. The important thing to remember was that she was safe, nothing had happened, and he wouldn't allow anything to happen in the future. She had disobeyed him by going out alone with Rawl-ings, although he understood she hadn't exactly meant to disobey him, and she wouldn't be making that mistake again. For the next few days, possibly even up to the wedding, every time she sat she would be reminded of her mistake and why she should not repeat it.

Back in control of himself, Gabriel pushed open the door.

Vivian was seated upon the cushions of the room's window seat, across the room. Immediately her head whipped around, green eyes glinting in the candlelight. The night rail she wore was very modest, billowy white fabric with lace at the high throat and wrists, which only made him want to strip it off of her completely. She was so wonderfully innocent in moments like this, so beautifully pale and wraith-like, and fragile-looking.

But he knew her bottom could turn as red as a cherry and the pink flesh between her legs would weep with her honey as it did.

"Vivian." They both studied each other for a moment, across the room. "Come here."

Slowly she got to her feet, walking across the room to meet him. The fabric of her night rail flowed around her—there was enough fabric in the garment to make two perfectly respectable gowns. Gabriel made a face.

"I hope your trousseau is not comprised of garments like this," he murmured, tugging at the silk ribbons holding the throat closed. "Not that you'd have much opportunity to wear them, anyway."

"I think it's pretty," she said, a little defiantly, although her hands remained at her sides, unresisting as he loosened the top of the gown.

"I think there's too much of it," he retorted, glad to see that she'd gotten some of her spirit back. While he'd enjoyed the way she'd turned to him after he'd sent Rawlings on his way, he liked Vivian obedient to him, not complacent. Grabbing handfuls of the garment, he pulled it over her head.

She was completely bare beneath it; those dusky rose nipples already standing out proudly at attention. Palming her breasts, Gabriel ran his thumbs over the little buds, teasing them as Vivian shivered with the attention. The way she looked at him when he touched her . . . Such avid admiration and adoration, it was enough to bring a man to his knees, to strive to be worthy of such a look. Giving her nipples a pinch hard enough to make her gasp, he let his hands fall away.

"Help me take my jacket off."

Vivian's hands trembled as she raised them to the buttons of his jacket. She'd never helped a man take his garments off before. It felt strangely exciting to help him with the fashionably tight sleeves of his jacket, revealing the emerald brocade of his waistcoat and the white of his shirt. How odd that removing this one item of clothing, which still left him almost completely dressed, could make her feel so much more unsure than being completely naked in front of him.

Loosening his cuffs, Gabriel began to roll up the sleeves of his shirt, a movement as exciting as it was anxiety inducing. "Go and bend over your bed, with your legs spread."

She didn't know if desire or fear was causing all the trembling in her limbs as she turned and made for the bed, moving quickly as if her own fleetness of foot would hurry along the process. Behind her she could hear the soft rustling of fabric as he continued to work on his shirt sleeves. Arousal curled in her belly as she wondered what she must look like, bent over and completely exposed to him. The bed was low enough that her legs had to be spread fairly wide for her to be comfortable laying her upper body across it. Cool air flowed across the heated flesh between her legs, making her uncomfortably aware of how wet she was.

Not that she was looking forward to being belted, she absolutely wasn't. She could only imagine how much it would hurt—she was sure it would be worse than a regular spanking. But she also knew how much pleasure it would bring him. And she was excited by Gabriel's presence, by the hungry look on his face, by her nudity in front of him, and the fact that he was going to punish her. Pain and pleasure, two staples of her life that had been missing since she left Mrs. Cunningham's.

She craved his touch, whether it be harsh or tender. Knowing she was going to be punished for her transgression was almost a relief, because once it was over she wouldn't feel so horribly guilty for disobeying Gabriel's order. Lord Rawlings had proven himself a complete scoundrel, and while she knew not all men would be like that, she shouldn't have gone off alone with him anyway. Gabriel had told her not to. She didn't blame herself for Lord Rawlings's behavior, but she did blame herself for disobeying Gabriel's directive, however innocently it had been done.

"So beautiful. And all mine." A tinge of awe touched his voice as he approached and ran his hand over her bottom. Vivian's entire body felt like a fire that had just found some prime tinder, sparks flaring at his touch. "I'm going to spank you, first with my hand, then with my belt. Twenty strokes with each."

Vivian sucked in a breath a little fearfully, but she could

feel her insides clench with excitement. While she hated to have disappointed him and she wasn't looking forward to being punished, she couldn't help but be aroused that he was here, in her room, and touching her. Finally.

Smack!

His hand came down hard directly in the center of her left buttock and Vivian cried out, muffling the sound in the mattress as she pressed her face into it.

Smack!

The blows were hard enough to sting, to throb slightly afterwards, but she knew very well they weren't nearly as hard as he could spank. This was a mere warm-up, a prelude to the true punishment, which would come when he was done with his hand.

Her legs began to ache with the effort of staying still, her bottom bouncing as the burn penetrated through layers of skin. Gabriel hit so much harder than Mrs. Banks! And perhaps, after only a few days, she had become unaccustomed to receiving any kind of punishment.

The swats rained down on her bottom, marching up and down the curved cheeks, covering them completely and turning her heart-shaped rear a bright pink. Gabriel's cock pressed insistently against his breeches, his self-control straining to contain his desire the same way the fabric was straining to contain his arousal. Vivian's muffled cries filled his ears and he could see nothing but her chastened bottom, slowly darkening in color. She jerked with the blows, especially when his palm found her sit-spot, but there was nowhere for her to go with her hips pressed against the bed the way they were.

When he reached the count of twenty, he crouched behind her, laying his hands on her rosy buttocks and digging his fingers into that soft flesh. Vivian squirmed and moaned, and then gasped as she felt his tongue slide between the slick folds of her womanhood. The heat of her bottom flared and mixed with the sudden pleasure he was eliciting from her tissues as he licked up her juices.

Gabriel knew he was confusing her senses; he enjoyed it. He roused her desires, noting the way her little clit swelled as he teased her with his tongue. Vivian's hips began to buck and move up and down in an ancient rhythm that pleaded for him to provide her with release.

Instead, he stood.

"Stand up, Vivian."

Slowly she pushed herself upright and off the bed, turning those glazed green eyes to him.

"Take off my belt, Sunrise."

Her bottom lip trembled as she realized he was going to make her provide him with the very implement he was going to punish her with. Gabriel enjoyed the way her slim fingers fumbled at the buckle, the way her breathing picked up, shallow with excitement as she slid it through the loops.

She hesitantly offered it up to him and he took it, holding it in front of her face.

"Kiss it."

The leather was soft against her lips but she knew it wouldn't feel so against her bottom. The spanking had left a warm tingling sensation along the surface of her skin and she was having trouble resisting the urge to rub her poor cheeks. What would the leather feel like, snapping down against her already raw skin?

"Turn around and bend over the bed again." Gabriel's voice was firm but gentle, the intense look in his eyes betraying his true feelings, even though he sounded completely unaffected by what they were doing. Glancing down, Vivian saw the outline of his cock pressing against his breeches. She wasn't sure whether or not to feel comforted by his obvious arousal as he punished her.

"Legs farther apart, love."

With a little whimper, she obeyed. She had tried to keep them closed, keep her body farther off the bed to give her more control over the situation, but there was no way Gabriel was going to allow that. The bed was at the perfect height to make it difficult for her to clench her cheeks with her legs spread the way they were, the perfect height to show off all the wet, pink flesh between her legs.

"Twenty with the belt. You will hold yourself in position. If you move out of position, that stroke won't count." Gabriel ran his hand over her bottom. She would be able to take the strapping easier with her skin warmed up than if he had just lit into her cold. "And, Vivian, what will you never do again?"

"Be alone with a man unless he has your approval."

"Good girl."

Thwap!

Vivian howled and shoved her face into the mattress, grabbing fistfuls of the blankets to keep her hands from flying back to cover her burning bottom. The belt felt like it had left a line of fire across her cheeks, a deep sting that covered more area and felt heavier.

Although her body tensed, her buttocks could only hold tension for so long in that position—it was too much effort with her legs spread to keep the muscles tightly held—and the moment her quivering mounds relaxed, the belt snapped across them again. Vivian cried into the mattress until Gabriel pushed a pillow into her face. She grabbed it, holding it against her upper body and burying her face into it.

Thwap!

Her hips moved up and down frantically, as much as they could against the bed, trying to relieve some of the deep, aching burn. She felt a little faint, wondering how much more she could take without moving. Knowing he would make good on his threat to re-do strokes was the only thing keeping her from trying to cover herself.

Strangely, it didn't even occur to her to try to scream or run. She needed this. Needed Gabriel to know she was sorry for disobeying him, and, more than that, needed the release from the fear and horror she'd felt when she'd realized Rawlings's intentions. At the time she hadn't been able to cry, hadn't been able to scream, but now she was able to do both, and it was a relief.

Her bottom was beginning to look mottled with the stripes from his belt across it. Gabriel had doubled the leather over in his hand so the end wouldn't snap around her hip, but he could tell this was not a punishment that was easy for her to bear. It wasn't one he particularly enjoyed giving out, either; he'd much rather demonstrate erotic pain to Vivian than deserved punishment.

"Please, please, Gabriel, it's too hard! I'm sorry. I won't do it again!"

"I know you won't, sweet."

Gabriel took his time, laying each stripe deliberately and with the same amount of force. Her bottom was absolutely crimson by the time he was done. Exhaling with satisfaction, Gabriel let his hand hover over the flaming red of her bottom and felt the heat emanating from it.

The idea of taking her now, with her cheeks redder and hotter than he was sure they would be for quite a while, tormented him. The need to claim her, to brand her inside and out with himself, was incredibly strong.

Letting her weep with relief that her ordeal was over, Gabriel ran his hands over her back, soothing and reassuring her. She slumped, her tears slowing and her breath returning to normal in response to his soft caresses and his approving murmurs. After several long minutes of his care, he opened the drawer in the table next to the bed, pulling out the oils he'd put there before her arrival. Coating his fingers with it, Gabriel stepped up behind Vivian and pressed two slick tips to Vivian's anus, swirling his fingertips around the entrance as he massaged her bottom with his other hand.

The sting of his hand gently squeezing her soft flesh contrasted sharply with the sudden stirring of sensations elicited as Gabriel teased her small opening. Although Vivian had become used to having that particular orifice touched and invaded, there was something different about the way Gabriel was touching her there now. It was gentler, more teasing, more erotic. Her insides clenched in reaction, her hips lifting and trying to press his fingers more firmly against her, her body craving to have him inside of her.

"Please," she begged when his fingers continued their slow caress over the sensitive bundle of nerves surrounding her crinkled hole. His finger pressed in slightly, but not nearly enough to appease the growing need inside of her.

Chuckling, Gabriel leaned forward, dropping kisses along her spine. She moaned at the tumult of sensation, from the burning sting in her bottom—which was being reignited by his firm caresses—to the sensual kisses licking a fiery track down her back, to the aching need in her core as his fingers teased but didn't satisfy.

"Please, Gabriel, more. Touch me more . . ."

She gasped as he pushed the thick digits into her tight hole, filling her uncomfortably but pleasurably. Vivian had grown accustomed to having her asshole played with following a punishment, and even if it still made her squirm mentally, she couldn't deny how much she enjoyed it physically. Especially when it was Gabriel touching her in such an intimate manner. She moaned, feeling the clenching of her pussy as he buried his fingers in her bottom.

After a few moments of Gabriel stretching her, his fingers dipping back and forth, twisting and stroking, Vivian wriggled, hoping he would now touch the soft, sensitive bits below that were aching to be stroked, to further pleasure's conquest over pain. The training at the school had done its work well—following her punishment, her body now ached for the completion of the cycle, the climax she had come to expect. She was ready for his hands and mouth.

"Please, please, please," she chanted, her legs spreading farther apart, hoping he would refocus his attentions. Even though what he was doing felt good, it was not what she truly wanted, not where she yearned to be touched. Where she yearned to be filled.

His fingers withdrew and her body quivered in anticipation, ready for his touch on her aching folds and throbbing pleasure bud.

What she was not ready for was the sudden pressure against her anus, much more insistent than his fingers had been and much thicker as well. Vivian gasped, her hips bouncing as the tight ring of muscle stretched, opening to the invasion.

"What? Gabriel, what are you doing?" The question ended in a high, thready gasp as he pushed ever so slightly into her body. Everything inside of her ached in a familiar and yet entirely new manner.

"Shh, love. I promise, you will still be a virgin on our wedding night. This is just another way to find our pleasure. You're used to the plugs. Now I'm going to show you what their purpose was—preparing your tight little bottom to take my cock." He withdrew slightly and then pushed forward, sinking deeper inside of her, pushing a burning pathway into her body. Her empty womanhood pulsed as he filled her in a far more perverse manner.

"Oh, but it hurts," she said, her words muffled in the sheets as she pressed her face against them, panting as he rocked his hips and thrust deeper into her. Opening for the intimate invasion did hurt, but at the same time her body responded eagerly to this decadent perversion. It felt different than the plugs, more yielding, and yet the thickness of his cock made her burn far more than the plugs ever had. Some part of her wanted him to stop, and another part of her wanted him to plunge in and fill the ache inside of her. She was as conflicted in this as she was in her response to his discipline.

He watched the ripple of muscle in her back as she shuddered, struggling to accommodate him. The pink ring of her anus had turned starkly white, stretched around the head of his cock, standing out from the deep crimson that he'd turned her ass. He had no doubt his sweet Vivian was now burning inside and out, but he would show her how good this could be for both of them.

"What else does it make you feel, Sunrise?" he crooned, pumping his hips gently as he pushed a little deeper inside her. Her muscles clenched and rippled as she moaned.

"So full . . ." She gasped the words out. Her back arched as his fingers stroked down her spine, which felt twice as sensitive as normal.

His whisper back was deep, husky, and filled with his own need. "It hurts . . . Does it feel good, too? Be honest, Sunrise."

"Yes," she whimpered, a blush suffusing her face at the admission. It shouldn't feel good, and yet it did. The intimate burn, the stretch, made the aftereffects of his belt seem very far away, but she realized she wanted to feel him deep inside her. She wanted to know what it would feel like, if it would satisfy the craving itch he had engendered. Then he pushed forward again and she groaned. Somehow it didn't hurt to have him go deeper, only that she was stretched so wide around him. The hands pressing down on her lower back, just above the burning skin of her bottom, held her completely still in place. There was no way to escape the intrusion of his cock, and for some reason that only made her pussy clench even more wetly.

"So beautiful, Vivian," he murmured, massaging her lower back with his thumbs to help her relax. "Your creamy skin and your hot, red bottom, swallowing up my cock . . . So bloody gorgeous."

Hips pressed against her bottom, his coarse body hair rasping against the sensitive surface, and she whimpered. He was fully inside her. Automatically she flexed, tightening and loosening around him, shocked to realize that her rear entrance could accommodate his entire rod. And it didn't hurt anymore, although it wasn't quite comfortable, either.

Then he began to pull himself out and the air seemed to rush out of Vivian's lungs as she clawed at the pillow in her arms again. It was as if the dragging sensation of his cock was scraping across all her most sensitive flesh, a sensation so strong it was overwhelming. She gasped and writhed, choking on her cry as she tried to understand the sensation.

When only his head was still inside of her, he began the long, slow process of re-entry. Vivian's body relaxed under his hands as he pushed back in, obviously finding it less uncomfortable than withdrawal. Gabriel gritted his teeth as he moved as slowly and gently as possible. His self-control was severely tested by the way she was gripping him so fantastically. Once he was buried deep inside her again, he ground his groin against her body, enjoyed her gasps and the bucking of her hips as he tormented her chastised flesh. He knew how sensitive her bottom must be, and now she was handling a sensory overload both from the surface and from deep inside her body.

"Oh, Gabriel!"

"Do you like it?" he whispered, leaning over her so he could feel the curve of her bottom pressing directly against him. He slid his hands under her upper body and easily found her breasts, squeezing and kneading them intently, confusing her senses even further.

Vivian let out a long, low moan. She did, but she knew it was wrong, what they were doing. Sinful even. For some reason that made her enjoyment even sharper.

"Do you want more?" he insisted, wanting her to ask for more, to beg for it.

"Gabriel . . . yes, please," she pleaded, giving in to the need inside her, and ignoring the small voice in her head that insisted this was wrong, that he shouldn't be doing such terrible, wonderful things to her, that he shouldn't make her feel this way. Her voice dropped to a husky whisper. "Please, more. I want it . . . I want you."

Triumphant, Gabriel pulled his hips back again and then pushed forward, emptying and filling her as she gasped and writhed for him. Her gorgeous red hair tumbled back over her ivory shoulders as her head flung back, pushing her breasts farther into his hand. Taking the tips of her nipples between his fingers, he pinched them as he began to move with more powerful thrusts, making Vivian arch again.

The sensations were incredibly intense, more so than she could have ever imagined even during the shocking intimacies of her training. Having Gabriel so deeply connected to her was wonderful, she loved feeling so filled by him, having him around her and in her, but it wasn't completely comfortable, either. It burned and pain sparked and flared with every thrust, both inside and outside. The rising tide of pleasure wasn't enough to completely stem the deep, burning ache in her bottom, and the slap of Gabriel's body against those swollen mounds only battered them further.

The muscles of her pussy and ass clenched and spasmed. Her hips moved in small ways, lifting up to meet his thrusts. Gabriel's warm breath was on the back of her neck, his panting filling her ears as he began to thrust in earnest. Vivian recognized the rhythm from when he used her mouth for pleasure, knew he was enjoying invading this other aperture into her body just as much, and that aroused her as well. She gasped and moaned at the shocking sensation of fullness, of him moving inside her so intimately.

Deep within her there was a coiling of ecstasy like she'd never experienced before. It wasn't the itch or the tingling she was used to, but a deeper, broader throbbing that swelled larger and larger in her lower belly with every thrust of his cock. The inner stinging had faded, her body adjusted to the rhythmic intrusion, and she found herself panting the way she did before she climaxed even though it didn't feel like any orgasm she'd experienced before.

"Oh, please, Gabriel! I think . . . *Oh!*"

His fingers pinched down hard on her nipples as her back arched and she wailed out with the overwhelming flood of sensations swamping her. Tears slid down her face, her overstimulated nerves screaming and buzzing as she came for him, her body swimming in ecstasy born of her punishment. It was heaven and hell, a chaotic mix of everything wonderful and terrible, and she thought she might actually pass out when she felt him swell up inside her.

Gabriel hadn't been sure Vivian would be able to reach fulfillment without some assistance, which he had been ready to administer. But he hadn't realized how well Mrs. Cunningham's Finishing School had trained her, how primed her body was for pleasure following punishment. Feeling her climax, knowing she was in the heights of ecstasy from being strapped and anally penetrated, stripped him of the last of his control.

He slammed into her body, hard and fast, groaning loudly as she rippled around him, joining her in her ecstatic climax. The first spurt of his cum emptied deep inside her bowels, her clenching muscles milking each hot jet of fluid from his aching cock. With a last pinch of her nipples he pulled away, opening his eyes so he could grip his cock and watch the final spurts of his orgasm land on her ass. The sticky, white fluid dripped over those crimson cheeks. The little hole closed up as he watched with satisfaction, her trembling body causing little streams of his seed to trickle down towards her thighs.

Gabriel felt supremely triumphant as he rubbed it into her skin. Not only had both of them been brought to their pleasure, but he'd marked Vivian irrefutably inside and out. She grunted a little as he rubbed her sore bottom, only barely understanding what he was doing as the sticky fluid was rubbed into her chastised skin.

"You were very good, sweetheart," he said, pulling her up and into his arms so he could turn down the sheets.

When he laid her down, Vivian whimpered and turned immediately onto her side, facing him. Her hand moved behind her to gingerly touch her sore bottom. Gabriel chuckled a little at the almost awed expression on her face when her fingers pressed against her burning backside. No, his little bride wouldn't be wandering off alone with any man again, and she would have a good reminder of why not for several days. There was a good chance she wouldn't be sitting comfortably until their wedding dinner, if then. She glanced up at him as he began to make himself presentable again, knowing he needed to return to his own chambers.

"Gabriel?"

"Yes, Sunrise?" he asked, looking down into those beautiful green eyes he had come to love so much. He thought he'd never seen her look more beautiful.

"Do you have to leave now? I know you always did at the school, but couldn't you stay?"

The request made his chest ache. He didn't know whether or not Vivian had the same emotions for him as he did for her, although he did think she must feel something for him, even if her emotions were grounded in the lust that had been trained into her. But that one little request made him hope for more.

"Of course, love, if you want I'll stay for a bit," he said, tucking the covers over her. He crawled onto the bed beside her, allowing her to snuggle up to him.

"I really am very sorry about Lord Rawlings," Vivian said. Gabriel found it completely natural to have her head resting on his shoulder. Tracing his fingers over her lips, he pressed a kiss to her forehead.

"You shouldn't be sorry for his actions, Sunrise. The man's an utter bounder. Just don't disobey my orders again."

"I won't," she said earnestly, tipping her face back to look at him. Gabriel took the opportunity to steal another kiss from her, and enjoyed the way she pressed herself against him as he did so. When he pulled away, she nibbled on her swollen, lower lip. "Gabriel? What did . . . what did we do tonight?"

"Sodomy. Also known as buggery," he said with a yawn. Vivian's eyes got big and he laughed, pressing another kiss to her forehead. "You'll become well acquainted with it, living with me, love. I want you in every way I can have you as many times as I can manage. But that's for after the wedding. Now go to sleep."

Vivian had heard others talking in whispers about sodomy and buggery before; she'd always thought it was a bad thing. It had been both wonderful and awful, just like her punishments. She didn't know that she would ever understand why her body craved such things, why they fulfilled her so completely, but the dichotomy satisfied her in a manner that she didn't think she could receive from pure pleasure. Her entire bottom throbbed, inside and out, and she shifted uncomfortably as she felt some of his seed leaking from her body and onto her thigh. She supposed it should be strange that she wanted to be held and comforted by the man who had strapped her and then taken her in an unnatural manner, but she felt warm and secure held by him. The tender regard that he treated her with was everything she had ever wanted—and she had started to secretly think the punishment and the pain was everything she hadn't known she wanted.

Closing her eyes, she enjoyed the feel of his arms around her as she drifted away into sleep, thinking how much nicer it was to be here in Gabriel's arms rather than back at the school alone.

CHAPTER NINETEEN

VIVIAN AWOKE WITH A WHIMPER AFTER SHE'D rolled onto her back, which had caused the ache in her bottom to flare to life with a sharpness that almost felt like a blow. Immediately she turned onto her side, but the damage was done. Her poor buttocks felt incredibly sore, throbbing dully as she clutched her pillow and breathed through the pain.

Vivian wondered if there was something wrong with her that she had enjoyed last night so much. Waking up alone, without Gabriel's strong arms and reassuring presence, she felt vulnerable. It had been wonderful falling asleep with him wrapped around her, secure in the knowledge that she had been forgiven for her ignorant but indiscreet disobedience.

Rolling onto her stomach, Vivian winced as her legs moved and various muscles protested—muscles she hadn't even known she'd possessed until now!

There was a light knock on her bedroom door and it pushed open; Vivian stifled her groan, peeking out from her pillow to see a pleasant-faced young woman in a maid's dress entering the room. She was not the maid who had been attending Vivian for the past few days.

"Good morning, miss," the young woman said cheerfully, seeing Vivian was awake and studying her as she went over to open the drapes covering the windows. Sunlight spilled into the room, indicating Vivian had slept later than she normally did. "My name is Penny. Lord Cranborne has hired me to be your personal maid. I've brought some cream that should help your bottom. He said you would have need of my services starting today."

"Oh . . ." Vivian couldn't think of anything to say. She felt horribly embarrassed that her new maid was already aware she had been strapped the night before, and yet the promise of some relief for the swollen skin of her bottom made her eager. When she thought about it, it seemed like another sign of how Gabriel cared for her; ensuring she would have what she needed to heal without having to explain to her maid why she needed it, ensuring she would have a maid who would understand and already have her orders.

Penny's self-assurance as she pulled Vivian's covers down and nightdress up, revealing the still-reddened cheeks of her bottom, was all too familiar to Vivian, and she submissively fell into the other woman's ministrations immediately. She sighed as the cream was smoothed into her hot skin, cooling it slightly and providing much needed surcease from the throbbing sensation. It was rather relaxing, after a few minutes, to feel Penny's fingers deftly stroking the cream into her cheeks.

The cream helped immensely. She was able to pull her drawers over her hips with only a little bit of wincing—although her new silk undergarments were quite soft against her abused skin—but she hissed a bit as she sat in front of the mirror for Penny to do her hair. There was something emotionally satisfying about the ache and discomfort in her poor bottom, even though physically it was still painful. It was as if Gabriel was constantly there with her, his mark on her skin. She'd spent so many mornings at the school looking for proof of the previous night's punishment and not finding any that it was almost validating to have such lingering effects now. Gabriel would be on her mind all day, as the state of her poor bottom wouldn't allow for anything else.

And she was grateful to him for providing a maid who didn't bat an eye at the condition of her buttocks. Penny hummed as she ran the brush through Vivian's hair, as if it were a completely normal morning, allowing Vivian to lose herself in the pleasure of having her hair brushed and thinking about her upcoming wedding.

When Vivian sat down at the breakfast table, much later than her usual hour, Gabriel was there waiting for her. He'd already gone for an early morning ride, a much more vigorous one than usual, as he'd had excess energy to work out after the extremely erotic dreams that had haunted him the night before. Apparently spending himself only once had made his desires rouse further, rather than sating them.

He stood and greeted her, smiling as she gingerly lowered herself into the seat beside his while he prepared a plate for her from the selections arrayed for them. After last night he was sure she would be famished, and he loaded it with all of her favorite things. When he lay the plate in front of her, Vivian looked at the contents and beamed at him, as if she was surprised by his knowledge of her preferences. Gabriel gestured to the footman to ply him with more coffee as he sat down beside her.

"How are you this morning, Sunrise?"

Color rose in Vivian's cheeks as Gabriel watched, fascinated. Perhaps it was her pale skin or red hair that caused her to blush so easily; he was still astounded by how quickly her cheeks could turn such a bright pink, despite the fact that she was no longer innocent in so many ways.

"Fine, thank you," she murmured, her eyes flitting around the room at the footmen lining the walls.

Gabriel chuckled. "Believe me, love, the staff of my father's house are quite familiar with seeing a woman who has been soundly disciplined." His look became sterner. "I won't tolerate lying, either."

"I am fine," Vivian hastened to say, her face turning even redder, the color clashing adorably with her hair. She stared down at her plate, unable to say the words while she was looking at the other people in the room. "The, um, cream my new maid used was, um, quite effective as long as I'm careful about how I move."

Laying his hand atop hers, he felt her pulse begin to pound beneath his fingers as he leaned in. He curled his fingers around her wrist, enjoying how frail and small her bones felt in his palm, the slight tremble of her body as her breath quickened and announced her arousal.

"And what about your sweet bottom, Sunrise?" he whispered in her ear. If anyone were to walk into the breakfast room at that point, they would have seen nothing but Gabriel whispering into his fiancée's ear; even her shocked gasp wouldn't have truly surprised any bystanders. After all, two days before their wedding, of course a man with Gabriel's reputation would be saying something scandalous to his bride. "How does that feel this morning?"

The stammer in her voice as she reassured him in a half-strangled whisper that she was sore but unharmed was absolutely delightful. Gabriel found himself becoming aroused all over again by forcing her to speak with such impropriety first thing in the morning; it was obvious she was shocked by his plain speaking as much as by the location and time of day for their conversation. Once they were married he was going to have a wonderful time introducing her to the pleasures that could be had over breakfast.

By the end of breakfast, Vivian was visibly shifting uncomfortably on her seat, from sitting so long during breakfast. When Gabriel suggested a walk through the garden, she accepted with relief. While walking might be slightly uncomfortable, it was far preferable to sitting.

Saturday morning dawned bright and fair, although Gabriel was already up and riding, trying to work off some of the pent-up energy he'd accumulated over the past two days. Seated on Lucifer, who danced impatiently beneath him as if sensing his master's mood, Gabriel stared off across Hyde Park.

Today he was finally going to marry Vivian, to claim her, and she would be his from this point onward. He would cherish and pleasure her, punish and torment her, and ensure she never felt the need to dally with another. As a former rake, although he already considered himself reformed, he knew how easily the women of the *ton* could pick up and discard lovers when their husbands were inattentive. That would never be a problem for him and Vivian. He would pamper her, adore her, and show her all the beautiful ways pain and pleasure could mix, finishing the education the school had begun.

For the past two nights he'd pleasured himself while remembering the feel of her soft flesh against his hands, the tight grip of her asshole as he'd deflowered it, and the hot seat of her bottom as it pressed against his groin while he buried himself inside her. The events of that evening were all he thought about whenever his mind drifted, and it seemed to be drifting quite often. He could hardly believe that tonight he would finally have Vivian as his wife and be able to enjoy every single part of her body. The ache in his groin made him shift in the saddle.

Lucifer stamped his foot impatiently and Gabriel laughed. His mount was as high-strung as he was.

Leaning forward, he patted the glossy black neck of his agitated steed. "Let's run, Lucifer."

With a kick and a shout of laughter, they were streaking across the park, straight into Gabriel's destiny.

Vivian's wedding morning was quite different from Gabriel's, although she was up nearly as early. Her body had fully healed over the past couple of days; certain spots were still tender when pressed, but the color had returned to normal and she could sit comfortably—cushions always helped. Penny had made herself completely indispensable. She was skilled at elaborate and flattering hairdos, and she was becoming quickly devoted to her kind and beautiful mistress.

It was through Penny that Vivian knew exactly what was going to happen to her tonight. The talk her mother had given her the evening before had been entirely unin-formative. "Lie back and let him do as he pleases." As if Gabriel would do anything else.

Even though her bottom had ached, she had felt a small surge of feminine satisfaction every time she'd sat down and been reminded of her punishment. It made her feel safe and watched over, cared for, even though she supposed in some ways that made no sense. Her pain and pleasure was a little secret between her and Gabriel. He'd touched and taken her body in ways she'd never even known existed, awakened cravings inside her that both horrified and enthralled her, and at the same time shown her every care and courtesy, revealed his playful nature, been so generous to both her and her family. She'd fallen in love with him. What she didn't know was whether or not he felt the same for her.

She supposed he must feel something. The strictures he put down for her seemed to indicate so. And he touched her and held her so tenderly, seeing to her pleasure as much as his own. Diana and Henrietta had told her that all the *ton* was agog at their love match and Gabriel's reformation of his previously wild ways. That, too, must mean something.

"There, miss," Penny said, pinning the last wisps of Vivian's hair into place. The elegant coils wrapped round the back of her head, making her neck look even more slender and long than usual. Her hair was like a flame in the early morning light, her eyes standing out large and stark. "You look beautiful."

Just then there was a knock at the door and Vivian's mother entered without waiting. Her eyes immediately went to her daughter, and the baroness cried out with wonderment and surprise at Vivian's beauty. "Oh, my. Oh, darling, you look glorious."

"Thank you, Mama," Vivian said, smiling as she rose to greet her mother. The baroness dabbed at her eyes with a handkerchief, sniffing as she looked her daughter over.

"I sent for a tray to be brought to us. I thought you might like to have a nice private breakfast," her mother said, smiling proudly.

"That sounds lovely, although I'm not sure I can eat. My stomach feels as though it's spinning," Vivian said with a light little laugh. Although she made it into a jest, she told the truth. Her nerves were quite agitated. In only a few more hours she would be a married woman, a countess and a future marchioness. She would no longer be poor. And she would be married to a man who enjoyed strapping her with his belt and then shoving his cock up her backside.

A tingle of excitement zinged through her legs at the thought, even though she knew it was perverse and wrong. It had felt natural and right with Gabriel. She enjoyed the mix of pleasure and pain she'd become accustomed to at the finishing school, and even more so when it was shared with him. But she still couldn't help but feel anxious about it all. Behind closed doors, he was more than willing to show her exactly what he wanted from her, and she was quite sure she could more than satisfy him there; her debut into society as a married countess seemed much more fraught with hidden dangers.

"Of course, dear, I remember I barely ate a thing before my wedding," her mother trilled excitedly. "It's perfectly natural to feel nervous. But you must eat something, we can't have you fainting during the ceremony."

"Of course not," Vivian murmured as she seated herself at the small table across from her mother. Penny let herself out of the room to give them some privacy. Heavier foods seemed completely unpalatable, and Vivian only put a few slices of toast and fruit on her plate instead of the eggs and kippers she usually preferred.

It was reassuring to hear her mother had been anxious on her wedding day as well, although the idea of fainting during the ceremony certainly didn't help to calm Vivian.

Over breakfast her mother chattered with excitement as Vivian tried to choke down her food. She didn't understand why she was so nervous; after all, it wasn't as if Gabriel would jilt her—he'd paid for her schooling and training just to marry her! And yet some nervous part of her worried he'd change his mind at the last minute. Then what would she do? Now when she pictured her future, his face was the first thing to pop into her mind, and she wanted the vision of her life she now had, with Gabriel and his strange brand of pleasure and eventually his children. Her view of the future had shifted considerably since she started her training at the school, but it was a shining vision that filled her with a deep well of satisfaction.

The wedding was painless, although perhaps not as swift as either Gabriel or Vivian would have liked. All of her doubts and insecurities had melted away when she'd entered the church and looked down the aisle to see him. Even from that distance she'd been able to recognize the look of possessive hunger on his face, the way he seemed to focus so completely on her that it was as if nothing else in the world mattered. And at that moment, nothing else had mattered to her but him, and she'd practically floated on her father's arm. The other people's faces and shining clothes went by in a blur.

She didn't see Emily dabbing at tears with a lace handkerchief, or the jealous countenance of Lady Astoria, the lustful glances of several of the lords in attendance, or even the bouncing joy of her younger siblings. They were part of the crowd, part of the scenery she must walk by to join Gabriel, standing at the alter watching her with an expression that made her feel breathless.

When she put her cool hand in his, heat surrounded her palm and fingers, despite their gloves, and she almost sighed as a feeling of rightness stole over her. Gabriel was just as affected, staring down into the fathomless depths of her eyes. From the moment she'd walked in the room, he hadn't been able to look anywhere else.

Gabriel barely heard a word of the ceremony, ignoring everything the priest said except for when he was expected to recite his vows, and Vivian hers. Vivian nearly faltered when she saw the smile that crossed his face as she promised to love, honor, and obey; she knew from the predatory look in his eyes when she said "obey" he heard it in an entirely different manner than most men would. And, as usual with Gabriel, that immediately made the area between her legs ache in a way that had become intensely familiar.

Their wedding breakfast was a torment. Gabriel amused himself by never relinquishing his hold on her, whether it be her waist, her hip, or her hand, and drawing small, teasing circles with his fingertips over whatever part of her he happened to be touching. Once or twice he even managed to brush the side of her breasts, making her breath hitch. Fortunately, no one seemed to notice how closely he was pushing the bounds of propriety—well, except for Lady Audrey, who gave him a sharp look, but Vivian felt fairly sure her new mother-in-law had only seen her reaction, not what Gabriel had actually done.

Intent on getting Vivian alone and all to himself as soon as possible, it was only the look in his stepmother's eye that kept Gabriel from throwing his bride over his shoulder and storming off with her. After all, he didn't much care what society thought, or even what her parents thought at this point. She was his and he wanted to claim her, with all the barbaric lust of his ancestors currently surging through him. But he wouldn't put it past Audrey, or his sisters, to bodily place herself in front of him and make him return to the celebrations, which would embarrass Vivian and could possibly hurt her standing, depending on how the gossips decided to tell it.

Which was probably why Audrey and his sisters were never more than ten feet away from him at any given time as he mingled with the wedding guests, gritting his teeth through a grin. His only satisfaction was in being able to keep his hands on Vivian's person without any outraged matrons screeching about impropriety. Even if touching her was its own special brand of torture, as it only emphasized that she was fully clothed and he wasn't going to have her to himself anytime soon.

As they spoke with their guests, Gabriel found his patience wearing even thinner. He did receive a momentary reprieve when they greeted George and Mary, the happy couple whose own wedding had marked the beginning of the path to Gabriel's and Vivian's. Unlike many of the backbiters and social climbers of the *ton*, they were both truly happy for Gabriel and Vivian.

"I take it the school was everything you'd hoped for?" George murmured quietly as Mary and Vivian exchanged kisses and compliments. Vivian's smile was more sincere, her demeanor more relaxed, as she spoke with her cousin.

"Oh yes," Gabriel confirmed, a true smile spreading across his own face. "Although, I think my choice of bride had just as much to do with it."

Chuckling, George clapped him on the shoulder. "Isn't that the truth?"

Although Gabriel would like to sit down and compare notes with George at some point, the wedding breakfast was certainly not the appropriate venue for such a conversation. Nor did they have the time, as there were far too many others that Gabriel and Vivian had to greet as well.

By the time they'd made the rounds of all the guests and Audrey had finally given him a discreet nod of dismissal, amusement quite clear in her laughing eyes, Gabriel had become quite adept at angling his body so no one would notice the bulge pressing against his pants.

"Thank God," he muttered, immediately grasping Vivian just above her elbow and practically dragging her towards the exit.

"Gabriel? Wait. What—where are we going?" she hissed at him in a frantic whisper, dragging her heels.

That was cause for spanking, he decided immediately, and they were going to have a talk about letting him drag her off whenever and however he damned well pleased.

"To my—our—home for some privacy. Immediately," he said, not bothering to keep his voice down. Off to the side he heard someone titter, but he didn't look to see who it was; with all the rumors about their love match floating around London, no one expected him to be anything but impatient now that they'd lingered long enough to satisfy the social expectations.

"But my family . . ." Vivian looked over her shoulder at them—they obviously hadn't noticed yet that she was being escorted out of the room—and then beseechingly up at him. He groaned as those wide green eyes stabbed straight to his heart. After the ceremony he hadn't missed his bride's joy in seeing her siblings, or her pleasure this past week at spending time with her parents.

Pulling her to him, he lowered his head to whisper in her ear. "Go and make your farewells, and I promise we'll see them again both before we leave for our honeymoon and after we return. We'll spend as much time with them as you want, once we return. You have five minutes, and then I am taking you out of here, even if I have to put you over my shoulder to do it."

The harsh, ragged quality of his tone and the way his hand tightened on her hip emphasized his point. Vivian was shocked at how aroused she felt by the image he put in her mind, even though she knew she'd never live down the shame of it. Was this what the gossip had meant when they'd talked about Lord Cranborne's "wild" behavior? Would he truly do such a scandalous thing at his own wedding breakfast?

One look in his molten silver eyes as he pulled away, and Vivian was quite sure that yes, yes, he would. He wanted to do the things to her that he did when they were alone at night, only now they were married and it was the middle of the day. She hadn't realized marital relations could be conducted before bedtime. Was he teasing her?

"Five minutes," he intoned again, perfectly serious.

Her mouth worked for a moment and then she whirled

away. Five minutes to make her farewells and then Gabriel was going to take her to her new home and do all the things he hadn't done to her yet. Make her a bride and a married woman in truth.

Warmth flooded her loins, heightening the color in her cheeks, as she hurried to her parents and siblings, her mind irrevocably focused on what might happen once she and Gabriel were alone again.

CHAPTER TWENTY

AS SOON AS GABRIEL SETTLED HIMSELF INTO the seat of the carriage, he pulled Vivian onto his lap, ignoring her squeal of surprise. Although the carriage ride was only ten minutes long, he intended to put those ten minutes to good use. He was determined that by the time they arrived at his house, she would be as aroused and anxious as he was.

"Ga—"

He cut off his name with a kiss, smothering the words with his lips and tongue. Vivian wriggled for a moment and then submitted, her body relaxing in his arms and inflaming his passions further with her quick acquiescence. She was warm and soft on his lap, one of her arms trapped against his body, the other pressing a hand to his chest as she kissed him back.

The bump and rolling of the carriage only served to press his groin against her soft bottom, and he groaned as the pleasurable friction taunted him. Reaching up to cup her breast, Gabriel wrapped his other hand around her waist and held her securely against him. Vivian practically melted in his arms as he pinched her nipple through the fabric of her wedding dress.

She couldn't believe Gabriel was touching her like this, in a carriage—even if it was closed—in the middle of the day. Somehow she hadn't thought he would even be interested in such activities except at nighttime. After all, hadn't her mother said her husband would visit her bed in the night? Hadn't her sessions at the school and his visitations always come in the evening?

Yet Gabriel's intent had been clear from the moment he'd wanted to leave their wedding breakfast. At first she'd almost thought she'd misunderstood, but now she knew she hadn't. She couldn't help but feel a heady rush of pleasure that he obviously wanted to touch and kiss her so badly, even if it was scandalous. The slightly shocked whispers as she'd been hurried from their guests should have bothered her, but they didn't.

"Oh!" she gasped. She writhed slightly as his lips left her mouth and latched onto her neck. Her lips felt swollen from his passionate kiss, her pulse throbbed as he sucked on the delicate skin of her throat, and she clung to him, her legs stirring restlessly as her thighs rubbed together in an attempt to ease the aching tension building between her legs. "Gabriel . . . Is this . . . Are we . . .?"

He chuckled, pinching her nipple tightly between his fingers and tormenting both of them as she let out a whimper of pain that made his cock jerk against the swell of her buttocks.

"No, sweet, I'm not going to deflower you in the carriage . . . but I am going to make you burn." The hand around her waist moved to her lower stomach, pressing erotically close to the area where she yearned for pressure, but not coming quite close enough. Vivian's body undulated, her hips reaching for his touch. "I'm going to make you burn for me, and when we get to the house I'm going to take you to our room, to our bed, and then I'm going to take my time."

Vivian couldn't find the words to tell him she was already burning; as often as she'd had her passions roused since she'd begun her marriage training, she had never experienced the full onslaught of passion Gabriel was unleashing now. Before this he'd always had to be so controlled, keeping his own lusts under a tight leash, and so had not been able to indulge himself as much as he'd wanted. Now his hands wandered, and even through the thick fabric of her wedding dress his touch burned her, every caress stoking the flames higher as she writhed for him.

Turning her slightly in his lap to give him better access to her body, Gabriel faced her away from him. He was disappointed he couldn't see her face, but now he could cup both of her breasts in his hands and slide his hand down between her legs. He arranged her so she had one leg on either side of his. He spread his legs and forced hers to spread as well, under her skirts, allowing her no pressure or friction against the swollen, sodden folds of her pussy. Whimpering, Vivian instinctively arched her back, which ground her bottom against her husband's lap, his stiff rod nestled in the cleft of her cheeks.

Fortunately for both of them, the ride between his father's house and his own was not long, or he might have truly lost all control and lifted her skirts then and there to have her.

When the carriage rocked to a halt, Gabriel gave her full breasts one last firm squeeze before gently placing her back on her side of the carriage to give them both a moment to recover. She looked absolutely delicious, her cheeks flushed bright red, her lips swollen, and her hair just disheveled enough to soften the elaborate coiffure. Her breasts heaved with every breath she took, her lips slightly parted as she sucked in air. The slightly dazed look in her eyes had every one of his masculine senses singing with smugness.

"Come, Sunrise," he said, opening the door and stepping down before turning back to offer his hand. "Time to go inside."

The absolutely wolfish grin that accompanied his words would have caused many a proper matron to swoon, it was so clear what his intent was. Vivian could only gape at him. Her senses whirled chaotically as the abrupt loss of his touch rendered her anxious. She wanted to throw herself on top of him, not step sedately out of the carriage like a lady. Right now she didn't feel at all like a proper lady should.

Blushing furiously, she accepted his hand and stepped down, trying not to look at the coachman, wondering how much he'd been able to hear. When they were in the carriage she'd completely forgotten about him, completely forgotten they were somewhere they could be overheard or discovered. Would there ever be a day when Gabriel didn't completely overcome her senses and sensibilities?

He didn't even look as though he had a hair out of place, his expression completely solemn except for the way his eyes burned whenever he looked at her. Other than that, he was the very image of a proper and solicitous husband. Whereas she felt wrinkled and rumpled, out of breath, and completely discombobulated.

Gabriel led her up the stairs before he swept her up in his arms to cross the threshold. Giggling, Vivian clung to him, but then she was only able to gasp in shock as he swept right past the servants who had gathered.

"I'll introduce you to your new mistress later, Mrs. Pringle," he called over his shoulder to the housekeeper, who watched him with obvious amusement as he carried Vivian up the stairs. Moaning with embarrassment, she buried her face in his shoulder as the housekeeper began to shoo the other servants away, doing her best to ignore the small encouraging cheers following them up to the second landing.

Even so, she couldn't summon anger over his high-handed ways; indeed, part of her thrilled at it. She'd heard some of the whispers about the purported love match between them and knew it had become true on her side. If Gabriel's actions were any indication, there was certainly more than just an arrangement on his.

Vivian's suspicions were even more on point than she realized; Gabriel was almost shocked at his complete loss of control, the fact that his desire for her had overridden any sense of propriety.

"I'll never be able to look Mrs. Pringle in the face after this," Vivian whispered into his collar, clutching at his jacket.

Laughing, Gabriel shifted her weight in his arms as he strode down the hall to the room they'd be sharing. "Of course you will, Sunrise. And like a proper housekeeper, she'll pretend she never saw a thing. Besides, I'm sure she'd be thanking you if she thought it was appropriate."

"Thanking me? For what?" Vivian asked curiously. She peeked out of Gabriel's collar as he paused, realizing they were now standing in front of a doorway, the door only partially open. Keeping her pressed against him, Gabriel shouldered it aside.

"For her winnings. I'll eat my hat if she's not one of the staff who bet I'd carry you off to bed without bothering with the niceties. Pringle's known me for years."

So busy looking around the room, Vivian didn't take immediate notice of his words. There was plenty to distract her; the room was incredibly large and airy, her trunks had already been piled against one wall, but the decor was decidedly masculine. Forest-green velvet draped against the large windows on the far wall as well as the bed; muted orange and rust cushions adorned the cream-colored window seat. A delicate ivory vanity, looking rather out of place against the darker woods of the other furniture, was set near one of the windows. Next to it was a chair she recognized as having come directly from Mrs. Cunningham's Finishing School, and even as she shuddered, she felt her insides clench in anticipation.

As Gabriel set her down, the meaning of his words finally punctured her thoughts. And she turned beet red. "Oh, dear . . ."

Gabriel just laughed. The smile that curved his lips was only visible for a second before he stepped forward and pulled her into his arms, lowering his mouth to hers. He was done with waiting to claim her. Vivian reached up to touch him, but he grasped her wrists in one hand, holding them behind the small of her back. She moaned into his mouth, pressing her body against him as her arousal flared back up with a vengeance. The fires had been banked, waiting, and now they roared to life, accompanied by the secure warmth that only came from knowing one's value, from acknowledging the meaning behind the act.

The kiss seared her with its intensity. She'd been kissed by Gabriel often enough to note the difference, although she didn't realize it was because he was no longer holding anything back from her. There was no need, as he no longer had to refrain from taking her virginity.

Step by step he backed her towards the bed, her satin curves pressing against him as she stumbled and tripped over her train, held up by his arms. He didn't mind in the least. He enjoyed the way her body moved against his, and was further aroused by the way she clung to him to keep herself upright. Torn between wanting to ensure she enjoyed this experience despite the pain of losing her maidenhead and wanting to bury himself in her immediately, Gabriel broke off the kiss and turned her around.

"Put your hands on the bed. Don't move them."

Vivian trembled as she did what he said, her legs automatically sliding apart to help her keep her balance as she bent forward. As she placed her hands on the dark green blanket spread over the bed, she couldn't help but notice how small her pale hands looked, her slender arms encased in the mint green of her dress. The darker forest-green almost seemed to make her skin glow.

Slight pressure against the base of her neck, and then it released, and lips pressed themselves against her revealed skin, Gabriel's body pressing into her from behind. She groaned as his weight rested against her, arms trembling as she held them upright. The fact that he'd only undone a couple of buttons meant he had to bend over her completely to kiss her neck, and his rigid erection dug into the soft flesh of her buttocks. She couldn't help but whimper in excitement.

A few more buttons, another kiss. He followed the pattern over and over again, trailing kisses slowly down her spine until he reached the top of her corset. Then he pulled the buttons apart much faster, and the gown sagged around her body as it opened for him.

"Stand up."

He pulled the gown from her arms and down her hips, and had her step out of it, leaving her in her corset, chemise, and drawers, still facing away from him.

"Hands back on the bed," Gabriel ordered, his voice more hoarse as he placed his hands on her hips and caressed them while she leaned forward again.

Knowing she was presenting her bottom to him, in a way that practically begged him to spank it, Vivian's emotions ricocheted wildly between excitement and anxiety. Would he spank her on their wedding night? The confusion, the anticipation, only added to her building arousal.

The laces of her corset pulled and loosened, allowing her to take deeper breaths, and then it fell from her body, joining her gown on the floor and leaving her only thinly covered.

"Stay like that. Just. Like. That." Gabriel's voice was rough, heavy with desire, and Vivian shivered as he stepped away. She missed his warmth immediately. The sound of fabric sliding indicated he was disrobing. Wanting to see him, wanting to know what he looked like under his shirt and pants, Vivian craned her neck around.

She only got a glimpse of broad shoulders, a muscled torso, and crisp black hairs scattered across his chest, before a sharp smack to her bottom had her head whipping back around.

"I told you to stay in place."

Smack!

He spanked her three more times before she cried out, her bottom stinging from the hard slaps, her fingers digging into the soft fabric of his blanket. The red markings across her skin, visible through the thin fabric of her drawers and chemise, made it even more difficult for Gabriel to pull himself free of his pants, as his erection had become hard to the point of almost being painful.

There would be plenty of time for her to look, touch, and explore to her heart's delight, once he'd sated both of them.

The smell of her arousal filled his nose as he pulled the pantaloons down over her hips and she lifted each of her feet to remove them completely. The red prints on her bottom were already fading to pink; between her cheeks her pussy lips were swollen, slick with her juices. Placing his hands on either side of the tempting lips, he pulled them apart, leaving Vivian gasping as his warm breath wafted across her sensitive inner folds.

Her elbows buckled and then collapsed, so that she was bending over with her bottom high in the air, her legs spread and her pussy parted, her head resting on her forearms. The airy fabric of her chemise slid up her lowered body, breasts hanging beneath her as her nipples rubbed against the silky fabric.

"Please," she begged, wanting him to touch her, to satisfy the throbbing need pulsing inside of her. "Oh, please . . ."

Although the idea of making her beg explicitly appealed

to him, it wasn't quite the same when Gabriel couldn't see her face. Besides, his mouth was watering with the need to taste her.

Honey, musk, and woman exploded on his tongue as he swiped it up her center. Her gasp filled his ears. With a growl, he delved back into her folds, teasing, tasting, and laving his tongue over her most delicate parts as Vivian's legs trembled. The sensations coursing through her were incredible, burgeoning and swelling inside of her, without giving her the stimulation she needed to cross the line. Pleasure built upon pleasure, her hips working as Gabriel feasted.

Then his mouth moved upwards, licking, sucking, his tongue sliding into her virgin hole and exploring as she gasped and clenched. The sensation was unlike the fingers she'd already experienced, less deep and yet teasingly pleasurable. She ached to be filled. The path of his tongue continued until he reached the star of her anus. Sensitive nerves buzzed and sang as he licked and sucked on the tiny hole, lavishing it with affection.

Vivian was lost in a sea of pleasure, working towards culmination in tiny increments that drove her wild. The rasp of Gabriel's tongue against all her most responsive parts, except the one she desperately needed, had her sanity teetering on the brink.

When he withdrew, with one last lick over her swollen, sodden folds, Vivian sobbed out a protest. She was pulled upright and her chemise yanked over her head before strong arms closed around her like steel bands, only momentarily, before tossing her on the bed.

Wide-eyed, she stared as Gabriel crawled onto the bed after her. His arms and chest were just as magnificent as the statues she'd seen at the British Museum, although none of the statues had the warmth of color his skin did, or the crisply curling black hair that adorned the flat planes of his chest and ran from his belly button in a line down to his cock. Beneath him, his erection hung full and heavy, so hard it was practically slapping up against his stomach despite gravity's pull. Angrily red and purple, it was pointing straight between Vivian's spread thighs.

"Oh," she said in wonderment, drinking him in with her eyes. His body pressed against hers, making both of them groan as his erection dug almost painfully into her stomach. Vivian's hands pressed against his chest, caressing. His skin was so soft over hard muscle, the wiry hairs so strange against her fingers.

Excitement throbbed inside of her as Gabriel slid down her body until he was level with her breasts. Her hands tightened on the hard flesh of his shoulders. Feeling his muscles beneath her fingers made her feel even more vulnerable. He was so much larger than she was, stronger, and completely capable of overpowering her at any moment. Yet she absolutely trusted him not to harm her.

The heavy mounds in front of Gabriel's lips were tipped with taut pink nipples, just begging to be kissed and sucked. Taking a breast in each hand, he squeezed and kneaded the soft flesh with firm fingers, wrapping his hands completely around each mound. He listened to his new wife moan as he sucked, gently at first and then with increasing intensity. Her whimpers were quickly accompanied by the writhing of her body, back and forth, and the thrusting of her hips in the air, seeking him out.

Gabriel's attentions became more forceful, almost painful, as the color of her nipples darkened from his ministrations. Vivian's body arched, seeking more stimulation, her eyes half-lidded as she watched him suckling at her breasts. She wished she could see more of his body, but watching the intense expression on his face as he touched her was incredibly arousing. Whimpering, she slid her hands over his shoulders, into the dark strands of his hair, touching every part of him she could reach. She was all too aware of how she was laid out before him, completely open to his hands and mouth, like a banquet for him to plunder.

One of his hands slipped down her stomach and slid through the coppery curls of her mound, teasing her as she gasped and jerked her hips upwards to meet the questing fingers.

Heat pulsed against Gabriel's palm as he slid one long finger into the silken vise of her body, stretching her virgin channel. He thrust his finger back and forth to mimic the sex act. His cock wept fluid steadily, coating the head and readying itself to breach her entrance, but first he wanted to ensure she was as ready as she could be.

He eased his finger mostly out, and when he pressed back in, it was with two fingers. Vivian groaned, her hands clenching into fists as her body stretched to accommodate the increased girth. The slight discomfort of being stretched reminded her of how it had felt when he'd taken her rear entrance after their engagement ball, but this was different, easier, more immediately satisfying.

His fingers curved inside her and found a spot that made her feel faint with pleasure. Her legs tried to close and pull him deeper into her. If only he would touch that spot again . . .

Lifting his head from her breasts, leaving her nipples

red and swollen from his attentions, Gabriel watched Vivian's face as he stroked the sweet spot deep inside her with the pads of his fingers, letting the base of his hand come to rest against her clit. As she moved her hips in instinctive rhythm, her clit pressed against his hand and she spasmed around him. Her lips parted and her eyelashes fluttered as she dug her fingernails into his shoulders, leaving little crescent marks on his skin.

He watched the pulse in her throat as her back arched, her neck elongating as she ground herself down on his hand, completely lost to her pleasure. Delicate pinks and reds suffused her face, her neck, her upper chest. Her breasts jiggled as her body began to shake. Although her legs couldn't close completely, they tightened about his thighs as she writhed for him. She sucked in a hot breath before she let it out on a scream.

Everything tightened and released. She convulsed beneath him in utter abandon as the pleasure washed over her. Nothing existed but the heat and the sizzling delight.

Then she was empty, but only for a moment, before something hard and thick began to push into her. There was a moment of stinging pain, like a snap, and then a feeling of fullness that amplified the pleasure she was awash in.

Gabriel groaned, his breathing ragged as he did his best to slowly sink into her, aware from her pleasure-glazed eyes that she might not even realize it if he truly hurt her at this moment. Fortunately, she was as wet and slick as a woman could be, her body welcoming him even as it trembled under the strain of accommodating his cock in her virgin channel. The thin veil of her maidenhead had provided no protection at all against his rampant cock;

only the slightest trace of blood streaked its length as he pulled out slightly and began to press in, deeper.

The sensation of being utterly filled had Vivian rocking as Gabriel buried himself inside her. She was barely aware of what was happening, only of the pleasure that swept through her, the long-awaited culmination of all his teasing, his caresses, his passionate kisses. With his arms braced on either side of her, Gabriel's body was hot and hard against her softer curves, the wiry hairs on his chest abrading the sensitized tips of her nipples.

When their groins finally met, she gasped at the sensation of having his hard body pressing against her clitoris while she was completely filled. The pain of losing her maidenhead had been swift enough not to bother her, even if she hadn't already become accustomed to experiencing some pain with her pleasure. Although her orgasm was receding, leaving her limp-limbed and satisfied, she could still enjoy the sensation of feeling Gabriel so intimately connected with her.

Then he began to move.

It was almost unbearably pleasurable as his cock dragged in and out of her tight sheath, his body rubbing against her sensitive lips and swollen clit, which were already buzzing from her climax. Vivian had learned those swollen tissues were much more responsive immediately following pleasure, and with Gabriel's cock inside of her, it was almost an overload of sensations.

When her eyes finally focused, it was to see his silver gaze staring down at her. His face was almost grim, jaw-locked as he struggled to keep control over his impulses, a battle he was slowly losing as her wet heat gripped him and rippled. The silken vise of her body, the satin of her skin against his, called for him to plunder, to ravage, to claim. Seeing her eyes, framed by those long lashes, watery with the tears from her intense sensations, was his undoing.

Gabriel groaned and gave way to his base instincts. Immediately his hips moved, harder, rougher, pounding into the softness between her legs, and Vivian cried out. Her training helped her—the combination of pain and pleasure as he thrust hard into her body was something she was used to, even if the manner in which it was being delivered was foreign to her.

When her legs started to tighten about him again, he reared back, sliding his arms under her thighs to keep them spread wide. The new position also had the effect of lifting her hips higher, allowing him to slide deeper, and he could watch as the glossy length of his cock, sheened with her honey, pumped between lips swollen tight around his girth. He could see every jiggle of her breasts, hear every sound as it crossed her lips, and see the way her coppery curls melded with his darker thatch of hair whenever he slammed home.

Leaning forward slightly, his body rubbed against her swollen clit, driving her higher and higher as his own lusts spurred him onwards. Since he had already taken her to her peak, he didn't feel the slightest ounce of guilt over concentrating on his own pleasure, but it didn't matter anyway. Vivian's body hummed with the sexual energy Gabriel had unleashed on her. Her innermost instincts thrilled at his handling of her body and his intentness on his own desires. She enjoyed being the vessel for his pleasure. It satisfied her in some primal way she didn't understand.

Watching his face as he leaned over her, she saw as the stony tension in his face fractured and then fell apart. His lips parted as he groaned in passion. Her insides tightened around him. She was utterly fascinated by the way his face twisted as he thrust hard into her—his ecstasy practically glowed from his dark features. It set off a smaller spasm within her, causing her to ripple and massage the length of his cock as he filled her with his seed.

Vivian moaned helplessly as Gabriel allowed her legs to fall and his weight came down on her, pressing hard against her clit and sending her into paroxysms of delayed pleasure. Her body milked him as he hunched over her, his back muscles rippling with the contractions of his own pleasure, until he finally slumped, almost boneless.

The weight of him took her breath away, but she liked it too. It was a comforting kind of weight. She liked the way he felt on top of her, as if he was enveloping her instead of the other way around; she liked the way her body cradled his, the way he felt as she slid her legs over his, twining her limbs around him. She ran her hands relentlessly over his back and felt his muscles flexing under her hands.

Soft murmurs were followed by kisses up her neck and finally to her lips, laced with such tenderness that it nearly sparked tears in her eyes. Gabriel's fingers slid through her hair, pulling pins out as he went. She hadn't even realized how uncomfortable they had become until he began to alleviate it. Spreading her copper tresses across his pillow, he smiled at a fantasy fulfilled. Vivian in his bed, with her glorious hair gleaming against the white of his sheets.

Leaving her lying there, eyes half-lidded and with a sleepy smile on her face, Gabriel got up to wet a cloth in the basin of warmed water his valet had left them, fore-sighted man that he was. Vivian hadn't bled much, but enough to tinge the cloth pink as he cleaned her. The lips of her pussy looked swollen and used, and her delicate inner thighs were reddened from being wrapped around his body.

The hazy, sated look in her eyes was of a woman well-pleasured. It was a look that made Gabriel's heart leap in his chest. He'd worried, after, that he'd been too vigorous, but if he had it hadn't mattered. She'd enjoyed it anyway.

"Are you sore, Sunrise?" he asked, dropping the soiled cloth to the side of the bed and spreading her thighs wider to look. He enjoyed that she still blushed at being revealed to him.

Fingers pressed against her lips, and she winced.

"A bit," she admitted. His fingers brought alive the ache in her muscles, which were unaccustomed to the use they'd been put to. But she didn't move to resist his touch—her hands lay passively by her head, arms up, and legs still spread to where he had put them. Gabriel couldn't resist gently caressing those sore, sensitive tissues until she gave a little moan and wetness spread across his fingers.

"I'll be more gentle tonight."

Vivian blinked, surprised, but too pleasure-lazy to truly show it. "Tonight? Again?"

Laughing, Gabriel crawled back up her body and lay on his side, pulling her into his arms so her face nuzzled into his chest. Vivian took advantage of the opportunity to wrap her arm around him, the other trapped between their bodies, and to rub her cheek against the rough hair of his chest. It felt as wonderful as she'd imagined to be held so by him, like this, unlike the other night when he'd still been clothed. His heat engulfed her, surrounded her in a cocoon of protection.

"Again, and again and again. As many times as I can have you, in as many ways possible, at all hours of the day," Gabriel said, dropping kisses across the top of her head, winding her hair through his fingers. A shiver went through Vivian, her thighs tightening together against the sore ache still residing there, and Gabriel laughed again. "I don't think I'll ever get enough of you."

"You won't?" The hopeful look in her eyes was filled with vulnerability and it was impossible for him not to answer it.

"This is a love match," Gabriel said gently, pressing his thumb to her lower lip, as if to leave an imprint on the full bow. "At least on my part. I think I might have loved you from the moment I saw you, although I didn't realize exactly what the emotion was. I only knew I wanted you, that I had to have you, to be the one to awaken your passions, to receive your admiration. And every moment since then, you've done nothing but draw me in deeper."

Tears sprang up and she closed her eyes, her throat working to choke back the relieved cry of joy she knew would make those tears spill over onto her cheeks. She'd never felt so happy in her entire life.

"Look at me, love." His voice deepened, roughened, and her eyes flew open to meet his silver gaze. The green flecks in his eyes were blazing. Fingers trailed over her cheek, gently, almost reverently. "There will be times I discipline you, times when I punish you for no other reason than the pleasure of hearing you scream or cry, but never doubt that I will always be there for you, to protect you, to adore you, and I will cherish every moment we spend together. You were mine from the moment I saw you, and now you've given yourself to me, and every single one of those bloody fools who bet against a love match are reaping what they deserve."

"I—" Her voice husked and she cleared it, determined to have her say. "I did not expect to find such happiness in my marriage. I did not expect to enjoy my training the way I did, or what came of it. This is nothing like what I thought my life would be, but I wouldn't change it for anything. I love you as well, with all my heart and all my soul. I'm yours."

The satisfaction that flashed in his eyes made her smile, joy suffusing her as he pulled her tightly against him. She nestled her head in his shoulder.

"Sleep, Sunrise. You must be tired after this morning, and you'll need your rest for tonight."

For tonight and all the nights to come. And mornings. Hell, she'd be lucky if he let her out of bed any time in the next week. Idly caressing her soft back, feeling the subtle play of flesh beneath his hands as her breathing deepened, he realized it had only taken her moments to drift off to happy sleep.

His wife. At last.